PRAISE FOR KEVIN J. ANDERSON

"Kevin J. Anderson has become the literary equivalent of Quentin Tarantino."

— THE DAILY ROTATION

"Kevin J. Anderson is the hottest writer on (or off) the planet."

— FORT WORTH STAR-TELEGRAM

"The scope and breadth of Kevin J. Anderson's work is simply astonishing."

— TERRY GOODKIND

"Kevin J. Anderson is one of the best plotters in the business."

— BRANDON SANDERSON

"One of the greatest talents writing today, Kevin J. Anderson is a master of adventures that are filled with dynamic, unforgettable characters."

— SHERRILYN KENYON

FANTASY STORIES
VOLUME 2

FANTASY STORIES
VOLUME 2

KEVIN J. ANDERSON

WFP
WORDFIRE PRESS

CONTENTS

When I learned that Shakespeare's famous Globe Theater had burned down during the initial performance of his play, Henry VIII, I began to sense the possibility for a story. When I discovered that the theater itself had been torn down and rebuilt using the same wood, and that some players may or may not have been murdered there ... well, I decided it just had to be a ghost story.

After having my fiction appear for years in numerous small press magazines, "Final Performance" was my very first professional sale, to The Magazine of Fantasy and Science Fiction.

FINAL PERFORMANCE

SCENE I

"London, this last day of June, 1613. No longer since than yesterday, while Burbages' Company were acting at the Globe the play of Henry VIII, *and there shooting off certain (cannons) in way of triumph, the fire catched and fastened upon the thatch of the house, and there burned so furiously as it consumed the whole house, all in less than two hours, the people having enough to do to save themselves."*

— THOMAS LORKINS, EYEWITNESS TO THE
BURNING OF THE GLOBE THEATRE.

Setting—London. Night. *The charred ruins of the Globe Theatre. Little remains of Shakespeare's playhouse: skeletal, blackened beams, the stone foundations. It is late November 1613—a light dusting of snow covers the ground.*

Enter Cuthbert Burbage, *half-owner of the Globe, brother of Richard Burbage, who is the famous actor of the Lord Chamberlain's Men, Shakespeare's company.*

S trange how silent London was so late at night. The houses surrounding him were dark, all candles extinguished for the night as sleeping townspeople huddled under deep piles of blankets. It was a cold November.

His breath congealed into thick plumes of steam as he walked, looking upward at the stars—intensely bright in the cold, crisp air. His left hand was kept warm from the rising heat of the lantern he carried, spilling out a small pool of dirty, orange light on the snow ahead of him. The numb fingers of his right hand groped among the folds of his coat pocket, searching for warmth.

Burbage's cheeks were flushed, and his ears hummed in the silence; his belly felt warm and full from the several tankards of beer he had drunk at the inn. The loud voices and forced laughter still rang in his ears. But everything else was silent now, the night air with barely a breeze, the thin covering of snow which seemed to muffle his footsteps. He had so little to do now—and it would remain the same all winter—with only his trips to the inn, until spring. In spring he and Richard were going to rebuild.

His footsteps impressed black marks on the new snow in Maiden Lane, and he stood before the ruins of the Globe. Only a few charred beams stood upright, painted white with a thin coating of snow—like the skeletal remains of some mythical beast. It was dark, and he could see little by the light of his feeble lantern: a pile of burned timbers and blackened foundation stone blocked his view of the stage.

A sadness filled him—perhaps the beer made him more susceptible—but it was an eerie, powerful, almost tangible emotion. This, the greatest theatre in London, which once had seated fifteen hundred people, now stood a pile of cinders and lonely ash.

No one had died in the fire, even though they had had a full house that last day. Well, one *had* died ... but not from the flames. Burbage had carefully covered that up: the brothers planned to rebuild the Globe, and superstition would drive people away from a playhouse where it was known a murder had been committed.

The external feeling of sadness strengthened, and waves of

despair and pain buffeted him, seeming to emanate from the ruins, like the cries of a mortally wounded animal in its death throes. Burbage frowned: he hadn't realized how much beer he had drunk. Now, perhaps, he understood the way Richard felt every time he came near this place.

But then Richard had always been the sensitive one, the one so filled with passion. At times, Burbage envied his brother, who was so sure of himself always, totally devoted to his profession as an actor. Richard's one desire was to perform on stage, and he did such a tremendous job. He lived for the Globe—Shakespeare himself had written many parts specifically for him to portray. Cuthbert Burbage had also acted on stage, only occasionally; but to him it was nothing more than repeating the lines he had memorized, picturing himself as a tool to move the play along. For Richard the characters were *real*.

It was not a hating envy he had for his brother, but a gentle one. Richard had no doubt as to his calling in life. The other Burbage was still waiting for his own calling. He had acted at times, when it was necessary; and he also managed the Globe Theatre, because his father had bequeathed it to Richard and him —and because he did a good job at it. His brother was a superb actor, and he himself was a shrewd businessman. The combination worked well, the previous success of the Globe had proved that.

But he wasn't sure that the loss of the Globe was the only reason for Richard's recent moody behavior, his anxiety. Being as popular as he was, Richard had little trouble acting in some of the other theatres in London. But Richard had seen something that night, when the Globe had burned, something that had shaken him badly. Burbage had waited for his brother to tell him, waited; but it had been five months, time enough for Richard's wound to heal ... or fester.

Perhaps things would be better come spring, when they could rebuild the theatre. Smiling vaguely, he remembered when they had first built the Globe, fifteen years before. Their father had built his own playhouse, the Theatre, in 1576—the first playhouse in all of London—in all of Europe, Burbage had heard (but who could possibly know all of Europe?). And on their father's death over twenty years later, the Theatre had passed on to Richard and Cuthbert Burbage—just as its lease ran out.

The landlord, one Giles Allen, was a singularly uncooperative man, despite Richard's impassioned speeches about an actor's need to have a playhouse in which to dissipate his creative energy, despite Cuthbert's tedious, patient negotiations. Allen had it in his mind to tear down the original playhouse because of "the greate and greevous abuses that grewe by the Theatre."

But the Burbages had turned the tables on him, tearing down the Theatre themselves and using the old wood, taking it to the south side of the Thames where they had erected the new Globe Theatre. Burbage chuckled aloud as he remembered Giles Allen, his face splotchy, almost exploding with anger, cheated out of destroying the playhouse himself.

His low chuckle seemed alarmingly loud in the deep silence. Around him, the snow seemed to muffle all other sound; even the wind had stopped. He tensed as his ears, numb from the cold, picked up a low sound, a strange sound. The thin blanket of snow had been left undisturbed since the last snowfall early the previous morning—only his own footprints left a trail to the ruins. He was the only one around—he had to be. The effects of the beer buzzed in his ears—perhaps they were playing tricks on him. He took another step into the ruins, stopping beside a blackened beam fallen at an odd angle. He rested his hand on the charred wood; melted snow ran along his fingers, carrying black particles of soot. He listened again, and he was sure. He looked at the snow around him—no one had entered the ruins in the past day.

Yet inside, unmistakably, he heard voices.

SCENE II

On December 28, 1598, Richard and Cuthbert Burbage "and divers other persons, to the number of twelve ... armed themselves ... and throwing down the sayd Theatre in verye outrageous, violent and riotous sort ... did then also in most forcible and ryotous manner take and carry away from thence all the wood and timber thereof unto the Banckside ... and there erected a newe plahhowse with the sayd timber and woode."

— GILES ALLEN, IN A LAWSUIT AGAINST THE BURBAGES IN MIDDLESEX COURT.

Setting—London. *The Globe Theatre, intact, before the burning. Morning. In the basement under the stage is Thomas Radclyffe, a young actor, rehearsing his lines, making sure he is satisfied with their delivery. He has been cast as Henry VIII in Shakespeare's new play,* All is True, *which will be performed for the first time at the Globe this afternoon.*

The basement is dim and shadowy, lit only by the light shining through the open trapdoor of the stage. It is cluttered with old props, a discarded mask of a ghost from an old play, costumes hang from sharp garment hooks on the wall beams.

Radclyffe closed his eyes tightly. He *was* Henry VIII. He filled his chest, thrusting it forward in a kinglike manner; he propped one hand on his hip. He imagined himself to be dressed in the garments King Henry wore in the portraits he had seen. His personality was putty, changing, fitting into a new mold, as an actor was required to do. He was almost ready.

His master, Havermont, had shown him this technique to *know* his characters, to *be* the people he was to portray. Radclyffe had been attached to Master Havermont almost seven years, lodging and boarding with the experienced actor since he had been ten years old. Thomas Radclyffe had been an extremely apt pupil—a bit impulsive, a bit impatient, his master had said, but Radclyffe wasn't sure now if the impressions he had given hadn't also been mostly an act.

After sending him through the typical women's roles—the bane of all apprentices before they started to sprout whiskers—Havermont had prepared him for the veteran actor's own particular types of parts so that Radclyffe could take his place at the time of his master's death.

And now Radclyffe had had the role of Henry VIII pressed upon him. Havermont had died suddenly; Radclyffe was not yet quite prepared, and perhaps he had let it go to his head a bit—his first salaried role, and it was *almost* the leading man. Radclyffe took it seriously—he always took his acting seriously—spending much of his free time down here, in the musty peacefulness of the basement of the Globe, where he could be totally alone, and let his dialogue fall into the quiet psyche of the theatre.

The lines came into his head—he was ready for them. He took up where he had left off the day before, trying to set his mind in the same mood. King Henry has just been informed that the people are outraged over a new tax, levied by the evil Cardinal Wolsey—no, not "evil," not yet, the King still considers him a trusted friend—Wolsey, played by Richard Burbage, the *real* star of the play, the part written by Shakespeare especially for Burbage. But the audience would go from the play remembering *him*, Thomas Radclyffe, Henry VIII.

He lowered his voice, taking on a forgiving, almost condescending tone, placing himself into the reality of the play. He is a king, he told himself, about to remove a tax he considers unjust, a tax which he has known nothing about, which Wolsey has placed upon the people but has just denied doing so. The King holds Wolsey as friend and believes him.

"'Things done well and with a care exempt themselves from fear; things done without example, in their issue are to be fear'd.'"

"*Louder.*" Radclyffe reacted instinctively, raising his voice.

"'Have you a precedent of this commission? I believe, not any.'"

"*More regal—more pride! With rising anger!*"

"'We must not—'" He paused, looking around the shadows of the basement, frowning. "Who is there? Who has spoken?"

"With rising anger! What is the next line? 'We must not rend our subjects from their laws, and stick them in our will.' This must be spoken angrily—not in a condescending tone."

Radclyffe became distressed, looking around the cluttered, cobwebbed shadows of the Globe's basement, but saw no one. He listened to the voice, trying to pinpoint it—but it was a whisper, an echoing mélange of voices.

"Where are you?" Then his eyes centered on something, propped up against the wall, a mask of a ghost, used once for the part of the ghost of Hamlet's father. He felt an eerie chill crawling in the skin of his back. "*What* are you?"

Radclyffe moved toward the mask slowly, afraid, but intrigued. *"A part of your profession. A muse? No, not quite so ... quaint. We ARE the Globe Theatre."*

Radclyffe picked up the mask, his fingers trembling. He looked to see if anything hid behind it—nothing. The frozen, empty mouth of the mask continued to pour forth its words.

"Thirty-seven years ago, James Burbage built the Theatre—the first playhouse in all of Europe. And then his sons Richard and Cuthbert Burbage tore it down and used the same wood to build this, the Globe Theatre. Can you think that all those performances, year after year, all those actors pouring their souls into these walls, could have no effect on the wood of this place? A part of it remains here. We are the soul of this playhouse—and you shall perform as we direct you when you perform on our stage, in our walls."

"No!" Radclyffe cast the mask back to the ground. The eye holes continued to stare back at him. Anger and pride sprang from his years of training. "I would be *no* actor if I did only as you tell me. My Master Havermont has taught me to be a great performer. He has shown me that I am to interpret the characters as *I* choose; I am to say the lines as *I* decide. The acting must come wholly from *me*, or else I am just repeating words. Master Havermont is right, and I cannot listen to you."

He had never doubted the existence of ghosts—nobody in London did. But he knew that ghosts were probably evil—and probably dangerous.

The voice paused, taking on a more sinister tone. *"You hold your dead master in high esteem, then?"*

"'The gentleman is learned, and a most rare speaker; to nature none more bound; his training such that he may furnish and instruct great teachers, and never seek for aid out of himself.' Indeed, I hold him in esteem."

"Then do you not think a part of him abides with us?" The voice was different now, familiar ... Havermont's voice.

"Be silent! I will believe that part of him abides with you—if you are truly the leavings of great actors—but it is a *bad* part, much like the scum on top of a beautiful pond. My master would never counsel me to listen to every whim of a spectator! I will speak *my* lines, with *my* voice, and *my* mind!"

Radclyffe turned, anger on his face, perhaps to cover his fear, and stormed toward the basement steps. Suddenly he was slammed against the wall by unseen hands and held there by a force he could not define. His eyes began to show fear. The voice came at him from every beam, every shadow.

"We have more power here than you think! You would be safer if you did not resist!"

Radclyffe used his anger again to push off the paralyzing fear. "'Be advis'd; heat not a furnace for your foe so hot that it do singe yourself!'"

Radclyffe flailed his hands in the air as if to fend off the unseen enemy, and he broke away, running quickly up the stairs.

SCENE III

"Yea, truly for I am persuaded that Satan hath not a more speedy way and fitter school to work and teach his desire to bring men and women into his snare than these ... plays and theatres are, and therefore necessary that these places and plays should be forbidden and dissolved and put down by authority."

> — JOHN NORTHBROKE, A CLERGYMAN,
> *A TREATISE AGAINST DICING,*
> *DANCING AND INTERLUDES WITH*
> *OTHER IDLE PASTIMES* (1577)

Setting—The uppermost floor of the Globe Theatre, just under the thatched roof. Raw beams cast odd shadows. Cuthbert Burbage is loading gunpowder into one of three cannons, props, which he is preparing as a stage effect for the afternoon's first performance of All is True.

Enter Thomas Radclyffe, *moving tentatively, looking nervous, a little shaken.*

Burbage kept his eye on the stream of black powder, pouring slowly so as to spill none of it. He heard the young actor approach. "One moment, Thomas ..." he said aloud, and thought he saw Radclyffe jump, startled, from the corner of his eye. Burbage inspected his work and looked at the other two cannons for a moment, then turned to face Thomas Radclyffe.

The young actor fumbled with his words for a moment, and found it easiest to say, "What are those for?"

"They are cannons, Thomas! Stage effects! You know, in the first act, when you, King Henry, and your party enter Cardinal Wolsey's palace all cloaked and hidden? Well, when the King enters, we shall fire these cannons—armed with only paper wadding, of course—to let the *audience* know that the royal presence has just arrived—and also to give them a little start!"

Burbage smiled, rubbing his hands together, then looked at Radclyffe, dissolving his expression into a frown. The young actor was pale and gaunt, obviously frightened. "And where is the bold, proud young actor who drives us all nearly mad with his outbursts of eagerness?"

Radclyffe seemed to fumble for words; he found different ways for his fingers to interlock with each other. "Well, Mister Burbage, sir, it is difficult to—"

"Speak!" Burbage snapped, not angrily, but with a tone of get-down-to-business that stopped all further stuttering from the young actor.

"Down in the basement—this theatre—Mister Burbage, there are *ghosts!*"

"*Hissst!*" Burbage turned him away, then looked worriedly down to the stage where some of the other actors were rehearsing. None of them seemed to be paying any attention. "King's deathbed, man! Hush when you speak of such things! Ghosts? If that rumor were to be unleashed, it would ruin us as surely as if we were to burn the place down ourselves!"

Burbage shook his head, concerned, then looked hard at Radclyffe. "Now, these ghosts—you have seen them? Where?"

"In the basement—I didn't *see* them, but rather heard them."

Burbage let out an audible sigh of relief. "The basement! Thomas, any man can get the jitters when he's alone down there among all the old props and shadows. The wood creaks a little, a few rats rustle about here and there. And your imagination makes the rest—"

"No! It wasn't like that, Mister Burbage! Not just odd sounds, but *words!* I had a conversation with the ghosts!"

"And what did these ghosts have to say?"

"They tried to force me to say my lines in different ways, making me act in their manner, and not my own. They tried to twist my talent, taking the ... the *life* out of my portrayal."

Burbage almost laughed but contained himself. "Most ghosts try to murder people, Thomas—but your ghosts want to be your acting coaches!" He saw the expression on Radclyffe's face, became serious. "Maybe it's Havermont come back to help you?"

"No!" Radclyffe looked angry, upset, downcast. "You don't understand! They are *evil*! They try to twist my acting talent to their own ends! I cannot perform that way!"

The young actor stopped and changed his emotions abruptly, saddened, almost accusing. "You can't understand—you're not an actor. You don't know what it means to me." He drew in a deep breath. "You don't believe me."

Burbage didn't. But he had enough tact to pause a moment, considering the best way to handle the young actor. He reached up to put a hand on Radclyffe's shoulder. "I know you, Thomas. I know that your temper is a little short, and that you are inclined to act without thinking sometimes. But I have never known you to have a wild imagination, and I have never known you to lie. Seeing this change in your mood, now, it is obvious to me that *you* believe what you say. But I ask you this, Thomas—say no word of this matter to anyone. If you must speak further on it, come to me, and only me. Surely you realize how this could ruin us if handled improperly. Any demon a man might find at the bottom of a bottle of ale would be seen as a ghost of the Globe—and people would flock away from this 'haunted theatre' as if it were a plague house! No, we must keep silent about this."

"But the ghosts will still be here!"

Burbage sighed. "Thomas, what would you have me do? I cannot get two strongmen and have them evicted as we would any other troublemakers!"

"Bring a bishop! Someone, anyone from the Church! To exorcise the ghosts!"

Burbage widened his eyes almost in shock. "A priest? King's deathbed, Thomas! Do you spend no time out in the city, or are you always sheltered here in the theatre? Have you not heard the Puritans' outcry against all places of amusement, theatres in particular? Did you not know that my father was forced to build the original Theatre outside the city of London because of the public outcry? And even then, he was brought before the London

Lord Mayor in the Middlesex Court more times than you can count on your hands. No priest would come near the Globe unless he wanted to burn it down. The Puritans would like nothing more than to hear that Satan has haunted our playhouse."

Radclyffe seemed to hear, but not believe. He lowered his voice, almost glaring at Burbage. "You and your brother should never have used the old wood from the Theatre." Radclyffe's face was angry, and he turned to walk away.

"Thomas!" Burbage called, worried. The young actor didn't turn. "Don't do anything rash!"

Radclyffe didn't answer as he disappeared down the ladder leading from the loft. Burbage looked after him for a long moment, folding his lips into a troubled frown, then he began to load gunpowder into the other two cannons.

SCENE IV

"Things done well and with a care exempt themselves from fear."

— WILLIAM SHAKESPEARE, *HENRY VIII*,
FIRST PERFORMED AT THE GLOBE
THEATRE, JUNE 29, 1613

Setting—the basement of the Globe Theatre. It is mid-afternoon on the day of the first performance of All is True. *Upstairs, offstage, noises can be heard as people file in to fill the theatre. The play will begin soon.*

Enter Thomas Radclyffe, *afraid, but moving with determination. He carries a torch he has made, naked fire pouring light into the darkness.*

He paused, swallowing hard, forcing his mouth into a grim, determined line, holding the torch in front of him like a weapon. He filled his mind with anger and obsession. Martyr—like Buckingham in the play. If need be.

"Hear me, ghosts!" Radclyffe's voice trembled, then gained in strength. "You are evil! You are oppressive! You stifle the creative expression of all actors—I must destroy you to save my profession. 'Ye blew the fire that burns ye!'"

He picked up the mask from the floor. "What? Are you silent? Have you fled?"

Radclyffe dropped the mask and crushed it under his feet, finding a small, inadequate outlet for his anger and fear. He heard the people above, waiting for the play to begin. Someone would probably be looking for him.

"You are brave, young actor—are you not afraid?"

"'Things done well and with a care exempt themselves from fear.'"

Radclyffe looked up to find the source of the voice—and saw another mask, a new one he hadn't seen before, propped in the corner of one of the beams, finely painted and detailed enough to look lifelike. Almost lifelike. It was Henry VIII, but subtly, hauntingly, familiar, with definite traces of Radclyffe's own face embedded within the features.

The young actor shuddered briefly, then steeled himself. "I will burn this theatre down and destroy the cursed wood which you inhabit. You will not harm me—I have chosen this time with care—for if you do, you will expose yourselves to all of London!"

He waited for a reply, hearing only the crackle of his torch in the silence, until the voice spoke again.

"Ah, but you forget, young actor, that we ARE this theatre ... and when we are filled with an audience—" Radclyffe's torch was suddenly snuffed out, plunging him into darkness. *"We are strongest of all!"*

And he felt a cold, icy grip, not quite like hands, around his throat....

SCENE V

"Will not a filthy play with a blast of trumpet sooner call thither a thousand than an hour's tolling of the bell bring to a sermon a hundred?"

— A PREACHER, STOCKTON, IN A SERMON
AGAINST THE THEATRE, 1578

Setting—the ground level of the Globe Theatre; the yard is filled with people, trying to get a clear view of the stage, which is raised above the crowd. At the entrance stands a placard announcing the day's play. Similar leaflets are scattered throughout London, tacked onto wooden posts, competing with many other announcements.

As people file through the single, narrow entrance, a man stands with a small box in hand, collecting one penny from all who enter. Those who are content to stand continue into the yard; those who wish a seat or a private box are required to pay an extra sum.

Cuthbert Burbage sits among others in a Twelvepenny Room, one of the best seats in the playhouse, with his guest, Lady Dalton. She is older than he, dressed in gaudy finery, decked with jewels. Burbage looks at the activity around him; he is impatient.

"If they don't start soon, we won't finish the play before sunset," he muttered to himself. "Can't have a performance without daylight, you know."

"Cuthbert, this is so exciting!" Lady Dalton peered excitedly into the crowd, as if to find out which of her social acquaintances had failed to attend the play, and how many had failed to get seats as exquisite as her own.

Burbage looked at her, scowling slightly. The Lady Dalton was rather rich ... and rather old, and rather dim. Damn his business sense.

"Is Shakespeare *himself* here today, Cuthbert?"

"Of course, he is—" Burbage snapped, "You don't think he'd miss the first performance of his new play?" He caught himself, placing some sweetness into his voice. "There he is, just across the yard from us ... see, in one of the other Twelvepenny Rooms."

"Sooo!" she cooed.

Burbage looked around uncomfortably: he wondered if Radclyffe had been found yet. The play had to start soon—he was afraid the young actor was going to ruin his first important role by chasing after ghosts in his imagination. Radclyffe—don't be a fool!

The noises of the audience waned like a dying fire after one of the Lord Chamberlain's Men stepped out onto the stage, speaking the Prologue. People smothered their random sounds, focusing on the words being spoken, waiting to be taken away to another reality.

And the play began.

Burbage leaned back in his seat, relaxing slightly, or at least seeming to. They wouldn't have started the play without Radclyffe, even though he didn't make an appearance until the second scene.

Lady Dalton seemed to be more interested in the audience than in the play. Burbage watched his brother Richard perform, strutting around as Cardinal Wolsey in all his evil glory—Richard enjoyed the villain parts at times, but then Burbage could never tell what his brother really enjoyed and what was just an act.

(Wolsey accuses the innocent Buckingham, the martyr, of treason, and has him arrested, to be brought before the King's court.)

The first scene ended, and Burbage grew tense again. He sat up, waiting the unbearable few moments. Why was he uneasy? The performance was of prime importance—Radclyffe knew that —he imagined himself to be a devoted actor, and he would never miss his first important role.

The audience background noise rose up quickly for a few moments but was dampened again as Scene II began. King Henry entered with pomp and glory—and Burbage finally felt at ease. After all, he should never have been worried. He knew Thomas Radclyffe—the young actor had been so proud of himself after receiving this part that he wouldn't have forfeited this performance for anything.

Yet Burbage squinted—and thought he saw something strange about Radclyffe's face. Of course, the makeup would have changed it somewhat—but he thought he saw sharp edges, shadows, almost as if Radclyffe were wearing a very detailed mask ... but no, he could see the mouth move.

Still, he felt uneasy again. Lady Dalton probably couldn't even see that far.

"What's happening, Cuthbert?" she whispered.

Burbage almost imperceptibly rolled his eyes heavenward. "This is the trial of Buckingham at the King's court. Queen Katherine has just entered to beg the King to withdraw a tax which takes one sixth of every man's possessions—"

Lady Dalton seemed to be barely listening. "Who's Buckingham?"

Burbage sighed.

The scene progressed. Radclyffe's voice was the same, but Burbage seemed to notice some special quality, a lilt, an intonation, which made the young actor's voice stand out. Burbage had never considered himself a theatrical critic—he heard the lines, saw which ones were delivered more masterfully than others. And people paid to see the performances—he drew his livelihood from that. But he hadn't felt any special drive, any special presence about acting. Until now, in Radclyffe's voice, he felt the very embodiment of a performance, the life, the calling—yet he couldn't pin it down. He couldn't say why, but he was somehow aware that Radclyffe was giving the best performance he had ever seen.

Richard, though, seemed to be acting strangely. There—he had just stumbled over a line. Richard had never stumbled over a line before, not in all Burbage's recollection. Was it jealousy? No, it was almost as if he were ... scared of something. But what would Richard ever be so afraid of that he couldn't successfully cover it up?

The scene continued, and Burbage felt a low buzz in the audience as the people remarked on how outstanding, how superb, the young actor was. What would have seemed an almost interminably long scene any other time, now held them enthralled.

And at last the scene was over.

He felt a tap on his shoulder. Burbage was startled and turned to find the man next to him pointing out into the corridor where stood a young boy, one of the apprentice actors of the Lord Chamberlain's Men. The boy looked agitated, pale, and sweating. He seemed unable to speak but gestured desperately for Burbage to come to him.

"Excuse me, Lady Dalton," he whispered in her ear. She smiled. "One of my actors wishes to speak with me."

"Oh, of course, Cuthbert—please hurry back."

Burbage went to the boy as the third scene began. They spoke in quiet voices. "What is it?"

The boy was trembling. "I've found him, Mister Burbage!"

"What? *Who?*"

"Come! Quickly!" The boy took his arm and drew him down the corridor through the curtains behind the tiring room, backstage, and to the narrow basement steps.

"What could possibly be down here, boy?"

"He is dead, sir! *Murdered!* Thomas Radclyffe, sir! He's hung up on the wall, by his neck—on one of the clothes hooks!"

"You're *mad*, boy! He's just been—"

They entered the dimness of the basement, surrounded by the muffled echoes of the performance overhead. Burbage didn't need to look very closely to see a burned-out torch on the floor, and a shadowy figure hung on the wall with its feet dangling off the floor. And the face was that of Thomas Radclyffe.

"King's deathbed!" Burbage gaped a moment, realized what he was doing, then composed himself almost immediately, thinking fast. The boy stood next to him. Burbage made his face firm and expressionless, but he felt cold.

"This ... could ruin us. A murder! At the Globe Theatre!" He looked quickly at the boy. "You have told no one?"

"No, sir! I thought it wisest to speak only to you!"

"Good! You are intelligent, boy. I have a gold piece for you if you tell no one. Not one word. If you *do* speak of this, I will find it very easy to destroy your acting career for the rest of your life."

"Oh, not one word, sir. Please don't feel you need to use threats, Mister Burbage."

"No … no. I know. I have to think of what to do. Keep quiet and be *sure* no one else comes down here. Calm. I must be calm. *We must remain calm.*" He sighed. "I'd best be back to the Lady Dalton before she says anything. Until I can talk to Richard." He heaved a long breath, then muttered, "Oh, deathbeds for the entire royal family! How are we ever going to patch *this* up?"

They walked up the stairs. "But, Mister Burbage—if Thomas Radclyffe is dead down here … then *who* is on the stage?"

Burbage paused, gripping the rail. "I don't know … and I am afraid to know."

He walked slowly back and seated himself beside Lady Dalton as Scene IV was just beginning. He gripped the arms of the chair to stop his hands from trembling. Burbage was surprised to find her watching the play.

She pointed to the action on the stage. "What are they having a party for, Cuthbert?"

Burbage tried to get his mind back on the play, to focus on something other than his cold fear. "Uh … the Cardinal Wolsey, my brother Richard, is having a great dinner at his palace, with many lords and ladies. See … they're all sitting around having idle dinner conversation, until—" He waited: it would have been glee and childlike anticipation in other circumstances. Trumpets sounded; drums rolled; and the cannons blasted, thundering in his ears.

And as his ears rung, Burbage thought he heard Thomas Radclyffe's voice, somehow—the real voice, not the false acting voice on the stage, this was different, a whisper running through his head, though not intended for his own ears.

"Now, we fight on equal terms."

Unseen, some of the burning paper wadding settled on the thatched roof, smoldering, kindling itself, setting fire to the roof.

The Lady Dalton squealed in terror at the cannon sound, then in delight. The audience, half-deafened, murmured in confusion.

On the stage, a company of cloaked and hooded strangers

entered, hiding their faces. Burbage continued to explain. "The Cardinal's guests think these are some foreign ambassadors—but they are really the King and his party in disguise. There ... that one is the King." Or is it something that I will never understand?—he thought to himself. There are more things in heaven and earth, Cuthbert Burbage, than are dreamt of in your philosophy.

"How do you know that's the King?" Lady Dalton asked.

"From the *cannons*—we wouldn't blast cannons for anyone but the royal presence, now would we?"

"Oh."

They watched as the hooded company made its slow procession across the stage.

"There, now Cardinal Wolsey suspects that one of the masquers is the King ... he says as much ... and he decides to unmask him...."

Burbage watched his brother walk on the stage toward one of the hooded figures, reaching up tentatively—more tentative than he actually should have been. He gripped the folds of the hood and began to draw it back.

"FIRE!" someone shouted.

Suddenly all hands were pointed toward the thatched roof which was in flames. Others took up the cry; tumult erupted. People fled toward the single narrow entrance.

On the stage, Richard Burbage cried out wildly; his face was white as a sculpture. The hooded figure was gone, the false Thomas Radclyffe, vanished; unnoticed in the uproar.

And flames began to devour the Globe.

SCENE VI

"... some of the Paper or other stuff wherewith (the cannons) were stopped, did light on the Thatch, where being thought at first but an idle smoak, and their eyes more attentive to the show, it kindled inwardly and ran round like a train, consuming within less than an hour the whole House to the very ground ... yet nothing did perish but Wood and straw and a few forsaken cloakes. Only one man had his

breeches set on fire, that would perhaps have broyled him if he had not by the benefit of provident will put it out with bottle ale."

— SIR HENRY WOTTON, EYEWITNESS TO THE
BURNING OF THE GLOBE THEATRE

"... while Burbages' Company were acting at the Globe the play of Henry VIII, and there shooting off certain (cannons) in way of triumph, the fire catched and fastened upon the thatch of the house, and there burned so furiously, as it consumed the whole house, all in less than two hours. the people having enough to do to save themselves."

— THOMAS LORKINS, EYEWITNESS TO THE
BURNING OF THE GLOBE THEATRE

Cuthbert Burbage found his brother Richard, much more shaken than he should have been from the fire, standing in the churning crowd around the flaming wreckage. Night was falling. A heavy beam collapsed in a shower of sparks.

Silently, together, they watched their Globe Theatre burn....

EPILOGUE

Setting—London. *Darkness. Cuthbert Burbage has entered the cold, snow-covered wreckage. Voices.*

He listened, creeping closer—the voices were strange and scattered, speaking a pastiche of lines from old Shakespeare plays. They didn't sound like children's' voices: in fact, they seemed to carry a great deal of emotion, sadness, loss.

He stepped around some fallen timbers and came in view of the burned-out remnants of the stage. In the shadows he saw strange figures, masked and costumed.

"What are you doing there? Who are you?" Burbage shouted,

his anger rising before he had time to think. He expected them to scatter and run like frightened children, but instead the figures turned to look at him.

Burbage stepped out from behind the wreckage and moved toward them. "Where did you get those masks?" he demanded, trying to place a tone of angry command in his voice.

The central figure turned toward him; he wore an old mask of the ghost of Hamlet's father, smashed-in but painstakingly repaired, blackened a little in the fire. He spoke in a deep, eerie voice, like many voices all in one.

"*We are the Globe Theatre, and we are almost dead. Do not disturb our final performance.*"

Burbage halted a moment, then stepped forward. "You are trespassing," he said coldly, standing directly before the figure, glaring at the mask. He saw nothing behind the eyeholes. Nothing.

They confronted each other in silence; and, unexpectedly, Burbage reached up to pull the mask off. And beheld the face of a leering skull, desiccated and fire-blackened.

Before Burbage could cry out, the mask was snatched away from his numb fingers and placed back on the figure's head.

Burbage felt cold, and his eyes misted over with terror and confusion. "*What* are you?" The words slid through his clenched teeth like a cold wind.

"*A truly talented actor leaves a part of himself, part of his soul, within the theatre in which he performs. This wood, these timbers, are from the very first playhouse in all of Europe, which has absorbed countless performances.... We are what is left.*"

Burbage first began to tremble. "*You!* Ghosts! You are what Richard saw! You killed Thomas Radclyffe! Murdered him!"

"*We acted only to protect ourselves. In vain.*"

Burbage stood motionless, only his thoughts whirling—fear, anger, confusion—and he could not function until he accepted his inability to accept. "I do not understand ... I cannot believe this."

"*You are not an actor. You will not understand.*" The central figure continued to stare at him with the frozen expression of the mask. *"Tell your brother Richard—he will understand. It will comfort him. He knows us, but he does not realize it. Tell him not to fear us."*

Burbage found he had taken one step backward, and another. The masked figure raised his voice. *"Leave us! To complete our performance!"*

Burbage felt his fear taking precedence over all his other emotions, and he took another step backward, staring at the troupe of spectral figures one final time. Then he turned to flee from the ruins of the Globe Theatre.

The wreckage of the Globe lay in Maiden Lane, covered with snow, until the winter of 1614 passed.

"And the next spring it was new builded in a far finer manner than before."

— MASTER JOHN STOW, *GENERAL CHRONICLE OF ENGLAND*

Rebecca diligently read most of my stories, across all genres, but after she'd finished quite a few, she gave me a near-impossible challenge: "Please write a story that has a happy ending! Something romantic for a change."

This was her Valentine's Day present.

FROG KISS

He had gotten used to it by now. The frog tasted cold and slimy against his lips, with a taste like brackish water, mud, and old compost. But Keric gave it a dutiful smack on its mouth, hoping that it wouldn't suddenly turn into the fat old king, who had also been enchanted, along with several more desirable members of the royal family.

But the frog just looked at him, squirmed, and then urinated on Keric's palm. Nothing. Again. He took a dab of red pigment from his pouch, smeared it on the frog's head, and then tossed the creature through the trees and marsh grass. He listened to it plop in another pool. Another one tried and failed.

Around him, the sounds of thousands of frogs croaked in the dense swamp, loud enough to drown out the whine of mosquitoes, the constant dripping of water, and the occasional belch of a crocodile.

Sweat and dirty water ran in streaks from his brown hair, down his cheeks, and avoided the frog slime around his mouth. He had caught and tested more than three dozen frogs already, but it would be years before he could find them all—and that was only if any members of the frog-cursed royal family remained alive in the deep swamps. A crocodile splashed somewhere out in the network of cypress roots and branches. Somehow Keric couldn't imagine the brittle old Queen Mother deigning to eat flies, not even if they were served to her by someone else.

When the evil wizard Cosimor had taken over the kingdom less than a year before, he had followed the traditional path of sorcerous usurpers by capturing the entire royal family and transforming them into frogs and then turning them loose in the sprawling, infected swamps of Dermith.

Cosimor had intended to tax the kingdom to its death, drive the subjects into slavery, and generally keep himself amused. But less than three weeks later the wizard had died choking on a fish bone—no vengeful curse, that; simply poor cooking. Now the kingdom had been left without any rulers, not even the incompetent but somehow endearing royal family.

Keric, who lived in a hut on the fringes of the Dermith swamps, trapping muskrats and selling the fur in the noisy walled town, had decided to try to find the royal family in its exile, free at least one of them with a kiss, and then count on his reward. A palace of his own, perhaps? Gold coins stacked as high as an oak tree? Fine clothes. He pulled at his dripping, mud-soaked rags. Yes, fine clothes first. And then perhaps the hand of one of the princesses in marriage?

He spat drying slime away from his lips. But first he had to catch the right frog—and they all looked alike!

He slumped down on a rotting log covered with Spanish moss, then looked across at the piled undergrowth to see a bloated old bullfrog sitting under a drooping fern. Plainly visible on the frog's back were three equally spaced dark blotches, just like the supposed birthmark carried by every member of the royal family! Was this the old king, then? The fat duchess, the king's sister? It didn't matter to Keric—the frog sat right in front of his eyes. It had always taken him too long to see what was right in front of his face.

He didn't want to hesitate too long. Keric shifted his body forward and then lunged, splaying out his mud-caked fingers. He skidded through a spiderweb, needle-thin fronds, and dead leaves, but the bullfrog squirted away from him. He scrambled and grabbed again.

He didn't see the girl until she leapt out from the bushes in front of the bullfrog, opened up the mouth of a large squirming sack, and swept the frog inside. The bullfrog made a croak of alarm, but then the girl spun the sack shut. "Got him!" she said, giggling. Then she sprinted away through the underbrush, leaving only disturbed willow branches dangling behind her.

"Hey!" Keric shouted and jumped to his feet. He ran after her, flinging branches out of the way. He splashed through puddles of standing water, squished on sodden grass islands, and ducked his head in buzzing clouds of mosquitoes. All around, the other frogs continued their songs. "That one was mine!"

"Not anymore!" He heard her voice from the side, in a different direction from where she had disappeared. He looked in time to see her running barefoot down a path only she could see. Barefoot!

Keric ran after her. He found himself panting and sweating. He had grown up in and around these swamps. He considered himself an exceptional woodsman in even the deepest parts of the morass. He could outrun and out-hunt anyone he had ever known. But this girl kept going at a pace he could not hope to match. He stumbled, he missed solid footing, he splashed scummy water all over himself.

"Wait!" he shouted. He heard only the crocodiles growling.

"If you'd look over here, you'd have a better chance of seeing me!" She laughed again.

He whirled to see her across a mucky pool, not twenty feet from him. Without thinking—since he was wet and filthy anyway—he left the path and charged across the way. "Give me my frog!"

Keric tried to run with both feet, but each step became more difficult as the ooze sucked at his boots. He had to get the bullfrog with the three spots. He *knew* it was somebody from the royal family. The girl probably didn't know what she had. Maybe she wanted to eat it!

He sloshed onward, but before he had gone halfway across the pool, he felt the muck dragging him down. He sank to his waist and found he could not take another step. He continued to submerge in the ooze. "Oh no!"

From the spreading cypress tree over his head, he heard the girl's voice. "You should be more careful out here in the swamps. Plenty of dangerous things out here. Crocodiles, water moccasin snakes, milt spiders bigger than your hand, poison plants." Keric looked up to see her sitting on one of the branches, holding onto the frog sack with one hand and munching on a dripping fruit in the other. "But you really have to watch out for that quicksand. That's especially bad."

"Would you help me out of this?" He looked at her. He had sunk up to his armpits and felt the cold muck seeping into his pores. The mud crept to the tops of his shoulders. Keric had to lift his head to keep his chin out of the ooze. "Um, please?"

"I don't know. You were chasing me." She finished her fruit and tossed the pit down. It splashed beside him.

"I'll tell you what you've got in that sack of yours."

"It's frogs."

"No, if you'll just let me kiss one of them I'll show you something magic!" He had to talk rapidly now. The quicksand had reached his lips.

"Oh, you mean *that*! Sure, I've got the whole royal family here." She reached in and pulled out another frog, this one sleek and small. It also had the three identical splotches. "You don't think you were the only one to get the idea for finding the frogs in the swamp, do you?"

Actually, Keric *had* thought he was the only one to think of that. Once again, the obvious was staring him in the face.

"But you were going about it all wrong," the girl continued. "You kept trying to kiss them out here in the swamp. Now tell me, just what would you have done if the frail and arthritic Queen Mother had appeared? Or one of the dainty princesses who would squeal at the sight of a beetle? How would you get them back? Makes more sense to me just to carry the frogs in a sack, go back to town, and then change them all back. Reward would still be the same, maybe more for saving them the journey."

Keric had to lean his head back to keep his nose and mouth above the surface. "Will you please help me now and give me advice later!"

She shrugged. "You haven't asked me the right question yet."

"What is the question?"

"Ask me what my name is! I'm not going to risk my life to rescue a total stranger."

"What's your name? Tell me quick!"

"I am Raffin. Pleased to meet you." She paused. "And what's your name?"

"I'm Keric! Help!"

She tossed a vine down that struck near his face. Keric grabbed at it, clawing at the slick surface of the vine with his mucky hands. But he managed to haul himself forward, toward the near edge of the pool of quicksand. He heaved himself out onto the soggy ground and shivered. He had lost his left boot, but he had no intention of going back to get it.

When he looked up at the tree, Raffin was gone.

After dark, when Keric remained cold and clammy but unable to light a fire, he saw an orange light flickering through the tangled branches. He followed it to Raffin's fire, then crept close to where he could see.

She sat humming to herself and holding four sticks splayed in the flames. Little strips of meat had been skewered on the wood and sizzled in the light. The bound bundle of royal frogs sat beside her. "Come closer and sit down, Keric. You're making enough noise at being quiet."

Angry, Keric came out of his hiding place and strode with confidence into her firelight. Finally, he sighed and shook his head. "I thought I was good in the swamps, moving silently, always knowing my way. I can't believe I am being so clumsy around you."

Raffin shrugged. "You *are* good. The best I've seen. But I'm better."

Her long pale hair must once have been blond but now had taken on the color of fallen leaves and dry grass. Her eyes looked startlingly blue within the camouflage of her appearance. Raffin had washed most of the grime from her face, arms, and hands before preparing her food.

Keric didn't want to imagine what he looked like himself.

Raffin took one of the sticks out of the fire and blew on the sizzling strips of meat. "Frog legs, filleted." At his shocked expression, she laughed. "No, just normal frogs. Don't worry. Would you like some?"

Keric swallowed. "I haven't eaten anything all day."

"Say please."

"Please. Uh, I mean, Raffin, may I please have some?"

"Of course. You're my guest. I saved your life. Do you think I'd refuse a simple request like that?"

He took the stick she offered and ate the crispy meat right off the bark so he wouldn't have to touch it with his dirty fingers. "What are you doing out here all alone in the swamps?"

"I live out here. Don't worry, I can take care of myself."

Keric could believe that. He guessed she was only a couple years older than himself.

"But I don't mind company once in a while." Suddenly, Raffin appeared shy to him. "Just listen to those night sounds, the frogs and the humming insects. Why would anyone want to live in the town?"

Keric frowned and ate the last piece of meat. "Then why are you trying so hard to get the royal frogs?"

"Because you are. I've been watching you for days. It's been fun. Besides, I have dreams of getting a prince of my own."

They talked for much longer after that, but Keric could get no better explanation from her. He felt the weariness from the day sapping his strength, making him drowsy. He interrupted what she was saying. "Raffin, I am going to sleep."

He saw her smile as he let his eyes drift shut. "Make yourself at home."

When Keric cracked his eyes open again an hour later, his body screamed at him just to keep sleeping. But he couldn't. He had something much more important to do.

Raffin had stayed beside the fire, which now burned low and smoky, still driving the mosquitoes away. She lay curled up on the ground, her cheek pillowed on her scrawny arms. She looked very peaceful and vulnerable. Keric frowned, but then thought of palaces and princesses and fine clothes.

The fire popped as two logs sagged, and Keric used the noise to cover his own movements as he crept to his feet. She had left the sack containing the royal family sitting unguarded on the other side of the camp. He shook his head, wondering why she had made it so easy for him.

He picked up the sack and slipped out of the firelight, starting to run as soon as he got out under the moonlit trees.

"Keric!" she shouted behind him.

He stopped trying to be silent. The marsh grass whipped around him as he picked up speed. Willow branches snapped at his eyes. He kept splashing in puddles or flailing his hands at large, flapping night insects.

"Keric, come back!"

He didn't answer her but started to chuckle. He could make it out of the swamp to his hut. He would go immediately into the walled town and kiss all the frogs, even the old Queen Mother, and bring them back before Raffin could find him.

He used all his forest skills to weave his path. He couldn't hear her following, but then he doubted if he would. She was too good for that.

Keric looked behind him as he ran, seeking some sign. Raffin did impress him with her knowledge of the swamps. She could teach him many things. He decided he would share his treasure with her anyway, once he got it, but for now he wanted to succeed on his own, to impress her that his own survival abilities weren't so trivial either.

He tripped on the tail of the first crocodile and could not stop himself until he had stumbled into a cluster of the beasts. Once again, he had been looking in the wrong place and missed what was right in front of him.

The crocodiles hissed and belched at him. Keric cried out. He could count at least seven of them, startled out of their torpor and suddenly confronted with something worth eating. An old bull scuttled toward him, looking as large as a warship. It opened its mouth so wide that Keric felt he could have walked inside without ducking his head.

He turned and searched for a way out. Hissing and snapping their enormous jaws, the crocodiles moved in. The old bull lunged. Keric leaped back, caught his heel on the long body of one of the smaller reptiles, and sprawled backward. Even the smaller crocodile chomped at him. Keric dropped his sack of royal frogs.

He scrambled to his hands and knees, looking for an escape. The moonlight made everything dim and confusing. He thought he saw a flashing orange light behind a sketchy web of cypress roots, but he concentrated only on the nightmare of wide, fang-filled jaws.

Raffin appeared and struck the snout of the nearest crocodile with her roaring torch. "Get away from him!" The beast hissed and grunted as it lurched backward. Keric blinked in amazement. In her other hand, Raffin held a pointed stick that she jabbed at the remaining crocodiles.

The beasts backed away. The enormous bull stood his ground and let out a deep growl from somewhere at the bottom of his abdomen.

Keric crawled to his feet, too stunned and frightened to be much help.

Raffin faced the bull's charge and shoved her torch at her attacker. The crocodile hissed and snapped at her, but she was quick with the end of her torch, touching the burning end to the soft tissue inside the reptilian mouth. Keric heard the sizzle of burning meat.

With a defeated roar, the bull backed away and then, in a final gesture of frustration and spite, he lashed out with his long snout and snapped up the tied sack of royal frogs. The frogs made a combined sound like someone stepping on a goose. The giant crocodile crunched down with his jaws, chomped again, then swallowed. After a satisfied grunt, the crocodile crawled out of the clearing and splashed into the water.

"I told you to be careful out in the swamps," Raffin scolded Keric. "Do I have to watch out for you all the time?"

Keric sat stunned. "They're all gone! In one gulp, the whole royal family!" He shook his head. "I never meant for that to happen."

Raffin took hold of his hand and pulled him to his feet. "The kingdom will do fine without them. They weren't particularly worth rescuing." She stared at him, but he continued to sulk. "Hey, it was fun while it lasted."

"No, I meant my reward. The gold, the fine clothes, the palace—"

"And what would you do with all that stuff?" She looked at him, then tugged at his old, mud-caked tunic. "Fine clothes? Are you seeking what you really want, or just what you think you're *supposed* to want? What other people tell you to want isn't always right for you."

Keric lowered his head, sighed deeply. He looked at himself and realized she was right. "If I had a palace, I suppose I'd just track mud in it all the time."

Raffin giggled. "It's not so bad out here, you know."

"But what about my princess?"

Raffin flicked her hair behind her shoulders and looked angry for a moment, then spoke in a very shy voice. "You could stay in the swamps." She paused. "With me."

Keric looked up at her and listened to the frogs and the night insects. One of these days he was going to learn to notice the things right in front of him.

Sword and Sorcery was a formative genre for me. I read E. Howard's Conan the Barbarian and Kull the Conqueror stories as well as the Marvel comic magazines with the same heroes. Other golden-age writers helped establish the genre—Fritz Leiber, Clark Ashton Smith, Leigh Brackett, C.L. Moore, mostly in the pages of Weird Tales Magazine*—and I read all of them as well.*

When the current incarnation of Weird Tales announced a special Sword and Sorcery themed issue, I couldn't have been more thrilled. This went to the very marrow of my storytelling bones!

I wrote this story during a winter writing trip to a cabin in Grand Mesa, Colorado. I would go out snowshoeing during the days, dictating scenes set in this cold and frozen fantasy world with ice temples and monsters buried in the glaciers. What a treat!

"Cold Ice, Red Blood" was also a bucket-list item for me, because even though I had grown up reading Weird Tales reprints, and I had submitted to the magazine numerous times, I'd never been published in its pages. This was my first appearance in Weird Tales, *and it certainly isn't the last.*

COLD ICE, RED BLOOD

—I—

In the thin mountain air, sunlight glinted off the frozen sculptures like a spark of life. People came to the high meadow from surrounding villages for the yearly ice festival.

Aramin had just finished a magnificent life-sized horse carved from a block of lake ice that fair workers had dragged over to the young man's small camp. He had paid them a copper coin for the labor. The money was dear to him, but he knew he would win the prize purse, and all would be good. His beloved Syla had all the faith in him that he could possibly need.

Ice chips lay strewn around the sawdust and straw on the ground. They would melt quickly as the day warmed, but the deep chill in the air would keep Aramin's work intact for a few days, long enough for others to see and judge before the spirit of Thall took back the water into his presence in the world.

Holding his chisel and rasp, he stepped back to study the figure, reluctant to declare a work completed, because Thall always kept tiny secrets of the universe he created and inhabited.

Next to him, though, Syla smiled at the work, her pale skin flushed pink, her pretty face beaming. When he saw her expression, he knew that the sculpture was finished and that it was good. "A perfect horse," she said in a voice that held rainbows of happiness, pride, and love.

Aramin sighed. "I knew it was a horse as soon as I saw the block of ice cut out of the tarn," he said. "I understood the shape of the creature within, but I couldn't decide whether it was a plow horse, or a war horse, or …"

"A wild horse," Syla said. "Like one of the mountain stallions that run free."

Next to the horse sculpture, he had carved smaller, less-ambitious ice figures: a leaping trout, a grazing sheep bursting with wool. The one he liked best was a formless swirl, like a cloud mixed with a waterfall. It was indefinable, captivating, his own attempt to create and capture a symbolic representation of Thall himself, the presence in all things.

Syla didn't understand that one, and Aramin wasn't sure he did either, but the form was what he'd seen in the ice when he began to carve, and the young man followed the inspiration. He freed what he saw.

His willowy wife went back to their cookfire, adding another cake of dung to increase the heat. Under her rabbit-fur cap, her thin braids were intertwined with dried flowers she had plucked in the mountain meadows that spring. She boiled a pot of meltwater to make flower-petal tea.

In the heart of each winter, people from all the high villages would make the trek up to the frozen tundra for the ice festival. Aramin and a dozen other artisans would show off their skills, making wondrous transient figures out of the ice. The sculptors would have to make the best of whatever chunks were hauled before them; each time Aramin would study the ice, let his thoughts go into the translucent material so he could *see* the figure that wanted to emerge.

Three elders would make the rounds and declare one of the sculptors the ice king, presenting him with a shawl of dyed wool and a purse of ten silver coins. Aramin had won twice already, and this year he felt confident—especially with Syla's encouragement, though she called him her ice king, regardless.

Each year, families would make the trip to admire the ice sculptures, drawn by sleighs or carts that could ascend the steep mountain path. Children played games around the festival meadow. Fur traders used the opportunity to sell warm pelts, and vendors roasted sausages or snow grouse; others sold mead or strong wine to keep people warm on the inside. A hundred visitors had set up hide tents and lean-tos, shared food and songs, and wandered about to admire the new figures, including Aramin's glistening horse.

Then the priest-soldiers arrived.

Well over a hundred warriors rode in on armored ponies. They wore fur and leather flashed with blue, signifying their allegiance to the temple of Thall. Some were mercenaries, others bonded warrior slaves. The soldiers spread out to reveal they were the escort party for a blue-robed priestlord, bald and bearded, who exuded a personality fully as cold as any of the figures on display.

A murmur of unease rippled across the festival meadow. Aramin stood nervously next to his frozen figures. Syla handed him a mug of her flower-petal tea, and they both stood silent and smiling, anxious but trying not to show it. "All are welcome at the festival," she said in a quiet voice, as if convincing herself.

The soldiers were silent and implacable as they moved about the camp. They clearly came from different tribes, some dark skinned with thick black hair, others with pale beards and cold blue eyes. All had muscles and scars that marked the length of their service. The priestlord, however, showed only withering skepticism as he walked among the ice figures. Frowning, he dismissed the work of Aramin's competitors, a harsher judge than any village elder.

When the priestlord approached Aramin's work, the young man tried to fashion a welcoming smile. Thinking quickly, Syla poured another cup of tea, strong now with the dregs from the pot, and she offered it to the stern man. He frowned at the mug and frowned at her before turning back to the sculptures. The priestlord said nothing as he glanced at the smaller figures, but his gaze lingered over the powerful wild horse. He nodded slowly. "You are clearly the most talented ice sculptor here. What is your name?"

"I am Aramin, my lord. From the village of Copka. And this is Syla, my wife." His voice and gestures revealed his nervousness.

The priestlord gave no indication that he had heard. Instead, he approached the amorphous sculpture. "And what is this? Are you not finished?"

"That's all there is, my lord. I meant it to represent the presence of Thall, who is everywhere and unknowable."

"Only a priestlord can know Thall in all his aspects." The bald man gave him a sour scowl. "I am Priestlord Issom."

Aramin feared that he had said something wrong. "I am just an uneducated man, my lord. I defer to your wisdom."

The priestlord remained dour. "You think Thall speaks to you?"

Aramin imagined that he stood on a sharp precipice. "I think Thall is everywhere and speaks to all of us, but very few can listen. You would know better than I, priestlord."

Issom pondered the ice horse for a long moment, then turned to a burly man beside him, a priest-soldier with bronze skin and blue-black hair. "I choose this man. Bock, guard him."

The big priest-soldier stepped closer to Aramin, who did not understand what was happening. Issom's words rang across the festival meadow. "I have found my sculptor." The escort warriors snapped to attention, as if they were bows that had just been strung, arrows nocked. "Eliminate these others. We cannot risk that the heretics might try to use their talents."

"What do you mean?" Syla said, confused.

With growing dread, Aramin realized that the warriors had taken up positions among the other sculptors, preparing for this.

Around them, screams started to erupt.

The priest-soldiers pushed their armored ponies through the encampment, raising weapons. Axes and curved swords struck down in a splash of bright red on the snow.

"Stop!" Aramin cried out. "What do you want?"

Issom turned, gave him a withering smile. "You. And I already have you."

The big warrior Bock stood in front of Aramin, not letting him move. Syla let out a shrill scream as she watched the slaughter. "But why? Those are our friends."

Once the rampaging soldiers were unleashed, they were not content just to kill the ice carvers. Their wives, their children were also struck down. Some of the weavers, cooks and fur traders tried to flee, but they did not get far.

Issom did nothing to stop the killing. "Thall wants no witnesses," he said.

It was a swift massacre. For good measure, the soldiers smashed the other frozen sculptures, the beautiful shapes that Aramin himself had admired, learning techniques from his rivals.

One of the closest soldiers glanced at the priestlord, who gave a quick nod. The soldier plunged his short sword through Syla's ribs and into her heart. Her eyes bulged, and she coughed out a bright rose of blood.

Howling in despair, Aramin lunged to save his wife, but Bock cuffed him on the side of the head. The young man reeled and dropped to his knees, and he could barely hear anything through the roar in his ears. On his hands and knees, he dragged himself closer to Syla's body. As he cradled her, she was still twitching, bleeding, but her eyes turned as milky as old ice. She managed to choke out, "Cold ..." before she died in his arms. Aramin let out a throat-rending scream ....

Sometime later, Bock wrenched the young man to his feet and hauled him in front of Priestlord Issom. The grim bald man looked satisfied. Aramin could not stop staring at three small droplets of blood that stained Issom's cheek. "Why?" Aramin groaned, and he kept muttering the question over and over, though he doubted that any answer could possibly exist.

"I need you for a massive task," Issom explained, "without distractions. You must use your entire heart and soul."

Aramin stared at the cold, lifeless body of his wife sprawled in the snow next to her spilled flower-petal tea. "I have no heart or soul."

Priestlord Issom didn't seem to hear. Instead, he turned to the big mercenary warrior. "Give me your amulet, Bock."

The muscular man withdrew a golden disk hanging around his neck. It bore the raindrop symbol from the great temple of Thall in the capital city. "Your dagger, your blood," said Issom.

Without hesitation, Bock slashed his thumb and spilled red onto the disk. The priestlord grabbed Aramin's limp hand, and before the young man knew what was happening, the sharp edge cut across his palm, releasing a scarlet flow, and the golden amulet was dipped in his own blood as well.

Issom handed the disk back to Bock. "This man, Aramin, is your ward and your responsibility. In the name of Thall, protect him against all threats so that we can accomplish our sacred purpose." The warrior hung the stained amulet around his neck again.

Aramin stared at the blood on his hand, then at the blood pooled around Syla. "Why?" he asked again.

"Thall has a great purpose for you," the priestlord said.

—II—

Mounted up, the priest-soldiers headed away from the festival camp. The mercenary warrior grabbed Aramin like a child and set him on the thin leather saddle in front of him. By the time the young man lifted his head to realize that they were leaving, he could not look back at the blood-strewn camp ... or Syla.

As they rode off, rocking on the back of the sturdy pony, Aramin's throat and eyes burned with grief. The procession went along the narrow mountain roads, climbing toward an even higher pass above the frozen meadow. Looking down the sheer drop-offs to the side of the steep path, he thrashed and tried to throw himself off the saddle, but Bock held him with a grip firmer than any ropes or chains. "I am responsible for you," the warrior said. "You will not harm yourself."

Aramin hung his head, clutching the rough mane of the pony. "Where are we going?"

"We ride," Bock said, without further details.

The nimble mounts plodded over a ridge and then down to a small mountain village next to a mine. At one time, there had been homes and a market square, but now all the dwellings had been burned to the ground. Blackened corpses were strewn along the streets—villagers and a few dead sheep. Even the brisk winter breezes could not clear away the last of the smoke, and the stench of ashes and rot permeated the air. Aramin stared, sickened; he had never been exposed to such horrible bloodshed.

Priestlord Issom rode at the head of the procession with his shoulders squared and bearded chin lifted. He didn't remark on the carnage as they crossed the village. Without turning back, Issom made a beckoning gesture, and Bock dug his heels into the pony's side, urging the animal forward. When they were alongside the priestlord, Aramin asked, "What did these people do?"

The priestlord looked at his captive's tear-streaked face. "This village, and others like it, served a purpose. We left this message for those who need to hear it. The heretics from Thall's main temple in Lessila must know that their cause is unjust and doomed to fail. You need to learn the message as well."

"You killed Syla," Aramin said in a bleak and empty tone.

Issom seemed to take it as a compliment. "It was a first step. I believe you will soon learn."

They rode through the wreckage of the town, passing charred homes, stables, the collapsing beams of a blacksmith's forge. Behind him, as if carved out of stone, Bock held him upright, made him look.

The priestlord continued. "We fought a great war in the capital city and tried to overthrow the heretic priestlords, those who erected their great sandstone temple and tried to contain Thall." Sneering, he stroked a hand down the beard that covered his chin. "They lied to the people and spoke their heresy. But even after great bloodshed, they withstood our siege, and I fell back into the mountains with this army of priest-soldiers. We are strong because Thall flows through my veins, and we will make our god strong as my own army is strong. We will come back and overthrow the heretics."

Aramin had spent his life in a small, isolated village and knew nothing about the priestlords and their temple in the capital. He knew that Thall thrummed through the air and mountains, and that no one could truly contain the presence of the god in a mere structure of sandstone.

The armed procession moved onward, and they passed through a second village near sunset. It was also burned, the people slaughtered. Behind him, Bock leaned close and said in his deep voice, "Another message."

Hearing him, Priestlord Issom glanced back at the captive. "It is a message for you, Aramin. We know where to find your village of Copka. If you do not do as I say, and as Thall requires, then I will send my soldiers to burn it to the ground, just like this one."

Aramin closed his eyes, sickened. With great effort, he kept himself from vomiting. The evil priestlord hadn't explained anything yet, and the young man dreaded what he would have to do.

The procession moved toward a higher pass, where the trail became so steep and rocky that the ponies had to climb in single file, and finally the priest-soldiers had to dismount and lead the animals. Sliding out of the saddle, Aramin felt weak and shaky, as if his bones were made of brittle ice. He could barely plod along the steep path. Without a word, Bock swept him up in a muscular arm and put the sculptor over his shoulder, carrying him like a sack of millet.

Once they reached the summit of the pass, the road widened again and the expedition wound its way into a hanging valley, an open expanse that had become a small city with hundreds of soldiers and rows of hide tents as well as a few permanent lodge structures built from wood and animal skins. The greasy smoke from numerous communal cookfires hung like a pall in the air. He also saw many squalid tents, little more than lean-tos, and fenced enclosures that held countless prisoners.

Issom sounded proud and confident. "As you see, sculptor, we have a large enough workforce for you to accomplish what I demand. You will have no excuse and no option for failure."

"But what is it I am to do?" Aramin did not possess any particular skills except for his knack of carving ice figures. He and Syla had eked out a living by tending their garden, two sheep and two goats in their quiet village, where neighbors helped out when needed.

On its lower end, the hanging valley spilled out into a steep gorge that revealed a flat valley far below, the brown lowlands crossed by caravans on their way to the capital city.

But Bock turned the young man by the shoulders and made him look at the head of the high-walled mountain cirque. "There."

Black cliffs were frosted by snow, framing a massive blue-white glacier, a living floe of ice and snow that had piled up over the centuries. The cold bulwark loomed above the hanging valley, as if poised to leap down the gorge.

"That will be our temple," said Issom. "You, sculptor, must see what that ice contains. Find Thall inside the glacier and carve out a great fortress of ice to reveal his fiercest aspect, monstrous and powerful." The priestlord raised his hands as if he could not contain his joy and energy. "Thall is frozen inside, and you will show him to all of us, and make a temple to prove that I am the greatest priestlord."

—III—

The wall of blue ice ached with a primal energy of the mountains. The glacier was alive, but sleeping.

"You have to see it and know it, sculptor," Priestlord Issom said, then commanded Bock to carry Aramin up to the head of the hanging valley, where they could stand before the ancient ice.

The priestlord closed his eyes as he faced the frozen cliff, drawing in deep breaths and exhaling steam. "There, can you feel it? Can you sense it? Thall is trapped in the ice, but you must tame him, free him." He turned his hard face toward the young man, and his smile was colder than the glacier.

Aramin remembered Issom's blank expression as he watched Syla murdered. "Thall is everywhere," Aramin muttered, "not only in that glacier."

"But you will find him *there*," Issom insisted. "You have access to hundreds of workers, a force that can create anything." He narrowed his dark eyes. "You must carve out a temple, shaped like Thall in his most angry and destructive aspect. Do this, and we can destroy the heretics from Lessila. Then Thall will be pleased."

"That is not how I understand Thall," Aramin said, not caring that his words defied this powerful man.

Issom struck him across the face. "Worms do not understand Thall! That is why priestlords exist. Carve my temple in the way you carved your other ice sculptures—or die."

Aramin closed his eyes, accepting. "Then kill me. You have already caused me pain greater than death."

Bock squeezed his shoulder with powerful fingers, as if crushing him ... but it was a caution, a warning, not a violent threat. "He can still cause you far more pain."

Issom was neither insulted, nor impressed. "The sculptor must draw inspiration from the cold and snow. Bock—bury him in the ice." He gestured toward a crack in the glacier. "That fissure there. Let him commune with Thall, so he can envision the glory of my titanic temple."

The priestlord turned away, not bothering to watch or gloat. Bock snatched up Aramin and trudged across the frozen ground away from the camp. Aramin's struggles invoked no ire from his mercenary guardian. They reached the looming glacier wall monoliths of ice had calved off and crashed to the base of the gorge below. Piled snow hung on ledges and filled cracks.

Bock brought him up to one such crack. Holding him with one arm, the bronze-skinned warrior kicked out a shallow trench with his boot. "You could freeze here, but it may also give you visions. I hope it brings what you need, sculptor." He tossed Aramin into the snow-filled crack. The young man sank part way, and his thrashing only made the snow engulf his lower body. Bock used his big hands to shovel more snow on top of him, burying him, suffocating him in white. Aramin's arms were pinned, and the frozen blanket constricted him. With his face covered by ice grains and lumps of hard snow, he couldn't see or breathe. He coughed, choked, and everything went black.

Then Bock brushed the snow away from his face.

Aramin gulped in a deep breath. "Don't leave me here!" he cried, but Bock packed the snow around his body, locking him in like a brick sealed into a wall with mortar.

"Thall lives in the cold," the warrior said. "He lives in the glacier ice. Let us both pray that he comes to you."

Aramin couldn't move; even his head was locked in place, his entire body engulfed in ice. The cold seeped through his garments and his skin, penetrating his bones. He let out a weak scream, but it only emptied his lungs, and he had a hard enough time breathing with the weight of snow upon him. His body convulsed with violent shivers. He closed his eyes, felt tears running down the side of his face, and they too, froze.

He thought of Syla and her laughter, how they would hold each other under fur blankets to keep each other warm. Their small hut did not demonstrate wealth, but rather love and comfort. Though his lips were blue and frozen, he could still feel her kisses as the cold prowled around him, penetrating deeper, stiffening his thoughts and turning his memories to frost.

His mouth watered and he could taste—actually taste—her sweet flower-petal tea. But then a different smell came to his numb nose, and he inhaled the sour coppery scent of spilled blood. The sound of screams rang in his ears, which roared from the cold. Syla's body had been left in the festival meadow with all the other slaughtered corpses, and now Aramin was far away, wrapped in ice, descending into a cold death as deep as the glacier. His lungs burned with the smell of charred wood and bodies from the villages that Priestlord Issom had destroyed. So much pain and death!

But Thall was also here, and maybe Aramin's spirit would go off to join Syla's and the others.

His shivering stopped as the deeper cold set in. The numbness filled his muscles, slowed his blood. He could barely even sense himself breathing. He remembered the beautiful wild horse he had seen within the ice block. He saw the image, remembered the inspiration, how he had looked at the frozen chunk with jagged edges from the ice saws that had cut it out of the mountain tarn. Syla had seen nothing in the murky block, but when Aramin looked long enough, he had caught a flicker of the horse, seen it move in his imagination, remembered the animal's joy and power of being wild, roaming free.

The trout carving had been the same, as well as the sheep. He had *known* what to carve. But the flickering amorphous representation of Thall had been a greater challenge. Though the other villagers and festival goers couldn't understand what he had produced, it was also much more gratifying. Aramin had seen Thall there and knew exactly what the image showed.

Who could know what Thall looked like? And why did Priestlord Issom demand that he create a fierce monster? Why would that aspect represent Thall? Yet he realized that it also did.

And as the clutches of his ice grave dragged him deeper toward a frozen death, Aramin pictured an angrier visage, a violent representation of all the terrible things that Thall could do —all the terrible things that Aramin *wanted* the god to do against terrible men like Issom.

Around him the glacier crushed him with brittle cold. The ice and snow pressed down, smothering him, grinding out the life in his heart. But at last Aramin envisioned what lay within this heavy bulwark of ice. He drew in a deep breath of ice crystals and blistering cold.

The snow suddenly cleared away from his chest, and the front of his tunic was seized in a powerful grip, ripping him out of the encasement of snow. Bock wrenched the young man's shoulders free from the white vise. His arms were numb, and he couldn't feel his cheeks or his lips, but he did gasp aloud.

The big warrior dug with his bare hands, clawing away the snow he had packed around Aramin, and finally levered the young man out of the crack in the glacier.

Aramin couldn't move, couldn't speak. Bock pounded his back, brushing away the snow and ice that caked his clothes. Finally, the sculptor wheezed out thin words like a faint winter wind. "Don't save me."

But Bock tossed him over his shoulder and strutted away from the glacier wall. "My amulet shares blood from both of us, and I swore to protect you. I must do as the priestlord commands, but I will not let you die."

Aramin was shivering violently again by the time they reached the camp. Bock took him to a tent on the fringe of the soldier dwellings near the workers' squalid lean-tos. The warrior dropped him to the ground by a smoky fire made of dung and twigs. Bock positioned him closer to the warmth as if he were nothing more than a ragdoll, then ducked into his tent to retrieve a warm fleece, which he draped over Aramin's shoulders. "Stay here and thaw. I'll bring goat soup from the cookpot."

Though Aramin couldn't think, he kept seeing the pounding vision inside his head, the savage aspect of Thall that dominated his thoughts with enough power and fury to drive away the image of Syla dying on the ground.

When Bock offered him the pungent soup, Aramin ate, simply staring down at the lumpy liquid and unable to concentrate on anything else. Finally, he looked up to see Priestlord Issom looming over him. "You have seen," the man said, not asking a question. "It is plain on your face."

"I know what lives in the ice," Aramin admitted, "and I can carve it for you."

With a huff, the priestlord nodded and turned away. "I will rally the work crews, and you will begin immediately."

After Issom departed, Aramin bowed back over his soup and muttered under his breath, "If you dare ..."

—IV—

Using a smaller block of ice no higher than his knee, Aramin carved a small representation of what he had envisioned. The sculpture was crude, but it conveyed the message: a fierce, fanged and primal monstrosity that could explode out of the glacier, an elemental force that brooded inside the wall of ice.

Issom regarded the carving and pronounced it satisfactory, but he had little interest in a small representational model. He wanted to see his real temple. The priest-soldiers lashed their whips, and the slave crews erected rope harnesses and scaffoldings. They hacked cubbyholes and steps into the sheer ice, excavating walkways and ramps up onto the main body of the glacier. The slaves used ice picks, hammers, and chisels to swarm over the frozen blue-white face like ants rebuilding their nest.

Like stonemasons quarrying granite, the workers sawed and chipped great blocks away, knocking them loose to send them tumbling from the front of the glacier and down into the gorge, where they would eventually spill out onto the plain below. Even in the star-filled night, when the temperature dropped further, the guards mounted torches so the workers could keep carving away the ice.

Visualizing the horror in his mind, Aramin directed the efforts and watched his vision manifest in the face of the blocky glacier. Now that the work was under way, Priestlord Issom was restless and energetic. Anything the sculptor requested, the soldiers made possible.

Pack ponies brought load after load of wood from the scrub forests below the tundra. After workers had carved out a small cave in the center of the glacier wall, Aramin had bonfires built, and flames roared all day and night, melting the ice, excavating a larger and larger opening. As the meltwater ran down the side of the glacier, it made the ice wall smooth and slick, pouring down like the drool of a slavering monster. Large icicles grew down from the roof of the newly melted cavern, sharp stalactites that looked like fangs. Aramin knew that Thall was guiding them.

A separate crew climbed to the top of the glacier, chopping and excavating a curved head above the yawning cave mouth. They lowered themselves with ropes and iron spikes pounded into the solid ice, and began scouring and polishing two circular sections the size of ponds—the eyes of Thall.

From the camp, Aramin looked up at the glacier headwall and watched the ice take shape. Weeks passed, and the numbness in his heart did not fade. His hatred toward the priestlord did not diminish, nor did he forget his sweet Syla. But he did watch the figure that was so prominent in his mind begin to take form in the glacier.

Issom stood beside him, nodding. He still treated Aramin as if he were no more than a pet, but now that he could see the work progressing, he expressed some satisfaction. "It is terrifying—and it fills me with pleasure, sculptor."

"It is terrifying," Aramin agreed, "and it fills me with dread."

A scream resounded from the glacier, and all the work stopped. The soldiers in the camp looked up, and the slaves gasped. Aramin shaded his eyes, gazing toward the vague shape in the ice just in time to see a worker with a load of firewood on his back slide off the steep ramp to the fanged mouth grotto. He screamed as he fell, dashed in a splatter of blood on one of the tremendous ice monoliths that lay piled at the base of the glacier.

After the dead man's lifeblood flared out like paint across the milky blue ice, a faint but undeniable shimmer of light awakened inside. The glow seeped out like frozen sunshine from centuries ago. It flickered, brightened, then faded like mist.

Across the excavation site the slaves muttered and gasped, all sensing the energy. The priest-soldiers held their weapons and backed away in fear and awe. But Issom smiled. "Thall has accepted our sacrifice! He is pleased with the blood—you witnessed it yourself, sculptor."

Beside them, Bock stood stony and implacable. His blue-black hair whispered about in the breeze, and his brow furrowed. The warrior seemed concerned, but did not speak.

Pleased, Issom reached a conclusion. "Now I know what we

are doing is right! Thall demands a blood sacrifice." He shouted to his soldiers. "Pick an old and frail slave—an expendable one. Take him to the mouth of the ice and sacrifice him there. Slash his throat."

The priest-soldiers rushed off to do their priestlord's bidding.

"No, don't kill my workers," Aramin pleaded.

Issom scowled at him. "I dare not go against the wishes of Thall."

A shaggy, gray-haired slave was seized and dragged away, his struggles ineffectual against the well-muscled men.

In horror, Aramin watched the soldiers carry the squirming old man up the ramp and steps to the open cavern mouth. They threw him down on the ice floor near the ashes of the old bonfire and slit the man's throat, then turned him over so he could bleed out across the ice. The sacrifice elicited another faint glow from within the glacier, and a stirring tremble made loose snow and ice patter down from the sheer ledges. But the glow soon faded, the glacier became stable again.

"Only one for now," the priestlord said dismissively. "Back to work!"

Cowed, the slave crews returned to the ice and began chopping away, melting and polishing, more tense now. To Aramin, the work seemed to have taken on a darker tone, a more ominous threat from the figure emerging from the glacier. Even the warriors muttered uneasily.

But Priestlord Issom was oblivious, or perhaps he just reveled in the sensation. "Thall needs to be strong," he said to Aramin. "He has shown us what he wants, and how we can preserve him inside our ice temple." He looked up. "We will make another sacrifice each day. One worker will be slain to give Thall the power of blood. We can awaken him, make him come forth."

"You can't kill all the workers!" Aramin groaned, thinking of the burned villages, the slain innocents who had just gotten in the way ... like Syla, like the other ice sculptors at the festival, the fur traders, the weavers, the children. "I need my workers if I am to complete the task you command."

Priestlord Issom was not convinced by the argument. "If the blood sacrifice strengthens Thall, then that will speed your work." He chuckled. "And if you wish to save more of their lives—then simply finish sooner."

—V—

As the monstrous god continued to emerge from the ice, blood sacrifice after blood sacrifice, the workers grew to hate Aramin as much as they hated Priestlord Issom. The young man could tell by their haunted glances. He could hear their whimpers and wailing from his own tent, which stood apart from both the soldiers and the slaves.

Each day as another innocent wretch was slaughtered in the temple mouth, a quiet flicker of light rose briefly from within the ice—acknowledging the blood gift, or was it a flash of rage from Thall?

Aramin wondered if the sacrifices would end if he became one final offering, if he flung himself into the rugged gorge below. But when he stood too close to the edge, looking with terrified intent at the long fatal plunge, somehow Bock was always there to prevent any harm from coming to him, even if it was self-inflicted harm ....

Aramin wanted to delay the completion of the enormous sculpture, so as not to serve the aims of the evil priestlord .... but each extra day cost the life of another worker. He did not know what Issom would do as soon as he completed the enormous frozen temple.

Or what Thall would do.

He slept restlessly, miserably, never sure which was nightmare and which was life. He shivered just listening to the moaning wind in the high empty valley. His stomach knotted as if a dagger twisted inside, no matter what he had eaten.

Now he woke to a whispered movement in the cold moonlit night. Hearing the sound of stretched fabric tearing, he sat up and saw the silver curve of a knife that pierced the side of his tent. A man with a pointed beard and blazing eyes tore the opening wider and thrust himself inside. He wore the blue uniform of Issom's priest-soldiers, and his glittering gaze locked on Aramin. The young man scrambled away, but the scream caught in his throat.

The stranger pushed himself inside the tent and raised the pointed knife. "You are responsible, heretic! You must die for what you do to Thall."

The attacker slashed sideways with his knife, and only by sheer reflex and luck did Aramin manage to avoid a mortal wound. He stumbled and rolled, but the tent trapped him like a large net.

The young sculptor lifted his chin and glared. He held up his hands in submission. "Do it! I didn't choose to be here." He had no weapons in his own tent, nothing with which he could defend himself.

"I do this for Thall." The assassin stalked closer.

Just then the tent flap yanked back, and Bock stood there with his sword drawn, looking like an angry bear. "You will leave him." He tore the opening wider, giving him room to move. Though Aramin's tent was larger than any of the slave lean-tos or the soldier huts, he still had very little space. With two great strides, the big warrior grabbed the young man by the back of the neck and tossed Aramin behind him like a discarded garment. "Out. Now."

The assassin slashed his long knife in front of Bock's face, but the warrior ducked back, and the razor edge missed his eyes. He snarled, "You will not kill Thall's chosen."

The assassin lashed out. "Heretic! Followers of the disgraced Issom. You will all die."

Aramin stumbled outside, tripped, and sprawled on his back. He rolled over and scrambled to get away. Shouts were rising in the camp, and other priest-soldiers came running toward his tent.

Inside, Bock kept the other man at bay. "You are the heretics. Priestlord Issom fought at the temple in Lessila, and I helped slaughter many of you."

The assassin threw himself upon the burly warrior, and their blades clashed.

Aramin pulled himself to his feet as more soldiers rushed in. Bock's sword cut a gash in the tent, and with brute strength he hurled the assassin through the gap. The would-be killer crashed to the frozen ground and sprang to his feet, whirling to fight as Bock surged after him. The assassin raised his blade to block his opponent, but the warrior lurched in with no regard for his own safety. He crashed his sword against the assassin's blade, then swung hard with the balled fist of his empty hand to smash the bridge of the enemy's nose. The man dropped as if he had been felled by a bludgeon. Blood spouted from his smashed nose, and one of his eyes bulged out as if the blow had knocked it loose from its socket.

Aramin swayed, then dropped to his knees, panting hard. Priest-soldiers swarmed up. Bock glanced at them, then glowered at the man who had tried to kill Aramin. "The sculptor is under my protection. You must pay the price." With only brief hesitation, he struck off the assassin's head.

Bock dragged Aramin to safety even as Priestlord Issom stalked up. "Spies and killers! Infiltrating our ranks! The heretics won't stop us."

On weak legs, Aramin stumbled along under the warrior's implacable urging. "I will find you a safe place to sleep near to me, sculptor. I stand watch." Bock touched the amulet with the dried bloodstains that hung around his chest. "You will not come to harm." It seemed less reassuring and more of a threat.

—VI—

Dangling in a makeshift rope harness in front of the monstrous ice visage, Aramin felt no fear as he gazed down the sheer cliffs to the gorge below. The skies overhead were gray and brooding, swollen with snow, but the threat he faced from Priestlord Issom was far more dangerous than any natural hazard.

The bulk of the ice-temple carving had been finished, the

glacier hacked, melted, and blasted away to reveal the massive hulk that Aramin had seen slumbering deep inside the ice—just like the wild horse he had liberated from its frozen prison, just like the trout and the sheep.

Thall was in all things, Aramin knew, no matter what the violent priestlords claimed, and he had found the god's presence as he climbed and crawled over the sheer glacier. He knew that Thall was powerful, and Thall was angry.

Aramin would finish his work, though—not for Issom or for his religious war, not because he was forced to do it, and not because it would ever make things right for the memory of Syla. No, he did it because now he felt Thall there in the ice, stirring.

With chisels, iron mallets, and rough rasps clipped to his harness, the sculptor dangled along the face of the primal monster he had excavated. Hanging next to him, encumbered by the ropes, Bock held a blazing torch. When Aramin directed him, the warrior would swing on his ropes over to a rough protrusion, then press the fire against the surface, like a battlefield surgeon cauterizing a wound. Glassy-smooth patches marred the blocky, scaled image that signified the god's face. In his mind, Aramin could see what needed to be changed, what parts of the frozen prison needed to be removed to reveal Thall for what he was.

Despite the thick ropes and the sturdy harness around his waist and chest, Aramin felt light as a bird as he drifted along the enormous ice sculpture. He grasped an ice protrusion and hammered on a rough spot, sending frozen chips flying into the air. He and his bodyguard had polished, melted, and shined the giant round eyes so that Thall could look out upon the world ... so that Thall could see what Priestlord Issom and his soldiers intended to do.

Bock hung close, gripping the torch as if it might keep him aloft. Even with his large muscles and numerous scars, with all the times he had faced death and all the victims he had killed, the warrior actually seemed anxious.

Aramin turned to him. "You seem nervous. I thought you did not fear death."

"I do not fear death," Bock said. "I fear falling." In his dark eyes, Aramin could see a depth of wisdom and understanding that he had not expected from a brutish bodyguard. "And I fear *you* falling." He twitched so that the dangling gold amulet swung out from his chest. "I swore to keep you from harm—my blood and your blood. Everyone heard that promise, as did Thall himself. If these ropes should snap, and we fall ..." He glanced down at the sheer drop into the black gorge below. "Then I hope that I fall faster and am dashed against the rocks before you do, because then at least you would have lived longer. Perhaps that would be sufficient for the gods to know that I kept my promise."

"Who knows what the gods consider sufficient?" Aramin said, feeling renewed bitterness. "Or if we have already failed them."

He looked up at the enormous angry face of Thall, at the quicksilver pools that represented all-seeing eyes, at the altar in the yawning cave grotto with icicle columns that represented fangs. He could feel the power in the temple, in the ice ... and in the mountains themselves. It was a power that Priestlord Issom and his armies wanted. But this manifestation was not at all like the ethereal formless void that Aramin had sculpted in ice at the festival camp.

Some work crews still labored at the temple, etching deep outlines of scales and lines of anger, but the carving was mostly finished. Aramin knew his work had neared an end.

As he hung in his harness, Bock looked in the other direction, down the gorge and out to the valley beyond. He spoke in a gruff voice that struck fear into Aramin's heart. "They are coming."

Bock gestured with his torch, and the young sculptor swung on the ropes, squinting into the cloudy distance to make out what the big warrior had seen.

The valley floor was covered with small figures, thousands upon thousands of soldiers that marched in ranks and set up a camp at the base of the mountains. Even from this distance, he saw some of the colors, waving banners that were wine red and yellow.

"The heretic army has come to engage us," Bock said. "We must tell Priestlord Issom, so he has time to prepare."

—VII—

Dark clouds gathered over the crags like boiling smoke, but they were filled with cold snow, ready to fall. The temperature plunged as the wind picked up, and sharp white flakes began to spit through the air. Upon learning of the distant heretic army, Priestlord Issom rallied his exiled soldiers. Battle horns resounded against the cliffs with blasts loud enough to dislodge white sheets of snow precariously balanced on high ledges.

After pulling Aramin and himself back up to safety from the face of the hideous sculpture, Bock had marched the young man to the priestlord's tent. Issom's face lit up with bloodthirsty anticipation as well as impatience. He rose to his feet and faced Aramin. "Is my temple finished?"

Somehow, the sculptor found the courage to stand straight. "It is *Thall's* temple."

"And I am Thall's priestlord. We created that temple to hold him and empower him. Now Thall must fight our battles for us and destroy the heretics who disgrace his name."

By slaughtering so many innocents, burning so many villages, Issom had already brought enough disgrace upon Thall. "The temple is complete," Aramin admitted. "I revealed the form within the glacier, the manifestation of Thall. My work is finished."

"And our fight has just begun." Issom glanced up at Bock, an implacable statue next to his ward. "Gather six priest-soldiers and we will go to the mouth of the temple. We must prepare against our enemy."

Aramin stiffened. "You sacrificed one worker every day, but now the temple is complete. The workers did as you demanded, and you promised to stop killing them."

"We will sacrifice no more workers," Issom grunted, then marched out of his tent. In the snow-flecked wind, he shouted to the ranks of his army, calling them to mount defenses and prepare for a march down to the valley.

The gray clouds spilled out more white flakes in the air like a cloud of cold gnats. Mournful breezes moaned along the rock faces and funneled through the gorge.

The exhausted and hopeless workers huddled under their squalid fur lean-tos, dreading the imminent storm. They leaned close to tiny campfires that provided more smoke than heat. The restless and angry priest-soldiers gathered their weapons, straightened their armor, saddled their war ponies, though it would be some time before the opposing army in the valley could pose any kind of threat.

The priestlord and his six priest-soldiers strode along the trampled path toward the headwall and the towering glacial temple. Bock ushered the young sculptor along, keeping pace in silence. The carved ice wall was a magnificent work, the best sculpture Aramin had ever done, but this time the prize was more than a dyed woolen shawl or a purse of coins.

The temple of Thall looked like the head of a snarling panther, a fierce dragon, and an uncontrolled whirlwind, all frozen together into the ice. Thall's form had been locked within the glacier for an eternity until the excavation work set the shape free and exposed the angry god to the mountain air.

Though Aramin had been given a fleece wrap, the cold penetrated to his bones. This frigid numbness, however, felt different from when Bock had buried him in the ice to make him have visions from the glacier. No, this was a deeper cold—a cold that was settling into the world.

Priestlord Issom's grin showed a row of white teeth as he stared at the snow-streaked temple. "It is everything I imagined Thall to be!"

Bock kept the young man moving, following Issom and his guards toward the temple, as if they were on a military operation. They climbed the wide ramp alongside the scaled and uneven face of Thall to reach the grotto overhang and its altar. Under the shelter, thick columns of ice hung down, sharpened by natural thawing into fangs and spears. On the floor, a heavy block of ice was where the monster's tongue should have been, its surface uneven and discolored, partially melted from the hot blood spilled there during the daily sacrifices. Aramin had lost count of the victims after the twentieth one, but he counted Syla and the unknown number of dead from the massacred villages as sacrifices as well.

Yes, Thall was strong.

The cold, still air inside the mouth grotto stank like a slaughtering pen when pigs were butchered for the winter. Issom reveled beneath the ice overhang, gazing out upon the gorge and the opposing army far away.

"Thall is here all around us," Issom announced. "We can feel him in the ice and in the air." He noted the pale steam wafting out of his nose. "And with our every breath." His blue garments looked darker in the overhang shadows. He raised his hands higher, and his fur-lined cape hung back to reveal a long dagger at his side. "Now Thall must be our warrior. We have fed him and strengthened him, but we must awaken him with one final sacrifice."

Moving swiftly, two of the priest-soldiers seized Aramin by the shoulders and threw him down onto the hard ice of the altar, so roughly that they knocked the wind out of him.

As the young man struggled, Issom continued to speak. "Thall blessed the sculptor with his visions of the god within the ice. Now we will repay Thall with this man's blood." He slid the sacrificial dagger out of its sheath.

Aramin wheezed and squirmed, but he did not have the strength—or the will—to fight off the priest-soldiers. He felt sickened, but not surprised. He had been fatalistic as the temple neared completion, and now his own blood would go into the ice of the glacier and its inner presence.

"You said you would not sacrifice any more workers," Bock said, his voice deep. His usual inflectionless tone held an edge of anger.

"The workers are safe," Issom said, "but Aramin is something else entirely. He is a part of this temple, and his sacrifice will provide the final spark we need."

Aramin rested his head back on the bloodstained ice of the altar and let out a rattling sigh. "Syla ..." He saw the leering priestlord lean forward and raise the dagger. From outside in the work area, Aramin had watched helpless workers slain here, day after day. He knew what would happen. He braced himself for the bright, sharp pain.

Then he heard a wet thrust and a sound like tearing meat. With a choking gurgle, Issom coughed out a spray of warm droplets onto Aramin's face. He saw the priestlord's bulging expression, a blade protruding from his chest. The long sword held the man's body upright as his arms twitched and flailed. Then the blade was withdrawn, and the body cast aside like a diseased goat carcass.

The big warrior Bock whirled with his bloodied sword as the other priest-soldiers gasped in disbelief. One wailed Issom's name as if he had just lost a lover.

Bock spoke no words, made no sound other than a grunt of effort as he struck again and again in the confined sacrificial grotto. He killed two of the guards by slicing off their heads before they could even draw their blades. One man charged at the warrior, and he sidestepped, striking a deep gash on the man's shoulder. He shoved the priest-soldier, so that he slipped on the ice floor and careened forward to plunge over the edge of the icefall, which was slick and melted from the bonfires inside the glacier.

"Get yourself out of the way, sculptor," Bock commanded, and Aramin rolled off the altar block. He fell to the opposite side as a priest-soldier swung his sword down, trying to cleave the sacrificial victim in half. The sword clanged against the dark, bloodstained ice. Another priest-soldier came in from the opposite side, hunting him. Aramin found himself cornered in the grotto.

Bock surged in, a whirlwind of steel. He struck down both soldiers from behind, then faced the remaining guard, who held up his sword in a pathetic attempt to defend himself. He sobbed after seeing the death of Priestlord Issom. Bock ran him through.

Aramin shuddered as he stared at the big warrior, the mercenary who had held him captive, dragged him along against his will, buried him in the ice until he nearly froze. "I swore not to let harm come to you," Bock explained. His voice held defiance, as if he felt he needed to justify his actions. "My oath was to Thall, not Priestlord Issom."

Shaking, Aramin nodded. His legs were weak, but he did not feel saved or rescued. He had always known how this would end, even if the details were unclear to him. The grotto was splashed with red. Priestlord Issom lay sprawled across the uneven altar, made into a supreme sacrifice. The slain priest-soldiers also poured more sacrificial blood into the completed temple.

Aramin took a deep breath and closed his eyes. His words were not loud, but a god could hear even the faintest of whispers. "Thall ... I set you free."

The deep blue ice of the ancient glacier began to glow.

—VIII—

The blizzard was raging when they emerged from the sacrificial grotto. Bock guided Aramin forward, leading him onto the snow-packed ramp from the glacier down to the high camp. White flakes whistled and spun around them, blurring their view of the mountains. With his other hand, the warrior held his bloody sword, ready to defend them against any priest-soldiers who might attack. Aramin staggered and slipped, but the warrior held him up. Finally, Bock sheathed his sword so he could keep his balance as they struggled away from the temple to more stable ground.

"No one saw what happened," Bock shouted into the wind. "The others in the army will not know Priestlord Issom is dead."

Behind them, the solid glacier began to throb and shimmer. Pale blue light seeped out of the frozen wall, not melting but thriving. The frozen temple remained fixed, but alive with cold and the vivifying presence of Thall. Soon, the glacier gleamed like a full moon. Silvery light leaked out of crevasses and fissures, showering upward like a spray of light penetrating a cloudburst.

Then the ice bulwark began to rumble and crack. Crevasses widened, and chunks of pale ice split off to tumble down the gorge. The enormous frozen sculpture started to move.

Shouts erupted from the camp. The workers wailed in fear, and the priest-soldiers sent out defiant challenges, some of which sounded like cheers, some like howls of victory, while others were deep-throated cries of terror.

The blizzard moaned around them. The packed ramp from the glacier shook and cracked, and Bock pushed them along until he finally reached the boulder-strewn hanging valley. The titanic sculpture in the glacier raised its head, opened its icicle-fanged maw. Even though its lungs were frozen solid from centuries-old packed ice, Thall let out a roar louder than the raging tempest.

Snow cornices broke off from the crags above, and small avalanches rolled down the cliffs in white feathery blasts. The monstrous head turned and cracked off more sheets of glazed frost. Thall's quicksilver eyes blazed with an inner blue glow, seeking an enemy.

When the warrior reached the snowy ground outside of the worker camp, he stopped Aramin, pausing as the young man caught his balance. "Can you run, sculptor? Run for your life?"

"I'll try." Aramin could not tear his eyes away as the great sculpture came alive and broke free of its glacial bonds.

"If you cannot do so, then I will be forced to carry you again!"

Aramin lurched into motion. In the camp the workers had scrambled out of their tattered tents and stared into the snow, trying to understand what they were seeing. The titanic figure of Thall roared again, making the mountainside shudder.

"Get away," Aramin called to them. "All of you."

"But the soldiers ..." one man cried.

"You need not fear the soldiers now," Bock said.

Priestlord Issom's warriors had gathered their armor and weapons. Some mounted their war ponies, but when they saw the animated glacier and the vengeful appearance of Thall, they staggered back. "It is Thall," one priest-soldier cried.

Others raised their blue banners. "It is Thall come alive to save us. Thall will destroy the heretics!"

But the living glacier broke loose from the cliff confinement and rolled forward, shedding blocks of snow and great monoliths of ice. Thall careened into the army camp like an uncontrolled avalanche, sweeping the soldiers aside, burying them under tons of rock and ice.

The blizzard blurred Thall's exact form, but Aramin thought that the horrific countenance was far more terrible than even he had conceived. The god struck and crushed all of Issom's forces, casting them into the gorge. Then the elemental figure rolled onward. The glacier blockade at the head of the valley was released, and many centuries of pent-up winter poured down.

Bock shook his head. "I do not comprehend Thall."

Aramin said, "Thall is free, and he is everywhere. He cannot be contained in a temple, and he fights those who tried to imprison him."

The blizzard roared and howled, and Aramin could no longer see. The workers were weeping, huddled in their matted coverings of white flakes. The slaves stumbled away from the camp clutching furs and blankets, nearly paralyzed with terror.

The rampaging glacier reached the edge of the gorge and crashed over the precipice. With all the energy stored inside the mountains, the liberated Thall leapt into the gorge followed by a seemingly infinite surge of snow. White waves rolled out of the mountaintops and poured down toward the valley and the opposing military force of priest-soldiers, who claimed that they, too, knew and controlled Thall.

The thunderous roar rolled on and on, magnified by the walls of the gorge: the sounds of an avalanche joined by the vengeful roar of a frozen god set free.

Aramin tried to make out any form in the amorphous flow of crashing snow and ice. For a moment, a glimmer reminded him of his small representational ice sculpture when he had tried to capture the infinite form of Thall.

Bock nudged him farther toward the rutted path on the other side of the hanging valley. "We must keep moving, sculptor. Find the mountain road and get to lower elevation. This blizzard is getting worse, and the storm can kill us just as much as the priestlord, or Thall."

Accompanied by the group of escaping workers, they pushed ahead until they found the snow-covered road leading out of the mountains. Though their footprints vanished mere moments after they left indentations in the snow, it seemed to Aramin that the blizzard itself thinned around them, forming a clear tunnel to show them the way.

He could not feel the cold anymore, but he didn't think it was from frostbite. The temperature around them grew more tolerable, the wind quieter. The other slaves seemed to realize their good fortune as well, and they hurried away.

Far behind them and in the valley below, Aramin guessed that the wild fury of the living avalanche would sweep across the other army with the same results.

"Where are we going?" Aramin asked Bock as the big warrior forged a path on the snowy road.

"For now, back to your original village." He glanced down at Aramin with a faint smile on his grim face. "I am not finished keeping you alive yet, sculptor."

Aramin accepted that. As he thought about it, he knew his answer. "And I am not finished living."

Even though I've lived far from the ocean most of my life, I've always had a fascination with seafaring stories, sailing ships and sea monsters and mysterious islands. My entire Terra Incognita fantasy trilogy is a nautical adventure, as is my novel Captain Nemo, *along with numerous short stories.*

When I was in high school, the rock album Point of Know Return *by Kansas fired my imagination, especially with its illustration of a sailing ship plunging over the edge of the world into a mysterious void filled with sea monsters. This story was my attempt to fictionalize the title track of that album. It remains one of my favorites.*

SEA WIND

The man held everyone's attention as he shouted into the milling, familiar chaos of the harbor, forcefully waving the stump of his right hand. For reasons I would always regret later, I stopped to listen.

"I have been sent here by the captain of the *Sea Wind*, a three-masted lateener lying at anchor in your beautiful harbor of Lisbon!" His voice was hoarse and gravelly, as if from too much shouting in his life. He stood tall on an old wooden crate, flanked by two burly seamen in fine sailing clothes, canvas trousers, striped shirts. The smell of salt breezes and fish stalls hung heavy around us. Many merchants and dock workers flowed around the obstacle, wrapped in their own business, but others paused to hear what the man had to say.

"The captain bids me to tell you that the *Sea Wind* is now taking on crewmembers for a voyage of discovery. We need twenty brave young men, and we will pay well."

Francis, my older brother, pulled me with him as he pushed through the loose crowd, weaving our way closer to the man on the crate, our own task forgotten. I held two mended iron hoops in my hand, fresh from the blacksmith, which our father needed for a barrel he was making. I knew we were expected back at the cooper shop promptly, and I tried to tell Francis, but he impatiently made me hold my words. Only a few people were actually listening to the man.

"Where are you sailing?" an unkempt man called out, lounging against an empty cart with a broken wheel.

The man with the stump turned toward the question. "We shall sail westward to the newly discovered island of Madeira, a paradise with jungles, flowers, and fruits, and birds the colors of jewels! Then we sail southward along the coast of Africa to rich ports and lands unknown, perhaps even the kingdom of Prester John himself!" He wobbled on the old crate. "Our own Prince Henry commanded us to discover the world—"

"*Prince Henry* himself commissioned your ship?" Francis scoffed.

The man smiled uncomfortably, turning to gaze down at my brother. The two burly sailors did not seem amused by the challenge. "The prince gave *all* men the task of exploring the seas, boy. Not two years ago, his own Squire Eannes successfully rounded Cape Bojador in Africa—what was once thought to be Hell itself, where men are black as charcoal because they stand so close to the sun, and the ground is a burning lake of sand! Eannes brought back tales of vast lands farther south—and the *Sea Wind* will go *beyond*, mark my words! To lands of untold riches—pearls as big as your fist, more gold than our ship can carry!"

He looked directly at Francis, pointing with the raw pink end of his stump. "Do you remember the stories of Marco Polo? Of the exotic places he visited, the adventures he had? Would you like to see lands never before beheld by the eyes of Christian men?" He paused and lowered his voice, adding an intense fever to his words. "Would you like to sail with us on the *Sea Wind*?"

The man made me uncomfortable, but Francis's eyes were glittering. He had caught the fever. I tugged on my brother's sleeve, but he stammered out, "How long ... how long do I have to decide?"

"The *Sea Wind* will set sail in four days; but we intend to gather the crew today. Are you interested, boy? Can you write your name?"

"Of course!"

I don't know which question my brother was answering. I was afraid for him, but Francis looked so sure of himself. One of the burly sailors handed him a stained piece of paper and a quill. Francis refused to meet my gaze and carefully wrote his name. Grandfather had shown him how to write it—Grandfather's name was Francis, too—but the old man couldn't show me how to write my name, since he had never seen what "Stefan" looked like.

The man from the *Sea Wind* smiled congratulations at my brother and rested his stump on his hip as if to say he would have shaken Francis's hand had he been able.

The iron barrel hoops in my hand had grown very heavy.

In the cooper shop, Father turned back to his work, away from Francis, struggling to quell his anger. His voice was gruff. "You can't go. You are my oldest son. I need you here." He began to arrange the staves for the barrel.

Francis wouldn't let his dreams be broken so easily. He gestured to me, even though I wanted no part of this. "Stefan knows how to do the work as well as I do—he can carry on! I *am* going, Father. This is what I want to do, to sail the seas and see the world. I'm old enough now." He paused, still waiting for Father to look at him, to face him. "Don't make me run away from home."

With a tired, defeated sigh, Father let the curved staves fall together with a flat clatter and stood up, abandoning the work. "How long?" He drew a deep breath, looking down at the barrel and then at me as if I were part of a conspiracy. "How long will you be gone?"

Francis seemed to fight back a smile, knowing he had won. "Maybe a year, no more. We'll sail down the coast of Africa, maybe even find a passage to India. I'll bring back more riches than we've ever had!"

Father wasn't as angry as I had thought he would be. Instead, he seemed resigned to the fact, as if he had been expecting this to come any day now, knowing his son's restlessness as well as anyone.

"If you're going to be gone for a year, then you'd better at least help me finish this barrel."

Francis breathed in awe as he stared at the *Sea Wind* lying at anchor in the harbor. "Look at her! Oh, just look at her." We sat on the wharf as the late afternoon sun turned golden heading toward the distant watery horizon. The waves brushed against the docks. The air was heavy with screaming gulls and the salty scent of the sea.

The masts of all the ships were like a forest on the water. The city of Lisbon stumbled downward from the surrounding hills like a staircase into the Tagus River where it met the ocean, forming a calm, sheltered harbor at its mouth. The *Sea Wind* rocked gently in the sleepy water, giving us a peek at the line of scum and barnacles crusted below the waterline. She was a magnificent ship, one of the largest in port—seventy feet from bow to stern—and could comfortably hold thirty men on a long voyage.

She had three raked masts, fitted with wide triangular lateen sails rippling in the wind, brushing against the spiderweb of rigging that entwined the ship. The *Sea Wind*'s hull was also finely decorated as an exploring ship should be to bear the pride of Portugal and Prince Henry the Navigator throughout the oceans. Her railing was painted gold, as was the stem, embellished with ornate feathers and curls.

Francis wrapped his arms around his knees as he sat, marveling at the ship he would call home for the next year, but I could see that wonder blinded his eyes. From looking at his expression, I knew my brother didn't notice that the gold paint on the railing was peeling and scarred by the graffiti carved there by other sailors. The ship creaked more than it should have in the gentle wash of waves, and the hull looked as if it might have shipworm. I squinted against the sun, and I could make out that the sails had been patched several times. The thick layers of barnacles at the waterline showed that the *Sea Wind* had been in the water a long time.

The wind picked up, and the ship creaked. "Francis ... what if you don't come back?"

"I'll come back."

"But you'll be out on the ocean, alone! Everyone knows about the sea monsters just waiting to prey on sailing ships! And you might sail off the edge of the world! You're going where no other vessel has sailed before."

Francis turned away from the ship, looking at me with scorn, but I could see the fear behind his eyes. "Stefan, somebody has to go. Somebody has to show the way, somebody has to dream. I talked to other sailors—the *Sea Wind* has voyaged south once before, but they thought they could never make it past Cape Bojador. They told me terrible stories of the bleak desert that pokes its finger into the sea, making the water dirty brown with sand and so shallow that the keel scrapes the bottom even twenty miles offshore. And they told me of barren cliffs of sandstone without so much as a weed growing on them. That was the edge of the world."

He blinked, swallowed hard to drive away his anxiety. "Or so they thought. So *we* thought! Until Squire Eannes rounded the Cape and came back to say there was more of Africa beyond ... and more, and more! It wasn't the edge of the world—instead, it might be a gateway to India! Somebody's got to go—you know that."

I saw a strange expression on my brother's face, not just a sadness, but an actual pity for me. "You wouldn't understand. You were always content with the excitement of Lisbon, with helping Father make his barrels, but you know I've always wanted to go to sea, how I've stared at the ships, heard the sailors' stories. I *have* to go. I don't have any choice."

Even though less than a year separated us in age, he seemed infinitely older than me. "I'll miss you, Francis."

"I'll miss you, too."

One candle in the corner guttered badly, flashing shadows like moths around the room, randomly switching the patches of light and darkness, but it was getting late and we would extinguish the candle soon anyway. Francis wanted to be in bed early, for the next morning he would go to board the *Sea Wind*—but I don't see how he could sleep this night of all nights. I would be lying awake myself.

Mother had already tucked our little brother Matthew into his basket of straw, supposedly to sleep, but the toddler could sense the tension in the air and his bright eyes watched as our family sat together in uncomfortable silence.

Father brooded by himself, not looking at Francis—I honestly didn't know if he approved or disapproved, if he were angry or sad.

Mother stared at Francis, as if she needed to say something but found it impossible to speak. Her fingers played nervously with a loose thread in her faded dress. Her dark hair was drawn back into a braid that was becoming undone, rampant hairs protruding wildly to shine in the uncertain candlelight.

"Francis ..." Her voice sounded uncertain. "We love you."

My brother obviously didn't know how to reply. On the other side of the room, little Matthew began bouncing up and down, shouting in his tiny voice.

"How long until I'm old enough? I want to go on a ship, too! I want to go with Francis!" When Mother ran to the child, she was crying.

After a long uncertain moment, Francis met the gaze of

Grandfather, his namesake. The old man sat in his chair, the one he rarely left except when he helped Father in the cooper shop. He was not yet too old to work. Grandfather spoke softly, which forced Francis to sit beside him in order to hear his words. I followed my brother, wanting to stay by him for every minute we had left together.

"Francis ... you have talked with the other sailors?" the old man said in a raspy voice. "You know what awaits you ... out there? In the unknown?"

Everyone in our family knew the story. As a boy, Grandfather had wanted to embark on a similar voyage, but before the ship had even left Lisbon harbor, he had tangled his hand in one of the winch ropes, crushing it, so that he was forced to return home without seeing the sea as he had hoped. Perhaps the old man now looked at Francis with envy, because he had a chance to complete the voyage his older namesake had never been able to do.

Francis had gotten good at his show of bravery. "I've heard stories of the abyss at the edge of the world where horrible creatures wait to devour unfortunate sailors. Of the great sea serpents and sirens and—"

"And the kraken? Have you been warned of the kraken?" The fearful look on Grandfather's face said that he would refuse to tell the story, whether or not my brother had heard it.

Francis looked up into the shadows where the walls met the ceiling, lost in his own imagining. "They say that when you are out there, and the sea turns dark, and the sky turns darker—you'll know. You'll know when the kraken has come, veiled in storms. And when the wind whistles through your rigging and tears at the sails, when the water foams and seethes—you'll know."

Grandfather pushed his face closer to Francis's. "And when black tentacles thick as a mainmast rise out of the water to wrap around your ship and *crush* it as if it were straw—and when the kraken drags you under, *screaming*, to feed his children—you'll know. And you won't ever return, Francis, but your bones will keep him company far beneath the sea, alone forever—for the kraken can never die."

Francis looked nervously around the room.

Grandfather sounded forlorn. "And we will wait for you here, a year, maybe two, and we will know what has become of you, Francis …"

"Oh, Francis!" I gasped, drawing a breath which was cold with shadows. The candlelight seemed to be dimmer than before.

A different light came into Grandfather's eyes. "But I know that no stories can change your mind. When that sea wind blows —you must follow it, you must go to the sea, answer your dreams. I know. There is no other way."

Francis smiled, undeterred. "You understand." He turned to look at Father, then back at the old man. "You understand."

Life was lonely without Francis.

He had left the morning before, looking both excited and afraid, waving from the side rails as the *Sea Wind* set sail away from Lisbon and out to sea. My older brother had been by me ever since I could remember, to talk with, to dream with.

And now I was alone.

Our small bedroom was dark, and the air was humid and filled with the raw scent of the wood slats Father soaked for his barrels. Light rain trickled against the whitewashed walls of our house overlooking the harbor. Faint echoes of thunder rumbled in the distance.

Francis was gone, in distant waters.

Baby Matthew cried in the corner, frightened by the storm. I heard Mother comforting him, whispering into his tiny ear. "It's just rain, little Matthew. The storm won't hurt you—it's far away. The storm is far, far out at sea."

The storm was out at sea.

I lay on my straw tick mattress, damp with sweat and rain mist, and I knew I would waste my time trying to sleep for a while yet. Silently, I crept to the window and moved aside the canvas curtain, cut from an old sail, so I could peer into the night. Ricocheting raindrops glistened on my face.

The cobblestoned streets were wet, reflecting distant flashes of lightning. The other buildings, every one of them a white box with narrow windows decked with flowers, perched on the steep levels of the city. I could barely make out the dark water of the harbor, and I certainly couldn't see the ocean. But the storm was out there, and so was Francis.

Is the sea dark now, Francis? And the sky filled with storm clouds even darker? Does the wind sing through the rigging and tear at the sails? Does the white foam boil against the side of the ship and crash on the deck? Is that roar of thunder your cry for help?

I could picture him standing at the rail, his knuckles white and his fingers gripping the peeling gold carvings scarred by graffiti, trying to hold himself steady against the screaming wind and crashing waves, peering down into the dark sea, pale with terror and waiting for the black tentacles of the kraken to reach up and smash the *Sea Wind*.

Francis!

Will you ever return to us?

Days later I found myself walking alone on the beach, far from the harbor. As if the storm had never been, the sun beat down to strike away my sweat. I wandered down the shore, looking for shells, for flotsam, for treasure. By myself.

The greatest loneliness was past now, and I was learning to be Stefan, instead of "Francis's brother." Father had begun to teach me what I needed to know as a cooper; and I was already becoming more independent. When Francis came back from his voyage, I might even be ready to embark on an adventure of my own. I could dream....

But I would wait for my brother. I would wait to hear his stories, the sights he had seen and the perils he had survived. Mother was already asking sailors from newly arrived ships if they had any news of the *Sea Wind* and when it would return. I could be patient and wait for Francis, though I would miss him.

The sun glared on the water, but I shaded my eyes to see a dark shape floating toward the beach, a piece of driftwood. I watched it bob along for a few moments and finally, when patience deserted me, I waded out to retrieve it.

I stood with warm water lapping about my waist, soaking into my coarse shirt. I looked at the wood.

It was a piece of wreckage, part of a ship, probably the splintered remnant of a rail. I turned it over, but in my heart I already knew.

Peeling gold paint ... scratched and obscured by sailors' graffiti.

The ocean made soft rushing noises, and I stared at the rail for a long time. Many ships had the same design, many ships could have shed that piece of wood—but in my heart I had no doubt.

Mother would continue to wait, day after day, for some word, watching for the *Sea Wind* to return. How long will you wait, Mother?

I let the driftwood slip back into the water and I pushed it away from shore. I knew I wouldn't tell her. For all she knew, all any of us knew, the *Sea Wind* was still out sailing to marvelous unknown places.

I turned and walked back toward the beach, washing the flecks of gold paint from my hands.

I've mentioned in other intros how much I was influenced by H.G. Wells and The War of the Worlds. *Wells published his novel in 1897, during the Mars craze inspired by astronomer Percival Lowell, who sensationalized the canals he saw on Mars through his giant refractor telescope in Flagstaff, Arizona.*

I researched Lowell and even visited his Flagstaff observatory. In one of the documents, I discovered a brief description of a plan developed by Lowell to dig giant canals in the Sahara, fill them with burning oil, to send a signal spectacular enough to be seen from Mars. I thought this audacious plan would be a terrific foundation for a story, and when I added Wells's Martians ready to invade Earth, it became even more than that.

This story, along with "Scientific Romance" in my first Fantasy Stories collection, form the core of my novel, Mr. Wells & the Martians.

CANALS IN THE SAND

Under the sweltering heat of the Sahara, Percival Lowell stood beside his own tent at the center of the camp and reveled in the clamor of his vast construction site. The excavations extended beyond the vanishing point of the flat desert horizon. Thousands of sweating workers—who worked for mere pennies a day—moved like choreographed machinery as they dug monumental trenches according to Lowell's commands, scribing a long line in the sand.

Lowell had seen the same on Mars, long canals, straight lines extending thousands of miles across the rusted desert. His own observations had absolutely convinced him that such markings must be indicative of surface life on a dying world.

Other astronomers claimed not to see the network of canals, that the lines on the disk of Mars were not there. It reminded him of the trial of Galileo, when the high church officials and Pope Paul V had refused to see the moons of Jupiter through the astronomer's "optick glass," denying the evidence of their own eyes. Lowell couldn't decide if his own contemporaries were similarly bullheaded, or just plain blind.

He took a deep breath, ignoring the pounding sun. The fiery heat and dust and petroleum stench practically curled the hairs in his mustache. With recently washed hands, he fished inside the front pocket of his cream jacket and withdrew his special pair of pince-nez, with lenses made of red stained glass. Through the copper-oxide tint, he could look out at the blistering and dead Sahara, seeing instead the scarlet sands of Mars. *Mars.*

How could one stand out here in the desert and not intuitively understand why the Martians would need to construct an extravagant set of canals to transport precious water from the melting ice caps down to their ancient cities? Water covered sixty percent of the Earth's surface, while Mars remained one vast planetary wasteland. The Martians' magnificent canals had endured as their world grew parched and withered with age, as their civilization mummified. By this time, those once-glorious minds must be desperate, ready to grasp at any hope.

Lowell strolled out along the well-packed path from the encampment to the long ditch his army of workers had dug in the shifting sands. Compared to what the Martians had accomplished, it seemed a child's futile effort, and it certainly wouldn't endure long—but then Lowell's canal was not required to.

It must remain only long enough to send a signal.

If Ogilvy's calculations were correct, Lowell had little time. He prayed his Bedouin workers would be fast enough. But he vowed nothing would deter him. After all, he had built his great Arizona observatory in a mere six weeks from groundbreaking to first light. He could certainly handle digging a ditch, even if it was ten miles long out in the middle of the Sahara.

Night on Mars Hill in the Arizona Territory, at an elevation of 7,000 feet, with clear skies far from the smoke of men. The big refractor and the observatory dome had been completed just in time to allow observations of the 1894 opposition of Mars.

Lowell spent his every free moment at the telescope.

His fellow Bostonian William H. Pickering, an astronomer for

Harvard, and his assistant Andrew Ellicott Douglass, both stood inside the chill, echoing dome of the Flagstaff Observatory, waiting for Lowell to relinquish the eyepiece. The wooden-plank walls of the observatory dome exuded a resinous scent. From where he sat in the uncomfortable chair, porkpie hat turned backward on his head and sketchpad in his lap, Lowell could sense their impatience.

"It is *my* telescope, gentlemen, and *I* will do the observing," Lowell said, not removing his eye from the wavering disk of the ruddy world, where fine lines appeared and disappeared as the seeing shifted in the Earth's atmosphere.

"Mister Lowell, sir," Pickering said, clearing his throat, "I understand your eagerness to use the refractor, but *we* are your professional astronomers, with the proper qualifications—"

Lowell finally turned, feeling annoyance heat his skin. "Qualifications, Mr. Pickering? I have exceptionally keen eyesight—and an exceptionally large fortune, which has built this telescope and pays your stipend. Therefore, I am fully qualified."

He snorted, looking down from his seat on the padded ladder and adjusting the porkpie hat on his head. "Perhaps if your Harvard had agreed to engage in a joint venture with me, Pickering, rather than calling me 'egoistic and unreasonable,' I would be more inclined to share. But instead, my own alma mater could not be convinced to do more than give you two gentlemen leave to work here, and then lease—*lease!*—me one of their small telescopes."

Douglass took a step back and looked to Pickering for his cue. Pickering, as always, cleared his throat and searched in vain for words.

Lowell's nostrils flared over his mustache. "You gentlemen are welcome to devote your nights to the study of the heavens at any other time, but this is *Mars* and it is at opposition. Please indulge this unworthy amateur." He turned back to the telescope, while the others shuffled their feet uncomfortably, and continued to wait. Within moments, Lowell had become totally engrossed in the view, his universe shrunk down to the tiny circle visible through the eyepiece.

Tact was a commodity that served little purpose when time was short. Lowell had selected Pickering, in part, because of his successful studies of Mars in 1892 at Arequipa in Peru. Pickering, a decent though somewhat stuffy administrator, had spent the winter of '93 in Boston supervising the design and construction of this observatory, which had been shipped out piece by piece to Flagstaff the following spring. Every bit of the project was a rush because Lowell demanded that the telescope absolutely must be functional by the time of the planetary opposition. Such a close encounter with Mars would not come again for many years.

Lowell drew a deep breath, shifted himself in his seat high above the observatory floor, and craned his neck. He fiddled with the eyepiece, and Mars stared back at him. He had the strangest sensation of being on the opposite end of a microscope, as if some immense being from across the cosmos were watching *him*, as someone with a microscope studied creatures that swarmed and multiplied in a drop of water.

His hands working independently, guided by the information channeled through the refractor tube, Lowell deftly sketched Mars, copying the lines he saw on the face of the planet. He had never been an armchair astronomer and would go blind before he ever allowed himself to be considered one. He and his staff had already recorded some four hundred canals on Mars—canals that other observers preposterously refused to see!

Lowell's outspoken beliefs had earned him much scorn, but no descendant of the great Boston family could remain quiet about deep convictions. In this case, and in many others, Percival Lowell knew he was right and the rest of the world was wrong— and he had proved it.

Well after midnight, his eyes burned. He flipped over the page in his sketchpad to where he had already scribed another perfect circle for a new map. Daylight hours were best used to prepare for the next clear night's observing.

Lowell noted that Douglass and Pickering had left

unobtrusively, and he hoped they were at least doing work at the other telescopes, since the seeing was so extraordinary this evening. He blinked, oriented his hand and a newly sharpened pencil on the map pad, then pressed against the eyepiece again.

A brilliant green flash leaped from the surface of Mars.

Lowell barely restrained himself from crying out. The flame had been a vivid emerald, a jet of fire as of a great explosion or some kind of immense cannon shot, a huge mass of luminous gas, trailing a green mist behind it.

Once previously, Lowell had seen the glint of sunlight on the Martian ice caps, which had fooled him into seeing a dazzling message—but it had not been like this. Not so green, so violent, so prominent.

Before long he witnessed another green flash, and quickly noted the exact time on the pad in his lap. His excitement grew as he formulated his own explanation for the phenomenon....

Several days later he received a telegram from Ogilvy, a prominent London astronomer, confirming the green flashes from Mars. Ogilvy himself had counted flashes on ten nights, while Lowell himself had recorded several others, which had occurred during the daylight hours in England.

Lowell knew exactly what the flashes must be, and he exhibited no reluctance whatsoever in telling others about his theories. Obviously, these brilliant flares were indications of stupendous launches, a fleet of ships exploding away from Martian gravity into space.

There could be no other explanation. The Martians were coming!

Work crews toiled day and night to move the sand, some complaining, some happy for the meager pay, some shaking their sweat-dripping heads at the insanity of this loud American and his incomprehensible obsession.

The Bedouins thought he was mad, as did many of Lowell's

colleagues. But the superstitious Bedouins understood nothing of the universe ... nor, for that matter, did most other astronomers.

He allowed no slacking in the construction for any reason. Shovels tossed sand up over the walls of the ditches; half naked boys ran with ladles and buckets, while camels strained to drag barrels of warm water along the length of the dry canal. Lowell supervised here, and he could only hope that the other two trenches would be completed in time to intersect with this one.

When the teams grew too tired to continue, he hired more. Lowell had spread his funds as far as Cairo and Alexandria. He had bribed port officials, paid for the construction of a new railroad out into the desert, leading nowhere, so that a private train could deliver supplies and workers to Lowell's canals.

The sand hissed in the breeze, glittering in the sun. A drummer pounded a cadence to keep the workers in a steady rhythm, like galley slaves. But they were being paid for this labor, and they had volunteered, so Lowell felt no sympathy for them.

Smoke curled into the air, carrying an acrid, sulfurous stench as brown-skinned men dumped wagonloads of hot bitumen into the newly dug trench. The sticky black mass would hold the sands in place, bind them into a thick, flammable mass. Still, the walls shifted, and the bitumen ran black and sticky in the heat of the day.

Grumbling, Lowell doubted the sloping walls of sand would hold if one of the great dust storms of the Sahara swept across the dunes. With one mighty breath, God could erase all of Lowell's handiwork, the fruits of years of labor and a squandered family fortune.

If only luck could hold until he sent his signal....

The great Suez Canal had been completed three decades earlier. For years the United States had discussed excavating a canal across Central America as soon as the government found some way to grab the necessary land. Lowell's own project was not impossible. It could not be impossible.

He strutted up and down the edge of the ditch, a dusty bandanna wrapped over his mouth, nose, and mustache. He recalled the ancient Hebrew slaves, erecting immense monuments for the pharaohs. But the pharaohs had had decades, even generations, to complete their enormous projects. Lowell had no such luxury.

The line in the sand stretched into a shimmer of mirage in the wavering air. Just a ditch, many miles long, extending to meet two other ditches in what his surveyors guaranteed would be a perfect equilateral triangle.

Back home in Boston, leaving the Flagstaff Observatory in the hands of Pickering and Douglass for the autumn, Lowell had calculated the absolute limit of his financial resources, determining the largest excavation he could complete, since the governments of the world refused to help in what they called his "crackpot scheme."

And still Percival Lowell had accomplished little more than a gnat, compared to Martian accomplishments, even allowing for the fact that their task would have been simpler, given that Martian gravity was only a third of Earth's. He had postulated Martian beings, therefore, three times the size of a human; in their reduced gravity, such Martians could be 21 times as efficient and have 81 times the effective strength of an Earthbound man. For such a species, the project of planetary canals seemed not unlikely.

Lowell's notebooks lay in the tent, but he had done the mathematics himself, letting the engineers double-check his work. Three trenches, each ten miles long, five yards wide, filled with liquid to a depth of an inch or so, equaled thousands and thousands of gallons of petroleum distillate, naphtha, kerosene. The convoys traveled endlessly across the Sahara: an impossible task, made possible—just barely—through the use of his great fortune.

It was a huge investment, but what better way could Lowell spend his money?

Douglass and Pickering had squawked when he had cut his generous allowance of funding for the Flagstaff Observatory down to a maintenance stipend. "How are we to continue our research?" their plaintive telegram had wailed.

"Come to the Sahara," he had replied, "and I will show you."

If Lowell succeeded in signaling the Martians, here and now, astronomical observatories around the world would never again lack for funding.

But they had to hurry. Hurry.

A blustery man, not intimidated by challenge, Lowell nevertheless found himself stuttering in awe when he met in Milan with the great Giovanni Schiaparelli—discoverer of asteroids and the original cartographer of the canals of Mars.

After spotting the green flashes, then laying plans for his great project to signal back to the Martians, Lowell had allotted himself half a year to travel to Europe and generate support. He had taken a first-class cabin on a steamer bound for England. Reaching London, he had sought out Ogilvy and immediately enlisted his aid.

The other astronomer had at first been skeptical that there could be any living thing on that remote, forbidding planet. Lowell, however, had been very persuasive.

Obtaining leave from his observatory, Ogilvy accompanied Lowell on his travels. Ogilvy's friend, a journalist named Wells, also asked to travel with them in hopes of getting a good story for his newspaper, but Lowell would have none of it. The newspapers had resoundingly ridiculed Lowell's theories about the Martian canals, and he wanted nothing further to do with reporters, not in the initial stages of a project of such importance.

The two men proceeded across the Channel and thence to Paris for an excellent dinner and conversation with the well-known French writer and astronomer, Camille Flammarion, who gave Lowell's idea a favorable reception. He beamed with pleasure to hear the Frenchman proclaim that Lowell's own theories about the canals and life on Mars had been "ascertained indubitably."

By train and private carriage, Lowell, and a wide-eyed Ogilvy —who had never previously visited the Continent—traveled to Italy to meet with Schiaparelli in his small villa.

Schiaparelli had been director of the Milan Observatory since 1862, where he had discovered the asteroid Hesperia, written a brilliant treatise on comets and meteors, and created his original maps of the Martian *canali* in 1877, only a year after Lowell himself had graduated with honors from Harvard. During that same opposition, the American astronomer Asaph Hall had discovered the two tiny moons of Mars, Phobos and Deimos— Fear and Dread. But using only an eight-inch telescope, Schiaparelli had exposed a more profound cosmic secret.

"When I originally drew my maps," the old astronomer said, struggling with his English, "I meant to represent the lines merely as channels or cracks in the surface. I understand that *canali* implies a different thing to non-Italian ears, suggesting man-made canals—"

"Not *man*-made," Lowell interrupted, extracting his pipe from its case and tamping a load of sweet tobacco from his pouch, "but made by intelligent beings, whose minds may be immeasurably superior to ours. Extraterrestrial life does not mean extraterrestrial human life. Under changed conditions, life itself must take on other forms."

"Yes, yes," Schiaparelli nodded, took a sip of his deep red wine, then a bigger gulp. He blinked his rheumy eyes. "But your subsequent observations have convinced even me, my friend."

Lowell leaned forward intently, lacing his fingers together over his knees. "I wish you could see what I have seen on the red disk of the Great God of War, Schiaparelli. Such wonders."

The old astronomer sighed. His rooms were filled with books, oil lamps, and melted lumps of candles in terra cotta dishes. A pair of spectacles lay on an open tome, while an enormous magnifying glass rested in easy reach on another stack of books.

"I can only imagine them. My own eyesight has grown so poor

that I must now occupy my mind and my time with the study of history. Though I can no longer study comets or meteors or planets, even an old man with dim vision can make astute observations of history."

"Tell him about Mars, Lowell, my good man," Ogilvy said, searching for something else to eat, and finally settling on some water crackers and old cheese left out on the sideboard in the Italian's dim rooms.

Lowell opened his mind's eye wide as he spoke in an oddly quiet and reverent voice, totally distinct from his usual booming, commanding tone. Thoughts of Mars still made him breathless with astonishment.

"You drew the canals yourself, Schiaparelli—narrow dark lines of uniform width and intensity, perfectly straight. Some even compose portions of great circles across the globe. As I view them from Flagstaff in my best refractor, they look to be gossamer filaments, cobwebs on the face of the Martian disk, threads to draw your mind after them, across millions of miles of intervening void."

Schiaparelli rubbed his eyes. "In my youth I, myself, never conceived them to be more than blemishes."

Lowell raised his eyebrows dubiously. "Geometrical precision on a planetary scale? What else can it be but the mark of an intelligent race? If we could respond in kind, would we not be morally obligated to do so, in the name of humanity?"

Ogilvy coughed on his cracker and looked about for something to drink, finally settling on a wicker-wrapped bottle of Chianti that Schiaparelli had opened for them. He poured sloppily into a glass on the sideboard, then took a quick swallow, only to renew his coughing fit. Lowell scowled at the British astronomer for shattering his spell of imagination.

He puffed on his pipe and settled back in the fine leather-bound chair. Outside on the open balcony, pigeons fluttered in the sunlight. Schiaparelli still watched him with an intent stare. Ogilvy began to page through one of the open history books.

"Imagine it, Schiaparelli," Lowell continued. "Think of a

parched, dying world inhabited by a once-marvelous civilization, beings with the science and ingenuity to keep themselves alive at all costs. Why, the very existence of a planetwide system of canals implies a world order that knows no national boundaries, a society that long ago forgot its political disputes and racial animosity, uniting the populace in a desperate quest for water. Water ..."

"And the dark spots, Lowell?" Ogilvy asked, turning back to the conversation. Schiaparelli drank more of his Chianti, amused and fascinated by the description. "Tell him about the oases."

Lowell stood up to stretch, placed his hands behind his back, and turned to the balcony to watch the pigeons. "Pumping stations, obviously."

The old Italian astronomer stared at where the walls of his villa met the ceiling, but he seemed to see nothing, perhaps only a blur with his used-up eyes. Lowell felt a rare flash of sympathy—losing one's eyesight must be the greatest hell a dedicated astronomer could imagine.

"But if Mars is so arid, Lowell, surely all the water would evaporate from these open canals long before it reaches its destination ... if the temperature is much above freezing, that is—and it *must* be above freezing in order for the water to be in its liquid state." Schiaparelli's forehead creased in a frown.

Ogilvy piped up, pacing the room. "And don't forget, my good man, the astronomical distances involved. If these canals were simple waterways or aqueducts, we would never be able to see them from Earth. They would be much too narrow. How do you account for that?"

Annoyed, Lowell turned to the Englishman. He and Ogilvy had already had this discussion in earnest several times, and again on the train ride to Milan. But he saw Ogilvy's raised eyebrow and understood that the other man had raised the question just to give Lowell a chance to explain.

"Ah, there is a simple answer for both questions," Lowell said, then paused to draw deeply from his pipe. "Almost certainly the lines we see are aqueducts with lush vegetation growing in irrigated croplands along the borders. The only remaining forests on Mars, towering high in the low gravity, sipping precious water from the fertile soil—much as the Egyptians grow their crops in the plains around the Nile. I estimate the darkened fringes of the aqueducts to be about thirty miles wide. This vegetation would not only emphasize the lines of the canals but would also shield the open water from rapid evaporation. Simple, you see? It is quite clear."

Ogilvy nodded, and Schiaparelli gave a distant smile. The old astronomer seemed more amused than impassioned by the concepts. Lowell came closer to his host, barely controlling his own enthusiasm. "My proposed plan follows a similar principle, Schiaparelli. The project I have conceived will take place on a much smaller scale, naturally, since I am but one man and, alas, our own Earthly civilization has no stomach for such dreams.

"I have already dispatched surveyors and work teams to the Sahara, in the flat desert in western Egypt. I will excavate three canals of my own, each ten miles long, across an otherwise featureless basin, to form a perfect equilateral triangle. A geometrical symbol impossible to explain with random natural processes, and therefore a clear message that intelligent life inhabits this world. To make them more visible, I must emphasize my puny canals with lines of fire, by filling the trenches with petroleum products and igniting them. It will be a brief but dramatic message, blazing into the night." His eyes sparkled, his voice rose in volume.

"But why this tremendous effort, my friend?" Schiaparelli asked. "Why now?"

Promptly, he and Ogilvy described the repeated green flashes, the launches of enormous vehicles, ships sent to Earth. Based on Ogilvy's observations and calculations derived from a careful scrutiny of celestial mechanics, Lowell believed he knew the travel time the Martians required to reach Earth.

Lowell's voice became husky. "As you can see, the Martians are on their way. We must show them where to land, where they will meet with an open-hearted welcome from Earthbound admirers of their past triumphs and their current travails."

Lowell took a deep breath and spoke with absolute confidence. "Gentlemen, *I* intend to lead that party. I will be the first man to shake hands with a Martian."

Finally.

Finally. Lowell had never been a man of extraordinary patience, but the last week of waiting for the three trenches to join at precise corners had been the most interminable time of his life.

Now, under the starlight and the residual heat that wafted off the baked sands, Lowell stood with his torch in hand, feeling like a tribal shaman, ready to ignite his weapon against the darkness, his symbol of welcome to aliens from another world.

The stench of petroleum distillates stung his eyes and nostrils. The chemical smell had driven off the camels and most of the workers, save those few foremen—mostly Europeans— who intended to watch the spectacle. On high dunes in the distance, the curious Bedouins had gathered by their own tents to observe. This would be an event for their storytellers to repeat for generations.

Working with his reluctant assistants Pickering and Douglass, Lowell had gone to a great deal of trouble to calculate the best time when the Sahara night would face Mars, so that his transient shout into the universe had the best chance of being seen—if not from the inbound Martian emissary ships, then from those survivors who had remained on the red planet.

Lowell turned to the telegraph operator beside him. Miles of overland cable had been run to the other vertices of the great triangle in the sand, so that the teams could communicate with each other. "Signal Pickering and Douglass at the other two intersections. Tell them to light their channels."

The telegraph operator pecked away at his key, sending a brief message. When the clicks fell into silence, Lowell stepped to the brink of his canal in the sand. He stared down into the bitumen-lined trench, the foul-smelling black mass that was now pooled with kerosene and gasoline dumped from enormous tanks that had been hauled across the desert by his private railroad.

Lowell tossed his torch into the fuel, then watched the fire spread like a hungry demon, rushing down the channel. The inferno devoured the dumped petroleum, hot enough to ignite the sticky bitumen liner so that the triangular symbol would burn for a long time.

Across the desert into the night, rifle shots rang out, signaling to other torchbearers stationed along the ten miles of each canal, who also tossed their burning brands into the ditch, so that the fire could engulf the entire triangle. Martians and fire, Lowell thought—what a strange combination.

Lowell's family had already made its mark on the world. Towns had been named after the Lowells and the Lawrences; his maternal grandfather was Abbott Lawrence, minister to Britain. His father, Augustus Lowell, was descended from the early Massachusetts colonists. His family had amassed its fortune in textiles, in landholdings, in finance. But Percival himself would make the greatest mark—on *two* worlds instead of one.

An unbroken wall of flame roared up into the night. He prayed the Martians were watching. He had so much to say to them.

Lowell found it difficult to sleep even long after the inferno had died down. He lay on his cot in his tent, smelling the dying smoke and harsh fumes, listening to the whisper of settling sand sloughing into the bottom of the trench from the burned walls. Far off in the Bedouin camp a pair of camels belched at each other.

In only a year or two, the shifting desert would erase most of his line in the sand, leaving only a dark scar. But if his intended audience received the message, Earth would be a dramatically changed place in that time, and his effort would not be in vain.

Lowell found his situation incredibly strange: he, a wealthy Boston Brahmin, now resting fitfully in an austere tent in the middle of a vast desert that had been made even more unpleasant by his own construction work.

Summoning images of beauty to his mind, he recalled his experiences in Japan, as much an alien world as this Sahara, perhaps even as alien as Mars. He thought of colors bright as enamel and lacquer, gold filigree and cloisonné, the heady perfumes of peonies and burning incense. He remembered being escorted along narrow avenues of carefully tended trees where an explosion of white petals drifted on the winds for the annual cherry blossom festival. He recalled the delicate ritual of a tea ceremony, or the thin atonal melody plucked out on a *biwa* as spiced morsels sizzled on a small hibachi.

During those years as ambassador to Japan, Lowell had lugged his six-inch refractor with him, staring, staring, seeing the Earth but watching the stars....

He had graduated from Harvard with distinction in mathematics at the age of twenty-one, and he had received the Bowdoin Prize for his essay on "The Rank of England as a European Power Between the Death of Elizabeth and the Death of Anne." He had traveled the world, studied the classics, experienced numerous foreign cultures, proved his facility in languages, even tried to join the fighting in the Serbo-Turkish War. What did he care that mere astronomers scorned his ideas?

Lowell had sailed for Japan in 1883, where he was asked to serve as Foreign Secretary for a special diplomatic mission from Korea to the United States—though at the time he had never even seen Korea. Returning to Tokyo, he had later been asked to help write Japan's new constitution.

Lying sleepless on his cot, he spoke aloud to the apex of his tent, where the canvas rippled in a faint breeze. "I have experience as an ambassador to foreign cultures. I have diplomatic credentials. How could the Martians be stranger than what I have already seen?"

The cylinder screamed through the air with the wailing of a thousand lost souls, trailing behind it a tongue of fire from atmospheric friction and a bright green mist from outgassing extraterrestrial substances.

Lowell burst out of his shaded tent to see the commotion under the midday sun. A burnt smudge of smoke smoldered like a scar across the ceramic-blue sky. Booms of sound thundered in waves as the gigantic ship/projectile crossed overhead.

"It's the emissaries from Mars!" Lowell shouted, raising his hands in the air. "The Martians!"

Like an exploding warship, the cylinder crashed into the desert with a spewed plume of sand and dust. Lowell felt the tremor of impact in his knees, despite the cushioning desert. He laughed aloud, yelling for Douglass and Pickering to join him.

After the burning of the enormous triangle, most of the workers had returned to their widely scattered lands, leaving only a few team bosses to tidy up the loose ends of the construction. Lowell had sold his now-useless railroad for scrap steel, giving the salvagers a decent percentage of the profits. The place rapidly turned into a ghost town, which some of the European bosses had quietly begun calling "Lowell's Folly." Pickering and Douglass had returned from the other two base camps to join him here. To wait ...

Now, as the dust settled in the distance, the other two astronomers ran up, their faces ruddy with sunburn and excitement. "We are vindicated!" Lowell cried. He clapped them each on the shoulder. "The Martians are here!"

The remaining Bedouin helpers fled the camp in panic, thrashing their camels to an awkward gallop across the dunes. *Idiots*, he thought. *Fools.* They did not realize the honor that had been bestowed here.

"The world as we know it is about to change. Come, let us put together an expedition. We must welcome our visitors from space."

The heat from the pit rose up in a tremendous wave, overwhelming even the blistering daytime pounding of the Sahara. Pickering dropped back, coughing, but Lowell plodded forward, hunched over, shielding his watering eyes. On an impulse, he reached into the pocket of his cream-colored suit jacket and withdrew his bright red spectacles, placing them over his eyes, seeing the world as a Martian would, the better to understand them.

Because of the residual heat, he could not get close to the crash site, and he felt a terrible dread that the Martian ship had exploded when it struck the ground, that all the interplanetary ambassadors had been obliterated by fire.

But then he heard faint pounding sounds within the metal-walled cylinder, mechanical noises, a soft unscrewing....

Finally, Douglass dragged him back. "It's too hot, Mister Lowell! We must wait."

With savage disappointment, Lowell stumbled away, keeping his head turned to stare at the smoldering crater through his red-lensed spectacles. "I have waited years for this moment. I can tolerate a few more hours—but not much longer than that."

His eyes stinging from tears not entirely caused by the blistering heat, he followed the other two men back to the main camp.

Douglass fetched some water, toiletries, and fresh clothes after sweaty hours spent in the dim shelter of their tents. He and Pickering ate ravenously of a quickly prepared meal, though

Lowell himself felt no hunger. His stomach tied itself in knots as he felt his life's work coming to its climax.

Lowell used some of the tepid water to shave, leaning over a small mirror. Then he changed into a fine new suit, and straightened his collar, keeping his gaze intent on the still-glowing pit visible through the propped-open tent flap. Finally, in the cool of the desert night, he told his two companions to wait behind.

"You can't go alone, man," Pickering said, after clearing his throat again.

"Nonsense." Lowell brushed the other astronomer's grasp from his arm. "It was my money that brought the Martians to this landing site, and I claim the right."

"That's the same argument you used with your damned telescope," Pickering muttered, but did not pursue the discussion. Douglass hunkered down, looking forlorn.

Lowell strode across the surrounding dunes in his black leather shoes, mulling over an appropriate speech, wondering if by some miracle the Martians might speak English. No matter, he thought. He had a knack for languages and would manage to communicate somehow.

Looking dapper, he approached the edge of the pit. He noted with fascination that the heat of the impact had been great enough to fuse some of the sand grains into lumps of glass. If the Martians could survive that, they must be prime specimens indeed.

He stood on the brink, looking down into the glow that lit up the crater as if it were day. A long, shiny lid had been unscrewed from the large pitted cylinder and lay on the blasted sands. Below, he saw clanking machines stirring, odd tentacled creatures moving about, exhibiting an industriousness no doubt born by their dire circumstances on Mars. Most remarkable, he saw, was a tall, newly assembled construction rising up on stiltlike, tripod legs. The heat was still incredible.

Magnificent! Lowell felt proud and overwhelmed to be

mankind's emissary. Now that they had reached Earth, though, the poor Martians could be saved.

Lowell hurried forward to greet the Martians. The wonders of the universe awaited him.

Kris Rusch has been one of my best friends for most of my life. I met her in an undergrad fiction workshop in college in 1981 and we've been close ever since, bootstrapping each other's careers, helping each other through ups and downs. She served as Dungeon Master for years as our gang of college friends played D&D every Sunday night. She was my "best person" when Rebecca and I got married. She's been my mentor, and I've been hers. Our writing styles and writing techniques couldn't be farther apart, and yet it works.

We wrote two novels together, Afterimage *and* Aftershock, *dark fantasy thrillers that featured a race of shapeshifters living in the redwood wilderness near Santa Cruz, California, who try to integrate among humanity. This story is loosely connected with that universe, a standalone piece that I still find gut-wrenching.*

CHANGE OF FACE
(WITH KRISTINE KATHRYN RUSCH)

—I—

I stand on the street below her apartment and watch as she rocks in the chair by the window. During the day, she leaves the shades up and the windows open. Sometimes she sings. Her voice quavers with a sadness I fear will never leave her.

She won't recognize me now, even if she looks out.

Early memories, they say, are the strongest. Ask all darklings, and they will tell you of their first solo change: the way the skin twists; the deep, arching, almost erotic pain; the creaks and groans as the bone structure shifts; and the sudden awkward sensation of wearing a rejuvenated, but different, body.

I, too, remember my first solo change. But I am only half darkling, and I remember something else:

The morning was cold in the forest. I sat at the edge of the group of darkling children, my feet buried in ferns. The teacher leaned on the burned-out stump of an old redwood, his personal scent evoking sand and old leaves. He was telling us all a story. But he kept glancing at me. He called me "human," although I was not. My father had rescued me from a human mother, bringing me back out into the forests. My father taught me little,

96

except to repeat over and over that I was the child of his blood, the child of his heart.

"Humans are strange creatures," the teacher said. His body that season was angular, with dark hair and long fingers. "They wear the same shape their entire lives and identify each other by sight, not scent. They don't believe in other species like themselves, yet they have more stories of us than we have of them. Humans will imprison you, torture or kill you. Stay away from them."

Most of the children looked at me, and a few moved away. Only a very little girl stayed beside me to prove she had no fear. "But he's human," she said, pointing at me.

"He is half-human, and if he survives his first solo change then perhaps he has earned the right to call himself a darkling. But if he dies, that will be another lesson to you." The teacher's deep voice sent shivers down my back. He continued talking of other things, but I stopped listening. I hugged my knees to my chest, feeling fear settle at the base of my stomach. Around us, the green-scented forest intertwined with life. The human city seemed very far away.

Perhaps I wouldn't survive the first solo change.

When I brought that fear to my father, he leaned against a tree that formed part of our small shelter and smiled. "You've been through three changes with my help," he said. "You're more darkling than they think."

And he was right. The change came three days later as a deep fog settled in the mountains, obscuring the trees and making the river's gurgle echo throughout the forest.

I felt the tingle at the base of my spine and called out for my father, but either he didn't hear me, or he refused to come. The first rending ripped through my ribcage, tugged on my arms, and pulled at my legs. Each cell screamed as it renewed itself.

I was going to die. I was human and I would die, half-formed and broken, like newborn babies who went through a change without the help of a parent.

My skin pooled around itself and my hair twisted, blowing

into my face. I felt the shift, seized it as my father had taught me, used it to bend myself into another form, a survivable form. The tingle grew into a buzzing around my head and the pain reached through me, grabbing each muscle, each ligament, each bone, pulling, pinching, and reforming until I thought I would explode. The explosion built, built, built—and stopped.

I staggered forward into the cool mist, tripping over a tree limb, wondering at my long legs and my short fingers. How rejuvenated I felt, reborn and made new again. An energy pulsed through me, and for a moment I thought I could survive anything.

"Father!" I shouted. "I'm a darkling now."

His nutmeg scent appeared out of the fog before he did. My father's new body—squat and large—strained at the seams of the coat he had put on that morning. "Not full darkling," he said. "Tomorrow I'll take you for a visit to the human city. When you grow, you'll have to choose between being a darkling and being human."

"I change, like all darklings."

"Yes. And you ask too many questions, and you cling like no darkling ever does." He had smiled, a secret smile that was his alone. "And you are strong."

But I am not strong at all. I still stand below my lover's window in the human city, gazing up at her in the rocking chair, torturing myself. I want just one glimpse of her face.

I hear my father's voice mixing with the teacher's of that cold childhood morning: *You are strong, human, more darkling than they think. Stay away from humans. They will imprison, torture, or kill you.* They will make you stand beneath open windows, because to go up the stairs is to confess that you made the wrong choice on the day you met Shelli, over one long year ago.

—II—

When I was sixteen, my first darkling lover left me for a boy who smelled of earthworms and tree rot. My father had his own concerns, and the rest of the darklings avoided me. I learned tree craft, oral history, and river fishing, I took other lovers and discarded them, according to the darkling way. I fathered two children in the forest, both of whom were raised by their mothers. Still I wasn't satisfied. Half human, half darkling, with urges that belonged to both or neither. I was never sure how to behave, or even what I wanted for myself. I had to choose.

I awakened one morning on a bed of leaves and dried redwood fronds, and I decided I would go to see the hustle and thrum of human contact. I had been to the city before, on several prolonged trips with my father, and he had showed me many of the things that are held important in human society. He taught me how to make a home, find a job, flit from class to class at night school, learning in snatches.

In the darkling community cache, I found old clothing that suited the tall, slender body I wore and took some of the money we stashed away for the times when we went to the city. Then I followed the river through the woods, veering off as the smells of the city became stronger: car exhaust mingling with wood smoke, human sweat and perfume, discarded garbage.

I wandered past the permanent-looking houses, the old Mission, and the clock tower, down to the Pacific Garden Mall. The strangeness swallowed me, and that day I became human, or pretended to be.

I sat on a bench and just watched for a while. People thronged among the caged trees and manicured bushes in the bright sun. Two cellists sat in front of the spaghetti restaurant and played. A woman walked by in heels and a navy skirt, intent, it seemed, on something far away. A flowery, alcohol-based perfume covered her real scent. A boy whose long hair smelled of sunshine rode a skateboard along the blocked-off streets. I had learned, in my previous visits, that every human, when asked, expressed a purpose, a reason for being. Darklings had no such purpose. Darklings simply were.

The cellists took a break, and I had a sudden craving for coffee that smelled thick and black and strong. I wanted some place simple, some place quiet. Few people sat in the coffee shop across the street, and even before I realized I had made a decision, I reached for the polished metal handle that smelled of the oil from a thousand hands.

I pulled open the door and felt the air conditioning kiss the sweat on my arms. The air tasted of metal, dish soap, and cinnamon. I crossed the worn linoleum floor and took a booth by the window, where I could see if the cellists returned. The seat was old and soft, the plastic scent buried beneath years of sweat, grease, and ammonia.

"Can I help you?" Her voice was quiet. I looked up.

She smelled of peppermint and moonlight. Her eyes had a downward cast, and I knew her skin would be like velvet to my touch. I felt a quick moment of desire, a darkling thought (*Take her now, or that body will escape you and become something else*), before I remembered that she was human. I smiled. "A cup of coffee. Black."

She tucked her notepad into her pocket and put her pen behind her ear. "That all? Coming right up."

She headed back to the counter with a light step. She poured coffee into a large mug and made a comment to one of the cooks. The sound of her laughter washed through me like the whisper of redwoods.

I gazed out the window. Three more boys on skateboards went past, followed by college students on bicycles. The cellists' chairs and music stands were gone. Perhaps I should have come earlier, given myself a chance to listen longer.

The rich aroma of coffee mixed with her peppermint and moonlight reached me. I turned as she set the mug down. "Do the musicians play here every day?" I asked.

She put a knee on the booth's other seat and gazed out. "I never notice anymore. They used to come in here."

"To play?"

"Oh, no." She smiled. "They would sit in this booth, drink coffee, and talk about music."

I recognized something in how her personal scent changed,

something I had been feeling all day. A wistfulness, a desire to be someone else. "Are you a musician?"

Her laugh had a derisive edge. She took her knee off the seat and stood up, as if she were going to leave. "I'm just a waitress."

"No one is 'just a' anything," I said. "What do you do on the days you don't come here?"

"Put my feet up." She wiped a strand of hair from her face and frowned, as if she thought the remark had been too curt. "Or go to Woody Allen movies."

"Woody Allen movies?" We had reached the end of my cultural sophistication. I had watched some television, but I had never been to a movie. I couldn't understand why anyone would sit in a large room, watching images flicker on a screen for two long hours, smelling the popcorn, the candy, the soft drinks, and the gathered people together in the darkness, crammed close to each other.

"You've never seen a Woody Allen movie?"

A flush crept up my cheeks. "I haven't seen many movies at all."

She stared at me as if she couldn't believe what she had heard. Behind her, a bell rang. She waved without turning, then looked back at me. "Is it something political, religious, or what?"

"I just never had the opportunity." I wrapped my hands around the coffee mug. Its ceramic sides warmed my palms.

"You haven't been in California long, have you?"

I smiled. I hadn't been in her California long at all.

The bell rang again. "Gotta get an order," she said and hurried away from me.

I sipped the coffee. The rich aroma lingered in my nose. I hadn't smelled anything so good in a long time.

A flautist and a violinist replaced the cellists in front of the spaghetti restaurant. I could barely hear the strains of music rising above the background street sounds. I would get a hotel room for the night, then search for a job and an apartment. This was an interesting diversion, to play human for a while.

"Listen, I'm going to a movie tomorrow."

I looked up, startled. The coffee's rich taste had dampened my sense of smell. She stood next to me and I hadn't even noticed.

"Maybe you could meet me there. It's *Annie Hall.* If you're going to start seeing movies, you may as well start with the best."

I savored the moment, as I had that first sip of coffee. No human woman had ever asked me to go anywhere with her before. "I'd like that," I said. "Where do I meet you?"

"You got a car?"

I shook my head.

"Then why don't you meet me here at noon? The movie's on campus. I'll drive you."

"All right."

She grinned and sprinted away. We didn't talk again that day, except to murmur a goodbye as I walked out the door. I didn't even learn that her name was Shelli until the next day.

—III—

We made love for the first time a week later. Her apartment was a small one-bedroom on the second floor of an old Victorian house not far from the Pacific Garden Mall. The place smelled of peppermint, cat fur, ammonia, and musty paper. Shelli had more books than I had seen outside of the library.

She took me into her bedroom. I had no plans to seduce her, afraid, I think, that our bodies weren't compatible even though I knew they would be. My half-darkling existence had proven that humans could be darkling mates.

Shelli undressed me slowly, with a sort of reverence for the body I wore, exclaiming about its thinness and the softness of its hair. She felt heavier, more solid than any darkling lover, more permanent, as if her skin were welded to her bones and her entire body were attached to the earth. When I sank into her, it felt like plunging into the warmth of the river.

Later, I found a job at a garden store—the people there loved my affinity for plants, though I rarely knew the human names for them all. The store seemed like the forest to me, smelling of flowers and earth, of fresh air and growth. I belonged there more than I had belonged anywhere, except with Shelli.

She and I passed through each day, eager to be with each other, and soon after that I moved in with her.

For the first time, I felt safe inside a permanent structure. For the first time, I lost my urge to roam. Life became like a series of Woody Allen movies: Each small event seemed to have an overlying meaning that I couldn't quite grasp, but which seemed very clear to Shelli and the others around me.

She told me once that she loved my spontaneity.

I loved her certainty.

Every morning, I promised myself that I would tell her about me and who I was. And every night I clutched her tightly, bracing myself for the change that had to come.

—IV—

That afternoon in the garden store I found a pink African violet that reminded me of Shelli. I set it aside and smiled each time I thought of it. A tiny thing to celebrate our third month together. Marking anniversaries was a human practice I was beginning to enjoy. When I walked down the street, I finally felt I had a sense of purpose.

I clocked out at five, tied a pink bow around the pot, and went out the back of the store. The alley was empty, dark with early evening, and smelled of dying plants. Through the rows of buildings, I could hear my cellists playing something modern and atonal.

The tingle at the base of my spine didn't alert me. I was so intent on crossing through the darkness to Shelli that I ignored the sensation altogether.

I had made it three steps across the alley when the pain ripped through me, long and hard and full. I stopped walking, preferring to concentrate on molding myself. I felt as if I were being torn from the inside out, broken and reformed. My father used to love the change, love its randomness and unpredictability, but it brought up the fear in me, the fear of death.

The flowerpot slipped out of what had been my hand and shattered against the concrete. My skin jelled, liquefied, and ran like chocolate in the sunshine. I screamed—once—then felt the transformation run through me, coursing inside my skin like blood. The lengthening stopped, my body shrank into itself. And when the pain ended, I was short and fat, lost in the clothes that Shelli had bought for my old body.

The back door of the garden store opened, and Tom, one of my coworkers, peered outside, he glanced at me and looked away, a habit he used when approached by panhandlers on the street. He closed the door again.

I got up. With shaking hands, I brushed the dirt from my clothes, then rolled up my long pant legs. I had to get to Shelli. I had to tell her. I hurried down the Mall, pulled open the coffee shop door, and stopped as Shelli smiled at me. She grabbed a single menu and asked, "How many?" in her most polite, and distant, tone.

I backed out, and continued backing away until I could no longer see the shop. Then I ran, tripping as my pant legs fell and my shortened steps missed their marks.

—V—

I went back to the woods and found no solace. I dreamed of cello music and peppermint perfume and Woody Allen's nasal voice. I even told my father about Shelli. He smiled at me. "You remember your first human like you remember your first lover. The experience is so different, so exciting. But she never would have believed your story of change, and she wouldn't have believed who you were, no matter what you said."

Shelli's eyes came back to me, the blank stare of non-recognition, the flat, polite tone in her voice as she looked at me in the doorway of the coffee shop. Humans didn't understand change. I would have had to leave regardless of what I told her. I stayed in the woods and tried not to think of her, declaring my experimentation with being human a complete and total failure.

I became a darkling again. I helped my father gather roots, herbs, and berries. We made poultices, ground spices, and stored food for the lean months. I took darkling lovers, seeking something solid, a woman who felt as if she were made of earth and water instead of air and flame....

Almost a year later, I found myself sitting on the same brick planter in the Mall again, watching Shelli's coffee shop.

At first, I told myself that I only wanted to see if she was all right. But it was more than that. The darkling teacher, in one of his many lectures about humans, had said they mated for life. The children had laughed. Darklings were like cats, sharing a casual affection, but moving from lover to lover, sometimes within the same evening. Change versus consistency; certainty versus spontaneity.

I pulled open the door of the coffee shop and felt the kiss of air conditioning again. The air still smelled of metal, dish soap, and cinnamon. A strange woman stood behind the counter. She brushed a strand of dark hair from her face and asked, "Just yourself?" as she grabbed a single menu.

I couldn't smell peppermint or moonlight. "Is Shelli here?"

"Shelli?" The waitress squinted and clutched the menu to her chest. "Oh, *Shelli*. She quit months ago."

My stomach lurched. I knotted my fingers together. "Do you know where she is now?"

"No. I'd only been here a few weeks when she left."

I nodded and pushed my way out the door. She was gone. Maybe the job had gotten bad for her. Maybe she had decided to go back to school, study acting or something.

I hurried through the crowded streets, ignoring the human scents of sweat and suntan lotion. Other bodies pushed against mine, but the jostling didn't disturb me. I finally turned on a residential street and saw the familiar tall Victorian home where Shelli and I had lived for such a short time.

Her name was still on the mailbox. I felt a thread of relief run through me.

"Help you?" A man stopped in front of me, smelling of oil and gasoline. His large hands looked as if they had always been stained black.

"I was looking for Shelli," I said.

"She's at work. I'm her downstairs neighbor."

I didn't know what to say. "I checked at the coffee shop," I said. "She wasn't there."

His half-smile now seemed a bit suspicious. "You haven't seen her for a while."

"No," I said. "I was going to surprise her. She took me to my first Woody Allen movie."

"She does love Woody Allen." He studied me for a moment. "She works at the spaghetti place across the street from the coffee shop. Changed jobs half a year back. Needed the extra money, you know, with Danny and all. She should be there now."

I thanked him and was about to leave when I stopped myself. "Do you mind answering a nosy question? Who's Danny?"

To my surprise, the man only smiled. "Her baby. I took her to the hospital for the delivery."

A shiver ran down my back. "A child? When was he born?"

The neighbor put his big hands on the mailbox, his fingers leaving marks in the dirt. "Must be about a month ago now. That was some night, let me tell you."

"I bet it was," I said and moved back along the sidewalk. I had left her alone with a child. Our child. I hadn't even thought it a possibility.

Fortunately, we hadn't had a change since the baby left the safety of her womb. I could help her and little Danny. I would have to.

—**VI**—

I walked through the city that night, trying to decide how to tell her, how to warn her about the change that was bound to come.

The child was only one-quarter darkling, and perhaps he wouldn't change at all. I knew nothing of genetics—how thin can darkling blood become before the change refuses to come? But if little Danny would indeed change with all the other darklings, then he needed to be guided through the process until his mind developed enough to control a change alone.

I had to talk to Shelli. She wouldn't know what to do, how to hold Danny's body in her hands and mold him, even as she was molding herself.

I slept for a few hours on the bench at the bus stop across from her house. When her bedroom curtains opened—a sure sign she was awake—I straightened my clothes, combed my hair with my fingers, and let myself into the foyer of her big house.

The hallway was dark and smelled of fresh-brewed coffee. I took the stairs slowly, my heart pounding in my chest. My father had said she wouldn't believe me. The thought gave me pause. My mother had been human, and he said she still lived. Perhaps he had tried to convince her of what he was, and she hadn't believed him. No wonder he didn't say much when I ran back to the woods. He thought that I was saving myself some pain.

But I couldn't run away any longer.

I took a deep breath and pounded on Shelli's door. I heard footsteps; then the door eased open as far as the protective chain would reach. I smiled at the familiar scent of peppermint and moonlight, mixed with something else, something milky.

"Yes?" Shelli asked.

Words left me, the prepared speech, the carefully reasoned arguments that I had worked on all night. Shelli's face peered into mine, her downturned eyes and strong lips. I wanted to touch her skin. I wanted to hold her. "I'd like to talk to you," I said.

"Who are you?" She hadn't moved, but her tone had changed. Now she smelled of fear.

"I ..." I couldn't blurt out the words. I felt the ridiculous phrase hang between us. "I know Daniel."

She laughed once. The sound was short and bitter. "Then you know that he left me."

"There's something you need to know about Daniel. It'll affect the baby."

The fear scent grew stronger. She braced herself between the door and the frame. "Does he know about Danny?"

My heart pounded. The lies made this even more complex. "He didn't know about Danny until a very short time ago."

"And you're here to tell me that he wants the baby, right? Well, Danny is mine. All mine. I had him alone and I will take care of him alone, do you understand?" She slammed the door. The sound echoed in the small hallway. I grabbed the knob, but it was locked.

"No! You need to listen to me! Daniel had some health— problems—that he might have passed on to the baby. Please—"

"Danny is perfectly healthy. The doctor says so." Her voice sounded muffled through the door.

"It's not something that will show up in tests. It's hereditary—"

"Get out of here or I'll call the cops! Get out."

A door downstairs opened. In the dark light, I could see her neighbor's silhouette. "Need help, Shelli?"

She wouldn't listen to me, yet, anyway. "I was just leaving," I said and hurried down the stairs. I had to figure out another way.

—VII—

I tried to talk to Shelli several more times. I left her notes, talked to her neighbors, and the police threatened me. I waited near the apartment, hoping to be close if something should happen. I took sponge baths in public restrooms, ate cheap sandwiches to stay alive, slept on the bus bench across the street from Shelli's apartment. I had to do something. My own search— to be human or darkling—had caused this. If I hadn't run away, perhaps I would have stayed with Shelli when it counted, helped her raise my son.

My father must have gone through this. He finally decided to take me. If I took my son away, I would break Shelli's heart a second time. If the child died ...

A tingle at the base of my spine woke me from my sleep on the bus bench. I saw that it was early morning, just before all the commuters went to work. The tingle persisted, and I suddenly knew that I had to move.

I got up, but my legs had fallen numb from the position I had slept in. I stumbled against the bus stop. The tingle expanded into a ripping pain, and I heard a shriek from Shelli's house. I was too late. I lurched forward. Shelli was crying for help.

My legs wouldn't carry me across the street. I collapsed in front of a parked car, my skin melting and reshaping as I subconsciously guided my body through the process. I wasn't thinking about my own change; I wanted to get up the stairs to help Shelli. I barely made it onto the curb when the transformation finished, leaving me taller and gaunt. An energy coursed through me, and now I bounded up the stairs to find Shelli's door open. Her downstairs neighbor shouted into the phone, demanding an ambulance. Shelli screamed in the bedroom, one long continuous wail.

I saw the thing in her arms: the mass of gelatinous skin, the arm sticking into what had been the baby's stomach, the nose bulging prominently out of what remained of his head.

I took him, thinking perhaps some remnants of the change would allow me to mold his skin. I cradled my son for the first time, tugging at his malformed limbs, trying to shape him into a child again. Please, I prayed to unseen gods, one more change. One more change. But it wouldn't help him. My son.

He was dead.

Shelli had stopped screaming. She took Danny from me and cradled him against her chest. Her eyes were empty.

"He's mine," she said. "He's all I have left."

I touched him, my hand trembling. He had died the way I had always feared, but not because of his human side. He had died because his darkling father lacked courage.

"Shelli—"

A siren echoed nearby, growing closer.

"They can't save him, can they?" Her fingers stroked his misshapen skull, the fringe of his fine hair.

"No," I said.

The siren stopped. Voices rose amid some clanking outside. Shelli pushed past me and carried Danny down the steps to meet the attendants.

I remained behind.

—VIII—

And so here I stand, beneath her window, watching, as I have done every night since Danny's death. *Child of my heart,* my father used to call me, and I finally understood what he meant. I am waiting, waiting for the tingle at the base of my spine again.

Sometimes I think I will run up the stairs, command her to watch me change. And when it is over, I will explain everything, who I am and how I have never really left her. Then I wonder how much more pain that will cause her.

Sometimes I think I will just sit here, for change after change, until she heals enough to come out on her own, begin her life again, for Shelli is constant, and she is certain. She will heal. That much I know.

The darkling teacher was not so far wrong when he called me human. A darkling would have left long ago. Even my father left the child of his heart. Love has no place in a changing universe. And darklings suffer enough pain without adding the constant ache of a breaking heart.

All my life I have tried to be either darkling or human, being instead a strange hybrid of both. I want to be human, to be with Shelli, but my darkling side interferes. I have lied to her, tried to be one or the other. Perhaps if I had told her so long ago, we would have had a chance. Danny would have had a chance.

Shelli sits in the window and rocks, looking out at the people below. Her voice, plaintive and low, slides over the words to

Brahms's *Lullaby.* I listen to her. I ache to comfort her grief, ache to share it—to feel her blame, her anger, and maybe, just maybe, her forgiveness.

A shiver runs down my back. I pause. Not a shiver, but a tingle. A tingle at the base of my spine.

I have only a moment to choose: change versus consistency, certainty versus spontaneity, human versus darkling. My body begins to shift.

Before I even realize it, I am bounding up the stairs. I want to tell Shelli I choose both.

I choose both.

I like humorous medieval fantasy. I would laugh myself sick while watching Monty Python and the Holy Grail *or* Jabberwocky. *I loved* The Princess Bride. *I even wrote my own medieval caper,* The Dragon Business, *about a band of medieval con men selling their services as dragon slayers—but there's no dragon. Or is there?*

Because I enjoyed writing that novel so much, a few years later I decided to continue the series with another caper featuring that lovable band of con artists and one former princess. In the back of my mind, I remembered writing a story a very long time ago about a ne'er-do-well prince who hid in the secret passages of his castle and concocted a fake haunting to scare away a usurper who had killed the rest of the royal family.

I couldn't remember any other details, and I couldn't find a copy of the old story, but I liked the basic concept. So I used that as the springboard for my next Dragon Business adventure, Skeleton in the Closet, *in which our scam artists are hired to haunt an old castle and frighten away a band of orc invaders.*

Imagine my surprise while ransacking all the archive boxes in storage to find contributor copies for these collections, when I uncovered the original old story of "Skeleton in the Closet," co-written with my small press friend Ron Fortier—published way back in 1980. It was quite a treat to re-read the original, which is completely different from the novel … but some ideas just stick with you. And it was good to reconnect with Ron again.

I hope this one gives you a chuckle.

SKELETON IN THE CLOSET
(WITH RON FORTIER)

Danis dropped his sack of stolen honey-rolls to the dirty floor of the secret passage, then strained on his tiptoes to see through the peephole. The stone blocks were cold and slimy, but Danis's frown of disgust was directed instead toward the food spread out on the castle's long banquet table. Luckily, Danis had managed to grab the honey-rolls for his own supper, hiding in the secret passage before the chamberlain could call the rest of the family to the banquet.

A long, ugly-looking dragon carcass (roasted too much, too—Danis could tell by the burnt edges on its wings) lay spread out on the serving table. Greasy, musty, stringy, smoky-tasting, all-around *disgusting* dragon meat—Danis didn't think anybody really liked it. But, out of deference to the brave knight who had so valiantly slain the beast, Danis's father King Adaeus was always proud to serve a banquet every damned time some hotshot warrior got it in his head to kill one of the reptilian monsters. Lord Ogfos, the slayer of *this* week's dragon, sat at the honored place next to the doddering old king.

Ogfos was fat and bald, with piggish eyes hiding deep in pink folds of skin. He probably didn't need a sword or a lance to kill a dragon—Ogfos could just challenge the beast to an ugliness contest and win every time. He wore a leather vest studded with iron knobs and a heavy broadsword at his side (even though protocol required him to sit unarmed in the king's presence). Ogfos had also brought more than the usual number of guards and retainers with him to the banquet—"but only as a protection against bandits and highwaymen." He sat now at the banquet table with a smug look on his face and a gleam in his eye.

Opposite King Adaeus sat the only man Danis considered to be more annoyingly stupid than the king—Sarvalas the astrologer, under whom Danis was still enduring his final year of "education." One night—out of the many cold and miserable nights the two had spent up in Castle Adaeus's tallest tower, staring at the stars—Danis had received a vicious rap on the knuckles because he dared to ask a question about a constellation not located on the zodiac. "If it is not on the zodiac, then it contains nothing of interest to anyone!" Sarvalas had then continued to explain (as Danis sucked on his stinging knuckles) how the positioning of the planets would affect the colors of butterfly wings and, by direct consequence, the flavor of the next season's wine.

From the protection of his dank hiding place, Danis stuck out his tongue at the astrologer, then turned away from his peephole to find a comfortable place to sit down. By the light of his flickering candle, Danis munched on a honey-roll as he tried to ignore the hum of the banquet room. He opened a heavy leather-bound book he had brought with him—a genealogy and history of Danis's family, tracing it all the way back to Kradus the Conqueror, over two centuries before. But the genealogy stopped abruptly with Kradus, and Danis couldn't find out why, or what had happened to his family before the reign of the Conqueror.

Danis's interest in the family tree stemmed from his need to know from whence he had derived his intelligence and wit. His father was an incompetent fool, and his brothers were all idiots; surely Danis was a throwback to some ancestor who had left his superior traits buried deeply in the family bloodline to emerge only now. Danis had convinced himself that particular ancestor was none other than Kradus the Conqueror—an enlightened, wise, benevolent, and all-around charming person, from what Danis found in the records.

While searching in the castle's small library for helpful information, Danis had found a map of Castle Adaeus's secret passages, which apparently no one else knew about. This wasn't really surprising, since so few people read anything these days. After all, as his brothers often said, with so many dragons to slay, so many peasant girls to rape, so many champion knights to hack apart, who had time for *reading?* Danis munched on a second honey-roll.

From the banquet hall he could hear Sarvalas's voice beginning the ritual dragon-feast soothsaying. Danis knew what was happening without having to look—Sarvalas was drawing out the dragon's intestines, tying them in knots, counting the lobes in the dragon's liver, all in order to read the future. (No doubt this practice helped the appetites of all those present at the feast.) Most kingdoms could afford both an astrologer and proper soothsayer, but King Adaeus seemed satisfied that Sarvalas could fill both positions. In the background, Danis could hear Sarvalas prophesying a long and happy life for the king, the royal family, all their friends, and generally everyone else in the world. The astrologer knew how to please his ruler.

The astrologer's words abruptly ended with a strange gurgling sound. Someone screamed. A racket broke out in the dining hall, as if one of Danis's brothers had decided to hold a jousting tournament on the banquet table. Danis sighed heavily, stuck his half-eaten honey-roll in the history book to mark his place, and stood up to peer through the peephole to see what all the commotion was about.

Sarvalas lay pitched forward in the dragon's entrails with a long arrow protruding from his neck. King Adaeus also lay dead with an arrow through his heart, pinning him upright against the back of his royal chair. Lord Ogfos was systematically slaughtering Danis's cowering brothers—the brothers were champion jousters, every one of them, but once the refined niceties of chivalrous battle were taken away, their hard fighting resolve turned into the consistency of a Christmas blood pudding.

Ogfos's guards milled about the banquet hall, killing the remaining members of Danis's family—aunts, uncles, cousins, people who probably weren't even related to him but who had pretended to be in order to gain the king's favor (and were now regretting having done so). But the tumult died now, as the people died.

Lord Ogfos strode to the dead king, pulled Adaeus's sagging head up and, with one sweep of the broadsword, severed it at the neck. Ogfos hauled the king's dripping head over to the banquet table and roughly set it upright on an empty silver platter waiting to be piled high with dragon meat. Grinning broadly enough to wrinkle the fringes of his bald scalp, Ogfos pried the crown from Adaeus's head while the king's dead eyes glared up at him. Ogfos looked smugly around the dining hall, then donned the crown. All of Ogfos's guards quickly dropped to their knees and bowed to the new sovereign, as did all the serving people who wished to live. Ogfos leered at them all.

Danis swallowed hard, grateful for how much he disliked the taste of dragon meat. Unfortunately, Ogfos would probably not be too happy when he discovered that a legitimate heir to the throne still lived—and under his very nose at that.

Oh well, Danis thought, at least he was going to have plenty of time to thoroughly explore the secret tunnels ....

The intricate network of passages throughout the bowels of Castle Adaeus—Castle *Ogfos* now—was quite extensive. The openings of the passages were very well hidden, and he had no trouble slipping out at night to steal whatever food and candles he needed. During the day he occupied himself by exploring the tunnels, spying on the new castle occupants, and trying to keep his mind off his not-too-promising future. He didn't feel a great deal of grief for his father or brothers—after all, Adaeus had been stupid enough to fall into an obvious trap, and Danis's brothers had been too inept to protect themselves.

At the moment, his knees complained bitterly as he descended the steep slope of one passage which mysteriously plunged downward to the level of (if not below) the dungeons. His candle spat out barely enough light to keep him from walking into walls, and the air was so thick and musty even the small flame seemed to have trouble burning. Danis felt as if the weight of the entire castle, with its fat and ugly usurper, would fall on his head.

The tunnel seemed to go on forever, and he doubted his un-battle-conditioned knees would be in any shape to let him climb back. But then, the young man didn't have much else to do—and boredom was poison to the sophisticated mind. When he finally saw the end of the tunnel ahead, he frowned and tried to think up a suitable curse, but nothing came to mind. The steep passage ended in nothing more than a little walled-up alcove. Thrilling. No hidden rooms, no treasure piles, only a dull brick wall.

But then Danis's brain came into play again. What were *bricks* doing down here, when the rest of the passage was made of slimy, hewn stone? The obvious answer came quickly to mind. This must be some dark secret Castle Adaeus had kept undigested within its intestines for centuries.

The bricks were crumbling, and the mortar was cracked and powdery, offering about as much strength as a pile of baked cobwebs. Danis easily knocked a hole in the wall with his fists and frowned down at his hands covered with dust and dirt. He wished he'd known of Ogfos's intentions beforehand—then at least he could have taken one final hot bath before hiding like a slug under a rock.

Danis thrust his candle into the opening he had made in the bricked-up alcove and peered around. Dust still filtered down, but he could see two rusty manacles hanging empty from the wet stone blocks and, under them, a human skull and a pile of disarrayed bones. Danis smirked. Castle Adaeus had, quite literally, a skeleton in the closet, some mysterious victim who carried a dark secret to which Danis would never know the answer.

"Um, excuse me, but are you disturbing my final resting place?"

Danis whirled to see a translucent man glowing with pearly light that clung to his tattered hair, ragged beard, and threadbare clothes. The figure looked like a walking sculpture made of glistening cobwebs.

"Who are you?" Danis demanded.

"Who are you?" the figure answered. "After all, *you're* the intruder here."

Danis drew himself up, trying to look formidable, but was unsuccessful. "I am the rightful heir to the throne, last survivor of the royal line—Ogfos the usurper has slaughtered the rest of my family, and I am hiding in these passages."

The figure sighed. "Oh dear, not *another* coup ..."

Danis frowned. "You mean there have been others?"

"Oh, it happens like clockwork every two hundred years or so. In fact, I am the last survivor—er, well, not really a *survivor* anymore—I am the ghost of the last survivor of the previous royal line, before Kradus the usurper butchered my family and took the throne as his own, forcing me to hide in these passages."

"Kradus ..." Danis gulped. "No wonder I couldn't trace my family line back any farther."

"Oh, of course not. And you probably didn't find any references to my family either," the ghost said. "It's common practice to strike all mention of the previous kings from the record. That way the usurper isn't constantly reminded of how he gained the throne. That is, if he has any conscience. Most usurpers *do* have guilty consciences, you know."

Danis digested the information, which gave him an upset stomach. "You said you fled to the tunnels when Kradus took over. How did you get bricked up here, then?"

"I hid in these miserable tunnels for almost a full year before I grew careless and let myself be seen when I snuck out to steal some leftover chicken. Kradus and his men hunted in the passages until they caught me—and when they discovered who I was, they chained me, here ...” The ghostly figure tried to caress the brick wall, but he seemed too insubstantial to feel anything. “Then they walled me up alive. Oh, dying was the most miserable part of it all.”

“Ick,” said Danis.

“And you are the last descendant of Kradus—my sworn enemy!” The ghost glared at him, then his expression changed. “But I’ll let bygones be bygones for now, because it’s been so long since I’ve had someone to talk to. My name is Parris, by the way.”

“Danis,” said Danis. He extended his hand, then thought better of it.

Parris was silent for quite some time, fidgeting, looking at Danis as if he weren’t sure of himself. Finally the ghost spoke. “Danis—do you think you could do me a favor? I know we just met and everything, but it would really mean a lot to me.” Parris continued without waiting for an answer, as if he feared that once he stopped talking, he would be afraid to speak up again.

“Could you—um, give me a proper burial? If it’s not too much trouble, that is. I mean, I’m tied to this place until my bones are laid to rest, and these tunnels have been rather boring over the past century. I’d really like to—to get on with whatever it is I’m supposed to be getting on with, now that I’m dead and all.”

Danis’s mind suddenly filled with the image of fat, ugly Ogfos sitting on the throne, stuffing his mouth with the delicate food cooked especially for the royal family. Danis rubbed his hands together. *Most usurpers* do *have guilty consciences, you know.*

“It would be a pleasure, friend Parris. But first I need a favor from you. Something to make you use your full ghostly potential —a final flash of glory for even the best of spirits to be proud of.”

Parris looked uneasy, but waited for Danis to finish. The young man said, “It was rather nice being a member of the royal family, and all the comforts that included. I want you to help me get my throne back.”

Parris turned almost completely insubstantial in his shock.

"Me? How can I do anything? I can't even pick up a handkerchief to cry in sorrow for your loss!" He moaned miserably.

"That's excellent! If you can moan like that in the dead of the night, we'll be in business! You forget that as a ghost, you have certain, ah, advantages over a mere human. Parris, my boy, between the two of us, *we* are going to haunt Castle Adaeus!"

Danis discovered his true purpose as he planned to recover his throne and all the royal goodies that came with it. His mind played mental passball with idea after idea, delighting in most of them, and gloating over many more. Boredom fled like the father of an illegitimate child, and Danis's prized intellect made his mental gears turn smoothly, winding Ogfos's fate more and more tightly.

Naturally, a thorough knowledge of all the current goings-on in the castle would be necessary if Danis was to formulate a suitable haunting. He delegated Parris as the main spy—since the ghost could easily escape through a wall if necessary—while Danis himself sat against the cold stone walls and did the hard work of detailed planning, intermingled with a healthy amount of daydreaming.

Danis had covered about half the list of everything he wanted to do once he won back the throne—after dwelling overlong on number seven—when Parris returned, sliding through a wall beside him. "I'm back! You know, all this flitting about really is sort of fun."

Danis wiped his forehead. "Well, what did you find out?"

"I just came from the royal chamber. Ogfos is busily directing his men to make changes according to his tastes. He thinks your father's bed is too small for his 'muscular' frame, and he ordered the seven best woodworkers and carpenters in the kingdom to construct a massive bed, twice as large as the one already there."

Danis gaped. "Suffering saints! He could bed half of his army on that thing!"

The ghost paused. "I don't believe it's the army he has in mind for bedding. Earlier he was in the company of two rather, er, *abundant* young maidens—charming creatures both, like matched bookends with long yellow tresses and ruby lips."

"Ah, the Casalane twins! They're the spice merchant's daughters, and my late brothers argued constantly as to which one had the greater appetite for fleshly delights. It's a contest they wage vigilantly, if town gossip is true. The merchant Casalane is a rather harmless, naive old man who brings them a mysterious spice from the wilds of Africa. The daughters have convinced him they love its mild flavor as a seasoning, though he can see nothing in it himself. But it's really the most potent aphrodisiac this side of the edge of the world. In fact, it makes all the old hags' boiled bat-wing potions seem like so much silliness."

Parris pondered this a moment. "Then the usurper Ogfos must have more courage than I had thought, since he gave the impression he intended to bed both of them at the same time."

"We'd best get to work at once, or else it might be too late. The Casalane twins could love him to death and spoil all my fun!"

Step one of Plan One began late that night, when Parris's bloodcurdling moans and shrieks shattered the uneasy peace of midnight. The ghost wandered through the corridors, flitting in and out of sight, letting the alarmed guards catch only brief glimpses. Most comical was the look on Ogfos's face as Parris strode through the usurper's bedchamber, popping out one wall and disappearing into another, interrupting Ogfos's nighttime entertainment in the process. Parris stayed to watch as the shaken usurper yelled at the Casalane twins and chased them (giggling) out of his chamber.

Meanwhile, Danis had slipped into the banquet hall and shot an arrow into the lord's chair. He found some thick red wine left uncorked on the long table and scrawled an almost-readable message in the bloodlike ink. "Death to Ogfos the Usurper. The Kradus family ghost demands vengeance!" The threatening message, tacked onto the arrow, would make a wonderful breakfast gift for Ogfos.

On his way out, Danis snatched some of the leftover food strewn over the table. The usurper must have executed the previous cook, who had served banquets for King Adaeus, since the food looked much better now.

After a day of rest and fruitful gloating, and after another night of Parris's wonderfully graphic moaning, Danis encountered a snag in his plan. "What do you mean you won't appear in the banquet hall during the next meal?" Danis barely remembered to keep his voice a near-whisper in the secret passages.

Parris stood his ground. "I don't want to be seen by all those *people*! If I liked to appear in front of everybody, would I have remained hidden in these passages for centuries? I'm shy! Look at me—I'm a mess! I look terrible!"

"Exactly! You're supposed to scare people—nobody ever heard of a cute ghost!"

"I'm not going to do it, and that's that!"

"But I've already drenched Ogfos's seat cushion with the wine!"

"No."

It took Danis almost an hour of "constructive coercion"— mainly by threatening that he would take Parris's decaying bones and strew them throughout the passages and the castle courtyard so nobody would ever be able to bury him properly. Parris finally conceded grudgingly. From that point on, the ghost rarely spoke, and when he did, his anger became obvious.

When Ogfos sat on his chair during the next meal, he found that his cushion, and the seat of his pants, had both been drenched with a sticky red substance. At the proper moment, a bedraggled-looking spectre appeared in the banquet hall, floating forward with a menacing finger extended toward the usurper. "You are dripping with the blood of the Kradus family! Ogfos must die!" He said the words with a nervous tremor in his voice, which most of the observers probably found frightening. Ogfos looked as if the haunting was beginning to get to him. The ghost vanished.

Later that day, the huge new bed arrived, causing more commotion than the ghost had. The seven best woodworkers and carpenters in the kingdom had labored nonstop for three days in order to fulfill the usurper's wishes. One had dropped from a stroke due to exhaustion; another had sprained his back while hauling the several-ton bed up the castle stairs and would be laid up for the rest of the season; a third had smashed his hand while setting up the bed and would never be able to do detail work again. The remaining four men labored with a block-and-tackle to set up the bed, and they watched their colleagues' injuries with grim satisfaction, for they were now the *four* best woodworkers and carpenters in the kingdom, and thus could charge much higher prices.

The huge, dark bed crouched on heavy legs that were decorated with ornate serpentine carvings detailing Ogfos's conquests (as concocted by the usurper and embellished by the woodcarvers). The gigantic bed lurked like a massive beast half-asleep in the royal chamber.

That evening, Ogfos kept himself so engrossed by breaking in his bed with the Casalane twins that he paid little attention to the loud ghostly moans outside his room—or perhaps the twins' effervescent enthusiasm drowned out all sounds except for their own heavy breathing.

And the same thing happened the next night. The rest of the palace guards were visibly jumpy, but Ogfos looked like a cross between a brick wall and a battering-ram. Danis, however, noticed occasional indications of the usurper's edginess, which made him suspect that his indifference was merely feigned, and that Ogfos was really terrified.

Danis begged Parris to appear before the people again, but the ghost would have none of it. Moaning unseen through the secret passages was one thing, but doing an encore performance in front of all the usurper's men was entirely another.

"I am not a freak, Danis! I am just your common, ordinary

ghost—it's not my fault you people have never seen one before. I don't *like* scaring people!"

"But you promised!"

"I promised to help you get your throne back. I *have* been helping! In fact, I've been doing more work than *you* have. But I never agreed to make a fool out of myself in front of everybody! I don't want the whole world to know I was never properly buried. Just keep your end of the bargain, if you please, and we can part as friends now."

"Parris, bear with me just a little longer. I need you to make one more appearance—speak a nice terrifying curse at Ogfos so that everybody in the entire castle can hear."

"Everybody in the entire castle! I refuse. I flatly refuse."

Danis tried to control his temper. He held his breath for half a minute, then stepped up to look through the peephole into the royal chamber where the new bed was already groaning with the strain. He tried to lighten the conversation. "I wonder how he can keep it up for so long—er, his stamina, I mean."

The ghost crossed his arms. "Danis, if you're going to make me appear in front of all those people, why shouldn't I just ask another guard or somebody to bury me properly? Then they'll come into these passages and find you. All will be lost—for you, at least, not me."

He sniffed. "Why don't you, then?"

They sulked in silence for the rest of the night.

While Danis watched through his peephole, with Parris brooding beside him, Ogfos surprised both of them. The bald lord stood up from his midday meal and withdrew a battered brass circlet that Danis recognized as the one Sarvalas the astrologer had worn (it had always left an absurd green line across his forehead). Ogfos strode down the length of the banquet table and stopped beside one of the guards. "I remember right," he said in a voice that sounded like crushed gravel. "You put the arrow in the astrologer's throat."

The guard nodded, trying to hide his puzzled expression. Ogfos took the brass circlet and mashed it on the guard's head.

"The soothsayer's spirit has passed on to you." His deep voice had a smug tone, laced with vinegar. "Tell me how to be rid of this ghost. Now. Or I shall liberate the soothsayer's spirit once more."

Danis could see the sweat blossom on the guard's forehead. Everyone around the table fell into a hush as the poor man tried to dig through the onion-like layers of his childhood memories and the ghost tales his mother had once told him. He closed his eyes and seemed to be calling on the soothsayer's spirit for advice, or perhaps praying for any type of salvation.

"This ghost is a poor lost soul, Lord Ogfos. He is vengeful, but harmless so long as he gets what he wants. His earthly body suffered terribly in death, and his bones were not buried properly." Danis noticed the guard's fingers were crossed so tightly his tangled knuckles looked white. "We just need to find his remains and give them proper burial, and all your troubles will be over."

Ogfos brightened, and pounded his fist on the long tabletop. "We must begin the search immediately! Look in every cranny in this entire castle, and then find more crannies to look in! Go! And let me know immediately about any bodies you happen to find." The guards scurried out of the banquet hall, last of all the astrologer/guard whose knees shook so badly he could barely walk. Lord Ogfos sat back in his royal chair, closed his eyes, and massaged his bald scalp.

In the secret passage, Parris the ghost clapped his intangible hands in delight, and vanished from sight.

Throughout the day the guards stormed through the castle, searching for anything that looked suspicious, hidden, or particularly interesting. Meanwhile, Danis scurried through the passages, desperately trying to find Parris and hoping the ghost wouldn't do what Danis thought he was going to. But it was a big castle, and neither the guards, nor Danis, found what they were looking for.

Uneasy and downcast, Danis spent the night spying on Ogfos's chambers through the peephole, hoping the wild bedroom antics would take his mind off his troubles. The castle corridors rang with a hollow silence, no ghastly moans and shrieks for the first time in almost a week.

Ogfos was nervous and edgy, more troubled by the lack of haunting sounds than he had been by the ghost in the first place. Though the Casalane twins remained as enthusiastic as ever, Ogfos could not perform. Cursing in frustration, he chased them out of his chamber.

At first they both looked playful, then turned sour expressions on the usurper as they reluctantly slammed the heavy door behind them. Out in the corridor they moved like blond spiders to the first pair of guards they encountered. The twins smiled in unison, each weaving arms about one man and leading him into a separate chamber to finish out the night—like sexual vampires, as addicted to fleshly pleasures as they were to the drug that made them so.

In the morning, Ogfos looked no better. He had not slept at all, and neither had Danis. The usurper's temper ran short, and at the next midday meal he hurled trays and platters when the head guard reported finding no mysterious hidden corpses in the castle. Ogfos bellowed for the astrologer/guard to be brought to him at once, preparing to make short work of the poor pleading man with a large meat-carving knife. But the astrologer/guard managed to shout that a corpse hidden for so many years would have to be lying in a secret passage somewhere in the castle. Ogfos pondered this as his arm hung in a half-completed downstroke of the carving knife, then he agreed. He released the trembling man and sent the rest of his guards off to pound on the walls, floors and ceilings in search of secret passages.

Danis felt as trapped as the victim in his former brothers' favorite game of Badger-in-the-Bag. With as many secret entrances as the passages had, he found it unlikely that even inept guards could manage to miss all of them. Parris was nowhere to be found, and Danis silently cursed the ghost both for being so timid, then for being so hotheaded. His imagination betrayed him, too, for instead of thinking of alternate solutions to his dilemma, his mind could only conjure up vivid pictures of being walled-up here, later to become a wandering ghost—just as the cretin Parris had.

In midafternoon, the guards pounding on the walls of the library—now stripped bare of books—accidentally broke into the network of secret passages. One man rushed to inform Ogfos, who looked both immensely pleased and relieved. The usurper called for the astrologer/guard in order to commend him for his wise counsel, but the man was nowhere to be found. Apparently, the guard had thought little of his chances of concocting a third believable story if no secret passages were found, and had fled the castle earlier that afternoon. He was never seen again, but later that year a wickedly smiling highwayman turned up at the local market fair trying to sell the astrologer's battered brass circlet.

Ogfos ordered all his men to pour into the passages and find the spectre's misbegotten resting place. He neglected to consider the intricacy of the passages, however, and within a short time most of the guards were effectively lost.

Danis would have to count on his own fast-thinking abilities as never before. Parris had deserted him, and he grimly set about taking matters in his own hands. If a real ghost had been too frightened to finish out the haunting, Danis would have to do it himself.

Before any of the guards could stumble upon him in the passages, he worked his way to the upper level of the castle and emerged into his mother's unused sewing room. No one had frequented this place since his mother's death years before. Unless Ogfos suddenly took an interest in needlepoint during the night, no one had any reason to enter.

By sundown he had returned to the passages, easily eluding the guards because Danis had a vague idea of where he was going, and they didn't. During the weeks of hiding, his royal clothes had degenerated to mere dirty rags, so he didn't look the slightest bit out of place as he slipped into the castle's pantry through the back way, dodging requests for assistance in preparing the evening meal. He loaded his sack with everything he thought necessary to transform him into a surrogate ghost.

Back in the passages, he sat with his back against the clammy wall, thinking about how much had changed since the first time he had sat here. He saw a dull glow in the distance and heard faint sounds. At first he thought Parris was returning, but then he realized it was a torch-bearing group of guards stumbling through the maze. He heard some vague curses, then the glow swung around another corner and vanished. Danis decided it was time to begin.

He stood up, put his mouth to the peephole of the banquet hall where Ogfos picked at his evening meal, and bellowed in his most threatening, booming voice. "Ogfos! You have made a grave mistake! I do not wish to be buried properly—I demand vengeance! I thirst for your blood, filthy usurper! Your guards are all hopelessly lost in my labyrinth, and you are helpless before me. Cringe! All is lost. You are lost. And you will not know whom I have chosen to be your instrument of death until it is far too late for you. Tonight you shall die." He made his voice the loudest, harshest whisper he could manage. "Tonight!"

Then he pushed his eye against the peephole to watch the effects of his speech. The serving woman dropped her dishes with a loud crash. Ogfos nearly jumped out of his seat, then looked wildly around him, but the echoing banquet hall had scattered Danis's words in random directions. Ogfos looked up at the ceiling as if waiting to see a flaming angel swoop toward him with a sickle, then he glared around suspiciously as if he saw enemies in every corner. The usurper hurried out of the banquet hall to lock himself alone in his room and wait out the night.

Danis smiled, and only the greatest caution kept him from whistling to himself. He returned to his mother's sewing room and began the next phase of Plan Two—juicy purple berries to deepen the color of his eye sockets and lips, strawberry jam to make his fingers look horribly red and sticky, and a heavy dousing of flour to make him pallid and cadaverous. He looked in a small mirror on his mother's old bureau and nodded in satisfaction, though he realized he would never be able to see a real ghost in a mirror anyway. A chill went down his spine—what if Parris was standing behind him just now? Danis whirled and saw nothing, except perhaps a faint vanishing glimmer out of the corner of his eye. He decided it was his imagination. *Leave the wild imaginings up to Ogfos*, he told himself. It was time to devote himself entirely to the business of haunting a castle.

After Danis reached the passage behind the royal chamber, he watched the ugly bald man for a while. The usurper sat on his huge custom-made bed, sweating profusely even from the pores of his scalp. The bed looked extremely damaged, as if about to collapse. The joints were loose, and the legs seemed to tremble in time with Ogfos's own trembling. The bed had been sturdily made, by the seven best woodworkers and carpenters in the land, but three consecutive nights with the Casalane twins was enough to destroy even the hardiest bed-worksmanship.

The usurper's eyes were red and bloodshot, as if someone had thrown the boiling water of terror in his face. He had not slept, he had not shaved, and his eyes remained as wide-open as peeled grapes. Ogfos had barred the heavy door to his room with a sturdy crossbeam, but did not take much comfort in the security. Just in front of the peepholes, four valiant candles sacrificed their light to the room, but failed to purge all the shadows. Having his rightful throne back would be fun, he thought, but not nearly as much fun as actually *getting* it back.

For added effect, Danis wandered through the tunnels surrounding the usurper's room, moaning at the top of his lungs in a poor imitation of Parris's style—but that was enough for Ogfos in his frightened condition. The usurper turned first one way then the other on the massive bed, which added its own protesting groans. When Danis stopped by each peephole and blew out three of the four candles, one by one, he could have sold tickets to see the look of abject terror on the bald man's face. Danis left one candle burning so he could see what he was doing; Ogfos fixed his gaze on the remaining candle, as if *willing* it to keep burning—which was fine with Danis, because the secret entrance to the royal chamber stood on the other side of the room.

The light remained very dim, and Danis stood in the shadows of the alcove as he whispered the usurper's name. The man turned, and his jaw dropped as he backed away.

"Ogfos—I have come for you. The time is now."

Suddenly a quiet scratching came at the barred door, followed by two mingled female voices. "Ogfos! It's us—let us in. We'll soothe your tension. You know we're good at that." Somebody giggled. "Come on, Ogfos. Open up!"

The usurper whirled to stare in honor at the door. *"No!"* Danis wasn't sure what the man was yelling at. More giggling came from behind the door. Danis's mind spun like a magician's top. He had intended to frighten the usurper into renouncing his throne and fleeing the kingdom. Still uncertain, Danis stepped boldly forward into the flickering shadows. "Ogfos—I am speaking to you!"

The tapping at the door grew more insistent. "Ogfos! We *know* how to get what we want …" The heavy crossbar jerked a little, then raised up completely by itself, moving eerily from its rests and away from the door before it clattered to the flagstones. Danis's eyes almost bulged out of their own sockets. The door creaked open a little, and two sets of long-nailed hands crept around the edge of the door. More sinister giggling echoed from the hall. "Ogfos—come play with us."

Ogfos gawked at the opening door, then gawked at the menacing spectre on the other side of the room, found neither alternative acceptable, and dashed to hide under his now rickety, but still beautifully carved, royal bed. Danis heard him whimpering. On impulse, Danis hurried to the side of the bed and bent down. He didn't know what the Casalanes would do, but he knew he could never have managed to frighten Ogfos as much as he was now. "Ogfos! Come out and I shall bargain with you."

Then the Casalane twins flung open the door all the way. "We're here, Ogfos!" They giggled, but in the dim light they could see only a shadowy figure standing by the huge bed. Danis turned to face the two women as they sprinted toward him. Not knowing what to do, he backed up against the bed just as they leaped up and playfully tackled him.

The massive bed, which had been built to withstand fire and storm and earthquake, could not bear the Casalane twins any longer. It gave a groan of despair and collapsed. The legs splayed outward like a newborn colt trying to stand on ice, and the massive bulk crashed down to the floor. Danis heard a muffled squish, but then he needed all his energy to fend off the amorous attacks of the two young women.

"Wait, this isn't Ogfos," one of the twins said, giving Danis a brief moment to catch his breath.

"Well, is it at least a male?" the other asked.

"You've never been too picky, sister."

"I? At least *I* don't need those specially made devices—"

"*You* designed them yourself, dearie."

While they were distracted by their bickering, Danis used the last of his energy to extract himself from their embrace and slipped off the bed. He stepped in something warm and wet on the floor.

"I'll bet if we gave him a nice bath he would look much more attractive." The twins looked at him, each raising hopeful eyebrows.

Danis backed away and heard the four remaining guards, probably aroused by the commotion, coming down the corridor. "Parris!" Danis whispered loudly into the air. "If you don't show up this instant, I swear I'm going to tell them the haunting was *all* my doing, and you will never be buried at all!"

Sure enough, Parris folded himself into the air of the room and stood wearing an uncertain expression. The Casalanes watched with interest, especially at seeing what appeared to be another man in the room.

Danis spoke quickly. "There are only four guards. Don't be shy. You *have* to tell them that you killed Ogfos, and that the rightful heir to the throne is up in my mother's sewing room. That'll give me a brief moment to clean up and look like a more presentable king-to-be. I hope these berry stains wash off."

He turned to the twins. "And you two, I can promise you more pleasures with more people than you've ever had (I think) if you'll just go along. Please?"

The Casalanes seemed intrigued enough by the possibilities, although they would have preferred to help Danis wash up, and agreed. He slipped back into the passages just as the guards burst into the room.

"I know I was mad at you, Danis, but I decided to give you the benefit of the doubt for two days. If by that time you hadn't managed to do whatever it was you intended, I would lead the guards to my resting place. Perhaps they would bury my bones and not bother you in the passages anymore. Knowing you, I'm sure you could easily slip out of the castle in the middle of the night and make a new life for yourself somewhere. Maybe even join the Church."

The young man snorted. "Danis the monk? No, thank you."

As the exhausted guards straggled out of the passages in small groups, Danis and Parris confronted each in turn and informed them of the new situation. As a suitable reward/punishment for both parties, Danis sent the Casalane twins to the ranks of the guards, where they could do with each other as they pleased.

Danis the King had Parris's bones removed from the passages and buried with full royal honors in the castle courtyard. Parris himself gave a stirring autobiographical eulogy, then went off to do whatever it was that properly buried ghosts were supposed to do.

The massive bed warmed the castle that winter, as it provided about two weeks' worth of firewood. The fire gave off a rather unpleasant smell, however, and Danis left it to be used by the guards in their quarters. The remains of Ogfos the usurper had been scraped off the bottom of the bed frame and added to the royal compost pit in the back of the castle.

Later that year, as Danis wallowed in the pleasures of being a king, he heard a hollow mournful wailing through the corridors. Although the servants assured him the sound was merely wind blowing through a chink in the castle walls, Danis ordered the usurper's body removed from the compost pit and buried in the local churchyard.

And the moaning stopped.

I remember haunting my high school library, turning the spinner racks filled with science fiction and fantasy paperbacks, mesmerized by the Frank Frazetta covers on the Edgar Rice Burroughs classics: Tarzan, John Carter of Mars, Carson of Venus, *the Pellucidar series. I devoured them, and they sparked a lot of ideas. I was the perfect age, and the memories were powerful.*

When the Edgar Rice Burroughs estate called for writers to pitch stories for a tribute anthology, The Worlds of Edgar Rice Burroughs, *I knew I had to write something for it. But it had been such a long time since I'd read those novels, I couldn't get the details right.*

Fortunately, my occasional collaborator, Sarah A. Hoyt, reads at a fiendishly fast pace. Together, we developed an idea that put Tarzan of the Apes squarely in the middle of H.G. Wells's Martian invasion from The War of the Worlds. *(See, I told you how much that novel influenced me!) The very idea sparked all kinds of excitement.*

The Martians might have had their heat ray, but Tarzan had all the animals of the jungle.

TARZAN AND THE
MARTIAN INVADERS
(WITH SARAH A. HOYT)

John Clayton, viscount of Greystoke, sat in a red leather chair in the study that had belonged to his ancestor. The setting would have seemed perfect to any civilized man, yet Lord Greystoke was uneasy.

In informal attire of shirt, trousers and waistcoat, he was more deeply tanned than one might expect, and his powerful shoulders seemed ill-confined by stylish garments. As he turned the page of the book resting casually on his knee, his movements gave an impression of grace and power not normally seen in his class. The Greystokes had always been exceptionally well built and powerful, however; the portrait gallery above gave ample evidence of a long line of strong-featured, muscular, grey-eyed men.

Yet in this comfortable, relaxing setting, the man flung himself from the chair, closed the book he'd been trying to read, and slapped it on the polished mahogany desk before pacing from heavy-curtained window to blazing fireplace. His steps were those of a beast uneasily confined in a human space and bound by human conventions.

As Lord Greystoke twitched the curtain aside and looked at the English night washed in a cold late-autumn rain, in his mind's eye he saw quite another landscape: the lush and untamed jungle of equatorial Africa.

Though he tried his best to look after his estates, speak to acquaintances at his club, or weigh in on issues in the House of Lords, he always felt apart from other humans. After his parents, Lord and Lady Clayton, had met untimely deaths in Africa, the infant John Clayton had been raised by Kala from a tribe of anthropoid apes. The young boy's ape-mother had called him Tarzan, meaning "white-skin" in ape language. He hadn't seen another human until the age of fifteen and not seen a white man until he was twenty, the age at which he had first worn human clothing ... and then everything had changed.

How odd it was to wear shirt and trousers, waistcoat and coat. How odd it felt to have a valet cater to his needs now. *Were it not for Jane*— Lord Greystoke thought, not for the first time, as he paced from the window to the fireplace. He paused to glare at the fire, that thing he'd once thought a living creature, the spawn of storm and lightning. The flames now sat confined in a stone-cased fireplace, just as Tarzan himself was held within this stone house, within his tailored suit, within the straining bonds of civilization and manners. Flaring his nostrils, he closed his eyes and imagined himself in his jungle again, swinging free from branch to branch, spending time with his friend the elephant Tantor, or Sheeta the panther, or even hunting with the Waziri warriors of whom he had become king. Now in the stuffy, clammy manor house, his skin longed to feel the warm breezes of Africa, and his feet wanted to be freed from the confinement of shoes. He could stand it no longer!

Overcoming his feigned Greystoke dignity, Tarzan had succeeded in divesting himself of shoes and socks and dug his calloused toes into the soft pile of the oriental carpet, when a soft knock sounded upon the door.

Tarzan looked up guiltily. "Yes?" He half-expected the opening door would reveal his stern, uncomprehending valet, but instead, he saw the delicate features of his wife, Jane Clayton, Lady Greystoke—the daughter of an American scientist who had come to Africa and there found Tarzan in his solitude. Had it not been for Jane ... Jane's face ... Jane's sweetness ... and the hold she had over his heart, Tarzan would never have come to England. He would rather have let the lands, fortune, and accolades fall to some relative, while he claimed his true jungle kingdom and the mastery of his anthropoid apes.

Jane's face creased in a smile, and a gleam of amusement danced in her eyes. "May I come in? Would I be quite safe entering the domain of the king of the jungle?"

Although normal expressions still did not come naturally to him, Tarzan gave her the best smile he could command. He extended his arm to her. "You are quite safe with me, Jane. Human or ape, I am always your husband."

She came swiftly to be enfolded in his embrace. "Don't I know that? Have I not seen you when you still didn't know how to form human words? And yet ..." Her hand caressed his powerful arm, feeling the muscles beneath the shirt. "You've always been human to me, the best of men."

His smile was now genuine. At that moment, he considered the freedom of his jungle well-lost for the sake of this.

Jane knew him all too well, however. "But you were dreaming of the jungle, weren't you?"

"Only a little," he admitted, and his hand gesture dismissed the surrounding countryside, tamed by sheep, covered in sheared grass, washed by rain. "I never liked the rain and cold, even when I was a little ap—*boy*, watched over by my faithful Kala." He kissed her forehead reassuringly. "Go to bed, and I'll be there presently. I'm only blue-devilled by the rain. I shall find a book to read, and I'll use it to lull myself to sleep."

She wished him good night and left the study, closing the door softly behind her. As Jane was well aware, Tarzan was often unable to sleep inside the house upon the too-soft bed, so he spent many nights beneath the boughs of a tree on his estate. For her sake, he always made sure to return to the house, dress in his night clothes, and be by his wife's side come morning.

Left alone in his study, Tarzan resumed his pacing, resisting the urge to head out into the rain-washed night. It was true he'd never liked rain, but sometimes he liked the inside of houses even less. His restless hands fidgeted with the numerous books on the shelves, and behind a row of dusty tomes, in a space he'd never before explored, he found a thin book. Out of curiosity, and remembering the many years he'd spent reading every book his late parents had left behind in the treetop jungle cabin, Tarzan brought out the small volume. It was a diary, much like the diary his father had kept. This volume purported to be the diary of … John Clayton, Viscount Greystoke. Another John Clayton? He carried the volume with him back to the red leather chair.

A quick perusal revealed that the diary belonged to a long-forgotten ancestor from the days of Queen Elizabeth I. After studying the unfamiliar spelling and wording, Tarzan realized that his forgotten ancestor, that other John Clayton, had been a privateer in the Drake mold who sailed all over the world, even to Tarzan's beloved Africa.

Reliving his ancestor's adventures, Tarzan forgot that Jane was waiting for him to come to bed; he even forgot the walls around him, and the sound of beating rain outside. Instead, he revisited the lush jungles, survived onboard mutinies, and imagined the bright pattern of the Southern Cross above.

Suddenly, however, his mood changed. His eyes narrowed as he read an ordeal his ancestor had endured, one that was more peculiar than even the many perils Tarzan himself had faced. With a furrowed brow, he read through the book. His toes unconsciously clenched the thick pile of the carpet. He turned the page to find a series of drawings, and stopped.

He took the small telescope from the mantel, but though he looked out the window, the overcast sky revealed no stars. Then Tarzan recalled his father's mechanical celestial sphere, a wedding gift to the elder John Clayton on the occasion of his union with the ill-fated Lady Alice. He displayed the precious artifact on its special table in the study, and servants kept it scrupulously clean and oiled, even without being instructed to do so.

Tarzan went to the celestial sphere and referred to the crude drawing in his ancestor's diary, comparing the notations. He felt a chill, and the deep tan of his skin became visibly paler.

His hand clenched into a closed fist. "It will not be allowed!" His tone would have frightened anyone who listened, but in the silent chamber there was only the sound of the rain against the window glass.

The butler was astonished at his enigmatic master's request so late at night. "Milord? But—"

"See the car brought around, Jones. I must go to London. At once."

"In a night like this, Milord? You'll not have enough light to see by, and you—" The man was more worried than rebellious, but Tarzan couldn't afford any delay. His eyes had first learned to see with no artificial illumination, and he had found his way through the jungle so thick that no glimmer of light penetrated to the lower levels. He would not be deterred by a rainy night in the English countryside. Pulling on his driving gloves and hat, he said, "Don't worry, Jones. I shall be well." He suspected the only peril ahead of him was a very boring drive at the end of which, with luck, he would secure passage to Africa.

As he got behind the wheel of his latest-model automobile, a single doubt assailed him. He ought, perhaps, to have told Jane where he was going. She would worry.

But if he revealed his plans, she might insist on joining him, and he could not put her at risk against such unearthly dangers. Tarzan, ape-man, Lord of Africa would have to face this threat for all mankind. And win. He would not let Jane or their son Jack become victims of such a terrible menace.

Next morning, Jane realized that Tarzan must have spent the night sleeping out in the rain, for he had never come to bed.

She was aware that in forcing civilization upon her wild husband, she had in some unknown way injured him. Other people thought that she'd redeemed a poor savage and bestowed the great boon of culture upon him. But Jane wasn't so sure. She remembered the sparkle in his eyes when he was in the jungle, and she wasn't sure that bringing him to refined, and confined, England was a good thing.

At the back of her mind she held the idea that once Jack grew a little older, they'd acquire a plantation in Africa and Tarzan would be able to disappear into the jungles he loved, now and then, while she would still enjoy the comforts of civilization. Someday.

But for now, Lady Greystoke had to go through the morning rituals without letting on to the household that anything might be wrong between them, or that she was worried that her very peculiar beloved hadn't managed to slip quietly back inside before dawn, as he always did.

She allowed herself to be helped into her clothes, and she approved the menus for the day with barely more than a glance. She visited Jack in the nursery and discussed with nurse how to break the young master's bad habit of sucking his thumb. She preoccupied herself, but Tarzan's continued absence was very odd. It wasn't like him to remain away from her for so long.

A few discreet questions revealed that no one had seen Lord Greystoke that day. Wondering if some accident could have befallen him in the seemingly safe environs of the manor, she hastened to his study to find a letter propped against the ornate celestial sphere. In her husband's handwriting, the envelope said only "Jane." She tore it open and found a single sheet of paper embossed with the Greystoke seal.

My very dear Jane, believe that I would not leave you like this if I had any other alternative. In an old diary I've found credible evidence that our world will shortly be invaded by a species more ruthless and determined than even our own—and I recognize all too well the place where they are supposed to land. My only chance is to go back to Africa and fight them there, before they reach the world of civilized men.

Doubt not that I will win this battle, my dear Jane—for I am Tarzan, Lord of Apes and Lord of Africa. I shall defeat these monsters who would use the creatures of Earth as fodder and slaves. And then I will come back to you.

Yours ever, Tarzan.

Beneath it, as an afterthought, he'd scribbled, *John C., Lord Greystoke.*

Jane stared in disbelief at the letter in her hands. What did he mean by the whole world being invaded? Countries got invaded, not worlds. She looked towards the mechanical celestial sphere, thinking of all those other worlds out there, and a doubtful frown formed on her delicate face. What if something came from those other globes to Earth? She shivered.

She noticed that Tarzan had left the paper askew on the desk, and his pen lying beside it, uncapped. Mechanically, she capped it.

Tarzan would have a head start of a night and a day, but it was clear where he was headed, one of the places familiar to him from his childhood. Which meant she knew where to find him. And she would. It was no part of Lady Greystoke's intentions to let her husband face a cruel invader alone.

"Jones," she called. "Bring our other car around."

Days later, Tarzan was let out of a small rowboat on the coast of Africa and he climbed onto the familiar shore, setting foot again on the land of his birth. Just breathing the air exhilarated him! He waved goodbye as the sailors rowed back to the steamer that had carried him here. He marveled that for once he had not met with mutiny or assassination attempts or other villains intent on eliminating him. Perhaps the very fact that he was here to save humanity from a terrible fate meant there was some protection from God or Fate.

Tarzan wasn't sure in which he believed. The anthropoid apes hadn't believed in much, though they did have some rites of their own—and it was to the place of those rites that he must now go.

As the ship steamed away, fast disappearing on the blue horizon, Tarzan removed all his garments. It was difficult enough to wear clothes in England, but it was torture here in Africa, where he should be home.

Knowing the ship would return for him in a month, he took care to fold the clothes and store them in the valise, from which he took his breechclout and his brass ornaments for arms and legs. Then, truly *Tarzan* again, he turned towards the jungle ....

Before long, he was swinging from tree to tree, following a familiar route. First, he had to go to where the old diary said the invaders' ship would land. There, he should find drawings on the wall, and then he would know for certain whether this had been a mere nightmare from his ancestor, or the truth.

The old treetop cabin was as Tarzan had left it, protected by the cunning lock on the door which made it impossible for the anthropoid apes or other wildlife to penetrate it. Sliding the lock open with the ease of long familiarity, Tarzan entered to find the interior largely undisturbed as well. He stowed his valise and looked wistfully at the bed where his mother had died a year after giving birth to him, and the place where his father had been killed. These reminders held no terror or sadness for him, since he'd never really known his parents. Having grown up among wild beasts, he had a very matter-of-fact view of life and death. Creatures lived and hunted and ate other creatures, and eventually one died and became food for others. He did not lament over it.

For a moment, he hesitated over his own purpose in racing back to Africa. If that philosophy were true, perhaps it held true in the greater universe, as well. Why was it any different for creatures from another world to hunt and kill the inhabitants of Earth? It was the order of nature.

His qualms were of short duration, however. Tarzan could apply such a philosophy to himself, as he had never counted himself much above the beasts. But Jane and Jack were also creatures of Earth, as were his many good friends, animal and human. Well did he remember losing Kala, his ape-mother. Though she had been rude and ugly, in the way of such things, he thought of her with all the bittersweet tenderness and respect that he would have lavished on his real mother, the late Lady Alice.

The thought that their lives should count for nothing made Tarzan's heart tighten in his chest. Yes, he would fight these invaders—not for himself, but for all the creatures of this Earth that he loved.

He was surprised to hear something heavy throw itself against the door of the cabin. He unsheathed his knife. He had killed lions and panthers with only his sharp knife and a rope. But when a soft growl echoed outside the door, he recognized the animal voice—Sheeta, the panther who, not so long since, had helped him rescue Jack and Jane when they'd been abducted by the dastardly Rokoff.

Tarzan *murred* back at Sheeta, conveying thoughts that could only be implied in the panther language, "Hello, Sheeta, my old friend and ally who helped me fight evil among the humans. I am Tarzan of the Apes, and I am back."

The soft *murr* that answered was all the welcome he could hope for.

With Sheeta following stealthily on the ground, Tarzan flew from tree to tree, suspended by ropes as he headed for the place he had read about in the diary. He remembered the site of his first great battle, where he'd killed Tublat, the unjust mate of his foster-mother Kala.

He had always thought of the place as a natural amphitheater, a part of the landscape like the mountains and hills and the ocean itself. But if his ancestor's diary was correct, this arena was not natural at all, but an alien construction, a landing pad for a sort of ship that could cross from one world to another. The idea should have made Tarzan's head spin, but he had already been forced to adapt his view of the world to include seemingly impossible things: wheeled vehicles, large cities, great industries. Adapting his mind now to the idea of yet another complex civilization that came from beyond the sky did not cause him any greater consternation.

The open amphitheater was circular in shape, and its unnatural strangeness was emphasized by the fact that it remained unencumbered by entangling vines and creepers. The encroaching jungle itself seemed to avoid the place.

The dense jungle choked off access, though, as if to deny any intruders. Giants of the untouched forest grew close, with matted growth clogging the spaces between their trunks. The only opening Tarzan could find into the level arena was through the upper branches of the trees. He knew his way.

Throughout Tarzan's childhood, the anthropoid apes had often gathered here. In the center of the amphitheater, he now saw one of the earthen drums built by the anthropoids for their strange rites, which have been heard by men across the vast unexplored jungle, but never witnessed. Tarzan was the only human who had ever seen the wild, frenzied revelry the drums inspired.

On moonlight nights, the anthropoid apes would dance in a rite that marked all important events in the life of the tribe: a victory, the capture of a prisoner, the killing of some fierce jungle denizen, the death or accession of a king. Here, prisoners were dragged to be killed and devoured. Here, Tarzan had defeated his first enemy and, later, had ascended as king of the anthropoid apes.

A long time had passed since then, and now another ruled the tribe, one who owed Tarzan fealty and who would recognize him as his lord. But before Tarzan would call on Akut and his people, he must first confirm that the strange symbols reported by his ancestor were indeed on the walls.

With his knife, Tarzan scraped at a half-buried wall of stone near the edge of the amphitheater. His wide knife revealed deep engravings in the stone: marks that represented the worlds encircling the sun, the larger rings of their orbits, and sharp triangle-shapes of the vessels that sailed between worlds.

Again he studied the ancient drawings and remembered the celestial engine at home which showed the alignments of those planets, and he had no doubt in his mind that his ancestor was correct. The engravings were clear, showing the movements of planets and indicating that when the planet Mars should be close to Earth and in just such an alignment, the ships of the Martians would fly to Earth.

Clearing more debris from the wall, Tarzan saw additional, more detailed drawings that the other John Clayton had mentioned but not copied: human captives being driven into the triangular ship, pictograms that showed them being forced to serve creatures with many tentacles and a confusion of eyes, and then being devoured by those monsters.

There was more, and Tarzan no longer had any reason to doubt the prophecy of his ancestor: if the Martian scout ship could get through, then the invaders would send an armada, intending to rule the Earth as overlords, as superior to humans as humans were to anthropoid apes.

Tarzan opened the well-thumbed diary, which he'd carried in his arrow quiver. What worried him most was his ancestor's warning, "They have a mind ray which can render you servile and mindless. Under its influence you will be unable to resist the enemy. Humans fall under this ray, but animals seem immune, and it was with the help of my faithful—" There a large stain blocked out the rest of the story, picking up much later with, "And thus, the space menace defeated, in peace and honor I travelled to England, bringing this warning to my fellow men, which alas none of them would believe."

An alien mind ray. Tarzan wondered if he was human enough

to fall under the influence of invaders, or if he still carried enough of the jungle within his heart and mind. Regardless, he must make sure that others stood ready to defeat the Martians and save Earth from subjugation.

If the mechanical celestial sphere was accurate, the initial ship would land tonight. He had very little time to gather his allies.

First, he explained the situation to Sheeta, as much as possible in the panther language. She understood that he would be fighting, and she knew to help him, and also that she was not to eat any of the animals of Earth, not in this battle.

Next, he visited Tantor the elephant, his old friend. The great gray beast remembered him, and Tarzan needed only moments to explain the situation, for elephants are as wise as humans. Tantor promised Tarzan that he would gather those creatures that were the elephant's fast friends: some tribes of monkeys, some birds, large snakes that slithered through the grass, and a tribe of wise old elephant matriarchs.

Meanwhile Tarzan went in search of Akut's people, the anthropoid apes who were descended from the ones who had raised him. At first, he worried that the new tribe leader would not remember him, and Tarzan would have to fight once more for his supremacy, but when he approached the tribe by a river, after the first moment of alarm in which the apes gathered children to themselves and flitted to the upper branches of trees, they recognized him and called out, "Welcome Tarzan, defeater of Kerchak, lord of the jungle, and friend of Akut."

Tarzan answered them by explaining that a great evil was coming from the sky and that they must defeat it. They were fearful of the news, but angry when he described the threat further. The entire tribe agreed to meet him by the amphitheater at moonrise.

Confident in his growing army, Tarzan went through the jungle on his own, to the nearby native village. When he'd been but a boy, he had convinced these savages that he was a supernatural entity, and they had appeased him by leaving out food as well as arrows poisoned with a fast-acting mixture. He feared that they'd fallen out of the habit after so much time had passed, but he found the arrows there in the little hut they'd built to revere him, and also fresh food.

Back home in England, Lord Greystoke would no more dream of eating leftover scraps than he would dream of sharing his dogs' kennels. Here, though, a different law applied. He ate the food, then he collected the poison-tipped arrows and returned through the high branches to his treetop cabin, where he restrung the bow he had taken long ago from a defeated enemy. He was preparing for a war against another world.

True, he could have brought a rifle with him and used that against the invaders. But he was more familiar with bow and arrows, and with its flash and explosion a rifle would give away his position. Yes, the arrows would be better.

He worried that the poison in the arrows would be ineffective against creatures from another world. But then he remembered the pictographs of the invaders devouring humans, and he reasoned that if the monsters could eat humans, then they must succumb to poisons of Earth.

When the moon rose over the ancient amphitheater, Tarzan was ready. Waiting in the crook of a tree above the ground, he felt and heard the animals of Earth nearby, also ready.

Before long, high above, there appeared a wheel of fire falling from the sky, a contraption that tumbled and made a sound just at the edge of hearing. Tarzan heard the first keenings of fear from the gathered animals, and he gave the shout of the great anthropoid apes, urging them to stand firm.

As the wheel of fire descended and finally came to rest in the amphitheater, Tarzan could tell that the supposedly natural arena had been designed to accommodate the otherworldly vessel. The triangular ship smoked, exuding acrid fumes; its walls were made of a black metal with a green sheen, and it gleamed wetly for all it had been on fire just moments before.

The ship remained quiet for an agonizing moment, and Tarzan wondered whether to command his animals to advance on it and stomp it flat before the invaders could emerge. But he reasoned that any such ship that could cross the vast space between the worlds must be hardier than the hooves and claws of the animals of Earth. He bided his time.

Then a tower emerged from the top of the contraption, emitting a light that seemed no natural light, but a glow that he perceived from the back of his brain rather than through the eyes. Tarzan stared at it, felt dizzy, but could not stop looking. Its effect on him was similar to what he had seen of a bird when faced with the hypnotic stare of a serpent. For a long, indefinable moment, he remained frozen on the tree branch, his eyes fixed on the light, and his mind filled with only a vague apprehension of danger and the stillness of death.

In vain, the tribe of anthropoid apes called out to him and asked what to do. In vain, Sheeta nudged him. In vain, Tantor let out a loud trumpet to demand his attention. But he could not respond. Instead, at the back of Tarzan's mind, he had a fuzzy recollection of the mind ray that his ancestor warned would render humans docile. *Humans.* He struggled, but he could not fight off the influence of the ray.

Then the Martians emerged from their ship, hideous things that brought a wave of nausea even to his fogged brain. Tentacled bodies that slumped and lurched forward, with dark oily skin that oozed a slime, leaving a trail behind them. And clusters of eyes that had looked upon alien skies which they had conquered, and sideways maws ringed with needle-like teeth, ready to suck and chew. They wished to be the new overlords of Earth, and their pulsing signal sent out an irresistible summons across the jungle.

Tarzan's stupor lasted an indefinite time, perhaps days, as he struggled—and then humans began to emerge from the jungle, making their way through the thick underbrush, battering down a new path. Natives both male and female, some of the women carrying little babes on their hip, utterly ignoring all of the wild animals gathered there by Tarzan. Instead, they marched forward singly or in groups, summoned by the terrible mind ray. And the hideous Martians waited there in front of their open ship to receive them as slaves, or as food.

He might have remained frozen forever, but then among the mass of dark-skinned natives clad in skins and tribal ornaments, he saw a figure clad as an English lady, and as the eerie moonlight fell upon her face, Tarzan recognized the beautiful features of his wife, Jane.

Two greenish-black horrors slithered forward to grab the slender arms of Jane Clayton, seizing her. She was too frozen to struggle as they began to drag her towards their sinister vessel.

Even though he was human by blood, the son of John Clayton Greystoke and the Lady Alice Greystoke, Tarzan of the Apes was not merely human. He was as much the adopted son of Kala the anthropoid ape, and his brain had been filled with habits and thoughts formed throughout his early life when he roamed the primeval forests of Africa—thoughts that were not bound by civilization.

Though he had struggled in vain against the force, this sight gave him a strength that no other force did, and he clawed deep into his own uncivilized *animal* heart to shake off the blind blankness of hypnotism. Just as his love for Jane had made a man out of the savage creature who had been reared in the jungles, now his love for his woman sparked a fierce fury in his ape-mind, a need to defend his mate.

As the creatures hauled his mesmerized and vulnerable wife into their alien ship, Tarzan at last managed to shake off the soporific effect of the ray. He arose with a cry that commanded all his animals to follow him. He jumped into the arena, racing toward, just as she stopped and shuddered, as though suddenly waking at the sound of his voice.

But Tarzan was not fighting alone. Monkeys swarmed forward to jump onto the entranced natives, knocking them to the ground and preventing them from boarding the ship. Birds of prey swooped in to harass the flailing tentacles of the startled Martians. Sheeta and two other sleek panthers bounded forward, driving a Martian to the ground, tearing greenish-black skin with their sharp claws, and spilling alien blood as well as slime. The aliens chittered and shouted, astonished at this unexpected and improbable resistance.

Still fighting off the cloying effects of the mind ray, Tarzan was only vaguely aware of Tantor's companions charging into the arena with deafening bellows. With a loud trumpet, a clever female elephant, supported by others, had charged up the sloped wall of the alien ship. With her trunk, she reached out and snapped the antenna from the hull.

In an instant, like the silence following a loud clap of thunder, the confusion was gone from Tarzan's mind. At the same time that the gathering natives stirred to life, awakening to their situation with fear and confusion, Tarzan shouted out an encouragement to all the animals. He plunged after his wife into the darkness of the alien ship, calling out in the tongue of the natives of the region, "These are cruel slavers from another world! They seek to imprison you—fight them!"

The creatures of Earth fought together, banding into a wild army that fought back against invaders from another world. In an army of fur, feathers, scales, and fangs, they struck at the scout ship that had landed in their jungle. Birds fiercely pecked holes in the metal skin of the vessel, and snakes slithered through. Howling, the great anthropoid apes pounded the ship and tore at the many-tentacled aliens with brute strength. Tantor and his elephant army crushed through the hull to free the few natives already in the ship. Sheeta's tribe gloriously crushed the aliens in their fierce jaws, then spat out the foul-tasting Martian flesh.

Tarzan, though, fought his own battle, following his wife's cries through the interior of the Martian vessel to an interior chamber in which a blazing glow shone from a vast apparatus surrounded by monsters who held Jane captive. They drew her toward the crackling glow, and now Jane fought back, trying to pull herself free of the tentacles, kicking, but in vain. Tarzan saw the shimmering blaze—and he wondered in horror if the assembled aliens meant to roast and devour Jane even now.

He let fly with his arrows so swiftly that he seemed to be everywhere at once. The poison-tipped shafts flew true, each one piercing an alien's slimy hide. He watched them slump one after another. Yes, indeed, the toxin was as deadly to Martians as it was to the creatures of Earth.

The invaders were in disarray, and Jane finally broke free of one captor, disentangling herself from the tentacles and lashing out with her boot to knock one of the aliens away; Tarzan shot it. But the other monster still held her, drawing her close and retreating toward the crackling glow, as if it meant to immolate itself along with her. Tarzan could not hit the Martian without the risk of hitting his own wife.

Instead, yelling a defiant roar of one of the great apes, Tarzan flew at the alien, his knife unsheathed. With a brutal slash, he severed the tentacle that held his Jane. Slime spurted, but she threw herself away, dropping to the floor. Tarzan plunged closer, ripping the knife sideways to hack off tentacles. The thing's sideways maw snapped at him, trying to lock needle teeth onto Tarzan's tanned skin. For a moment, the remaining tentacles held him fast in a death grip, and the jaws snapped shut, trickling silvery venom.

But he bit and he clawed, and he broke his arm free to raise the knife high. He brought it down, plunging the sharp point into the mass of staring eyes. He drove the hilt as hard as he could, shoving the blade deep into what must have been the Martian's brain. The alien shrieked, and greenish-blue ooze spurted out. The heavy, slime-coated creature slumped in an ungainly heap on the floor.

Tarzan panted, and he looked around to realize that the chamber was now filled with the creatures of Earth. All the other aliens lay dead.

As his sweet Jane rushed into his arms, he held her. Seeing himself dripping with alien ichor, he cautioned her, "Careful, my love. I'm covered in alien blood."

"It doesn't matter to me. This was a time when Earth needed a savage to defend it," she said, her hair in disarray and her own clothes stained with slime. "For savage or civilized, you are always the best of men, and the only one I'll ever love."

Long into the night around the amphitheater, the creatures of the jungle, for once at peace, celebrated the death of the alien enemies. All found something to eat in the wreckage of the ship, be it the aliens themselves or the plants that the aliens also ate.

Days later, in quieter times when Tarzan and Jane had returned to the treetop cabin in the jungle, they woke together after a sound and untroubled sleep. In a sleepy voice, Jane mused with a self-deprecating laugh, "And to think I came to Africa to save *you* from these aliens."

"And you did, my dear." He wore only his breechclout and barbaric ornaments, yet he had the manner of the most respected nobleman. "But for the sight of you, I would have remained hypnotized by the creatures, and I and all my friends would have perished. Just as your love saved me from a life of eternal savagery, so did your presence save me from alien enslavement." He smiled at her. "Now let us enjoy our days here in the jungle, so I can remember who I really am, while we wait for the ship that will take us back to England—and to Jack. In the meantime, let me share with you my jungle domain, just as you have shared civilization with me."

This story brings together two of my favorite fictional characters—Jules Verne's Captain Nemo from 20,000 Leagues Under the Sea *and* The Mysterious Island, *and Mary Shelley's Frankenstein monster. You'll meet both of them in other stories through these volumes.*

At the end of the classic novel Frankenstein, *the monster leaps off an ice-locked ship and drifts away on an ice floe into the Arctic, vowing to throw himself into a funeral pyre.*

In 20,000 Leagues Under the Sea, *the* Nautilus *is trapped under the Arctic ice caps.*

Just imagine an encounter between the two of them! I had to fiddle to make the timing work, since Shelley's novel was published many decades before Verne's, but that was easily fixed with a little imagination. They form a terrific fictional team.

THE STRANGER ON THE ICE

The *Nautilus* was trapped in the cold grip of Arctic ice. The white landscape had solidified as solid as cement, holding the submarine boat in a death grip above the surface.

Nemo had climbed outside onto the platform wearing his cork-lined jacket, pulling up the fur-insulated hood. The outside air was as fresh as broken glass, and with each breath he could feel the cutting cold. During the few hours of spring daylight, the clear sky above the polar regions was mockingly blue, but he knew from grim experience that Arctic storms could howl up in no time, out of nowhere. Even in his thick mittens, Nemo's fingers were cold, but he did not want to go back into the vessel's stuffy interior—not yet.

With a spyglass, he searched the monotonous bleakness, but saw nothing of interest, no hope. This frozen plain would be open water after the spring thaw, but now the ice remained unbroken, frozen over again.

During his exploration of the world, traveling countless leagues under the sea, Andre Nemo had traveled deep into the polar circle. Their vessel had resupplied at hardy fishing villages on the coast of Greenland, and more recently at a rugged settlement on Svalbard. The *Nautilus* had ventured through spring cracks in the icecap, navigating toward magnetic north, following Nemo's compass and his curiosity.

He knew his crew would give their lives for him, after he had risked his life to liberate them from the horrific prison camp of Rurapente. While held captive by the evil Caliph Robur during the Crimean War, Nemo and his fellow prisoners had been forced to construct this submarine warship—and they had escaped, stealing the *Nautilus*. Now, exiles from the world, they had voyaged the seas, battled a giant squid, found the sunken city of Atlantis, saw the wonders of the deep with their own eyes.

Drawn by the shimmering aurora of the Northern Lights, Nemo had allowed himself to be lured north, and then farther north still. The icecap had cracked in the early thaw, leaving wide chasms that his adept pilot could navigate. They had mistakenly believed that the weather would continue to warm, that the Arctic Ocean would become more navigable, week by week.

But a malicious twist of cold had descended upon them. Fortunately, the *Nautilus* had surfaced into the open air so he and his crew could observe the polar glory, but before they realized their danger, the temperature had plunged, and the ice crevasses had frozen over again. Now the armored submarine boat was caught like a fly in amber.

The head of the watch, Brian Courdoin, climbed out to stand beside him on the platform. "Captain, this reminds me of when we were caught inside that iceberg off Antarctica."

"I remember it well, Brian." In times of tension and stress, Nemo used first names. His crew was a devoted team rather than a regimented army. As prisoners of war in Crimea, the men had had enough of military excesses and the abuses of command. "This time at least we're above the surface, and we have enough air."

"True, Captain," said Brian, "but if these plates shift they could crush us like grinding jaws."

As if to emphasize his point, the armored iron hull groaned as unseen tides shifted the ice.

"We've survived worse," Nemo said.

Brian blew cold steam out his cracked lips. "That we have."

Out in the stark emptiness, Nemo was startled to see a black dot of movement. Thinking it was some mote in his eye, he raised the spyglass, careful not to touch the cold metal eyepiece to skin, and adjusted the focusing tube.

It was a large, dark figure shrouded in furs, riding a dog sled across the frozen terrain.

He handed the spyglass to Brian, who was just as astonished. "Who would be out on this landscape? Where did he come from?"

Upthrust through the snowfield, the *Nautilus* would have been obvious to any traveler. The stranger snapped commands and pulled on the reins. The team of wolflike dogs dragged the sled along on clattering rudders, approaching the frozen vessel. The front cargo bed of the sled was filled with lashed-down packages and provisions.

Nemo had faced unexpected encounters before, some of them joyful, others more dangerous. Alas, the dangerous encounters were more common.

He called down into the vessel, telling his men to prepare rifles, but not to bring them up yet. Nemo would not be the aggressor. He'd had more than his fill of war.

The dogsled came toward them on a straight bearing. As the barking and yipping dogs came to a halt beside the frozen vessel, Nemo kept his eyes on the stranger. The man was at least six-and-a-half feet tall, covered in a patchwork of furs that made him look like a bear. In the shadows of the hood that covered his head, Nemo could see dull yellow eyes peering out. The stranger seemed as fascinated by the *Nautilus* as by its captain.

After a long silence, the man spoke in a deep resonant voice—in English. "I did not expect to find company out in this wasteland."

"Nor did I." Nemo switched from his customary French. "Are you friend or foe?"

"Such a harsh environment makes foes of all of us, but unlike these wild dogs, humans can choose to put aside those base instincts. I make that choice. I have seen, and caused, enough violence in my existence."

Nemo was taken aback by the stranger's educated words and manner. This was no wandering native hunter of seals or reindeer. He took a risk. "An admirable choice, sir. As a human, I also prefer alternatives to conflict. Life is fragile."

"Fragile?" He seemed powerful, but not aggressive. "When life is forced upon you, it is exceedingly difficult to take away." The words puzzled Nemo, but before he could ask, the stranger continued, "I also have had my fill of conflict or vendettas. That is why I live alone up here … but after so long, conversation with someone from the civilization I left behind would be a worthy diversion."

Nemo invited the stranger aboard the *Nautilus.*

After Nemo introduced him to a wary crew, the mysterious visitor said, "I have no name."

Nemo laughed out loud, which elicited a troubled and surprised reaction. He explained to the stranger, "I am Nemo— and my name literally means No One."

"Something we have in common, then." He pulled down his fur-lined hood. In the electric light of the *Nautilus,* Nemo was shocked to see the craggy face. It was a horror of scars, jagged lines and lumps around his brow and his eyes. His ears looked as if they had been detached and sewn back on. He glanced around as if daring the crew to voice questions, but no one did.

Nemo said only, "You'll find no judgment here, sir. We've all survived the horrors of war, and most of us carry our scars on the inside."

The stranger turned his attention to the submarine boat. "Your vessel is a grand work of science."

Nemo led him along the narrow corridors, explaining how the *Nautilus* had been built as a battleship for an evil man, and now his crew had no families to return to, no lands that would take them back.

He invited the stranger into the salon near the bow. The viewing windows, which normally looked out upon schools of fishes or tremendous coral reefs, now showed only the wall of ice. Still knowing nothing about how this scarred man lived alone in the Arctic Circle, Nemo opened a bottle of port from their stores. He felt sociable now, though if they remained trapped for another month or two, his crew would be reduced to starvation rations of tinned biscuits and salt pork.

The stranger said that he was not hungry, explained that he ate little. The two sat in their chairs, curious, awkward, hesitant. Finally, the big man ventured, "Your science has brought you here. You must think it can perform any wonder."

"Some wonders, yes," Nemo said, and his thought grew dark. "But science also created the great guns, explosives, and war machines that I saw ripping our world apart. Science has made war all the more terrible. I respect science, but I am not enamored with it."

"Good," said the stranger. He had not yet deigned to take a sip of his port. "I am also familiar of the harm that science can cause."

Nemo drank, feeling the warm sweetness in his mouth. "One must admit that medicine has worked wonders, however—saved many lives. That much at least I can admire."

The stranger's scarred face sank into a troubled expression. "I am not so enamored with science and medicine. Some of the mysteries of life should remain mysteries."

Nemo warmed to the debate. "But what about discovery for its own sake? I'm an explorer, a naturalist. I document things that all humankind should know."

The stranger sat bunched and tense, and Nemo noticed more scars on his wrists and hands. "I've had my fill of learning the answers to mysteries. Thus, I stay here in exile."

"Why are you in exile?" Nemo asked.

The stranger downed his glass of port in one gulp, as if angry.

"Because I am not a natural man like you are. I am a product of science. I was made, not born."

Nemo's stomach knotted. "You mean you are an outcast."

The dull, yellow eyes looked up at him. "I murdered my maker's young brother, and then I murdered his wife on their wedding night. I did it out of revenge, for what he had done to me."

Nemo felt a chill. Power and danger rippled off this man in waves.

"He pursued me to the ends of the earth to get his own revenge ... and I finally strangled him on another ship trapped in these frozen Arctic waters. I am a monster...."

Nemo sat like a rabbit staring at a viper, waiting for the strike. He had a pistol in the table drawer nearby, but he doubted he could reach it in time.

The stranger looked away, stared at the ice outside the viewing window. "I vowed to throw myself on a funeral pyre, and that should have been the end of it, but I decided that such an escape was too easy. My guilt demanded something different. The persistence of life ... even the life forced upon me is still precious."

The chair creaked as he lifted his bulk up. "I see I make you uncomfortable, Captain Nemo. Your crew is already anxious. I need not add to their worries. I'll be away now. A storm is coming, and I should find my shelter."

Nemo followed the big, scarred man as he walked down the metal corridors toward the hatch. Though he was reluctant to host a confessed murderer in the confines of the *Nautilus*, he would not send him to certain death, either. "Where will you go? What about your dogs?"

"I have redoubts and shelters for all seasons," the stranger said. "I've survived alone for many years, and I'll survive for many years more."

Nemo followed him out of the hatch, and the stranger swung down to where the sled dogs were huddled against the rising breezes, making impatient noises. In the distance, Nemo could see ominous white clouds on the horizon, snow and ice crystals blown up by harsh winds.

When the big man reached the sled, he loosed the bindings of his cargo. "I'll leave you some provisions. I don't need them all." He left several packets on the hard snow for the *Nautilus* crew to retrieve, then pulled his dogs in line. Without a word of farewell, he set off across the white landscape, and Nemo stared after him as the winter storm came in.

The storm raged for two days, and the wind-blown snow only locked the *Nautilus* more securely in its tomb of ice. Nemo and his crew were warm enough, although the energy from the banks of chemical batteries could not suffer the drain for long.

When the air grew close and heavy, they had enough potassium hydroxide powder to scrub the carbon dioxide, and hydrolysis produced sufficient oxygen for their needs. Once the storm passed, they could vent the submarine boat and refresh their atmosphere.

When the raging winds finally stopped, his men took turns below the hatch to chip their way out. Finally, when he climbed out to stand in the open air again, Nemo's heart sank when he saw that the vessel had been nearly engulfed in slabs of ice and snow. His greatest fear was that they would be trapped forever.

He kept holding to his belief that the weather would turn soon, that the ice sheets would break and shift in the overdue spring. But some parts of the Arctic Ocean never thawed....

He directed his restless, agitated crew outside to work. They had to maintain their hope. The men wore cork-lined jackets, heavy mittens, and furs over their heads; they lined up in teams with pickaxes and shovels to hack away at the stone-hard snow. With furious determination, they hammered away at the slabs against the metal hull, excavating a portion of the vessel. Ice chips splintered and flew, and the men redoubled their efforts to dig a hard narrow trench. It was the work of desperation.

Nemo took his hand with a pickaxe as well, building up a sweat, warm and sore and distracted. Eventually, though, they all understood that the ice was frozen *beneath* the *Nautilus* as well. Unless the ice sheet itself broke apart, the submarine would remain imprisoned.

He heard the yipping dogs before he saw the sled approaching across the snow. His men paused in their labors to look up as the burly fur-clad stranger came toward them. The dogs strained against their traces, pulling a heavy load.

The scarred stranger gripped the handle in front of him and swayed, as if he could barely stand upright on the footboards. He called out to Nemo's crew, "I brought food."

The sled ground to a halt near the piled chips of ice and snow from the excavated trench. In the sled's cargo bed, Nemo saw the bloody carcass of a reindeer.

The stranger left the sled and staggered toward them. He wheezed with effort as he explained, "If you are trapped here until spring, your men would fear starvation." His dull yellow eyes swept across the uneasy crewmembers on the snow. "And starving men can turn into animals."

The reindeer had been ripped open. Long gashes split its side and belly. The dark blood had frozen, and the animal's eye was glassy as ice. Nemo felt a chill. This big stranger who had already confessed to murder; had he somehow torn the wild animal apart?

The dogs barked and shifted, tugging at their harness, and Nemo saw that the big man's furs were also ripped, soaked with blood from deep gashes. He took three wobbling strides and collapsed in the snow.

"Call Dr. Dyer!" Nemo shouted. "Help me carry him inside the *Nautilus* to the infirmary."

Three men bore the bulky form through the hatch and down into the warmer chambers of the vessel. The stranger was barely conscious, but he continued to struggle, refusing help. If he hadn't been so weak, they would never have brought him aboard.

Nemo followed, trying to get answers that would help the doctor. "Were you attacked? How were you injured?"

In a dry, resonant voice, the stranger said, "One of the big white bears ... killed the reindeer ... and it did not wish to relinquish its prey." The heavy lids closed, and breath rattled out of his throat.

Sean Dyer, one of the British prisoners from Rurapente and now the *Nautilus*'s surgeon, guided them into the small infirmary. "Good lord, he's been shredded!" The men placed the wounded stranger on the medical table. "Help me get these furs off of him."

Using surgical knives, Dyer cut the frozen bindings and broke away the iron-hard blood. The stranger roused himself enough to fight back, pawing at them with his large, mittened hands. The doctor yelled for help, and the crewmen held the patient down.

Dyer and Nemo finally peeled back the furs, as if they were skinning an animal, but when the surgeon exposed the stranger's bare chest, he gasped and swore. Nemo caught his breath in disbelief, and the other crewmen backed away.

The polar bear had carved deep gouges into the stranger's chest, but that was not the most horrifying part of his appearance. The man's torso was a patchwork of scars, jagged lines with rows of ugly suture marks, as if he was a crudely stitched quilt made from scrap pieces of humanity.

The stranger blinked his yellow eyes and lifted his head. His black lips twisted. "Away!" He shoved the doctor, making him stumble into the bulkhead.

Nemo dared to come closer. "You've been grievously wounded. We're trying to help you—heal you. This is a doctor."

"I despise doctors," said the man.

"I can't leave these wounds untended," said Dyer.

Nemo leaned closer. His heart pounded, but he kept his voice calm. "I see your scars, and they do not matter to me. But those wounds must be tended, or you will die. You brought us food, and we owe you a debt of gratitude. Let Dr. Dyer patch you up."

"He is already a patchwork," muttered the surgeon.

"I am greater than the sum of my parts," the stranger said in a rumbling voice. Then, with an exhausted sigh, he slumped back and grudgingly accepted Dyer's ministrations. The surgeon pulled the long wounds together and bound them with neat sutures that were far more masterful than the other scars that covered the man's body. Finished, Dyer wrapped the injuries with gauze and tape.

The stranger grunted his thanks. Nemo convinced him to rest, if only for an hour, though the big man was anxious to leave.

One of the *Nautilus* crewmen had done his best to clean and patch the torn furs. Brian Courdoin came in with bloody hands to report that the reindeer had been butchered and the meat brought aboard, with the offal fed to the dogs.

Nemo said, "That will feed my crew for weeks. We may survive thanks to you."

"The persistence of life," said the stranger, donning his furs again. "My dogs will be happy for the meal. They are hardy animals, used to the Arctic ... but they are still fragile things."

In contrast, he had regained his former strength in almost no time, and he insisted on departing. He answered no more questions, revealed nothing else about the mystery that surrounded him.

Nemo felt an odd connection to the nameless stranger who acted as their savior. Out here in the frozen wasteland, a man's past meant nothing. They were both outcasts and exiles in their own way.

After another ten cold days and long Arctic nights, the mood of the crew had grown heavy, and they felt inevitable fate weighing down on them.

Then the weather turned.

Nemo sensed the difference in the impossibly frigid air. Long-awaited spring, which had gotten lost in the polar emptiness, now returned as if to catch up with the calendar. As he stood outside on the platform, he could hear cracks and booms off in the distance as ice floes separated.

At first the crew whispered, then they cheered. They could feel hope again. "We might escape from this prison after all," Nemo announced.

But he knew the shifting ice could mean destruction instead of liberation. His engineers tested the chemical batteries, measured the remaining charge and made sure the drive train and engines had enough power to get the *Nautilus* propellers underway the moment the ice released its grip.

Despite his adherence to science, Nemo also needed to gamble. How much energy could he expend to free the ship and still have enough to propel them down into free water once the ice broke up? He connected battery cables to the outer hull, applying the output of the stacked batteries into resistance heating. It would warm the metal plates and melt a film of water around the *Nautilus*.

Outside, his crew fell to work again with pickaxes and shovels, excavating more of the trench around the ship. The clatter of iron tools against hard ice was punctuated with additional explosive sounds as the thick icepack slowly awakened. Caught up in a frenzy of determination, his men could taste their imminent escape, though the *Nautilus* was far from freed.

"It's only a matter of time, Captain," said Brian, who was panting after a hard shift of wielding a heavy axe.

Nemo wasn't so sure. The movements of the icecap were capricious. "We are fools to think we can be stronger than Nature."

"Not stronger, Captain—that's folly." The crewman blew out cold air through his lips. "But smarter."

The big nameless stranger arrived one more time while they worked to free the *Nautilus*. Now, the sled dogs looked haggard and weary, and two of the harnesses were empty, but the fur-clad man pushed the animals to greater speed by lashing his whip.

As Nemo walked across the ice to meet the stranger, he turned back to look at the *Nautilus*, saw his beautiful armored vessel like a trapped sea monster. The electrical resistance heating had melted off the rime of ice, and the ship could move a little within the jaws of ice. But it was by no means freed.

When the sled arrived, the stranger swung himself off the foot rails and stood by the tarpaulin that covered the cargo. "Tell me, Captain Nemo, can your vessel's hull withstand heat? I might be able to free it from the ice."

Nemo didn't know what he meant. "The *Nautilus* was made to charge into naval battles and withstand cannon fire. In my extraordinary voyages, I have taken it near underwater volcanoes where the water boils and the lava creates jets of steam." He stepped closer to the sled. "What did you have in mind, sir?"

In the distance, the boom and crack of splitting ice sounded like Arctic thunder. The stranger looked over his shoulder. "You may have your chance soon enough."

He snapped one of the lashing cords with a twist of his hand and pulled off the tarpaulin to reveal crates of oily, greenish-black rocks with a jumble of rough edges.

Nemo easily recognized the substance. "Coal! How did you find coal up in the Arctic Circle?"

"The Norwegians have opened mines on Svalbard, excavating deposits there. The villages are mainly seal and walrus hunters, but they also produce coal that is loaded aboard intermittent cargo ships. The locals burn it in stoves to heat their homes and cook their food." His scarred brow furrowed. "I thought you might make use of it here."

Nemo picked up one of the rough-edged chunks. "Yes, we could distribute the coal in the trench around the hull. Once ignited, it'll burn hot enough to loosen the ice." He frowned. "But I don't know how thick the ice is."

"Open water is not far down. I've watched crevasses appear in my journey here," the man said. "I raced across the ice, and it was ... hazardous. I lost two dogs."

"I'm sorry," Nemo said. This man lived in self-imposed exile, yet he had assisted them three times now.

"Fragile life." The stranger turned to his sled. "Come, let us distribute the coal and make the attempt." He guided the dogs up to the *Nautilus,* and Nemo's crew unloaded the crates, using shovels to distribute the loose coal around the submarine boat. Nemo used some of their spare kerosene, which burned hot enough to ignite the hard black fuel.

As the ring of rubble burned with thick black smoke, the orange flames seemed out of place in the blue-white environment. Nemo instructed the workers to retrieve their tools, while others climbed back aboard to check the systems and prepare the engines, ready for anything.

Loosely anchored to the hard snow, his dogs were restless and whining, as if they could sense the instability of the icepack.

Nemo stayed outside with their strange, ugly comrade. As they stood together watching, he felt a thrill as he saw the armored vessel shift, settling into the softening ice. "It might work ... my friend."

"Friend ..." The scarred man looked at him, puzzled. As if the idea made him uncomfortable, he walked away to inspect the line of burning coal.

As the stranger moved to the stern of the vessel, two crewmen reported to Nemo that the *Nautilus* batteries were back up to charge, that the engines were ready. They had gathered the last of the tools, and one man carried a coil of rope over his shoulder. With rising anticipation, Nemo moved around in the other direction, trying to see if the jagged bow was nearly freed.

Behind them, the sled dogs barked and howled, snarling. Two of them fought with each other, and in their struggles they uprooted the anchor pin from the hard snow. The dogs bolted off with the empty sled, racing across the white landscape as if pursued by demons.

Nemo yelled, but he could not stop them. At the stern of the *Nautilus,* the big stranger shouted a command, but the dogs did not obey his voice.

A louder sound drowned out the gruff voice—a rumble, then a shuddering snap. Nemo saw a midnight-blue lightning bolt zigzag through the flat white ice, like an arrow shooting toward the *Nautilus*. The frozen sheet split apart, and the fresh chasm widened. Arctic water welled up.

Nemo shouted a warning that was far too late to be heeded. The big stranger staggered away, but he could not outrun the shifting ice. Near the *Nautilus*'s stern, the floe split beneath his feet, spread apart—and the man fell into the deadly blue water.

"No!" Nemo yelled, and he turned to the crewmen beside him, seeing the coil of rope. "Run! We can help him."

The men dropped their picks and shovels and raced with Nemo across the ice to the fresh crevasse. They had to look, had to try, though there was no possible hope. The big stranger had vanished into the frigid depths, and no one could survive immersion for more than a few seconds in the Arctic water.

The dogs had raced far away with whatever supplies or blankets the man might have had.

The *Nautilus* groaned as the frozen plates moved, and it listed at an increased angle. From the hatch platform, Nemo's crew waved and yelled for them to run back.

At the split in the ice, Nemo dropped to his knees at the edge and stared into the bottomless slash of water. The crewmen stood at the crack with blank expressions and the clear understanding there was no hope.

Nemo grabbed the rope from the broad-shouldered man and threw the end into the water, though he knew it was a fruitless exercise. He felt sick.

Suddenly, the rope grew taut, as if some big fish had snagged it. The crewman with the rope staggered back, nearly sprawling into the water himself. Nemo and the second man grabbed him, and all three braced themselves, pulling hard.

Down in the blue depths, he could see a figure—the big man hauling himself hand over hand along the rope. "Pull!" Nemo shouted, and he and the two crewmen staggered back.

With his own strength, the scarred stranger dragged himself

to the surface, then reached out a big hand to clutch the ice. He pulled himself up out of the water.

Nemo and his companions grabbed the sodden furs, heaving to get him onto the icepack, though they were convinced the stranger must be dead already. The cold would kill him in seconds.

"I'm sorry," Nemo groaned. "You helped us, but it cost you everything."

Shuddering and shaking, the mound of wet furs heaved as the man dragged himself on hands and knees. A crust of ice had already formed around him, but somehow, impossibly, he lurched to his knees, then rose to his feet. He drew his beefy arms back and shattered the ice that crystallized on his furs. His skin was gray and pallid as death, his lips blue-black from the cold, but his yellow eyes were alert.

"Life is persistent, Captain Nemo," he said. His teeth weren't even chattering.

"Get him aboard the *Nautilus*. We must warm him!"

The stranger shook himself again and stood straight and tall. "No, I will stay here."

"You'll die," Nemo said.

More crew shouted from the *Nautilus* platform. "Captain, we have to go now! The ice beneath us has broken!"

"Your vessel is free," said the stranger. "I helped buy that for you. Don't waste it."

He turned, but Nemo grabbed at his arm. "Come with us. You'll be safe. We can drop you off at any port you like, but I can't leave you here."

"You will leave me." The stranger brushed away more chunks of ice. "I have been out here for many years, and I'll remain in exile for many more. I intend to keep my solitude and keep my peace. The world does not want me—it has proven that time and again."

"I understand how you feel, but we are alike in many ways, you and I."

The stranger's craggy, scarred face turned to him. "No, Captain, we are not alike—not even in the most basic of ways ... for you are human."

Nemo didn't know what he meant. "We're all human."

"No, I was *made*—stitched together by Victor Frankenstein, brought to life by electricity and science. I don't belong in your human world. I have been out here for half a century already, and I expect to be here for much longer. When life is forced upon you, it is exceedingly difficult to take away."

From the *Nautilus,* the shouts grew more strident. The nearest crewman tugged at Nemo's arm. "Captain, the ship is free. We need to go before the ice closes again."

"Half a century," Nemo said to the stranger. "That's not possible."

"My maker pursued me up to the Arctic Circle, vowing revenge," said the stranger. "He took refuge aboard an English exploration ship that was trapped in pack ice ... and I killed him. That was 1818—and I have been here since."

"1818," Nemo said, his voice faint with disbelief. "But it is 1870!"

The stranger chose a direction at random in the emptiness, and began to trudge away from the wide blue crack in the breaking ice. "Years mean nothing to me, Captain Nemo. How does one measure eternity?"

He marched away alone in the white wilderness.

The crew dragged Nemo with them, and he finally turned and ran. The boom of breaking ice resounded in the air. The coal fires had sputtered out as the crack widened like a loosening pincer. Ahead, he heard the thrum of the submarine engines, the whir of the propeller.

From the platform, he could see Brian waving. "The ship is free, Captain! Hurry!"

They scrambled up the iron hull rungs and crawled down into the hatch and sealed it above them. Nemo wasted no time before he shouted orders. "If we've broken loose of the ice, then dive!"

The helmsman angled the rudder, spun up the propeller, and the submarine vessel shuddered loose of their frozen prison. At last, the *Nautilus* submerged into the cold, free depths.

Nemo doubted the chill would ever be gone from his bones, though, as he thought of the man he had left alone in his Arctic exile.

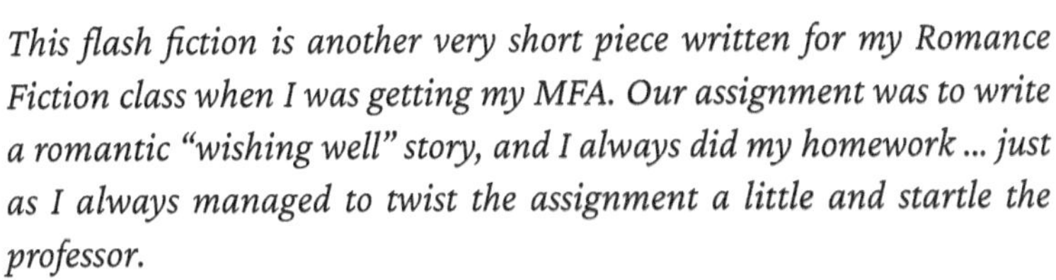

This flash fiction is another very short piece written for my Romance Fiction class when I was getting my MFA. Our assignment was to write a romantic "wishing well" story, and I always did my homework ... just as I always managed to twist the assignment a little and startle the professor.

MAKE A WISH

He sat at the edge of the still fountain with a handful of bright copper pennies. Bright shiny memories.

Randy came here every day, out of habit. He plucked one of the coins from his palm, looked at the reflection of sunlight, and tossed the penny into the still water. Sinking slowly, it came to rest among the other coins thrown by lovers and optimists.

He saw Shira's face, the bright smile with one nicked tooth, the scattered freckles that somehow made her even more beautiful. For the cost of just a penny, he could remember her laughing—often at his foibles, but usually with shared humor.

Randy remembered what it was to be lonely, not desperate but just adrift. Shira had been a wonderful friend at first—always friends before romance, then lover, then love of his life.

He threw another shiny penny, which brought back memories like magic, a wish come true, as it splashed in the fountain.

Randy had never been much in the way of social graces, but Shira understood him. They could talk for hours about things that mattered to him, and things that didn't but fascinated him nevertheless. They played role-playing games together with a bunch of his other friends, mostly male, and finally—hoping for the best, but expecting little—he had asked Shira to help him find a girlfriend, someone special. After they sat together in a coffee shop, talking over exactly what Randy was looking for, in the end he summed it up succinctly with "Someone just like you."

He jingled the pennies in his hand, tossed another one in: Shira treating him as a Pygmalion project, teaching him how to talk to girls, how to talk to *her*.

Another penny submerged with a splash: Their first romantic dinner, the wine and candlelight, the grocery store rotisserie chicken and packaged salad, because that was the best Randy could do.

Another penny: Their first kiss. Then their best, most passionate kiss. Then their millionth kiss ... they were all special. There weren't enough pennies in the world to help him remember all of those.

Another penny, another memory: a whitewater rafting trip where they both got drenched and couldn't stop laughing.

Someone had once called them an odd couple, because Shira was so out of his league. While Randy had tried to stammer out a clever answer, Shira defended him. "What's wrong with being odd?"

He gazed at the coins at the bottom of the fountain. He was alone today, but at other times couples would come here, charmed, laughing, casting their hopes and dreams into the wishing well. Randy knew about hopes and dreams.

Their first apartment, decorated with a Star Wars theme of course, just because.

Their wedding, where everyone was encouraged to wear Renaissance Faire garb, which earned them disapproving clucks from their parents, but delight and support from their friends.

The pennies were going fast now, each memory priceless, but costing only a cent. And when his hand was empty, with only one last copper coin between his fingertips, he tossed the penny in, making his strongest wish.

"Go for it!" Shira had always said. "What do you care what other people think?"

It was inevitable, the one memory more vivid than any other, no matter how much loose change he spent on recalling the rest of their lives together. The penny splashed in the water, and it became a flood of sound, the crash of metal, the shatter of glass, the car rolling over, twisting into the guard rail and into the trees. Then the pattering sound, which became a silence around them so deep that Randy was sure he could even hear the blood flow.

Make a wish ...

How many times Randy had wished that he could have been the one killed in the car accident that day. He would have given anything to switch places, to let Shira survive instead of him.

With his pennies all gone, Randy used his one good hand to roll the wheelchair back away from the fountain with all its coins, all the memories and dreams, beneath the still surface. There wasn't any magic here after all.

Wishes didn't come true.

In other volumes in this set, I've introduced readers to my series set in the strange, creepy Wisconsin farming town of Tucker's Grove. As I continued writing stories about Tucker's Grove, I fleshed out the history of the tow, from its founding in the 1800s to the modern day. This story bridges the two time periods, influenced by the wonderful Richard Matheson novel (and equally wonderful film) Somewhere in Time.

Even across history, sometimes lovers get to have happy endings. Sometimes they don't.

MIRROR, MIRROR
ON THE WALL

Clouds congealed in the sky like a smoke pudding. The weather report on the TV news talked about severe storms, heavy rains on the way.

Thunderstorms fascinated Peter D. the way a rattlesnake fascinates a mouse, and he stood in the shelter of the old house's front porch watching the clouds, smelling the ozone in the air, waiting for the crack of lightning and the roar of thunder. He could sense a raw, elemental power just waiting to be unleashed on the thirsty cropland.

If piddling Kansas twisters could transport little girls to the Land of Oz, he thought, what could the whim of a big-blast Wisconsin thunderstorm do?

The first raindrops smelled like metal as they came down. When a stray horizontal gust splattered him with raindrops, Peter D. pulled open the screen door and darted back inside the farmhouse. Within moments, heavy rain began to rattle the rippled windowpanes.

As the storm built, the ancient Waltercroft house creaked and groaned. At least the tornado siren from nearby Tucker's Grove hadn't sounded—not yet. Peter D. empathized with the people who had lived in this same house a century before. He tried to transport himself mentally into the past, smelling the dampness in the air, the wood of the old house. How could he write about history, even a piddling history of Rutherford County, if he didn't *feel* it? It sounded like some creative-writing class exercise.

In the hallway Kathy tugged his arm. "Come on, Peter D.—we're alone at last. Better make the best of it." She used her playful voice. She was 23, half a year older than himself, both of them fresh out of college with liberal arts degrees, neither having the slightest clue what they wanted to do with their lives.

Only an hour ago, his eccentric aunt Lillian had driven away on her Florida vacation as what she called a "doozer" of a storm built overhead. While Lillian was gone, he and Kathy would house-sit and work on their local history book that his dear old aunt had convinced her women's club to sponsor.

Now he turned to Kathy, stroked her short brown hair. "Why, what did you have in mind, ma'am?" he drawled in what he considered to be a passable Rhett Butler imitation. They had been together for two years, yet still found opportunities to act like high-school sweethearts. "This is a respectable old house. We should act appropriately."

Kathy arched her eyebrows. "Appropriately? The original owners must have fooled around sometimes."

He slipped his arms around her waist and glanced up at their reflection in the antique hall mirror. Aunt Lillian once told him the mirror had been hanging in that hallway undisturbed, open and glazed as a dead man's eye, for more than a century (and she should know, he thought, since she was almost that old). "Look at us, the perfect couple."

The thunderclap sounded like the eruption of a Midwestern Mount Vesuvius. A jolt ran through the walls, threatening to knock the entire Waltercroft house off its foundations. The lightning flash, simultaneous with the thunder, was blinding, disorienting, powerful.

Peter D. found himself sprawled on the hardwood floor, knocked flat as much by the sound as by the blast itself. He rubbed at the blotches of color that danced in front of his eyes.

Kathy lay next to him, trying to focus her eyes. He grabbed her shoulders. "You all right, Kath?"

"Just rattled." She sounded confused. "Listen. Did you hear something?"

"My ears are ringing louder than an out-of-control stereo." Peter D. shook his head to knock his brain back in place.

"—struck by lightning," a young man's voice said.

"What if the roof is on fire?" A woman's voice this time, frightened, followed by a sudden gasp. "Will! How are we ever going to explain you being here?"

Peter D. got to his feet and helped Kathy up. The voices were coming from the hall mirror. "What the hell?"

The decor shown in the reflection did not match the actual things in Lillian's home. The furniture looked old-fashioned, but the pieces themselves were new. Peter D. turned around to see Aunt Lillian's TV on its imitation-wood stand, the paperback historical romances strewn on the coffee table, curio shelves on the walls filled with ridiculous knick-knacks from the old bat's world travels. None of those things showed up in the mirror.

The young couple talking in the reflected parlor were definitely not Peter D. and Kathy.

"She looks like Jane Seymour in *Somewhere in Time*," Kathy whispered.

"Somebody better start playing the *Twilight Zone* theme."

"It's raining too hard for the house to catch fire," said the young man in the mirror. Will? He looked about twenty years old, with blond hair and a few wisps of beard. "It'll be all right, Audrey. I promise." He placed his hands on her shoulders, projecting calm confidence.

The young woman was seventeen or so, quite pretty, with big eyes and long brown hair wrapped up in an intricate bun, leaving a few curls to hang at the sides of her face. She gazed at Will for a moment, then slid into his arms for a hug.

Peter D. raised his voice to the mirror. "Hey, can you two hear us?" The figures in the reflection did not react, even when he repeated the question in a loud shout. "I guess not."

With her face pressed against Will's faded work shirt, Audrey's voice became muffled. "You should get going now—Nels will be home soon."

"He doesn't even care about you."

Audrey drew back in alarm. "He *owns* me! You'd be a thief stealing one of his possessions—and he has the right to shoot any thief he catches in his own house."

"He doesn't have the right to ruin your life."

Audrey kissed his continuing scowl away. "He saved my life, remember? Please don't make things worse by getting yourself killed."

As Audrey hurried the young man toward the front door, Will glanced at his reflection in the hall mirror. He seemed to stare directly through Peter D. "Something's wrong with your mirror. I can't see my reflection."

Audrey was concerned only with getting him out of the house. "Nels will know how to fix it. Now you have to go."

Before the door swung shut, the young man called, "See you next Wednesday!" and Peter D. could hear a horse and wagon departing. Audrey didn't even look at the mirror on her way to the parlor, where she sat in silence, trying to compose herself.

"From their clothes, I'd place those two in the mid-to-late 1800s." Kathy headed to where boxes of old records and local books sat on an enormous dining room table in front of seven potted geraniums. "We've got three names—Audrey, Nels, and Will—connected to this house. With all the research material your Aunt Lillian left here, we should be able to find out something." She was always the "hard facts" person, while Peter D. considered himself the "creative genius in training." For a project like this, they were a perfect team.

Not long afterward, another voice came out of the mirror. "Damn storm hit me half an hour before I got to Tucker's Grove."

Nels was a tall, sturdy man of about forty, his light brown hair just on the verge of turning gray, with rugged features that showed no hint of softness. His blue eyes glimmered with a common-sense intelligence. His flannel shirt and overalls were faded and worn to the point of being comfortable. By the careful way Nels wiped his boots on the front rug and looked around the foyer of his house, Peter D. imagined him to be a hard-working man.

Soaking wet, he carried a brown paper package, which he had shielded with his body in an effort to keep it dry from the downpour.

Audrey stopped several steps away from him, well out of reach—trying to hide her fear? discomfort? Peter D. couldn't tell. "You'd better change your clothes. You're getting the floor all messy." Her voice held nothing more than the required emotion as she said the required comment.

"I still need to do some chores outside. I just ... stopped in to see you."

A long silence.

"How was Bartonville?" She was obviously forcing herself to talk to him, but the chill in her voice was obvious.

Nels extended the package to her. "I got you some sewing material. You can make a new dress."

She stepped forward to take it from him, tugged on the strings and brown paper to reveal a pale, flower-print material. "Thank you, Nels," she said with no warmth or genuine thanks. She retreated toward the parlor with her package.

"Who was here?" he said quickly.

She froze, her back to him. "Who said anybody was here?"

"I can see the cart tracks out front, Audrey. Who was here?"

Audrey finally faced him. "Mrs. Litch came, from church. Just after the storm." Peter D. thought he saw defiance in her eyes as she told her bold lie. "She wants every family from around town to make one square for a community quilt they're going to auction off at the church. That's why she was here."

"She couldn't have come *after* the storm." Nels kept his voice carefully even, though he seemed charged with more static electricity than any thunderstorm. "There's only one set of wheel tracks in the mud, leading out from here. And a dry patch where a wagon sat during the storm."

Fear sparkled in Audrey's eyes. "Maybe she came before the storm, then. I can't remember. We were talking." Then, with a hint of exasperation, she added, "Shouldn't you be out doing your chores?"

Peter D. noticed Nels clenching his fists as he turned and pushed his way back through the front door.

During the next three days, Kathy buried herself in the names and dates of Rutherford County, poring over the data and waiting for her mental junction-boxes to throw the proper information into the proper places.

Before leaving for Florida, Lillian had gathered all the local historical documents she could find: birth records, death records, tax records, court records, even a boxful of yellowed letters, diaries, and postcards gathering dust in the attics of those "nursing home fixtures" Aunt Lillian resented so much. Everything was grist for Kathy's data-crunching mill, raw material to be digested into a detailed story that Peter D. would tell with all the verve he could muster. Kathy chewed the pink erasers off pencil after pencil—it helped her concentrate, she said.

"Want to hear a rundown of everything we can get from names and dates?" She tapped her pencil on the legal notepad where she had jotted her thoughts. "Nels Waltercroft, born March third, 1854; married Leilah Miller in 1880—he was twenty-six. He built this house, and the two of them lived in it for ten years until Leilah died. Seven years later he married young Audrey Bailey. She was seventeen, he was forty-three. Audrey died on August 25, 1897—less than a year later. Nels never married again and died in 1901."

Peter D. paced the room, tapping his fingertips together as he painted a picture in his mind. "How did any of them die?"

"These death records aren't very explicit."

He looked over her shoulder to scan the notes on the yellow pad. "What about that Will guy?"

"No way of knowing. No last name, no other concrete information. I can't work miracles."

"I beg to differ." He gave her a peck on the cheek.

Peter D. stationed himself in a folding chair where he could watch the mirror. Restless, he waited for something important to happen. He toyed with Aunt Lillian's enormous collection of knick-knacks, even tried to read one of her romance novels, and kept Kathy supplied with fresh pencils.

"This really gives me insight into how boring life was in those days." Peter D. said. "No TV, no video games, no stereo, no internet, nothing to keep you occupied at all. Get up with the sunrise, go to bed shortly after sunset, unless you feel inclined to light a lamp. Just listen to how quiet the house is! It's enough to drive you up a wall."

At the moment, in the mirror, Audrey was alone in the house, writing in some sort of diary. "No wonder so many people kept journals ... although why anyone would want to relive an uneventful day is beyond me." He stopped as an idea occurred to him, then looked closer at what Audrey was doing. "Wait a minute! I've seen that book before."

He hurried to the boxes of records, shuffling through them until he held up a faded brown book and flipped to the front page. "Audrey Waltercroft's diary."

Thrilled, Kathy took the book from him, flipped pages, looked for dates. "She didn't write in it every day, so the entries are sporadic. They start a little before she married Nels." She thumbed through the journal to where the writing ended, leaving half a book of blank paper. "And the last entry—an interrupted one—is dated Saturday, August 21, 1897."

Peter D. did the math. "That's only four days before she died."

Her eyes darted along the neatly written words on the first several pages. "Listen to this—the Bailey family home burned down when she was seventeen. Nels came to help put out the fire and rescued Audrey from the burning house. Later, when the Methodist church took the family under its wing, Nels asked Mr.

Bailey for his daughter's hand in marriage, in gratitude for rescuing her."

Peter D. snorted. "As if she *owed* it to him!"

Kathy could not take her eyes from the pages. "Well, it makes a lot of sense, given the time. Audrey was old enough to be married, and Nels Waltercroft could certainly support her. Remember, her family had lost everything in the fire, and Audrey was one more mouth to feed. Nels offered to take her away from all that, so her parents consented. Good deal for everyone."

"If you say so."

Kathy bent closer to the faded handwriting. "I'm reading from Audrey's diary now: 'Nels is a good husband, in his own way. He provides for me, but he doesn't love me, or at least he never shows it. I want the man that I marry to love me with all his heart—like Will does. I have always loved Will. He's such a kind and loving person. Even the animals love him! Will is going to be a horse doctor. He finds hurt animals and tends them. We were going to get married, but we'd decided not to tell our parents until he saved up some money. That was before the business with Nels.

"'Will and I still see each other every Wednesday, when Nels goes to Bartonville to pick up supplies. It's our only chance to be together, but better that than nothing.

"'I know that what Will and I are doing is wrong—but what Nels did to me was wrong, too. I don't have to feel guilty! I love Will, and that's all the reason I need.'" Kathy frowned, turned several pages, then closed the book. "The entry just stops there ... and it's the last one."

"A little anticlimactic," Peter D. said. "But it sure explains the frostbite I got when Audrey and Nels were talking."

In the hallway, Audrey's voice came from the mirror. "What are you doing here? It's Saturday!"

Will laughed. "Nels is in town, so I figured he wouldn't be here."

"But he could be back any minute—"

In the mirror, the young man had a definite swagger. "Nope. He's getting the horses shod at the blacksmith's, and he's having a wheel fixed on the wagon. He'll be gone all afternoon—and *I'll* be right here. Come on, it's a beautiful day. Let's go for a walk down the lane."

After they went out through the front door, Peter D. saw that Audrey had left her diary open on the table.

When Nels returned home later that afternoon, Audrey did not come to greet him, merely acknowledged him from the kitchen. As the man strode into the parlor, his pale blue eyes were drawn to the open diary on the table like iron filings to a magnet. He moved silently over to pick up the book, his forehead furrowed with curiosity. He began reading the latest entry.

"Uh-oh," Peter D. called from his chair by the mirror. "Nels just found the diary."

Kathy hurried over. "*Everything's* in there."

Nels's eyes went wide as he continued to read. First his expression registered shock, disbelief, then horror. His big hands trembled and clenched as if he were trying to rip the book in half, then he squeezed his eyelids shut so tightly that he squeezed out tears. But he kept silent all the while. Nels stood rigid for a full minute until he managed to compose himself. He closed the book with an awkward gentleness and placed it under some papers at the bottom drawer of his writing desk. With calm deliberation, he locked the drawer.

"I guess everybody can't be the perfect couple, like we are," Peter D. said.

Nels gripped the back of a chair as if he needed support, then cleared his throat. When he spoke, his voice was surprisingly firm, loud enough for Audrey to hear him in the kitchen. "I saw Mrs. Litch in town today."

Silence hung in the air for a moment before Audrey's reply came from the other room. "Oh? What did she have to say?"

A long pause, and Peter D. waited for the man to throw his accusations, to expose his young wife's lies. Nels took several long breaths and said instead, "She said she looks forward to seeing your quilt square completed."

Suddenly, the pieces fit together in Peter D.'s mind. "Hey, Kath—you said the last entry in Audrey's diary was on a Saturday, right? And it was an interrupted one? In the mirror, *this* is Saturday. And Will interrupted her this afternoon while she was writing ... and now Nels has locked the diary away. I get the feeling Audrey isn't going to be writing in it again."

"The plot thickens." Kathy snapped her fingers as an idea occurred to her, and she shuffled through a pile of papers until she found the one she wanted. "I should have thought of this before. On August 25, 1877—the same date as Audrey's death—a William Jacobsen, age twenty, also died. August 25, by Audrey's diary, was a *Wednesday*."

"They always met on Wednesdays," Peter D. said.

Kathy looked at him with wide eyes. "Aww, no—Nels? This Wednesday?"

"They're going to be murdered in four days. And all we can do is wait, and watch."

The following day he and Kathy observed as poor Audrey searched frantically through the parlor for her diary but did not find it. Peter D. paced the front hall, angry, sad, and helpless. He tried shouting to the young woman, pounding on the mirror glass, but could not get her attention. Audrey moved unsuspecting, one day at a time, toward the date of her death.

"Hey, mirror, mirror, on the wall! How can we stop this from happening?" Peter D. said. He received no answer, and he got the feeling there would be no fairy-tale ending for Will and Audrey.

He saw Nels's mood steadily darken. The man's eyes were puffy and red, bloodshot, as if he passed his restless nights plotting instead of sleeping. He and his young wife barely spoke to each other. Audrey must have sensed that something had changed, but she refused to broach the subject.

Now that they knew the exact dates, Kathy found an entry in the Rutherford County court records: "Nels Waltercroft acquitted of the murder of his wife Audrey and her adulterous lover William Jacobsen." During the brief trial, Nels had offered the diary as evidence of their affair, which was all the straight-laced judge needed to see. The book had survived locked away in a court vault until Aunt Lillian resurrected it for their historical project.

On Wednesday morning Peter D. watched the mirror with growing horror when Nels left, as he always did, supposedly off to distant Bartonville. Not long afterward, Will appeared, taking Audrey in his arms and leading her into the parlor. The young woman needed his comfort and his love with a level of desperation she had not showed before. Will dismissed her worries, but Audrey seemed more fearful than ever. She told him what Nels had said about Mrs. Litch, how he should have caught her in the lie, and how her diary had now gone missing.

But Will erased the fear from her eyes as if she were a bird with a broken wing that needed mending. He brushed away her tears, stroked her cheeks to calm her. They began to kiss on the sofa, steadily becoming more caught up with each other.

These two reminded him very much of himself and Kathy, a couple meant to be together, and he admired Will's strength and confidence, his ability to show his love. Peter D. would have made wisecracks instead, trying to get Kathy to laugh.

The young couple in the mirror were already doomed. They had been murdered more than a century ago.

And it was going to happen again in only a few minutes.

Peter D.'s stomach churned, and his pores wept tears of sweat. "I hate feeling so helpless!" He clutched one of Aunt Lillian's inane knick-knacks—a cheerfully painted vase that said "Greetings from Puerto Rico." He should have taken Kathy off on a sunny vacation somewhere rather than staying here in this house with dreary historical records and old tragedies.

Standing close to him, squeezing his other hand, Kathy stood engrossed in the mirror. She choked back a muffled cry as the door opened silently and Nels entered the front hallway, cradling a shotgun in his arms. Tears streamed down his weathered cheeks, and his whole body trembled. His skin had a grayish tinge, as though he were about to be sick.

Peter D. nearly crushed the Puerto Rico vase in his sweaty hand.

Nels strode forward like a thunderstorm and loomed in the hallway, staring at the two kissing in the parlor. His face twisted into an anguished expression, and he let out a bestial cry.

Audrey looked up and screamed. Will tried to turn in his shock.

Nels raised the shotgun and pressed his eyes shut as he squeezed the trigger.

Peter D. hurled the knick-knack at the mirror. "No!" It was the only thing he could think to do.

The roar of the gunshot sounded simultaneously with the crash of breaking silvered glass as the vase struck the mirror.

Another violent jolt went through the Waltercroft house, and a roar of thunder detonated in the air. When the mirror shattered, the whole house writhed on its foundations. Splintered glass reflected random timelines in different directions, bouncing possibilities into alternate futures, leaving the future to change the past.

And *Now* changed instead.

Lillian hesitated, then decided to hang up the phone, leaving her nephew's number undialed. Writing a history of Rutherford County would have given Peter D. a chance to showcase his writing talent, but she was sure he'd make some derisive joke about the project. Better if he never even knew of her silly idea.

Here in Rutherford County, local historical landmarks were few and far between, now that the subdivision builders had torn down the old Waltercroft house. Even the locals had little interest in forgotten people from an unremarkable past.

In the cramped kitchen of her "senior" apartment, Lillian

went to the coffee maker and poured the untouched pot of old coffee down the drain before starting a fresh batch. Lillian never drank coffee, but she loved the warm, roasty smell of a brewing pot. It helped ease the annoyance of being trapped in an old timers' complex—"Prep School for the Nursing Home," she called it. But she had nowhere else to go.

Lillian had uncovered many fascinating Tucker's Grove stories to share with Peter D., excellent fodder for a historical book, in her opinion. As his aunt, Lillian had always felt free to give him ideas for novels, hoping he would take up writing again. Given Peter D.'s creative streak, he must be bored in his dead-end job as a bartender. She wanted to be supportive of the poor boy, but her goof-off nephew had been moody and withdrawn since he'd broken up with Kathy. She had always thought the two made a wonderful couple.

Lillian kept waiting for him to snap out of his funk. "Here's a wonderful romantic story about the old owners of the Waltercroft house," she wanted to suggest to him on the telephone. "A young girl was torn from her true love and forced to marry a cruel old farmer, but the girl never stopped loving her young beau. Corny, right? When the farmer found out about the affair, he took up his shotgun and went to confront them. But—surprise!—he was struck by lightning on his way to kill the two. Struck dead by a bolt out of the clear blue sky. Not a cloud in sight. Can you believe that?"

Of course, Peter D. would have groaned and rolled his eyes, dismissing the tale. "Yes, I know it's a true story, but people just won't believe it. Too much of a coincidence for fiction. There has to be some *reason* for things like that to happen."

Oh well, she supposed he was right. Lillian wished Peter D. could be happy. He and Kathy had been so captivated by each other, so in love, just like the young couple in the story. She sighed. Things change, and sometimes there's no explanation.

The bitter smell of coffee began to fill the kitchen.

Remember Heavy Metal Magazine? *Or the animated movie? I even owned the terrific soundtrack double album. That magazine was a hallmark of my college days, with its garish covers, spectacular monsters, and beautiful buxom women (scantily clad and scantily armored, but warriors nevertheless). For a nerdy kid, it was pretty aspirational.*

Looking back at that magazine, I realize that much of it would not be considered "appropriate" today. But some of the larger-than-life characters and epic, bombastic stories are so over the top that I can still enjoy them for what they are.

One of those grand characters was Colt the Outlander, a big, brawny guy with more muscles than brains and lots of weapons, including his favorite hand grenade. He is accompanied by two drop-dead-gorgeous women, who are quite likely smarter than Colt, and they are in control of more than he realizes. The stories are all set in a harsh post-apocalyptic world, like what you'd see in Mad Max.

Through WordFire Press, I worked with the Aradio Brothers, creators of Colt the Outlander. They had spent years tirelessly drumming up interest in Colt, trying to develop a TV show, feature film, or animated series. Through WordFire, they published a new Colt the Outlander novel written by Quincy J. Allen, and I wrote an original Colt novella.

The Aradio Brothers let me play with their fun, colorful, and studly character, and I created a wild tale. Sit back, engage the entertainment portion of your brain, and go for a ride.

COLT THE OUTLANDER: THE BLOOD PRIZE

—I—

The badlands of Neb-6 sprawled out in a bleak but breathtaking vista of spiral canyons, tan rock spires, abandoned mining operations, and all-too-rare green oases.

Colt paid no attention to the alien view. His eyes were focused on the targeting cross.

Riding high in the open wind on the back of his hover-hog, Colt felt the massive levitation engines thrumming as he straddled the engines with his legs. He adjusted for the vibration as he squinted at the fine hairs, zeroing in on his target. He nudged the throttle to move in closer, and the Razorback sliced through the air like a knife sliding into the gut of a combative bounty.

Closer ... closer ...

The lens of the targeting cross focused in on the nasci, one of the hideous rodent-scorps that infested the canyons out near the isolated and automated power plant Dar-Zeta. Colt saw two males and a much larger female scuttling through the shadows of the ravine floor.

The critters were hideous: rat-like heads with arachnid eye

clusters and sharp teeth, bodies covered with long venomous porcupine spines that gave them a round and fuzzy appearance … if seen from a distance and out of focus, with very poor eyesight. They had multiple articulated legs and a segmented, upcurved tail tipped with a deadly stinger.

"Ugly bastards," Colt muttered as he took aim. He had seen and tolerated plenty of ugly things before. The key point was that nascis were a pain in the ass, reproducing swiftly and chewing up power-transmission cables from the Dar-Zeta plant.

It seemed like a good day to do some cleanup and pest control. And target practice.

He lined up on the male on the left, the ugliest of the three, and wrapped his gloved hand around the familiar worn wood stock of the antique lever action rifle. He grinned so wide that he was just asking for bugs to cover his teeth.

Before he could fire, another shot rang out, an incinerating blast that struck the male nasci body core, splattering gooey meat all over the rugged canyon wall, as if someone had planted a grenade in the middle of an overripe melon. Multi-jointed limbs and the curved arachnid tail flew in all directions like twigs blown in a storm.

"Dammit, Brem!" Colt shouted. "That was my target."

The other two nascis scuttled in a panic, racing for shelter, and Colt frantically tried to line up his next target.

"I have never seen you hesitate before, Colt," said the slender beauty with long dark hair as she zoomed her hover-bike in beside his. She coolly aligned her sniper rifle for another shot.

"I wasn't hesitating. I was enjoying myself." He fired twice, annoyed that he was distracted enough to miss the other male until his second shot. He was careful to kill the thing, not vaporize it. No body, no bounty.

Calmly, Brem lined up the large female which had taken shelter among tumbled boulders. The female nasci was using her clawed legs to tear into the pebbles and dirt, excavating a safe burrow. From his angle, the shot was bad. Unable to hit the creature, Colt shot the boulder instead, splitting it in half.

Brem worked precisely with him. The instant after he fired, she sent a perfect shot that struck the female nasci's head, drilling through the rudimentary brain and killing it instantly. "Teamwork, Colt."

"Teamwork," he agreed. "I like it when we do things together. Lots of things."

He smiled at all the fond memories: he and Brem, he and Jenna, he and Jenna and Brem … With two beautiful women, the combinations seemed endless, so long as all three parties had good imaginations. And they had very good imaginations.

"Let's round up the critters and pack them in the tow-pod," Colt said, wheeling the Razorback about in the air, skimming a hairsbreadth from the sheer canyon walls. As he dove down toward the dead nascis, Brem followed in her more-unwieldy Mamba, and the two came in to land on the canyon floor.

Back at the Crow's Nest, Colt's headquarters, their mechanic TK—for Tommy Kowalski—had repaired and modified the salvaged Mamba craft for Brem, a normally graceful hover-bike now made less aerodynamic with the integrated tow-pod attached to the rear. Today, they needed the tow-pod to pick up all of the nascis they killed.

The engines of the Mamba were a higher-pitched whine than Colt's hover-hog, but Brem had always been more stealthy, needing less vehicular muscle than Colt. She was an assassin, and a very good one, a perfect team member for an outlander and bounty hunter. Colt, with his background as a massively successful cage fighter, mine worker, and security goon for the Velvet Curtain brothel, liked to get in the thick of things, personally.

As they both swung off their bikes and crunched toward the dead, ugly critters, Colt rolled his shoulders, laced his fingers together, and cracked his knuckles. "I think that's seventeen for the day already, and it's not even midmorning."

"Eighteen," Brem corrected as she opened the hatch of the tow-pod to reveal the dead rodent-scorps packed inside.

Colt grimaced at all the dead creatures. "When I became an

Outlander, this wasn't exactly the sort of bounty I had in mind, but it'll bring us some good coin. A bounty is a bounty." He cocked a grin toward Brem. "Besides, it's a lot of fun."

"Yes," Brem said with a completely businesslike expression. "A lot of fun."

The owners of the power plant Dar-Zeta paid fifteen argentums per dead nasci just to clean up the canyons and stop the things from chewing on the power cables.

With his gloved hand, Colt picked up the corpse of the second male nasci, the one he had killed, and lifted up the dead thing, careful to avoid its poisonous spines. Its multiple legs dangled, and thick brownish-red blood dripped from cracks in its cauterized wound. He tossed the nasci into the tow-pod.

"Not much room left in there," he said. "Of course I could use my boot to stomp them down and pack the bodies." He looked at the splotch and smear of the exploded nasci on the canyon wall. "Better knock the score back down to seventeen. This one's not intact enough to qualify for a bounty."

Brem tossed her long dark hair behind her. "All the parts make a whole," she said, quoting some philosophy that Colt didn't care about. "It is all one being."

"It's a bunch of unrecognizable pieces, but go ahead and scrape them together. Maybe Dar-Zeta will give us a partial payment." Colt kicked some of the rock debris away to expose the more neatly killed female. He picked the thing up by the back of its neck and held up the rounded swollen body. "Ecch! I thought I've seen ugly before, but this wins the prize."

The belly of the female was covered with swollen blisters, nodules as long as Colt's thumb, dozens and dozens of them, and they all looked ready to pop. Each one squirmed slightly from something inside. "This one's got some kind of disease." He hoped it wouldn't decrease the value of the carcass.

"Not a disease. Those are its young, all ready to hatch. I think they burst the pustules and tear their way out of the mother's belly, then eat the carcass for their first meal."

"Then it looks like you did mama a favor." Colt made a

disgusted sound as he tossed the female's corpse, squirming pustules and all, inside the tow-pod and closed the hatch. "Looks like we've got a full load. Let's head back to the Crow's Nest. If Jenna's back from her run to Casbah City, maybe she'll want to join us for an afternoon run. We always have a lot more fun together when it's the three of us."

—II—

According to common wisdom on Neb-6, it was unsafe for a woman to travel alone in Casbah City, especially a beautiful woman with a perfect figure who was unafraid to show it, crinkly blond hair, blue eyes, and a face that could launch a starship. But all bets were off if that woman was Jenna Connor, and she happily convinced anyone who thought otherwise.

Such "convincing" was often loud, painful, and exhilarating. In fact, Jenna sometimes looked for opportunities to make her point—unless she had something more important to do.

After two days of buying supplies and taking care of some personal business in Casbah City, she wanted to get back to the Crow's Nest and Colt and Brem. She had only a few bruises from her time in Casbah City, as well as a new stash of weapons and ammo, materials for a range of interesting explosives she could play with, and some food supplies.

Now, leaving the city and racing out into the sprawling dry rock expanse of the badlands, she buzzed along in her refurbished Mamba hover-bike, which TK had rebuilt as a companion to Brem's. Fifty feet above the parched ground, at maximum altitude, always pushing her equipment to the limit, she raced among fantastic rock pinnacles, twisted hoodoos, and pointed stone monoliths. Out in the open badlands there were plenty of sights to see, as well as plenty of places for an ambush.

According to common wisdom on Neb-6, it was unsafe for a woman to fly alone across the badlands. And idiots were always testing that fact.

Two incendiary-tracer rounds rang out from the rock

outcroppings above. Explosions erupted from the rock and sand as her Mamba soared past. Both of the blasts missed, which gave Jenna some inkling as to the caliber of her would-be assassins.

She hunched over the Mamba's controls, dodged in the air, swooped right then banked left, knowing that even idiots could get lucky once in a while. From the opposing rock pinnacles on either side of her passage, two pursuit Jackals dove down like falcons after prey, and Jenna had no intention of becoming prey.

As she raced ahead, the buzzing engines of her Mamba became a jarring whine. She continued to fly evasively.

More potshots streaked past her, but they all missed. These people were amazingly incompetent.

Unless they weren't trying to blast her to pieces.

And that meant they wanted something else.

Out here in the middle of nowhere, Jenna had to imagine she was just a target of opportunity. They couldn't possibly be after her in particular. Could they?

Up ahead she heard the grating, rattling roar of high-powered engines. Two more armed Jackals launched from shadowy alcoves in other rock spires, closing in. It was an ambush, all right.

Crap and double crap! With a third helping of crap on top of that.

Instead of just flying and fleeing, Jenna decided that she would enjoy the encounter more if she opened fire herself. Her Mamba was loaded with two forward-linked light machine guns and one smaller-caliber aft scatter gun, although it was much harder to fire from her backside.

She targeted one of the bastards ahead of her and fired repeatedly, embarrassed that it took her three shots to bring him down.

Her aim went foul because she winced and twitched as a lancing, burning pain went up her left arm. It wasn't from being struck by one of the attacker's weapons. No, this was something else, a hot flash, a lingering and annoying aftereffect from the violet fever that had afflicted her as a child. The majority of violet fever victims died, some horribly, but she had recovered and was now immune. Once every four years or so, the hot flash twinges flared up, causing her great annoyance.

That was the real reason Jenna had volunteered to go into Casbah City alone, hoping to find some quick treatment.

Right now, the timing for the painful twinges couldn't have been worse.

As her third shot struck home, she watched the rider on the Jackal tumble away as his fuel tank exploded from Jenna's rounds finding their mark. One down, three to go. The fireball dissipated into smoke, shrapnel, and body parts. She didn't have to worry about that one anymore.

Now it was Jenna versus three idiots, and she liked those odds.

Unfortunately, she didn't see the last Jackal lying in ambush in a small cave alcove in a rock spire as she whooshed past. The hunter's shot rang out, and either he had better aim or better luck. The incendiary round drilled through the rear engine of her air-bike, knocking it offline and on fire.

At least it didn't explode ... yet, but, uncompensated, the second engine sent her into a wild, smoking corkscrew. Though Jenna wrestled with the controls, her hover-bike took an inevitable nosedive toward the rocks below.

She made a split-second decision and saw she had no choice but to abandon the Mamba. Before she ejected, Jenna triggered her automated distress beacon, a burst signal that would go straight to Colt, wherever he was, as well as to the Crow's Nest headquarters. They would find her, if it wasn't too late.

Or, if it *was* too late, at least Colt and Brem would kick ass and get their money's worth in revenge. Jenna didn't have time to ponder the alternatives right now.

Checking to make sure she had her two Kodiak sidearm pistols as well as her trusty bash-axe, which she had named Dozer, Jenna sprang off the careening, doomed hover-bike and punched the activation pad on the bubblechute harness strapped to her back. Tumbling through the air, she spread her arms and legs in proper position, and the cushioning bubblepack inflated around her. But since she was so close to the ground, the bubblechute did little to slow her plunge. She slammed into the barren desert, rolling and rolling. The layered bubbles burst when they reached their maximum tolerance, slowing her momentum, and Jenna finally bounced to a halt.

Springing back to her feet, ready to fight, she tore away the tattered polymer film, discarding the expended bubblechute. She drew her two Kodiaks and stood ready, spreading her legs in a fighting stance, and faced the four buzzing Jackals that dove down toward her.

She opened fire, one pistol in each hand, but the Jackals were coming in fast. Two of her shots grazed the lead pursuer and sent him into a wild tailspin, but the other three came in hot, blasting the ground around her. The bandits clearly meant to intimidate rather than destroy her.

Jenna was not intimidated easily, and she certainly didn't intend to surrender.

Though she had knocked one out of commission, the other three Jackals were not damaged, and they seemed more intent than ever on taking her. She had hurt her own arm in the fall, which made her aim shaky, and she missed the next round of shots.

A hot flash flare-up made her shudder again as she cursed the charlatan Dr. Bulbo in Casbah City who had sold her the treatment for an exorbitant number of argentums, promising that it would work. "But it might take a few days, maybe even a week for you to feel the full effect." Hell, even untended the flare-ups usually lasted no more than a few days, so Bulbo could have given her breath mints for all she knew.

Breath mints, in fact, might have been more effective, because she could have given them to the scumbags trying to shoot her down right now.

She stood alone, ready to fight. She wished she hadn't lost her entire load of explosives and weapons on the Mamba. She could do without Dr. Bulbo's medicinals right now, but her arm was bleeding from a gash, blood dripping onto the ground.

The lead Jackal she had damaged crunched to the ground not far away. Jenna assumed that one was out of commission, but the other three circled around and came back, shooting, demanding her surrender. Jenna kept firing her Kodiaks, deciding not to shoot at the bike but instead aiming at the chest of the lead pilot. The pistol blasted a hole so wide through his sternum she could see sky through on the other side. He tumbled off headfirst and made a small crater in the ground as his bike crashed behind him.

The last Jackals came toward her, and a net dangled between them. Jenna didn't like the looks of that at all. She stood her ground, raised the Kodiak in her right hand, because her left arm was bleeding too much to keep her aim steady. She shot and scorched the underside of the right-hand Jackal, making him swerve, which tore the net.

Jenna had bought herself another couple of seconds. She tracked the flight of the second Jackal, steadying her aim. "Got you, bastard."

Then she heard a crunch of rocks behind her, a heavy footfall, and she whirled to see the bandit-pilot who had survived the nearby hard landing of his Jackal. When she turned, he charged forward, holding up a club. She swung the Kodiak, fired off a shot, but too soon. The projectile missed him.

His club didn't miss her head, though.

She saw stars, and then the black of night inside her head, but she didn't see the dusty ground as she collapsed face-first onto it.

—III—

With Brem following the Razorback, Colt headed home, glad for the tow-pod full of dead rodent-scorps. They were worth fifteen argentums each. Once back at the Crow's Nest, Colt looked forward to spending the rest of the day and night, and probably the next day, satisfying himself with good food, good booze, and good sex. That was the point of it all, and he liked to have realistic goals. He had been with Brem and Jenna long enough to know the ladies had similar goals.

An urgent distress signal spoiled those plans. Instantly alert, Colt looked at his screen. Brem raced her Mamba up close to his hover-hog. "It's Jenna!" she shouted above the roar of the engines and whistle of the wind.

Colt was already adjusting course, swinging around. Brem followed him, as if their two hover-bikes were welded together. "We'll go get her," he said. "Full speed. Every second might count."

They both knew Jenna would never cry wolf. If she had triggered a mayday signal, it had to be a Class-friggin'-A distress. He didn't want to hold back with the Razorback's bigger and more powerful engines, roaring on ahead of Brem. But she did something to her engine output, hunched low over the controls so that her long black hair streamed behind her like an inky comet's tail. She streaked forward, nudging past him, and Colt cranked the throttle as they circled around the spiral canyons, gaining maximum altitude so they could streak forward unimpeded, like avenging angels, toward the coordinates where Jenna's distress signal had ominously fallen silent.

Though the distance was great, they had arrived at the crash site within an hour. Unfortunately, Colt knew it was an hour too late. He had convinced himself that it wasn't something as simple as engine trouble, and Jenna wouldn't go down without a fight. He seated his goggles over his eyes as he and Brem split up, circling in a search pattern. They found soot marks and a crash site, but the debris belonged to a Jackal of unknown origin, not Jenna's Mamba. The wreck of her hover-bike was a little farther along, and its explosion had left a blackened divot in the desolate ground.

"She would have been hauling explosives," Brem pointed out, "to fill up our stockpile."

Colt nodded. Plenty of people would have seen that flash. He hoped Jenna hadn't been blown to hamburger in the air. But then he saw the tatters of a polymer bubblechute, and he brought the hover-hog down toward the ground. Below, near the wreck, he spotted figures moving, humanoid shapes wearing rudimentary garments, dusty tan to blend in with the badlands. With a flash of anger, Colt wondered if these were the bandits who had shot down Jenna.

Hearing the approaching air-bikes, the figures looked up, but they didn't scatter in a guilty panic. Instead, they just looked up and stared at Colt and his powerful Razorback.

He recognized their sleek alien features with large eyes, smooth faces covered with tribal markings. The males had prominent head dressings around their elongated heads and colorful totems draped around their necks. The females had glossy, lovely hair, perfect feminine curves, and piercing eyes.

These were Creed, the native inhabitants of Neb-6, who lived in an uneasy peace with the human settlers on the world; the sweeping colonization that had occurred centuries ago to mine Neb-6 of hallekite, the valuable mineral that had made the Babylon jump-gate technology—and thus interstellar travel and colonization—possible. But that was before the Great Darkness that had cut off Neb-6 and left all the survivors here to scramble and rebuild the remnants of civilization from the scraps and leftover trash. Only the strong survived, and the native Creed were strong.

But so was Colt, because he had been raised among the humanoid alien race after being orphaned as a baby. He would fight them if he needed to. He would force them to tell what had happened to Jenna.

But in his heart, he doubted the Creed had caused this. In his experience, heinous ambushes and treachery usually meant *humans* were involved.

He left the Razorback parked and hovering on the ground. Brem stood her Mamba next to his and stepped off, carrying her Osprey sniper pistol. Colt took his massive handgun, named Hammerhead, and also slid Tusk, his wide-bladed combat knife, into its sheath at its side, just in case he needed close-in bloody work.

The five Creed—two males and three females, all hunters— stood together around a site where a battle had obviously taken place. Nearby, a dead man lay sprawled on the ground wearing a drab, blood-soaked jumpsuit with a large hole blasted all the way through his torso.

The Creed looked wary, but not combative. They were all tall, taller than Colt, even the females. They had a human appearance, but exaggerated, with large eyes, and flat noses, rich silver-gray hair, and crimson skin. The bright tribal pattern on one of the males was much more prominent than the others.

Colt the Outlander spoke to the foremost male in a guttural but nonthreatening voice. As a young boy, Colt had grown accustomed to their language, their culture, and their fighting style. He was ready to fight now, and all five of these Creed would know it. They could smell it in his sweat and in his anger.

"Where is my companion?" he demanded. "Did you shoot her down? Did you see what happened?"

"Neither," grunted the male. The female hunters also shook their heads. They held their long spears at an angle, flexing their bodies like supple willows. The other male hunter sniffed along the rocky ground, searching. "She came down here, though."

The other male signaled for attention from twenty meters away. Colt and Brem sprinted over to where the Creed gathered around crimson splashes on the ground. "Human blood," said the Creed leader. He bent down and inhaled a deep sniff. "*Female blood.*"

Colt looked at the sprawled uniformed man dead on the ground. "So it's not his blood? We know that she was injured somehow—if not killed?"

"It is not that man's blood," said the Creed male. "There is another smashed Jackal farther down the canyon. We claim salvage rights."

"I claim my friend," Colt said. "You can have the damn wreckage. I just want to know where to look for her. Where did they take her?"

The huntress Creed bent down and rolled the dead man's body over with her large hands. The bandit's face was slack and scarred. One of his eyes had been gouged out, now fused in a long-healed scar.

"He must have been a terrible shot," Brem said.

Colt admired the clean hole right through the center of the dead man's chest. "We know Jenna's a good shot."

The male Creed leader squared his shoulders, and his headdress ruffled in the warm dusty breeze. These were nomadic hunters and scavengers out on the badlands. Colt had never considered the Creed to be a particular threat, though he knew the humanoid aliens were out for their own interests.

The male's flat nose flared as he sniffed, inhaling deep of the air. "I believe they took her that direction." He gestured vaguely to the southwest. "Approximately seventy kilometers in a ring of mountains, an old mining outpost was overthrown and turned into a fortress. Peridot Basin. They might have gone there."

Colt was surprised. He slid his goggles up on his forehead and scratched at the tattoos along the side of his face, calling attention to the markings the Creed had placed there. Such markings forged a bond between Colt and the natives, even if it also drove a wedge between him and the rest of civilized humanity.

"Peridot Basin? It's been over an hour, and you can tell all that just from smelling the fume trail?" He knew the Creed were amazingly gifted in wilderness survival skills, but this went beyond any of his imagining.

"No," said the male hunter, then kicked with his right foot at the jumpsuited chest of the dead man on the ground. "I learned it from this. These markings are from Peridot Basin. The slaves overthrew it, killed the company owners, and have turned it into an unbreachable fortress. That's where they've taken her."

Colt nodded his gratitude. "Take all the damn salvage you can find. We're going to go get our friend." He turned toward Brem. "Terms like 'unbreachable' just bring out the competitive spirit in me."

—IV—

Jenna awoke with a splitting headache, surrounded by beautiful naked women. And somehow, she sensed that was not a good sign.

She turned from side to side on the hard bed, feeling a lightning bolt of pain through her brain. The bandit thug must have split her skull, and now she felt thick cloth wrapped around her head, some rudimentary bandaging. An IV tube left a pricking sensation in her left arm, and she saw red filling the tube, a thrumming pump, a polymer bag swollen with blood. At first glance, Jenna couldn't tell which direction the blood was flowing, into her or into the bag. This seemed to be some kind of bizarre brothel/medical center.

She realized she was scantly clothed in strips of translucent cloths, just barely covering her private parts, and lying on a medical cot, strapped down. Her body had been cleaned ... but not bathed and perfumed as if to impress some male customer. It felt more like she was being prepped for surgery.

She groaned, and two of the stern-looking, perfectly formed women came closer. They were clad only in filmy reddish garments that made them appear functionally naked, and their breasts, hips, thighs were so exquisitely shaped that they had to be artificially enhanced. While she stared, Jenna identified the fine white scars of the bodily alterations.

"The bitch is awake," said a redhead at the head of her bed. "Call Madame Qoo."

A raspy female voice answered from the corridor. "I'm coming! Make sure she's strapped down. Lordex went through a lot of trouble to get this one."

"Lordex went through a lot of trouble for all of us," said the redhead with a proud sniff. "That's why we're grateful and we serve him."

The woman who entered from the corridor exuded power as well as perfection. "That one won't show any gratitude, though," the woman said. Madame Qoo? She, too, wore a sheer filmy garment, except hers was gold in color. "We won't bother to recondition her. Lordex has very specific plans for her body and all its parts."

"Good," Jenna said, squirming but restrained by the straps on her wrists, "because I'm making plans for him, whoever he is. And I'll deal with you, too."

As Madame Qoo came closer to leer at her, Jenna got a better look ... and wished she hadn't. Though the woman's body was achingly lovely, the beauty ended at her neck. Madame Qoo's face would have made a dorrox spit.

"Are you running some kind of a brothel, a white slavery operation?" Jenna sneered. "You can try to recruit me, but I guarantee you won't get many repeat customers asking for my services. They'll all have their throats slit."

The redhead slapped her as she lay bound on the medical table. "Be grateful for the opportunities Lordex and Madame Qoo give us."

"I've had opportunities," Jenna said, still struggling. "This isn't one of them. And you can have better opportunities as well." She tried to see all the other artificially gorgeous women in the medical center.

"We've had far worse ones, too." The redhead straightened, lovingly ran her palms over her breasts, her waist, her flat abdomen. "I used to be a mine rat, as were all of us. Dirty, stuck underground, unable to breathe. And if the cave-ins didn't kill me, the fumes would. The mining company didn't care, so long as we brought up enough ore. None of us here at Peridot Basin had a life expectancy greater than twenty ... until Lordex freed us all, and Madame Qoo gave us a new opportunity."

"Sounds like they deserve a Humanitarian of the Year award," Jenna said. "I would applaud, but my hands are tied." She jerked her arms, trying to free her wrists. Pain throbbed through her skull as she thrashed. The redhead slapped her again. The woman seemed to enjoy it; Jenna did not.

Madame Qoo came forward. "Enough of that." She fiddled

with the IV cannula in Jenna's arm and removed it. "That's another bloodbag filled. We'll drain a third one out of her later. She can lose a lot more and still hold onto life. Get her ready. We'll take her to Lordex. He wanted to wait until she was fully awake."

Jenna snarled, "I look forward to meeting him. Keep my clothes off, so I can show him that there's no need to perform surgery on me, unlike the rest of you. My body's pretty damn perfect as it is."

Madame Qoo's squarish, bovine face sported a frown. "Under other circumstances you would be correct, but we don't want your body—at least not in the sexual sense. Lordex has other uses for it, and he will take great pleasure from you, regardless."

"I intend to pleasure Colt with my body. Lordex can go to hell."

Madame Qoo stood by as the beautiful female attendants worked around Jenna, preparing her, strapping her down tighter and folding the bed so they could wheel it out of the medical chamber. "He wants revenge."

"Boring," Jenna said, but she was also perplexed. She frowned. "I've pissed off plenty of people, I don't deny that. I'm a demolitions expert, and there's often collateral damage, sometimes accidental. But I don't recall ever having had dealings with Lordex before. What did I do to him?"

Madame Qoo gave her a withering glare. "You survived the violet fever."

—V—

After racing overland throughout the afternoon, keeping low so as to avoid being seen by spotters, Colt and Brem hammered southwest at breakneck speeds toward a line of jagged, black volcanic outcroppings. Ahead, they saw the stark venting towers, fences, holding tanks, and processing stacks of what had once been an enormous mining and smelting operation. From a distance, as the Razorback and the Mamba flew into the deepening velvet of sunset, they could make out additional fortifications and blockades around towering gates.

Colt throttled down the roar of his engines, and the Mamba's whine also died down to a whisper as they both cruised in at a low idle. The two hover-bikes followed the line of mountains, muffled by shadows to remain out of sight of any Peridot Basin sentries.

Since Jenna had been alone out in the badlands when she was abducted, the bandits would not likely expect pursuit, certainly not this soon. But they had underestimated Colt's determination.

Approaching the Peridot Basin complex, Colt could not help but admire the immensity of the structure, the gigantic company facility which had now been converted into a fortress. He had heard of the Peridot facility a long time ago when he was a young man working down in the mines for a rival company. During his years of cage fighting, he'd learned that Peridot Basin had fallen offline, disappeared. Apparently, the company owners were even more ruthless than most operators, and the slaves had risen up. Now the inmates ruled the asylum. Colt had no idea what the Peridot workers had been doing all these years, nor did he care. None of that had been his business ... until they made it his business by kidnapping Jenna.

Idling in the sheltering camouflage of rocks, Brem swung off her Mamba and stared toward the imposing fortress. She used her own far-seeing lens, while Colt adjusted his goggles, zooming in to study the imposing gate. He and Brem both considered in silence, assessing the target, the defenses.

"Jenna's on the other side of that," Colt said. "We have to go get her."

Brem replied, "How do you propose we do it? Just go through the front door?"

Colt shrugged. "That's the most straightforward way, and I've always been a direct sort of person."

Brem nodded. "This bounty will be a lot more difficult than bagging a few nasci out in the wild."

"Damn right, but I've never shied away from a tough score." Colt looked at Brem. "And neither have you."

As full night fell, jagged shadows stretched out from the volcanic peaks to enclose the mining operation. Colt and Brem made their plan, which basically amounted to blasting their way in, finding Jenna, and fighting their way out. It seemed a good enough solution, so long as Colt didn't think about it too much.

Brem said, "We don't know what size of an operation they have in there. Is it a full-fledged slaving headquarters? Do they constantly kidnap loners and bring them back here? Or was Jenna singled out?"

"We can make polite formal inquiries once we get inside," Colt said. He went back to the weapons bin in the rear saddlebag of the Razorback. He unlatched the bin, rummaged among the small and powerful machinery of death, and withdrew his favorite grenade. Jenna had told him to save it for a special occasion.

Jenna was a savant when it came to explosives. She had built or modified all the weapons Colt used in his bounty hunter work. Although each package contained incalculable amounts of death, precisely metered out according to Colt's needs, she was astonishingly careful with her work, even obsessively so. While she'd always had a penchant for destructive chemistry, she hadn't always been so lucky, nor so meticulous. In an accidental explosion, Jenna had killed both of her parents, rendering herself an orphan when she was fifteen.

But Jenna provided Colt with all of his weapons now, and she had instructed him in their use. She taught him about each grenade, telling him its yield and its purpose. He had an affinity for them, even an affection. Jenna had made Colt see that each grenade was part of the team, part of the family.

In this case, to rescue Jenna, it seemed appropriate to use his favorite one.

As full night fell and all of the bright station lights and security illumination blazed brightly, Colt and Brem eased their idling hover-bikes toward the main barricaded gates. Peridot

Basin had been closed down for the night like some kind of medieval fortress from an old Earth fairy tale.

Tonight, Colt would tear down that fairy tale.

Moving with silent engines and only the levitation packs activated, he and Brem crept closer to the gate, sounding no alarms. They waited, watching. The isolated fortress had few sentries, no obvious movement, but they heard noises from inside. Crowds of people lived within Peridot Basin, but Colt couldn't guess how many. Dozens, hundreds ... thousands? He hoped he didn't have to kill them all—but they *had* taken Jenna, after all, and he had his priorities.

Beside him, Brem was grim and philosophical, ready to do whatever was necessary. She nodded to him, and he looked back at the tall, imposing gate. No sense waiting any longer.

Jenna could hold her own in a fair fight, but this was by no means a fair fight, and he couldn't guess what might be happening to her in there right now.

As he stared at the supposedly impenetrable barrier, he held onto the hand grenade, adjusted its yield, and set the timer. "It's showtime, my little friend. Fly. Do your stuff." He activated the motivator, then released the grenade.

It shot forward, spinning through the air with a building hum as the light brightened. Colt did a silent countdown as Brem watched intently.

"Knock, knock," Colt said.

The grenade struck the towering gates and detonated. The rippling blast of concentric, supercharged shock waves destroyed the barricade as if it were a dry cracker, hurling the center inward while the sides crumbled and collapsed in a roar, opening a portal into the brightly lit industrial fortress.

Echoes from the explosion rang out around the jagged volcanic peaks like rumbles from a blackstorm.

"I'm usually more for the stealthy approach," Brem said. "But have it your way, Colt."

Alarms and sirens began to howl inside Peridot Basin.

He grinned as the flames died down, proud of the little

grenade and its final flash of glory. "We've announced ourselves. No sense being fashionably late."

He roared the Razorback's engines to full power and throttled forward, while Brem raced the Mamba beside him. The smaller hover-bike still looked unwieldy with the tow-pod levitating behind her, but she kept up with his speed. Her long black hair flowed behind her.

Inside the mining company complex, people rushed forward in a frantic, disorganized response. Some of them were burly guards wearing repurposed company jumpsuit uniforms, just like the victim they had found sprawled near where Jenna had been abducted. Many of the others were beautiful women—far too many beautiful women, all of whom looked far too perfect to be natural. And they were certainly not dressed for mining work.

Brem said, "If they have all those gorgeous ladies, why did they need Jenna?"

Colt raced forward on the Razorback. "Some people just can't have enough—which is not necessarily a bad thing, if the feeling is mutual." He flashed a glance at Brem's beautiful face, thought of Jenna, then he scowled. "But if it's slavery, then I don't care how much blood we have to spill until we get her back."

Colt readied the hover-hog's front weapons. The linked Gatling guns and heavy machine guns armed. As he roared forward through the blasted gates, the blatting ionized exhaust sounded like gunfire as it echoed around the compound.

He and Brem pulled into the middle of the surging crowds. When he saw he had their attention, Colt said in a light, conversational tone, "We're looking for a friend of ours."

He opened the Razorback's front saddlebag, reached in, and grabbed the object there, digging his fingers into the clumpy strands of greasy hair. He pulled out the severed head from the corpse they had found at the crash site and held it high. The man's face was slack and distorted in death, but his scarred-over eye socket was quite distinctive. "She was last seen with this guy. Anybody recognize him?"

—VI—

Five of the perfect biologically resculpted women "escorted" Jenna out of the infirmary to her meeting with Lordex. "Escort" seemed an appropriate, if ironic term, since that was exactly the service these women had been designed to provide. Jenna was still barely clothed and bound by her wrists, apparently helpless ... which she supposed made her captors relax, and therefore had made them underestimate her.

Granted, she would have felt more badass if she had her Kodiak sidearms or her bash-axe Dozer, but she herself was enough of a weapon. If she got a chance, she would make them see that. Already, using a ragged fingernail, she had begun to fray one of the wrist cuffs, working silently and quietly, maintaining a carefully neutral expression. Her fingertip was bloody, but she kept sawing, and she felt the cuff begin to part. It was only a matter of time.

They made their way to the upper observation headquarters tower in the middle of the barricaded complex, a high central tower once used by the mining company, where their administrators would lord it over the enslaved worker rats. Lordex had turned that headquarters into his palace.

As they approached the upper deck of the central headquarters tower, the beautiful escort women were smiling and chattering.

"Lordex saved us. We would do anything for him," said the redhead who had slapped Jenna twice.

She struggled against her bonds. "Yes, I can imagine he's a sweetheart."

The other woman sneered. "What you can't imagine is how awful our lives were down in the mines. Now, after years of surgery, hormones, and implants, we've all become beautiful, ready to go out into the world. Thanks to Madame Qoo, every one of our women is well-trained and highly desirable."

Walking beside the folded medical chair where Jenna was bound, Madame Qoo said, "We've sold a steady stream of them to the brothels in Casbah City, Bootleg Springs, Jericho Flats, even a handful of smaller Dodger towns, if they can afford it."

"So you're slaves," Jenna said. "You're sold as whores."

"The argentums we get from our women finances the rest of the surgeries and builds our fortress here. It's a price every single one of them is willing to pay."

The redhead narrowed her green eyes. "From the tone of your voice, bitch, it sounds like you think that's an awful punishment. Lordex rescued us from the mines. Our gratitude knows no bounds."

"And I've helped arrange it," said Madame Qoo. "I negotiate the best price. And Peridot women are getting a well-deserved reputation all across Neb-6."

"Never heard of them," said Jenna. "And don't think I'm not familiar with brothels. We have plenty of business connections." She struggled against the bonds again, keeping up the pretense. "I will not be a whore—not for Lordex, not for anyone."

"That's not what we have in mind for you, dear," said Madame Qoo. She carefully pulled a silken, translucent hood over her head, adjusting it to hide her ox-ugly face. Jenna wondered if the madam was ashamed of her looks—deservedly so. The other woman leaned closer and explained, "Lordex made the rest of my body perfect, but he doesn't wish to gaze upon my ugliness."

"Why didn't he just finish the job?" Jenna said. "Or was it too much of a challenge?"

"Nothing is too much of a challenge for his biological sculptors," she said. "But he wanted me to maintain my humility. The perfect body is a promise of what I could become, while my original face is a reminder of where I *was*."

"How philosophical," Jenna said. "You should talk to my friend Brem."

The escorts carried her into the high-ceilinged headquarters deck of the tower, a cavernous chamber where many other burly workers and guards were dressed in the old uniforms of Peridot Basin, as well as numerous well-endowed women who had been physically enhanced to become perfect prostitutes. Whether slaving away in a mine or indentured to a brothel, Jenna thought either one sounded like a deep, dark hole.

The high HQ deck was like a prison guard tower, with broad observation windows looking out across a wide fenced complex garishly lit after nightfall. Peridot Basin inhabitants moved about in the main area inside the gates, performing incomprehensible tasks.

The most shocking sight was Lordex himself.

The leader of Peridot Basin sat on a raised dais. His body was enclosed in a chair that had been altered and folded to hold his distorted form. Lordex's wide nose looked like an onion that had been stomped flat, and the skin of his face was a landscape of sores, warts, and lesions. His eyes were scabbed over and swollen with scar tissue. Bristly hair sprouted in random patches, only a few of which were on top of his head. His lip had been pulled down and hung open, creating a perfect trough for saliva to ooze out.

His body looked equally disgusting and distorted. His spine was twisted, as if someone had tried to fold him into a very small container. A translucent sack of blood, half-empty, dangled from a metal tree-holder at his side, and the tube ran into his arm. Jenna guessed it must be her own blood.

With one glance at Lordex as they brought her chair up to the dais, she turned to look at the hooded Madame Qoo. "And he thinks *you're* ugly?"

At the right side of his modified chair, Lordex reached down with a gnarled arm into a small bin, curling his hooked fingers to pull out one of Jenna's Kodiak sidearms, holding it up for inspection. "Nice weapons. It'll be good to add them to my collection." He dropped the Kodiak, then rummaged around before pulling out her bash-axe. "This looks interesting ... and threatening. Whatever it is."

If his twisted grimace was meant to be a smile, he didn't do it very well. "It's called Dozer," she said. "I'd like to introduce you personally sometime."

He laughed, and behind her fabric hood, Madame Qoo laughed as well.

Lordex squirmed in his seat as he leered at her, then he winced. His skin flushed, and he snarled and swatted at his own face and arms, as if to drive away a swarm of stinging gnats. The distorted man breathed heavily, slurped his own saliva through his twisted lip, then finally turned back, glaring at Jenna. "Your blood is helping."

She tugged against her frayed wrist strap. "What the hell do you want my blood for? Does it taste good?"

"Your blood is special, just like you are special, Jenna Connor."

"Men tell me that all the time." She kept working with her fingernail, sensing that the frayed cuff was almost severed, but she didn't let anyone notice. "You're surrounded by beautiful women, even if you had to make them yourself. What do you need another one for?"

"Not for that," Lordex said. "You're special because of the violet fever. You survived."

"Yeah," she said defiantly, "and I still get hot flashes. What is it to you?"

He slurped spit. "I survived as well, but I was not as lucky as you. After the epidemic years ago, a few were lucky, like yourself —and the lucky ones are damned hard to find now. I've looked all across Neb-6, and I was glad when Dr. Bulbo sent us your details."

"What do you need survivors for?"

"Because I'm a survivor, too, but look what the disease did to me!" He raised his voice to a roar. "There are a dozen more just like me. You got off easy, Jenna, but now it's going to get a lot harder for you." He chuckled, which caused an extra burst of drool to come out of his twisted lip. "*Your* blood has the antibodies I need to keep the resident clusters of the virus under control. And I am going to milk you dry until I get a large stockpile for my personal use. But that's just a stopgap measure. I'm going to have your liver, which will turn my system around. Maybe I'll take your heart too, depending on what the other bids are."

"What other bids?" Jenna said.

"The other victims like me. Each one will pay a fortune to just have a piece of you, Jenna. And, oh my, we're going to cut you up into lots of little pieces. A lung here, a kidney there ... a pancreas, for someone on a budget. Maybe your eyes." He shrugged. "Who knows? We haven't even begun to advertise yet."

Nearby, Madame Qoo nodded under her concealing hood.

"Each one of your organs carries some of the antibodies, and the other survivors believe they might be cured if they have them." He shrugged, and his entire twisted spine rolled. "Doesn't make much medical sense, but they'll pay, and they'll hope."

He winced again, and his face flushed. He swatted at his skin. "Damn, it burns! The fever is still trying to get its revenge. But once your liver starts producing the antibodies I need, it'll bring the violet fever under control."

"Dream on," Jenna said. "I still get the hot flashes, too." She didn't admit that it was only once every couple of years.

"Hope springs eternal," Lordex said. "And when you look like me, you have to be an optimist."

Outside, at the front gate of the compound, a sudden explosion cracked through the air.

From the observation windows of the headquarters tower, Jenna could see a bright flash as the massive barricade blasted inward. Seeing the shape of the bright shockwave and hearing the rumble, Jenna smiled. She knew exactly which type of explosive that had been, exactly which grenade.

"That'll be Colt," she said. "And you're about to be very sorry."

Her ragged fingernail finally cut through the last threads and broke one of her arm cuffs.

—VII—

The crowd of angry people rallied in the compound as Colt and Brem raced in, but they were outmatched. Peridot Basin had resources and weapons, but the two were ready to use the destruction they brought with them.

Holding up the severed head, Colt only had to repeat his

inquiry twice, punctuated with a few gunshots and two smoking bodies. Brem took out her sniper pistol and blasted another guard, who brought his own sidearm to bear.

"Now, I asked politely," Colt said again from his rumbling hover-hog. "Tell me where my friend is."

Soon enough, a squealing guard pointed to the high headquarters tower and its broad bank of windows. The people inside must have already seen the blast and the intruders, so Colt knew they had to move. He nodded to Brem. "That's where we have to go. Let's move."

Tossing her long dark hair behind her shoulders, Brem fired up the Mamba's engines and angled toward a long rampart that snaked its way upward, connecting to the tower. Colt followed with the roaring Razorback.

As an afterthought, he let the people down below keep the severed head.

They rose like projectiles to the high citadel, from which Lordex observed the entire compound like some wizard in an ancient fortified tower. Some of the guards below opened fire at them, but the shots went astray. Several impacts even *spanged* off the outer reinforced walls of the headquarters tower.

Hunched over their bikes, Colt and Brem hurtled straight for the wide bank of windows, glowing brightly from lights and people inside. He hoped Jenna would be in there. And probably a bunch of scumbags who needed to learn a lesson.

"Do you suppose it's enhanced glass? Blast resistant?" Brem asked. "We could splat like a bug on a windscreen."

Colt opened fire with all of his front mounted guns, blasting the transparent barrier, which shuddered then shattered, crumbling away in small shards and lumps of liquefied crystal.

"Nope," he said. "I think we'll get through just fine. Full throttle!"

Side by side, they roared through the opening Colt had just created, heading into the fresh chaos.

Colt didn't like to overthink what he was about to do. His eyes drank in the situation: armed guards dressed in Peridot uniforms, a surprising number of beautiful and scantily clad women, the dais on which sat a hideous lump of a man—and Jenna, dressed in translucent red strips of cloths, strapped onto a folded mobile medical bed.

Colt liked to see Jenna semi-nude, of course, but under different circumstances, and all the attractive women distracted him now. But seeing Jenna gave him a clear goal, and he knew exactly what he had to do. He could always bother finding out the answers later. If ever.

With the explosions outside and the alarms, Lordex and his guards all turned toward the main viewing window, reacting to Colt and Brem's splashy arrival at the towering gate.

Jenna used that second of distraction to rip her arm free, tearing the last threads in the restraint and reaching over with her bloodied hand to yank off the other cuff, freeing both hands. *Idiots*, she thought, and glad for it.

Then the glass windows exploded inward. Searing blasts of energy weapons came from the Razorback as well as Brem's Mamba. The two hover-bikes roared into the cavernous chamber.

Her feet were only loosely bound. The female escorts and Madame Qoo had been very sloppy. Within seconds, she was free.

Lordex gurgled toward Colt, "Stop them! Guards! Open fire!"

Uniformed men inside the upper headquarters deck began shooting.

Jenna sprang from the restraining bed and leaped for Lordex himself in his twisted throne chair. She yanked the bloodbag from its metal tree-stand and threw herself upon the twisted, sadistic leader of these people. She grabbed the tube filled with her blood and whipped it around Lordex's neck like a garrote, astonishing him. He had been so focused on Colt's attack, he had expected nothing from his naked imprisoned woman.

She cinched the tube tight around his throat and yanked hard, cutting off his windpipe. He thrashed, flailed, and clawed at the tube, but his body wouldn't work right. Furious, she pulled tighter, trying to strangle him, but decided that would take too long.

Still cutting off his air, Jenna reached into the bin beside his modified chair, blindly rummaging until her fingers closed around the handle of her bash-axe. "There you are, Dozer." She pulled it free and raised it over her head. "I'd like you to meet someone."

In a single powerful arc, she swept it down to hammer all of the exotic weapon's force upon the center of Lordex's chest. His sternum was the bullseye. The impact reverberated like an earthquake throughout his entire body with such force that blood squirted out of both ears in small red jets.

When Jenna felt the impact through her arm, it was one of the best sensations she had experienced.

Hunched over the hover-hog, Colt blasted with his quad forward guns, mowing down the armed guards who were shooting haphazardly at him. He rocked the Razorback to the right and left, dodging the inept blasts.

But when he saw several taking aim at Brem, he got really pissed. He found new targets, and three of those shooters transformed into red steam and splatters of meat.

In the mayhem, he did his best to avoid harming the incongruously beautiful women. But when several of them, including a furious-looking redhead, screamed curses at him and snatched up weapons from the fallen guards to take potshots at Colt, he changed his opinion to considering them acceptable losses, or just plain enemy sympathizers.

The only beautiful woman he focused on right now was Jenna.

She had already gotten herself free—no surprise there—and he saw her hammer the twisted monstrosity of a man who had apparently taken her hostage. He dropped the Razorback toward the dais, landing next to her.

For her own part, Brem circled the Mamba inside the high-ceilinged headquarters chamber, making tight turns. She deployed an innovative strategy against the mob of Peridot inhabitants. As angry crowds surged toward the dais where Jenna had just killed their leader, Brem flew above them and cracked open the tow-pod behind her.

Spiny, venomous nasci tumbled out, covered with gore, dead yet still deadly. A rain of rodent-scorps dropped among the crowd, causing a panic. The poison-tipped spines pierced the Peridot fighters, and hooked stinger-tails also caused damage.

Worst of all, though, the egg pustules on the belly of the pregnant female nasci had burst and hatched while they were stowed in the tow-pod. The hungry little creatures had devoured part of their mother's carcass, and now the smaller but frenetic rodent-scorps swarmed everywhere. The things obviously decided they liked fresh human meat better than their dead mother. People ran screaming and shrieking.

Landed at the dais, Colt swung himself off the Razorback and pulled out his massive Hammerhead gun. Jenna flung her arms around his waist and pressed herself against him. She cast a disgusted glance at the hideous man who lay slumped and broken in his chair. "He's dead, Colt. I already took care of it."

But Colt knew this man had abducted Jenna—and no one got away with that so lightly. He aimed the Hammerhead at Lordex and blew two large smoking holes through his chest. "Just to make sure."

Jenna gave a brisk nod, drawing satisfaction.

Madame Qoo ran about shrieking, flailing her arms, and firing one of the not-so-lucky guards' machine pistols in the air. Her head and face were still enveloped with the mesh hood, which was now covered with four of the nasci hatchlings, each as large as an outstretched hand. With sharp articulated legs, the ravenous creatures poked the fabric, and they bit downward, chewing at Madame Qoo's hair and face.

"Get them off! *Get them off!* GET THEM OFF!" she screamed. Running blindly, still squeezing off bursts of gunfire into the dais, she staggered, nearly collapsing into Colt and Jenna.

He whipped out Tusk and swept sideways with the long killing knife, using all his strength. The sharp blade bit into her neck and sliced cleanly through her skin, her jugular, her spine, and out the other side. Madame Qoo's covered head tumbled off and rolled down the dais steps, scattering the nasci hatchlings. Her beautiful body collapsed like a wet rag.

"There, I got them off," Colt said.

The guards and women had run screaming from the headquarters tower. Others tried to stand their ground and fight, but more shots from Brem's forward weapons array either scared them off or killed them. During a lull in the confusion, Brem swung around, stabilized her Mamba in the air, and dropped down to the dais next to Colt and Jenna. "Are you all right?" she asked her partner.

Jenna nodded, then she winced as another hot flash rushed through her, but it was smaller than the previous ones. This outburst was dying away, with or without treatment from the traitorous Dr. Bulbo from Casbah City. "I'd be a lot more comfortable at home, though." She looked at Colt. "I lost my Mamba. Give me a ride?"

Stepping closer, Brem scowled down at the bloody corpse of Lordex. "Is this the man responsible?"

Jenna nodded. "Yeah. He's an asshole. *Was* an asshole. We killed him."

Brem pulled out her Osprey sniper pistol and fired twice, blowing another two holes in the man's torso. "Just to make sure," she said.

Colt fired up the Razorback and climbed aboard. "Let's get out of here." He positioned his goggles over his eyes and nodded toward the blasted bank of windows. "Out the way we came."

After retrieving her Kodiaks from the bin beside Lordex's chair, Jenna swung up behind Colt. "I still don't have my clothes."

"I'll take you shopping in Casbah City later."

"I'll get chilly during the ride."

He looked over his shoulder as she wrapped her arms around his waist. "Just press close. That'll keep you warm."

And she did.

The hover-hog and the Mamba raced out through the smashed window and into the night.

—VIII—

Back at the Crow's Nest, Colt couldn't get his clothes off fast enough, although ostensibly his first priority was just a hot shower. Good thing Brem and Jenna both needed showers, too, so it became a relaxing and cooperative experience all around, with much steam, soap, and laughter.

Once they were clean, relaxed, and exhausted again in an entirely more pleasurable way, Colt set about pursuing his other important priorities with the two women, namely good booze and good food. After their adventure, Colt considered it a good opportunity to dust off one of his best bottles of Elcar brandy. Though Jenna had lost her supplies from the last run, they still had plenty of gourmet supplies they could easily serve among themselves.

Preoccupied, their engineer TK hurried into Colt's private chambers, his hair mussed, biting his lower lip. "I think I've got options to replace Jenna's Mamba. The salvage yard is full of components we've collected over the past year, and I can put a new one together. It'll even be souped-up—" He paused and stared at the three of them lounging on the broad bed among the rumpled sheets. Colt and the two beautiful, dangerously competent women all looked up at him.

"Can it wait, TK?" Colt asked.

"Yes ... yes, of course. I'll adjust the specs and bring you a more formal proposal tomorrow."

"Tomorrow," Colt said, "but don't wake us up too early."

After TK had left, Colt equally shared the last of the brandy, and they all savored the warm, sweet burn.

"All those nasci carcasses would have brought in enough aggregate bounty to pay for a month of supplies, Colt," Brem said.

He sighed, but didn't let himself be bothered by it. "Whether or not we got paid for the work, at least we eradicated a bunch of those pests. Power station Dar-Zeta will be happy at least."

Jenna climbed next to Colt and snuggled close. "Sorry you lost that bounty on my account, Colt."

He shrugged. "Aww, it was mostly target practice, anyway."

Brem slid close on the other side. "It was quite exciting in its own right."

"There must be some way I can make it up to you." Jenna leaned over and kissed him. He could taste the brandy on her lips.

"I'm sure we can all think of something," Colt said.

Percy Bysshe Shelley's poem "Ozymandias" always resonated with me, a great and powerful tyrant from an ancient empire, whose fame and power are lost in history with nothing left but crumbling ruins out in the desert.

In a much more modern inspiration, the Dream Theater song "Lost —Not Forgotten" from their album A Dramatic Turn of Events *is also about a horrific tyrant who may not deserve the fame he claims. I had this story on my mental back burner for several years until I wrote it as a rich and colorful sword-and-sorcery story.*

THE REIGN TO COME

Emperor Shaksus the Incomparable was dead, throwing his entire empire into turmoil. He had reigned for forty years, but his death was unexpected at the age of only 61. He died not from secret poison in his food or from a knife slipped into his back; Emperor Shaksus the Incomparable, a healthy bull of a man, had died of a failing heart as he relaxed for an evening in a steaming bath.

Unfortunately, even given his supposed prowess in bed with the beautiful concubines in his harem—all of whom he serviced quite regularly and vigorously, according to snickered whispers around the court—Shaksus had no heir, no children whatsoever. And although he insisted the fault must lie with the women, lest anyone dare question his virility, the obvious evidence suggested that the emperor's seed simply refused to take hold in any womb. Thus, the prosperous empire that stretched from the ocher mountains in the east, the white desert to the south, and the fertile lands of rival kingdoms to the north and west, was left without a leader.

The powerful court wizards knew what had to be done.

A spectacular funeral pyre raged for three days on the apex of the Temple of the Sun God, sending a banner of greasy, black smoke into the sky to signal a time of mourning. The body of Shaksus had long been consumed, but the temple priests had kept adding fuel to the flames along with the occasional body of a slave just to keep the fires bright. Messengers rode to the corners of the empire commanding one full moon cycle of respectful grief. But the court wizards knew they could not distract the people for long, and so they put out the call far and wide.

A new emperor had to be found.

Dressed in rags, but his very best rags, Aykin stood in the long line that stretched across the square leading to the dark and ominous arched openings of the Emperor's palace. The ornate, imposing structure towered over the capital city, but now stood mostly empty, the functionaries and concubines evicted, the windows covered with black cloths. Crows circled the tallest pointed towers.

Aykin stretched up on his thin legs, brushed dark, unruly hair from his brown eyes, and tried to peer around the shoulders of the burly, but dumb as a barrel, candidate who waited stoically in front of him. "I wish the court wizards would hurry," he muttered. There must be at least a hundred people ahead of him. "They haven't seen the best yet. I'll surprise them, I will." His bravado and confidence elicited no response whatsoever from Dumb As A Barrel. Aykin turned and flashed a grin at the well-dressed merchant behind him in line. "You'd best go home and see to your business. Once the court wizards interview me, they'll know who to choose as the next emperor."

The merchant gave him a withering sneer. "I don't believe the court wizards ever suggested that arrogance was a valued quality for leadership."

"Arrogance?" Aykin laughed. "I call it ambition, confidence, a clarity of vision. I know in my heart I'd be a good emperor. I'd make our land strong and wealthy."

The merchant assessed his rags, his frayed sandals, his unkempt hair. "It doesn't appear that you've put any of your skills to practice."

"I need the resources," Aykin replied. "I know I can do it."

When the court wizards had sent out a call for candidates, requesting to interview any person of any station who believed he could serve as the best new emperor, Aykin had made up his mind. What did he have to lose?

His mother had died on the streets when he was young, and he had never known his father. Who was to say he didn't have royal blood? Pampered nobles didn't know anything about real life, about survival, about making do. Aykin did. For several years he had led a band of street thieves, and they survived by their wits and their quick fingers. They had never been caught, although eventually—petty thieves being inherently unreliable—they had each drifted off on their own.

With the throne of Shaksus now vacant, Aykin saw his chance. Since he was unschooled, he only knew the muddled oral history of the empire, but he was aware that imperial dynasties had changed again and again over the centuries, often through wars, conquests, and assassinations, but other times exactly like this— the one fittest to serve, as chosen by the court wizards. Using inexplicable magic, they could pick the most suitable new emperor for the good of the land—and they were rarely wrong. Aykin knew they would not make the wrong choice once they spoke with him.

Rushing to offer himself for the position, the young man had taken the time to wash the grime off his face using the scummy water from a horse trough, and he had combed his shaggy hair with his fingers. He possessed a knife to defend himself, but the blade was so dull it had only made a mess when he tried to cut his hair. Thus, rather than looking noble and presentable, Aykin would have to make himself wild and wily, unpredictable, someone the armies and the citizens could cheer.

First, he had to convince the court wizards. He had to make his case.

"I wish these people would move faster," he muttered, again trying to peer around Dumb As A Barrel. The line of hopefuls shuffled forward, and Aykin saw one of the rejected candidates emerge, head down, from the dark archway of the emperor's palace. It was an older man, a wise scholar who held a bandaged hand close to his chest. He scurried away, paying no attention to the jeers of the crowd. Most of the people filling the plaza outside the palace had no interest in becoming the next emperor, but they were happy to mock those who failed.

Aykin drew a deep breath, reminding himself that he wasn't going to fail.

That very morning, after the court wizards issued their call, he had rushed to the middle of the capital, wanting to be the first in line. If he had made it, that would certainly have saved time and trouble for the empire, because then the wizards wouldn't need to interview so many other people. But he had found more than fifty people already there, all of whom fancied themselves of imperial quality.

So, he had to wait. All day. But showing patience was a good example of his abilities as a great leader. Patience. Yes, he would counsel himself for patience.

Another timid-looking candidate entered through the palace archways to meet the wizards. The rest of the people stood under the baking sun waiting and shifting. Aykin looked around him at the city, the tiled roofs, the whitewashed walls, the colorful pennants showing the eagle symbol of Emperor Shaksus. Black crepe and mourning fabrics still dangled in front of many windows.

Before long, the next candidate failed, left in disappointment, and then another entered past the two muscular guards. The line crawled forward. Aykin waited, and waited. Still fifteen more people in front of him.

A wine-seller with a brass cup and a skin full of a sour vintage walked down the line, offering drinks for two coppers. Although Aykin was sorely tempted, he didn't have the coins; he reminded himself that soon enough, when he was emperor, he would drink the finest wines. Soon enough.

The merchant behind him bought a cup from the wine-seller, sipped, then grimaced and dumped the red liquid on the flagstones.

Across the plaza the crowds swelled, then dwindled throughout the day. The people were ready to cheer their new emperor as soon as he was crowned, but they were not, in fact, enamored with the long and tedious process. Neither was Aykin.

His stomach growled; he had not eaten in two days. He was hot and sweaty. As the court wizards rejected candidate after candidate, he moved closer and closer to the marble steps and the arched palace doorway above. Finally, late in the afternoon, he reached the shade of the moving shadow from the high towers, but the temperature had already begun to drop. Aykin was determined to stay there all night long.

The door loomed closer as each person entered and left. Some never even departed, perhaps exiting through a different doorway, or maybe being kept on as staff members for the new administration, but the next volunteers were called in to state their case. Aykin knew the new emperor had not yet been selected, and his hope remained bright.

Vendors walked by with meat pies, tempting them with savory aromas. If he was free and running through the streets Aykin would have snatched one, but he restrained himself. That wasn't fitting behavior for a future emperor.

At sunset, when the evening bells tolled from the apex of the Temple of the Sun God rang out, the silent burly man in front of him, Dumb As A Barrel, turned and simply left the line, walking away without a word. Though surprised, Aykin hurried up to take his place in the line. Only five more people stood ahead of him before the two guards who blocked entry with their braced spears and grim expressions. He was close. His heart began to beat faster.

When he finally climbed the steps and stood above the plaza, he turned to look back, astonished to see the hopeful applicants who had gathered throughout the day. The line stretched all the way across the vast square, and beyond into the main promenade street where Emperor Shaksus had hosted great parades, then continued into the winding streets of the city. All those people would be so disappointed as soon as he was crowned the new emperor.

When his turn was called, a portly man dressed in purple silk robes entered the palace, marching past the guards with his head held high and a grin on his face as if he meant to charm the court wizards. Half an hour later, he scuttled out, his head down holding a cloth-wrapped hand, and vanished into the gathering night shadows.

Aykin stepped forward. Only two more ahead of him! As the night gathered, the chill set in, but he knew that tonight he would sleep in imperial beds, surrounded with silks, perhaps even beautiful women. He would have a feast. He would never again feel hungry. He wouldn't have to cheat or steal to survive. But he had proved he was willing to do what must be done, and often emperors needed to make difficult decisions. Even his shady past might be something worth noting.

The next two candidates were found wanting, just as Aykin expected. Torches and lanterns began to glow throughout the city, and thousands of sparkling bright eyes shone in the gathering darkness. And when it was his turn, Aykin stepped up to the two stony-faced guards with their crossed spears. He was accustomed to guards sneering at him, calling him a street urchin, a beggar, or a thief (all of which were true)—he was used to it. Now they showed no disgust when they looked at his rags or his unkempt hair. Aykin was another qualified applicant, and they had seen many things since the death of Emperor Shaksus.

He raised his chin and waited, knowing he would be called next. The reign of Emperor Shaksus had been long and stable, different from the fire and bloodshed of other emperors. The history scrolls would not record many accomplishments from the mostly placid and unremarkable reign of Shaksus, and Aykin already began to think of how he would want his own name written for posterity. Aykin the Magnificent? Aykin the Undefeated? There were so many adjectives.

Finally, the guards separated their spears and stood apart to let the young man enter the great gallery of the huge palace. He swallowed hard and strode into the giant echoing chamber, reminding himself how long he had waited for this. His tattered sandals made whispering noises across the polished tiles. Torches surrounded the walls of the great reception area. Ahead, under the vaulted ceiling, shimmering braziers lit the empty throne where Emperor Shaksus had sat.

Robed in crimson and emerald green, the three court wizards faced him. The three wizards had shaved heads and voluminous beards. They wore heavy amulets, golden chains, and multiple rings with large polished stones. They looked weary, even bored. No wonder, Aykin thought, since they had already dispensed with so many applicants today.

With a spring in his step, he spread his hands to greet them. "I am Aykin, and I am your next emperor."

The three wizards stood in front of a beaten copper basin on a tripod erected between the shimmering braziers. They did not react to his boastful claim. Without waiting for them to ask questions, Aykin continued, "I am clever, I am ambitious, and I understand the people because of my common upbringing. This gives me advantages that—"

The central court wizard raised a hand like an executioner's axe. He spoke in a deep, gravelly voice, "Silence! We've not yet begun."

Aykin quieted himself and shifted from one sandal to the other. "I will be the greatest leader. I promise. Ask your questions."

The wizard on the right, the gauntest of the three, drew a jeweled dagger in his left hand. The blade was slightly curved, its edge polished so sharp that it was a silver whisper of steel. The gems in its hilt glinted in the light of the brazier.

"We don't need to ask questions," said the wizard. "Your blood will tell us all we need to know."

Aykin's heart skipped a beat. Was it some kind of test to see if he would show fear, or did they truly mean to attack him? He stood his ground. The opposite wizard took a step closer. "We don't need to ask you questions, because people lie, and we need the truth."

"I would never lie!" he lied, but then caught himself. He lowered his voice. "What is it you need to know?"

"We must see the reign that is to come before we can make our decision. What will you do as the next emperor? How will you lead the land? How will you make us prosper? Under your leadership, will this empire thrive or diminish?"

"It will thrive," Aykin said.

"We shall see." The wizard with the knife stepped forward and grasped Aykin's hand. The young man instinctively jerked it away, but the wizard held firm. "If you can't pass even the simplest of tests, young man, then you are dismissed."

With a huff, Aykin shoved his hand, fingers outstretched, toward the bald, bearded man. "I will do anything to become emperor. I'll show you. What do you need?"

"Your blood." With a quick sharp slash, he drew the blade across Aykin's palm. The young man yelped with the bright sting of pain, and the wizard pulled his hand over the empty beaten-copper basin. The blood spilled down into the bowl. Aykin felt the throbbing hurt, the pulse of his heartbeat, as the blood flowed out to cover the bottom of the basin, dripping and dripping until it had reached a level that was smooth and still.

Fascinated, Aykin stared down into the dark red emptiness in the shallow bowl. "What did you do that for?"

The wizards gathered shoulder to shoulder. "We must see the reign to come. We will see the kind of emperor you are."

They began to hum, and the light from the braziers crackled and brightened. Aykin felt a tingling of magic in the air. He couldn't take his eyes away as he looked down into the blood-filled basin. The dark surface shimmered, rippled, and he blinked, seeing shadows there, movement. Then images formed, and Aykin recognized himself—not himself as a street urchin, but himself as an *emperor*.

"Behold your reign," said one of the court wizards. They all watched intently. Aykin stared while as-yet-unwritten history played out before his eyes.

After Aykin the Magnificent took his throne as emperor of the land, he wore fine clothes, slept in an expansive bed with numerous enthusiastic and talented women. He was far too young to worry about finding a princess to marry.

He thrived on being the new ruler. Aykin got his feet under him for the first year of his reign, and he began to understand just how much unquestioned power he wielded. This was everything the young man had dreamed of.

For months, Emperor Aykin traveled from city to city, exploring his empire, learning whom he ruled, assessing which parts were weak and which were strong, which lords were sycophants and which might be problematic. Even though he had no shortage of advisors and counselors, Aykin had learned from his time on the streets—with all the friends who had helped him, then disappointed him—not to trust anyone.

He even found a few of his street-scamp friends, elevated them to positions in his government. His long-lost companions were giddy with the unexpected opportunity, but sadly proved to be inappropriate for their roles. One young friend was a particular embarrassment, caught stealing from the treasury and smuggling gold coins out to secret hiding places. Aykin couldn't understand the foolishness: the man had everything he could need, why should he bother to steal?

When his legal advisors instructed him that any thief must have his hands chopped off, Aykin accepted the punishment since he was, after all, the emperor and must be bound by laws. Even though his former friend pleaded for mercy, Aykin insisted the sentence be carried out, and the young man's hands were laid out on the chopping block, then severed with an axe and a scream. Wailing, his handless friend howled curses and insults at Aykin, and then the court advisors pointed out that the penalty for insulting the emperor was death. Since the muscular executioner was still standing there with his bloody axe ready, Aykin had the boy's head chopped off, too.

That night, the rest of his elevated friends ran away in fear, many of them taking coins and jewels as they fled. So Aykin put out a warrant for their arrest, and they were subsequently hunted down and executed, not just for the thievery but because they must certainly have cursed his name as well.

After his first year, Emperor Aykin had explored the boundaries of his empire, inspected his lands from the white powder deserts and the rugged mountains to the borders with the fat and fertile kingdoms to the north and west. He felt discouraged and saddened to see the limits of his empire, knowing there was so much more to the world.

Tutors had instructed him on the history of the empire, the conquests and defeats of the previous leaders. Emperor Shaksus had not expanded their lands at all during the forty years of his reign—in fact, he hadn't even tried. Shaksus showed almost no ambition, content with the empire as it was. Aykin decided to make his mark now that he was in command of the imperial treasury as well as the large standing army. He funded the military, trained his cavalry, increased recruitment, enlarged the armories, and six months later, in the warmest summer months, Emperor Aykin launched an exploratory sortie over the border of the weak neighboring kingdom of Daraka.

The Darakans were mainly farmers and shepherds. They had no fortresses along the border and they had grown soft after decades of peace. When Aykin's initial sortie proved successful, conquering villages and expanding his territory into rich farming lands, the emperor was so pleased that he called his generals and expanded his army by promising lands and riches to the new recruits.

His massive army marched forward with no warning. Previously, Emperor Aykin had withdrawn all diplomatic ties with Daraka, so their attack was swift, relentless, and unexpected. Before the autumn leaves had even finished falling from the trees, Aykin ruled all of Daraka. He had killed the king, taken over the castle in the capital city, and dispersed his own troops at strategic points throughout Daraka.

By now he decided it was time for him to get married, and because his advisors told him that the best way to consolidate the rule of two great kingdoms was through marriage, he took the hand of the princess of Daraka—a spindly yet pretty young woman named Cereline, who was red eyed and wild with grief after the defeat and execution of her father, the Darakan king. Aykin was sure she would come around, so he married her anyway. When she threatened to resist, he had her drugged so that she was in a stupor throughout the entire wedding, but cooperative enough during the ceremony and in bed that night.

The alliance between Aykin's empire and the kingdom of Daraka was now cemented, and his wealth and power had grown.

To the north of the newly conquered kingdom, there were rich gold and silver mines, which Aykin commandeered. In a clever and wise decision, he exploited the mines by drawing new workers from the commanders of the defeated Darakan army, sending them underground to dig gold and silver ore, which further enriched the treasury of his ever-growing kingdom.

After conscripting the Darakan soldiers as well as sending out a wider call to arms among his own people, Aykin kept making plans. And after winter was over he launched another offensive during the mud and rain of spring, which stretched the boundaries even farther. His troops swept across the lands beyond the Darakan border; they pillaged the countryside, burning villages, conquering one district after another, demanding fealty from the town lords and petty princes.

Once, when he came back to his imperial bedchamber drunk from celebrating yet another victory, Princess Cereline tried to kill him. He easily drove her off and afterward kept her locked in a guarded room by herself. Later, she tried to take her own life, since she could not take his, and she failed in that as well. Aykin grew impatient with her, but he needed an heir and, rather than letting her kill herself so he could simply take another, more cooperative wife, he fell back on drugging her in the evenings before having her brought to his bedchamber. Even so, it still took him three months to get her pregnant.

After another neighboring kingdom fell—mostly because they surrendered in terror—Emperor Aykin faced the defeated king. He realized that the easy conquest had come about because these people feared him, and fear, he decided, was a sharper weapon than a sword.

So, he reached a decision. When the defeated king bowed before him, Emperor Aykin took a curved scimitar from one of his loyal guards and personally struck off his head. The shock spread rapidly to surrounding kingdoms. Some forged alliances to build up their own armies, but the wise ones rushed emissaries back to Aykin's palace with sworn statements of surrender and loyalty.

Aykin absorbed land after land without spilling a drop of blood (except for the necessary pillaging his guards and soldiers caused, but that was to be expected). As his armies swelled with all the new recruits pressed into service, Emperor Aykin marched on the lands that had pulled together to resist him. His unstoppable wave crushed all those who stood against him, and in only a few years he doubled and then tripled the size of his empire. He built garrisons throughout the newly conquered lands, as well as his original empire, simply to maintain the peace, because many were jealous of his success and made halfhearted attempts to overthrow him. But they all failed.

He led a bloodbath across the continent, building immense fortresses, erecting giant monuments so that history would remember Emperor Aykin the Magnificent, the Undefeated. He built a pile of skulls plated in gold, from each enemy who had stood against him and failed. Under his leadership, his vision, and his strength Aykin's empire became the richest, most powerful, most feared empire in all the world and in all of history.

The images in the beaten-copper basin faded as the blood blackened and congealed. Young Aykin stood giddy and astonished by what he had seen. "That is my reign," he asked in a whisper. "I will accomplish all that? I will make history. I will make our empire incomparably strong."

Grinning, he blinked and looked up in amazement. He knew he was the correct successor to the weak and unambitious Emperor Shaksus. The court wizards would crown him then and there, and he would begin his reign now that he knew what to do.

Instead, he was surprised to see all three wizards staring at him with eyes wide, their lips curled downward in revulsion. "We have seen your reign to come."

Their reaction annoyed him. Drunk with the immensity of all he had just seen, Aykin lashed out. "You will obey me! You have witnessed my power."

The court wizard raised the curved silver blade. "After so many years of peace and prosperity, we certainly don't need another ruler like that!"

Before Aykin could retreat, the wizard plunged the long sacrificial dagger into his chest, then stabbed twice more just to make sure. The young man reached up with weak and watery fingers, clasping at his wounds as he fell to the floor. He knocked over the tripod and spilled the beaten-copper basin, but his own blood made a much larger puddle on the polished stones in front of the empty throne.

Shaking with alarm and disgust the three court wizards called for guards to take the body away and clean the mess. "He has no place in our history."

Together, the three wizards cleansed the basin and propped up the tripod. They washed their bloody hands with perfumed water while the guards removed all signs of the street urchin. Finally, they gathered their courage and called out to the arched doorway of the palace. "Send in the next one."

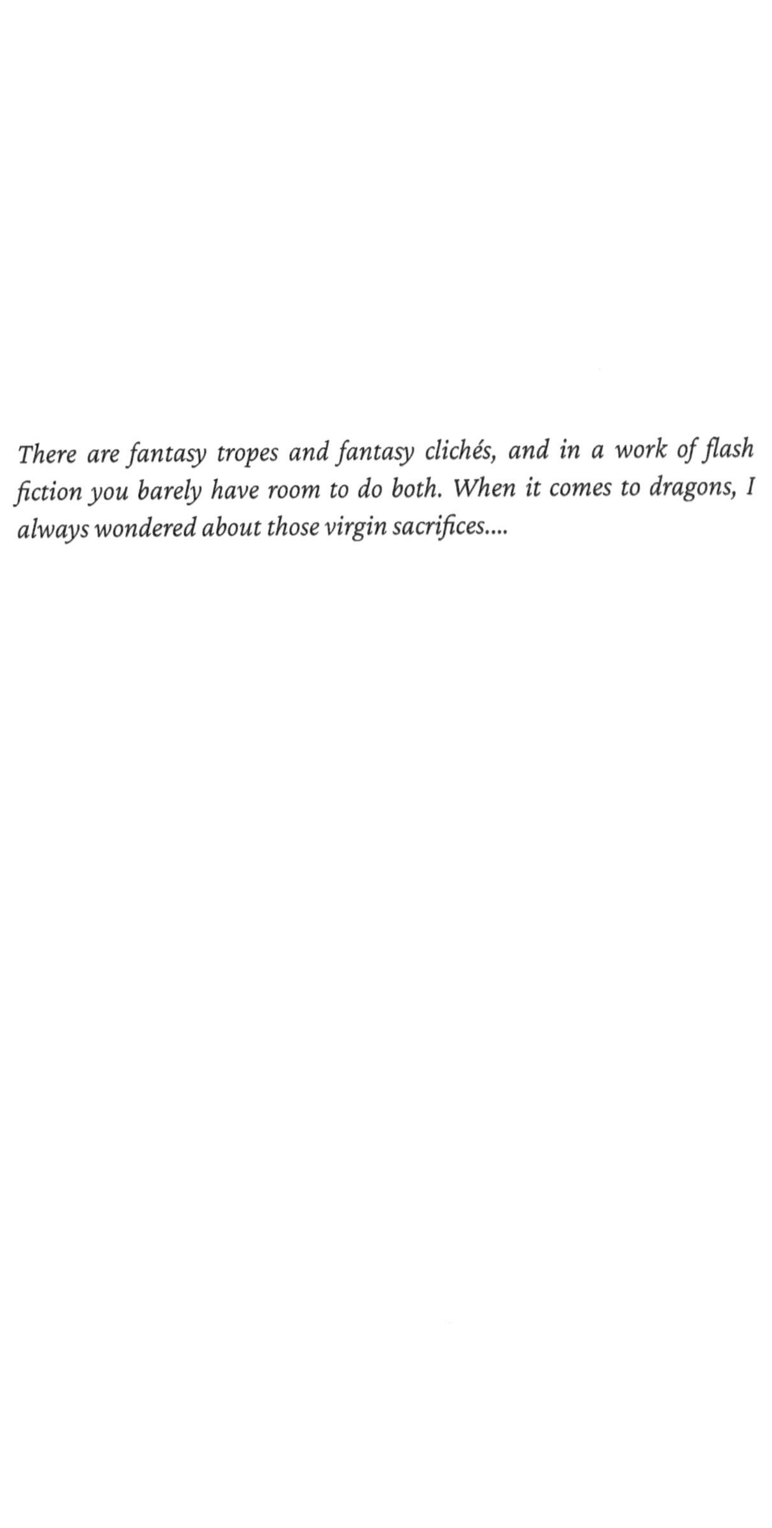

There are fantasy tropes and fantasy clichés, and in a work of flash fiction you barely have room to do both. When it comes to dragons, I always wondered about those virgin sacrifices....

THE SACRIFICE

The foul-smelling mist exhaled from the cave opening, a swirl of brimstone and smoke. A soft reptilian growl echoed, low and steady. The dragon was still sleeping, but when he awakened, he would be hungry.

The young woman, the virgin sacrifice, struggled against the ropes that bound her to the stake. Her wrists were already raw, but she couldn't get away. She waited for the monster to emerge, to devour her.

The charred bones strewn about the lair—crushed skulls, cracked femurs drained of marrow, curved rib cages—gave evidence of previous meals that had not satisfied the beast.

She tried to be strong, straining and grasping against the bonds, but she didn't dare twist too hard, because that might make her wrists bleed, and blood would certainly draw the dragon. A tear stole aimlessly down her cheek, but she forced herself not to whimper. The fear, too, would bring him out.

Months ago, the dragon had awakened from its ancient slumber and terrorized the countryside. With broad razor wings, it swooped down on the shepherds' flocks, roasting sheep and leaving charred fields. It attacked the villages next, setting thatched roofs on fire, burning cottages to the ground, feasting on any victims it could seize.

When the priests consulted their holy texts, they knew there could be only one solution to appease the dragon: a virgin sacrifice, a pure young woman offered to keep the beast at bay. And the townspeople, her own people, had turned on her. They chose her because she was the least important, an orphan with no one to speak on her behalf. Though she was pretty, kind, and well loved, she had no dowry and was not likely to find a husband anyway. She had no say in the matter.

Now she was tied to the stake before the lair, waiting, doomed, sure the dragon would soon emerge, a nightmare of scales and fangs and deadly fire. And it would see her there, a sacrifice.

But all she could think of was the brave knight and his kisses, his reassurances ... how he had held her the night before. It was their secret. None of the villagers suspected.

But she wondered if the dragon would know ...

My interest in the legends of the sea reached its apex in my epic fantasy trilogy, Terra Incognita—three doorstop novels and crossover rock CDs. The sprawling story dealt with voyages of exploration, the monsters of the deep, as well as religious fanaticism and intolerance. It's some of my most powerful work.

Even though the Terra Incognita novels had dozens of main characters and multiple side stories, this tale insisted on being a standalone—a close-minded "prester" (a priest) who is confronted with a mythical creature that his faith will not let him believe in.

MYTHICAL CREATURES

The prow of the *Compass* cut the rough gray waters like a knife carving a Landing Day roast. Prester Ormun closed his eyes and drove away all his pleasant memories of the traditional holiday ... or any other family memories, for that matter. Those were behind him now; only bleak settlements on the scattered Soeland Islands lay ahead. The prester had a difficult path to follow, even if he did not understand God's reasoning behind it.

The ship's damp sails creaked and sighed, and he felt the cold spray on his face, blown by the coming storm. Dobri, the bright-eyed cabin boy, came up beside him, leaning over the bow to peer down into the choppy waves. "Are you looking for *sylkas*, Prester? They say sometimes you can see them in the whitecaps just before a squall."

"I do not believe in *sylkas*. And neither should you." Prester Ormun knew that for a young man like this, the world was filled with mysteries and wonders, but also ignorance. It was his appointed task to enlighten the people of the islands.

The cabin boy squinted at the sea, which looked leaden under the thick sky. "They're real, Prester—beautiful women with golden hair or seaweed all over their bodies. Other sailors have seen them."

"I don't care what other sailors say. *Sylkas* do not exist. It is written in the Book of Aiden that God created the peoples of the land, but only fish, seals, whales, and sea serpents inhabit the sea —no intelligent creatures. I can show you the Scriptures, if you like." Since Ormun knew the cabin boy couldn't read, the proof would be lost on him.

Dobri was both disappointed and skeptical to hear the prester's pronouncement. He had grown up in a small fishing village, and this was his first voyage away from home; he wanted to believe all the wondrous, imaginative stories, whether or not they were true. Now the boy gazed ahead, intent on spotting one of the imaginary *sylkas* so he could point out the creature to Ormun.

With a pang, the prester realized that his own son Aleo would have been about Dobri's age now....

A large wave gushed over the *Compass*'s bow, and the cabin boy scuttled away, but the prester did not try to avoid the splash; instead, he let it wash away his past again. His family was gone, and nothing remained for him in the city of Calay. That was why he'd been sent across the rough waters to the bleak Soeland Islands. A new chance ... a last chance.

The church's prester-marshall had sent Ormun to preach among the roughshod and hardy islanders; he would bring them the Book of Aiden to comfort the people in their storms and cold northerly winds. Ormun accepted his first mission with neither enthusiasm nor complaint. He was humble enough not to expect redemption, but he did hope to achieve something positive with whatever remained of his life. That he was all he asked God for....

Back in Calay, before he became a prester, Ormun was a shoemaker with a wife and two children, a home, friends—a lifetime ago, or a year ago, depending on whether he measured time by a calendar or the gulf in his heart.

The gray plague had swept through the Craftsmen's District, as it did every few years. Shops closed their doors and latched the window shutters. But Ormun had his family to feed: his son, his daughter, and his wife, a dark-haired, tan-skinned beauty named Risula. And so, he kept working, while others hid.

He never knew which customer exposed him to the plague. Ormun lay shivering in bed for days while his family tended him: Aleo, only twelve years old, acting as the man of the house, Risula giving him salty broth to drink; even little Essa brought him flowers that she'd picked outside.

Ormun gained strength day by day, then suffered a relapse, falling back into a deep fever, sleeping like the dead, drenched in cold sweat. His last murky memory was of Risula shushing their daughter and leading her away, telling her to let her father sleep. And then his wife had started coughing....

When his fever broke, Ormun emerged from his coma, very weak, and he could barely open his crusted eyes. His throat was parched, and he called out for water, but heard nothing. The house seemed quiet, much too quiet. After he gained enough strength to crawl out of bed, he found his family huddled together, dead, victims of the fever that he had somehow survived.

Ormun had walked away from his home, wandering the streets in a daze, until he finally came upon the kirk. He stumbled inside, and the local prester cared for him, read to him from the Book of Aiden. It was then Ormun decided what his mission in life must be. The gray plague had left him with an empty heart, no laughter, and no love. He clutched onto his service to the church like an anchor of hope, read the Book several times through, and debated with great fervor. When the kindly local prester could no longer answer his questions, he sent the gaunt and intense Ormun to the main kirk in Calay, where he met with the prester-marshall himself.

Cast adrift in life, Ormun begged the church leader for a new course to set. The prester-marshall did not try to explain God's personal message for Ormun, didn't pretend to reveal the purpose behind all the pain he had suffered. "I know a place where you can be of service. The Soelanders need you, and I think you belong there." He anointed Ormun a prester and presented him with the Book and the fishhook pendant that was a symbol of their faith.

No one called Soeland a pleasant place to live, but that mattered not a whit to Ormun. He took his Book and his letters of passage, and begged a bunk on the *Compass*, which was ready to sail back for the islands....

Now the sea grew rough, and waves rocked the vessel. Captain Endre Stillen came to join the prester, looking troubled. He was a red-bearded man with a muscular chest and potbelly as hard as a wine cask. "Your cabin would be more comfortable, Prester. No sense staying out here in the storm—the weather is going to get worse."

"Discomfort doesn't bother me, Captain," Ormun said.

Stillen shot an uncertain glance to the anxious cabin boy who hovered nearby. "Dobri says that you don't believe in the mysteries of the sea." He raised his bushy eyebrows.

"I do not."

"The ocean is vast and uncharted, and we've all seen things we can't explain. I'm as inclined to believe in *sylkas* as in anything else. If nothing else, it gives me hope to know that those dark waters might contain benevolent creatures, should anything happen to my ship."

"I don't need mythical creatures to give me hope, Captain. The Book of Aiden says that *sylkas* don't exist, so therefore they don't exist. It doesn't matter what tales you've heard or what you think you've seen."

The conversation reminded Ormun of a recent outspoken stargazer who had adapted a seaman's spyglass so he could stare at the stars and planets in the night sky. The astronomer convinced himself that he saw tiny satellites circling one of the planets—an impossible idea. To prove his assertion, the stargazer had asked the prester-marshall to observe for himself; but the church leader refused to raise the spyglass to his eye. "The Book of Aiden tells us that God made the world as the center of all things, so therefore other satellites *cannot* circle one of the tiny planets in the sky. I have no need to look, when I already know." He handed the telescope back to the baffled astronomer. Ormun thought it was an amazingly profound demonstration of the prester-marshall's unshakable faith. He only hoped he could be as worthy someday.

Seeing that the prester's mind was set, Captain Stillen chose not to pursue the argument. "Those legends are a vital part of Soelander life and folklore, Prester. You'll be in for some lively discussions when you get to the fishing towns, that's for certain."

"I'm not afraid of debate."

The captain ordered the sails trimmed against the squall. As the winds picked up, waves hammered the side of the ship. Most of the crew hurried belowdecks before the rain started to sheet down.

Dobri yelped, pointing off to starboard. "I saw one! Look, Prester—it's a *sylka!*"

Ormun froze, wanting not to look, *almost* strong enough to refuse, but he couldn't help himself. He turned to where the boy pointed—and that was his weakness, his failure.

While he looked in the other direction, a rogue wave swamped the bow and gushed over the rails with enough force to knock him overboard. He reached out, grabbed for anything, and his fingers caught the slick wood, but couldn't get hold. Then the rush of curling foam bore him overboard into the wide gulf of the sea.

Prester Ormun sucked in a breath to shout for help, but he swallowed a mouthful of salt water instead. Flailing, sinking, he coughed and retched as the wave crest bore him upward, then plunged him under again. He clawed at the water with his hands, seeing grayish light above. His face burst from the waves again, and he drew in a deep breath. He rose and sank, completely lost, adrift. His heavy woolen shift pulled him down.

In the pouring rain he spotted Dobri and Captain Stillen struggling to their feet on the deck. He caught a glimpse of the cabin boy, his mouth open in dismay as he saw the prester in the water. Dobri waved and shouted.

Ormun raised his hands to signal, but the seas were too

rough. Currents whisked him farther from the ship. The *Compass* could never send out a boat to rescue him.

He tried to stay afloat, but his arms and legs felt leaden. His shoes—good leather boots that he had made in his own cobbler shop long ago in that other life—filled with water. He was going to drown out here.

Oddly, he didn't view the thought with any particular terror, but he did feel a heavy confusion. God's course for him had been so clear—to spread the word out in the Soeland Islands. What was the purpose of saving Ormun from the gray plague only to let him be swept away by a capricious wave, drowning before he even had a chance to preach to his new charges?

He went under again, struggled to the surface, caught another breath. Letting go, he let himself be flung about by the waves. Barely able to think, he experienced a paradoxical sense of calm and peace.

Then clammy hands grasped him from below. A firm grip took his woolen shift, cradled his head, buoyed him up to where he could breathe. But Ormun didn't want to breathe. He struggled and fought against the strange figure below, but he was too weak.

In the end, he simply surrendered to the water and the mythical savior that his imagination had created in his last moments of life. Prester Ormun sank into the darkness, trying to remember a prayer.

When Prester Ormun awoke, he smelled fish in the dank and cold air around him. Dried saltwater plastered his hair to his head, and he had to pry open his crusted eyes. Before his vision adjusted, he rolled over onto his knees and retched, puking up foul-tasting saltwater.

He saw that he was in an empty cave at the waterline, which looked out upon the open sea. Outside, the waves sounded like drumbeats against the algae-encrusted rocks that he could see beyond the cave opening. With a start, the prester realized he was naked, his woolen shift spread on a rock nearby. The cloth was stiff and salt-encrusted, but reasonably dry. He shivered and pulled his clothes back on, hiding his nakedness.

He noticed four gutted fish on a flat rock next to him, along with a pile of oysters and clams, all of which had been pried open, ready for him to eat. Weak and starving, Ormun devoured the food without thinking, without tasting, and he felt reborn, as when he'd emerged from his fever after the gray plague. Now, however, questions clamored in his mind, and he looked around, trying to understand what had happened to him.

A figure swam in the sea outside the cave. It seemed human at first—until the creature hauled itself onto the rocks and climbed dripping into the cave. Covered with luxurious locks of golden fur, it was obviously female, with rounded breasts covered by matted weeds. The face was narrow and ethereal, with large brown eyes —soulful eyes, like those of a sea lion. She smelled of salt from the sea. Her lips curved in what was an unmistakable smile as she saw him awake and looking at her.

Ormun squeezed his eyes shut and felt for his fishhook pendant in a protective instinct, but the religious symbol was gone. Perhaps it had washed away when he'd been swept overboard, or perhaps this *thing*—this *sylka?*—had stolen it, fearing the sign of Aiden.

Ormun opened his eyes again, but the creature was still there; he had expected her to vanish like a mirage-shadow. She came forward to squat near him, briny water trickling from her fur, and he struggled away. The *sylka* picked up the empty oyster and clam shells and cast them out of the cave, then she turned back to scrutinize him, like a raven fascinated by a shiny object ... or a predator deciding how best to devour its prey. A thrumming sound echoed from her throat, a call that was at once mysterious, mournful, and hypnotic.

When the creature edged closer, Prester Ormun backed away until his shoulders struck the cave wall. "You're not real!"

The *sylka* trilled at him. Her eyes showed a yearning to

communicate. She repeated the sound and chirruped with a higher note at the end, like a question.

"You're not real." Though he could see the *sylka*'s form as if she had been sketched from the logbook of a delusional sea captain, could smell her musky iodine odor, and hear the sound she made, Ormun clung to what the Book of Aiden taught: That God had blessed *mankind* with intelligence, giving only His *chosen children* the minds to understand and worship Him. All other creatures of the land and sea were lowly animals. In another verse, the Book specifically denounced mermaids and *sylkas* as distractions for a devout man, superstitions unworthy of a true follower of God.

But now Ormun found himself faced with the contradiction. The Book of Aiden stated plainly that this *sylka* could not be here. Ormun had read those words of scripture with his own eyes ... yet those same eyes showed him this impossible creature. Right here.

Back in Calay, the prester-marshall had instructed him in the use of rational thought. If this *sylka* truly existed, then the statement in the Book was in error. A small error, perhaps—and how could anyone know all the mysteries and all the creatures in the vast sea?

Yet one error in one verse was as bad as a thousand errors, for either way it proved that the Book of Aiden was flawed.

And because it was the word of God, the Book of Aiden could *not* be flawed. Therefore, that one verse, and all verses, had to be correct. By definition.

Hence, the *sylka* could not exist, and she was not there. He stared hard at her, willing the illusion to go away.

The *sylka* hunkered down and continued to gaze at him with mournful eyes. She let out a series of complex musical trills, but Prester Ormun closed his eyes and covered his ears.

The *sylka* left the cave several times throughout the day, diving into the sea and swimming away. She always returned with fresh fish, oysters, or abalones for him, all of which he ate suspiciously. Ormun used the empty abalone shells to capture dripping water that trickled from the moist rocks of the cave. It tasted gritty and dirty but soothed his parched throat.

Each time the mythical creature went away, Ormun tried to convince himself that she was only an illusion brought about by delirium, perhaps a relapse of the gray fever. Then the *sylka* returned, and they would stare at each other again....

He feared she might bring back others of her kind to show them the strange captive she had hauled from the stormy seas—but, again, the prester knew that couldn't happen, because *sylkas* did not exist. There were no others. Each time she came to him, she was alone ... and so was he.

When he felt strong enough, and desperate enough, Ormun made his plans and waited for the *sylka* to swim away again. The creature slipped out of the cave one afternoon, and Ormun decided it was time to escape—if he could. He ventured out of the opening and climbed up on the rocks, hoping to find some landmark that would tell him where he was.

If this was one of the Soeland Islands, Ormun could make his way inland, where he might find people—a fishing village, a shack, or a boat dock. But when he scrambled up the algae-covered boulders above the tide line, he saw that this island was merely a tiny patch of land, an elbow of reef that barely rose above the waterline—a few acres of forlorn boulders and tufts of misplaced grass. He could see the full swatch of land from end to end, side to side. The island was empty. He was alone.

Staring at the watery horizon with tears burning in his eyes, he discerned the gray hummocks of other islands in the distance, larger shores that might be inhabited ... but they were much too far away. He could never swim that far, and if he tried to escape, he was sure the *sylka* would come after him, grab his legs, and drag him beneath the water. He still didn't understand why she had saved him in the first place.

As he stood there in empty dismay, the *sylka* rose out of the surf and climbed onto dry land on the other side of the islet. Silhouetted in daylight, she looked like a seductress, her form voluptuous, the golden kelplike fur haloed by the sun. Ormun had looked at women once, had found Risula so lovely that she made him dizzy with desire ... but he had been a different man before the gray fever—someone without the same convictions, without the same priorities. He averted his eyes.

The *sylka* came toward him, clearly alarmed to see him out of the cave. On land, her movements were ungainly, like a seal's, although he had seen how sleek and lissome she was in the water. When the creature urged him back to the cave that was his prison, he recoiled at her touch, but could not resist. He saw no point to it; he had nowhere else to go.

Back in her lair, the *sylka* was intent on showing him something. She trilled, inducing him to come to a dank alcove in the rear of the small cave. Under a weed-covered overhang, she had piled rocks to create a protective barrier, a sort of nest. The *sylka* looked at him with great wonder in her eyes as she grasped the rocks with her webbed hands and lifted them away one by one.

Beneath the protective barrier rested a group of pulsating, grayish spheres, pearlescent objects, each one larger than a ripe melon. Ormun counted five of them grouped together with loving care, moist with a filmy membrane—a clutch of eggs! The creature's young. She was reproducing, about to unleash five more of her kind into the world!

Obviously the *sylka* wasn't entirely alone out there in the waters. Ormun imagined her out in the gray cold sea, at night, letting out her trilling song, calling a mate from across the waves. Did she lay her eggs here in the cave and wait for a male to spray his milt on the clutch like a frog? The very idea made him shudder with disgust.

The *sylka* inhaled and exhaled wet burbling breaths, and she crouched closer, cooing. The creature extended a pale finger and stroked the nearest egg. Her touch activated something within, a sparkle in the air accompanied by the smell of ozone, and Prester

Ormun felt an overwhelming sense of importance and hope—a magical, unnatural connection.

On the egg's shifting metallic surface, he saw distorted images, like memories seen through the fever fog. The *sylka* touched a second egg, and a third, and more images formed on their reflective shells ... the prester's hopes and possibilities from the lost part of his life, things she could not possibly know about him.

Ormun saw the blurry, uncertain features of his son Aleo, laughing, full of tales of fish he had caught or beetles he had collected. The second eggshell displayed sweet, doe-eyed Essa, who loved to pick the flowers that grew in meadows just outside the city. And exotic, beautiful Risula.

But the last time Ormun had seen his family, they were dead, plague-ridden, their bodies huddled on the floor of their home, while he shivered in a coma on the narrow bed. Now, he gasped a quick, perfunctory prayer, but he continued to look. He knew he should turn away, even though those faces made his heart ache.

Sensing his reaction, the *sylka* trilled with happiness.

Then Ormun realized these visions were not just memories, for he saw Aleo as a young man, standing with a thin and pretty red-haired woman. They held each other, kissed—Aleo's wife-to-be? Ormun saw another maiden with fresh-picked flowers in her hair, unmistakably Essa, just at the edge of growing up. He saw Risula cradling another baby—her own, or a grandchild?

The eggs held possibilities, a wellspring of the future.

"No," Ormun whispered, drawing away. "No, this never happened! This can't be." He covered his eyes. The *sylka* was distraught, not understanding his reaction, but Ormun clung to strength within.

The images that pooled on the shells of her eggs did not represent the path that God had chosen for him. He had endured the pain. He had read the Book. He had fought for understanding and acceptance, like a pathfinder hacking through persistent underbrush, rather than taking a simple and easy trail that did not lead where he wanted to go. These elusive memories were not *his* memories, and that future did not belong to him.

"No," he said again.

With obvious disappointment, the *sylka* piled the rocks again over her eggs.

Even though the prester understood his mission now, he feared he wouldn't have the necessary strength. As he shivered through the cold, damp night while wrestling with his thoughts, Ormun once again told himself that none of this was *real*. Maybe he had actually drowned when the wave swept him overboard, and this was his test before God let him enter Heaven. The only thing that had kept him alive after the plague, the purpose that allowed him to get through one day, then the next, was the anchor of his faith, his dogged belief in what the prester-marshall had taught him. If he abandoned that, then he would be abandoning everything he had left.

The eerie, tempting images he'd seen in the *sylka*'s eggs—his family, his happiness, a bright future—none of that was true. How he longed for what he saw in those illusions, wanted that reality more than anything else he could ever imagine. But that, in itself, was what warned him. *His* wishes did not matter: It was about what God wanted. Ormun had to be strong, and his only strength was his faith.

On the fourth morning after being washed overboard, Ormun watched the *sylka* return to the cave, climbing out of the water. As the creature sloshed toward him, she looked excited, gesturing with a webbed hand. When the prester didn't follow, she hurried back to the cave opening and stared out to sea, then trilled a sharper sound, more urgent than her soothing music. Ormun felt compelled to look out upon the sunwashed waters.

In the channel between the islands, close enough that he could see the sails and rigging, a two-masted vessel cruised in from the north. He even recognized the lines, the look of the hull, the cut of the sails. It was the *Compass*! Maybe Captain Stillen had come back to look for him, or maybe this was just the ship's regular return route through the archipelago.

Thrumming, the *sylka* looked at him with her limpid eyes. Ormun's heart lurched, and he knew the time had come. This was the crux, and he clung to the truth like a man grasping a lifeline. He had not dared to pray for a chance at redemption, to demonstrate his devotion and his acceptance—and now the sailing ship had returned! The *Compass* would rescue him.

He lurched to his feet, uttering a prayer of thanksgiving. The *sylka* gestured for him to hurry, and by her demeanor and bright expression he guessed that she intended to swim out to the *Compass*, draw the attention of the sailors, and get Captain Stillen to change course to the islet. This creature had already rescued him from drowning, and now she would save him from being marooned on the small island. She turned away, looking out to sea.

Ormun picked up one of the melon-sized reef rocks, held it in both hands, and brought it down with all of his strength on the back of the *sylka's* head. He bashed as hard as he could, and her skull was much softer than the rock. The *sylka* collapsed, letting out a mournful hooting sound, and Ormun struck again.

He stood tall and dropped the rock on the floor of the cave. "You don't exist." If the captain, the cabin boy, and the rest of the crew saw her, they would not have the strength to cling to their faith. Ormun had no other choice but to save them from their own gullibility.

He went to the back alcove, pulled away the rocks piled over the clutch of eggs, and gazed down at the quicksilver pooling— the reflections that were mocking echoes of a past that was already gone and a future he would never have. Useless and dangerous, a mocking temptation. Prester Ormun was strong enough to avoid fantasies, no matter how attractive they might be. He knew his life's course.

Ormun picked up another rock and smashed the first *sylka* egg, obliterating the illusions of things that might have been.

Then he destroyed the rest of the clutch, one by one, until he felt safe again.

When he was finished, he was surprised to discover that the *sylka*'s body still lay on the cave floor; the dripping slimy fragments of broken eggs remained strewn about their nest. Now that he had passed his test of faith, Ormun expected them to vanish instantly, but he didn't search for, or want, explanations. It was time for him to be rescued, to return to his role as a prester preaching the Book of Aiden. The Soelanders needed him.

Ormun carried one of the abalone shells as he scrambled out of the cave and onto the high point of the small islet. There, he jumped and waved, seesawing his hands in the air, trying to get the attention of the *Compass*. He caught the bright sunlight with the shiny interior of the shell, flashing a signal. He yelled until his throat was raw.

And finally—finally—he saw pennants raised on the mainmast, and the ship turned toward the rocky island. Someone had seen him.

When the *Compass* anchored at a safe distance from the islet, Prester Ormun watched the ship's boat lowered, saw men rowing toward him. Though he was not a good swimmer, he dove into the water and struck out to meet the boat partway. He recognized the boy Dobri at the front of the boat, and two sturdy Soeland sailors pulling at the oars. The prester flailed in the waves, swimming as far from the islet as he could.

He needed to be away from the persistent imaginary remnants of the *sylka* and her eggs. He didn't want any of these men from the *Compass* to see the evidence, otherwise they would be deceived by what they wanted to believe.

Gasping and exhausted, Ormun reached the boat, and his heart swelled with joy. Dobri leaned over to catch his hand. "Prester, we thought you were dead!"

"I thought I was, too," he said as they helped to haul him aboard. "But I survived, and now I know that God still has more work for me to do."

The cabin boy laughed, and the sailors rowed back toward the

Compass. Ormun was too tired and shaken to tell his story, and he still had much to think about before he revealed anything.

When they tied up to the sailing ship, he climbed aboard to congratulations from Captain Stillen. "We couldn't believe it, Prester! No man ever survives out here. How did you make it to that small island? We were just continuing our passage among the islands, but Dobri spotted the flashing light."

"An abalone shell," the prester said.

The captain admired his cleverness, and Dobri added, "I was at the bow looking for *sylkas* when I saw it."

"*Sylkas* don't exist, boy," Prester Ormun said, more convinced now than he had ever been.

But while the crewmen took him to change into dry clothes, the prester watched Dobri hurry back to the bow with a spyglass in hand. Seeing the boy's eager willingness to believe, he felt only sadness and disappointment. He had to teach these people the truth, no matter how difficult it was.

Nevertheless, Dobri continued to scan the waves, always looking, always hopeful.

I'd never been asked to write a story for a coloring book before.

My writing student and friend, Tanya Hales, creates charming artwork that she puts together into coloring books funded by Kickstarter. For her second volume, she asked writer friends to create a very short story to accompany an illustration.

Tanya assigned me a drawing that showed a two-headed dragon, lava monsters, and a flustered-looking knight. Challenge accepted!

And I only had 300 words to set up and tell a story involving all those pieces.

I wrote a very tight piece of flash fiction, then edited and whittled it down, then whittled it again, until the story finally fit in the word count.

I liked the idea so much that I reshaped and incorporated it into my novel Skeleton in the Closet.

THE QUEST PRIZE

N ow we're in the thick of it," I said, in my best Knight-in-Shining-Armor voice.

"Isn't that what you wanted?" asked Ruk, one of the two mercenary dragons I had hired for this quest. "To prove your bravery and win the hand of the beautiful princess?"

"The idea sounded better in the tavern," I admitted, "after a few tankards of ale."

"We still get hazard pay!" insisted Rul, the other mercenary dragon. "Increased wages as promised."

"I didn't sign up for this," said Ruk as we faced the oncoming horde of lava beasts.

"Nevertheless, it will be a battle for the ages," I said, trying to sound brave. I held up my sword and glared at the fiery things lurching toward us and the erupting volcano in the distance. "Think of what the minstrels will sing about us."

"We won't be able to hear it if we're dead," said Rul. "Besides we're too big, and most taverns won't let two full-grown dragons in."

I knew that even with my full armor, the lava beasts would cook me like a hard-boiled egg if they came too close.

I was already a well-established knight, with smallholdings of my own, a trophy room in my castle with jousting-award ribbons. But I was lonely, and I decided I wanted to marry up. When the king offered the hand of beautiful Princess Lyra to the knight who proved himself worthy through great deeds, I vowed to win her hand.

But when I went to the throne room and bowed to the princess and the wise old king, I didn't think Lyra was all that beautiful, with a horselike face, stringy hair, and a spoiled-brat sneer when she looked at me. Nevertheless, when I had gone on my sacred quest, the king blessed my sword and gave me a generous traveling stipend (I think he was eager to marry off his daughter, and I was the only brave knight who had risen to the challenge in more than a month).

So I went out and captured a few brigands, saved a damsel in distress or two, but that wasn't sufficient. But when it came time to face a horde of lava monsters raiding the countryside from their hideout in a local erupting volcano, I knew I needed to bring in some extra firepower. So, I hired these two intimidating though rather mild-mannered dragons, Ruk and Rul. The scaly beasts were down on their luck and charged a surprisingly reasonable fee for their mercenary services.

The attacking lava monsters, though, did not seem impressed with my two hench-dragon sidekicks.

"Look," said Ruk, "they have open hands. Isn't that a friendly gesture among humans? Maybe they're just waving at us."

Then the horde began hurling lava globules. Magma splashed and exploded on the ground all around us. Thankfully, the fire creatures had piss-poor aim.

The dragons roared and belched out fire of their own, blasting back against the lava beasts, but the things only brightened, feeding on the fire.

This wasn't going to work as planned. Not at all.

As they surged closer, and I could feel the heat shimmering like a furnace, I thought about Princess Lyra, her horselike face, the sneer of perennial contempt on her face.

"Well, the princess isn't all that pretty," I said.

"Agreed!" said Ruk, flapping his enormous wings, but the great breeze only fanned the flames of the advancing monsters. "Meet back at the tavern!"

"They have an outside biergarten this time of year," said Rul, "and it's big enough to fit all of us."

I agreed that it was the best end to our quest. We retreated, deciding how we would spin the tale to the other tavern patrons. "First round's on me."

For Clockwork Lives, *Neil Peart and I wrote a version of* The Canterbury Tales *set in the unique clockwork world from our bestselling and award-winning novel,* Clockwork Angels. *We wanted to tell additional stories about the many characters that we loved. One of them was particularly close to Neil's heart, drawing on his decades of drumming for the legendary rock group Rush.*

We developed a lovely story about a drummer who begins to lose his ability to play music through a degenerative disease, so he invents a robotic clockwork percussor that can keep perfect rhythm. The climactic scene from this story inspired our entire novel, Clockwork Destiny.

Now, alas, one more detail makes this story additionally poignant. Not long after Clockwork Lives *was published, Neil himself was diagnosed with terminal brain cancer. Re-reading the plight of our ailing drummer character in "The Rhythm Method" feels far too prophetic.*

THE RHYTHM METHOD:
THE PERCUSSOR'S TALE
(WITH NEIL PEART)

The first time I saw the Clockwork Angels, they inspired me. I had just moved to Crown City to become an instructor at the Alchemy College, and the city was full of strangers. When thousands of people crowded shoulder to shoulder in Chronos Square to see the angels, I felt a sense of community, a sense of anticipation.

After full night fell and the stars appeared overhead, the people filled the city square, muttering with excitement and love, vibrant with anticipation. Wisps of sweet-smelling smoke wafted from vents in the ground, vapors exhaled from the underground coldfire nexus that powered Crown City. The fumes made us dizzy, disoriented, but also euphoric—ready for the Angels. Globes of coldfire light hung suspended around Chronos Square, bathing the crowd in angelic illumination. The Watchtower, with its great clock, stood over the crowd like a fortress of benevolent time and order.

As if from an invisible signal, we all held our breath, turned our faces upward, and watched the high tower doors ratchet open like curtains drawn back on a cosmic play. The immense Angels glided forward on smoothly oiled gears, four beautiful ethereal figures carved from permanent stone, the most perfect machinery, animated by quintessence. They were flawless.

They spread their clockwork wings, and one after another they dispensed pearls of wisdom that might have seemed like platitudes when read in skeptical daylight. Even now, that night's recitation is engraved in my memory, spinning out in the unearthly voices of the Angels in turn—*"Be kind, for everyone you meet is fighting a hard battle."* With the dizzying smoke around us and the euphoria of the crowd, though, the words penetrated our hearts as well as our ears. *"Beginning a task is hard. Finishing a task is harder still, but far more satisfying."*

The people gasped. Some of them wept. And when the Angels raised their wings, we all lifted our hands in a fruitless attempt to reach them.

It was amazing. It was a miracle ... and yet I realized the performance was missing a fundamental element. I was inspired then. I *knew* what I had to do, why I had been brought here to Crown City.

The Clockwork Angels captivated us all—but there was no music. I could improve on that.

Although it had no bearing on my career assignment, I'd always had perfect rhythm. I could keep time with absolute precision, like the unwavering pulse of a sleeping infant. I could feel the beat of everyday activities. Tick-tock. I needed no metronome. When I couldn't sit still, I would tap out an impatient beat on a tabletop or on my leg, which annoyed nearby people. They didn't hear the same intrinsic beat of the world. They called me restless, fidgety.

I was a respectable man from a respectable family in a respectable town on the outskirts of Crown City. I studied to become a professor, learned the basics of alchemy. My family paid the appropriate fees, and after I passed the appropriate tests, I was brought in as an instructor to the Alchemy College, which should have been enough for any man.

I settled into the instructors' dormitory, comfortable in my new rooms and ready for a new school year. I pattered out my satisfaction on a tabletop, prepared my lesson plans, and—now that I'd been inspired by the Clockwork Angels—considered adding music to the curriculum. Did not an adept drummer "keep perfect time?" And wasn't that exactly what the Watchmaker wanted?

My classes were like all the other first year classes, with my novice pupils performing standardized experiments, testing reactant powders and metals, growing crystals from saturated solutions, dissolving organic substances in the most potent acids. I taught them how the world's basic elements could be assembled and reassembled into any imaginable substance. The movements of molecules had their own rhythm.

Throughout my first semester, there was very little music at the College, save for the drumbeats I heard in my own head. Music wasn't forbidden in Albion, but neither was it encouraged. The common people had their own instruments, their own songs, but the Watchmaker himself would never express his happiness by bursting into a tune. He simply considered music irrelevant.

When poring over old class records, I was surprised to discover a forgotten part of the curriculum, a discretionary class that no professor had taught for some years, and thus it had fallen into obscurity. "Fundamentals of Music." It was perfect! I immediately contacted Professor Gruber, the chief alchemist priest, requesting permission to teach the music course, saying that it would broaden the students' experience and knowledge.

Professor Gruber was skeptical and, above all, curious. He summoned me to his office. "There must be a reason this course is no longer taught," he said.

I had to force myself to sit respectfully still and not tap out a beat on my leg. "Perhaps because there was no qualified teacher, sir. I studied the old syllabus, and I believe I have the proper knowledge."

The chief priest frowned down at the papers. "I'm not sure, Professor Russell. Such a class might distract the students from more important pursuits. Music in the abstract? Think about the average person. What use would they have for rhythms and melodies? At the Alchemy College, we focus on science."

"Then I will teach the *science* of music, sir," I said. "Don't you see? Music *is* mathematics—so many intricate systems, the orderly arrangement of notes and chords like formulas, the logarithmic interrelation of harmonies, the geometric patterns and structures of the orchestration—aligned to a strict physical premise of *time*. Surely the Watchmaker would approve.

"The conductor's tempo is the clock, unwavering and unstoppable. Like a grand-complication timepiece, each instrument in the orchestra must play its part in synchrony, each musician meshed in that perfect, ticking pendulum. And there is the emotional resonance in the listener—like *alchemy*." I paused, saw to my dismay that much of my excitement was lost on him.

"It still sounds like only a metaphor to me," said my superior, but he indulged me with a long sigh, signing the paper so that I could prepare my class. "We will consider it an experiment."

My first class was small, only eleven students, and five of them were there as their fourth choice since they had not qualified for the topics that interested them. But I was happy because the class itself allowed me to study and refine my own knowledge, quantifying the things I knew by instinct and giving names to the rhythms I could sense in the universe around me.

And it established a precedent, giving me opportunities for more advanced classes.

But I needed the devices to create music. I discovered that if I described a musical instrument to my colleagues as a *scientific* problem—a resonant cylinder of a certain fundamental note, a membrane with tunable qualities, a soundbox with certain harmonics—the younger alchemists would take it as a technical challenge appropriate for the higher-level classes.

Soon I had invented and assembled an orchestra's worth of tuned drums, chromatic bells, steam-powered horns, and more.

Long strings stretched across whole rooms, each one plucked by rotating plectrums driven by coldfire steam.

But I had to teach my students something the Alchemy College considered "worthwhile." Those grand designs I heard and visualized would have to wait until I could express them in some greater arena. An audience. But that day would come. Surely it would be perfect enough for the Clockwork Angels.

So I instructed my students in harmony and melody, but the study of *rhythm* excited me most of all. At the front of the classroom I set up an arrangement of drums, and I would start each class with one big *boom* on a mounted bass drum. Having attracted their attention, I silently counted a slow three bars, then hit it again. *Boom!* After the same interval, I struck the drum a third time, and by then we could all feel a pulse.

As the students listened, I added a counter rhythm on a small, snappy drum, with the bass drum still punctuating every third one. A foot pedal activated a drone with rippling harp-like harmonies, and I brought in quick flurries of *rat-a-tats* on small melodic drums. Seemingly out of time, they slashed across the pulse in a jagged onslaught that raised my own adrenalin.

Some of my students showed a genuine aptitude for the subject, but most exhibited a just-as-genuine lack of interest—not hostile, merely perplexed.

After all my labors and my technical successes with the new instrument designs, I was surprised to become an object of scorn and ridicule among the faculty members. Some of the senior professors mocked me for wasting time with something as esoteric and useless as music—"corrupting our youth," they said, "distracting them from more practical matters when they should be trying to strengthen the Watchmaker's Stability." I defended myself by presenting the mathematical basis for musical theory, but they just sniffed, calling music a mere "pseudoscience," unlike the rigorously proven science of alchemy.

After much justification and debate, I convinced Professor Gruber to extend my class for another semester. I was so pleased with his answer that I felt jittery.

But when the jitters continued throughout the next month, I sensed that something entirely different might be wrong—with *me*. I held out my hand and watched it shake and tremble, as if my nerves were fighting against a thousand clashing drumbeats. It frightened me. I could make the tremors stop by sheer force of will, but they would return. I told no one, but my fear increased as the dread realization began to dawn on me.

I was losing my rhythm.

Though music was my passion, most of my teaching was in basic alchemistry. I would walk among the laboratory tables and watch as the students crushed mineral powders, dissolved salts, and burned crystalized distillates. I made my students perform each step themselves, and in that way, I could hide my tremors.

It was some kind of degenerative nerve disease. When I saw the best physicians in Crown City, they had no cure for my malady. They gave me potions to counteract the tremors, but the drugs only made me logy, my tongue thick, my vision blurred. I don't know if the tremors stopped, but I was too lethargic to notice them. I decided that was not an acceptable cure at all.

Yet without the potions, my condition grew worse. When I tried to perform interlocking counterrhythms with my connected musical instruments, my fingers, hands, and feet betrayed me— lost their rhythm, lost their time. The tick-tock of my life had slipped a gear tooth. I could no longer control what I needed to do. My sadness increased. How would I ever present the Watchmaker with my grand dream of music for the Clockwork Angels if my own body was an asynchronous wreck?

In my private offices I had a metronome that kept perfect time, swinging back and forth, clicking off the beats. Always before, such devices were superfluous to me because I could hear the rhythm so perfectly in my head. But as I sat by myself holding my wooden stick and trying to match the beats, my hands trembled so much that I kept missing time.

Few of my students could hear the intrinsic beat as anything more than theoretical—they didn't even know what they were missing. But I had always heard that constant tick-tock drumbeat, as reliable as the pounding of my own heart. And now that I was losing it, I found the idea far more heart-wrenching than never to have known it at all.

It was terrifying.

But fear can either destroy a person or make him rise to new levels. I went out to see the Clockwork Angels again, and as I raised my hands with all the others, dizzy from the sweet smoke in Chronos Square, their words poured into my mind. *"All is for the best in this best of all possible worlds."* At first the tears streaming down my cheek were hot and bitter—all was not for the best in *my* world—but soon I wept for a different reason than all those other ecstatic worshippers. I had been inspired again! I still knew what I wanted to do, but I would have to achieve it in a different way.

The Angels, those perfect clockwork goddesses built by the Watchmaker, had surpassed what he himself could do. Though the loving Watchmaker was himself slightly more than human— we all knew that—the Clockwork Angels exceeded even him.

Now that my body had demonstrated its frailty, its unreliability, maybe I could create a substitute as well. Something better than myself.

If every clock ticked out a perfect beat, then perhaps a clockwork mechanism could be expanded into a machine to keep time with the music I felt in my heart, a clockwork drummer whose very existence was to demonstrate the mystic rhythms of the universe for everyone to hear. Not just a metronome's mathematical perfection, but shifting rhythms that pushed and pulled like gravity, tides, or solar winds.

A rhythm could drive forward with intense energy, or relax into a gentle cadence. And oh, the tension when two such rhythms were combined, the upbeats straining against the downbeats. Sublime! If I could not be that drummer to teach the students and show the Watchmaker, then my artificial percussor could do so in my stead.

I went to the chief alchemy priest to give him the sad news that I no longer felt adequate to teach the rhythm and music class. "My health is deteriorating, sir. I have seen several physicians already. And it would be best if ..."

Professor Gruber made an annotation in his logbook, but didn't seem the least bit disturbed. "All is for the best, Professor Russell. Take each day and use the extra class hour to rest and recuperate."

Yes, I needed the free time, but I didn't choose to rest. With maddeningly shaky hands, I designed my creation, assembling a thousand small pieces of basic steam technology, hydraulic engineering, interlocking clockworks, based on all those instruments and mechanisms I'd asked the engineers to design for my first music class. Wheels within wheels motivated armatures, pistons, ball joints, spiral arrays that ratcheted down to finer and finer movements.

It would be perfect, exactly what I needed the Watchmaker to see.

During the intricate assembly process, I had to fabricate stabilizing tools because the tiny screws and bolts fell from my shaking hands. But those who live with adversity are forced to learn either patience or despair, and I refused to despair as I saw my beautiful percussor take shape before me.

I used muffled caps on the drumsticks so the racket would not disturb my fellow professors—or even alert them to what I was doing. I added coldfire to the small boiler inside the torso chamber, powered up the mechanism, and set the articulated arms in motion: smaller gears for faster tempo, larger pistons for heavy bass drumbeats. Making adjustments, I felt a growing delight despite the fact that my own tremors increased, possibly due to exhaustion or stress.

The percussor was my surrogate rhythm keeper. He could do what I could no longer accomplish, and he kept perfect rhythm. I knew he would exceed even my best.

Seven months later the artificial drummer was complete. I had tested and programmed for all possible tempos and counterrhythms. Clockwork controllers allowed every rhythmic subdivision or polyrhythm, and could trigger any number of sound producers—drums, horns, strings, and cymbals, all of my own invention. Ah, if this could be integrated into the Clockwork Angels!

But the percussor still wasn't ready for his debut. He had the programming and the well-oiled intermeshed gears, but he was missing one thing. While music is a science, as I had demonstrated by deconstructing it into pure mathematics, music is also *art*—and for that my percussor needed a soul.

As a professor of alchemy, I had access to forbidden materials, including the College's well-stocked chemical vault, and I had the authority to requisition any items I needed. The Red Guard stationed at the door knew me, and he assumed I must be preparing for another laboratory class. I knew exactly what I needed.

Inside the vault, the well-labeled shelves were stacked high and stocked well with all the known combinations of elements, arranged according to a rudimentary periodic table. But what I needed rested on the highest shelf in a sealed case marked with a honeybee symbol—precious, immeasurably valuable, and so misunderstood.

I climbed a ladder to reach the high shelf, set the tumblers of the lock with the proper combination that only alchemy professors were allowed to know, and opened the container with hands shaking even more than usual. Bathed in the pale white light that was life itself, I removed a tiny fragment of the stored *quintessence.*

That was exactly what my percussor needed.

When I prepared my demonstration for important faculty members, I invited the Watchmaker himself. The other professors thought it was just a courtesy, never expecting him to come, but I claimed that this was a most vital exhibition, something of importance to the Clockwork Angels. I needed to show him for myself—how else could I make my case?

I felt weak with relief when the ancient man arrived accompanied by three members of his Black Watch and the highest-order alchemy priests, as well as Professor Gruber. Even if I hadn't suffered from the degenerative palsy, seeing the Watchmaker in person might have set my entire body shaking.

But I was ready. The precious quintessence had the effect of strengthening me as well, energizing me, and I felt more in tune with my own rhythm. At least temporarily. I would have used more of the substance myself for such a crucial event, but I didn't dare. My percussor needed it.

For the demonstration, I had set up my clockwork drummer in one of the empty auditoriums. The percussor was all brass and copper, bright with coldfire, venting trickles of steam as the boiler built up to optimal energy levels. Regardless of my own anxiety, the mechanism would drive through the performance without a flaw. My multi-armed percussor ratcheted into its initial position, articulated arms bent, drumsticks raised, all components of the kit arrayed around the central torso. Hidden within, the quintessence burned bright.

My job was to introduce the percussor and then wait nervously as my creation performed. Would the Watchmaker hear the rhythms and see what was missing in his Clockwork Angels? I could only hope!

"My gracious observers, at this college I have taught a class in the mathematics of music, the mystic rhythms of the universe, the clockwork beat that ticks away inside all of us. But my own human frailty makes it impossible to achieve the perfection that existed only in my imagination. The best part of being human is that we can strive to create something better than ourselves." I nodded toward the great man. "Just as our loving Watchmaker created the Clockwork Angels, which embody more grace and beauty than any mortal can hope to achieve, this device can add even more grandeur to the Clockwork Angels, fill the silence that accompanies each performance, and make them *better.*"

The Watchmaker looked at me fixedly, as if I had insulted him, then turned his attention to the clockwork percussor. His ancient parchment skin was drawn tight across his face. I had hoped for a paternal smile.

I felt the tremors returning, and I badly wished I had another bit of the quintessence, just a small dose, to calm my nerves, but right now all of the precious substance was inside the percussor.

I stepped back, swallowed hard, and activated the percussor. My heart was pounding louder than any drum I'd ever heard. "This piece is titled *Exaltation.*"

Just as I used to begin my earliest classes at the Alchemy College, the percussor seized their attention with a single deep *boom!* The silence that followed seemed to hang heavy, expectant, impatient. Then came the next loud *boom!* as the bass drum continued to repeat in slow pulses.

Other instruments joined in—rhythmic slashes and melodic bursts, expanding chords and flourishes of bass notes. The percussor was a melody of mechanical movement, smooth joints, gliding pistons, all in perfect rhythm. My amplification chambers could project a sound across the room or make it hover in mid-air above the listeners' heads. I smiled to watch them swivel in unison when their eyes were drawn by the acoustic illusion, as if they would *see* the sound I had manifested there. Even the Watchmaker turned his head.

I even dabbled with how to create color in the sound—just tinges so far, but I hoped some of my listeners—especially the Watchmaker—might sense an azure chord, a prismatic arpeggio, or a harp gliss that sprayed out in golden sparks. With coldfire steam that emanated from the mechanism I created sensations of cold and heat, damp or arid air, which further amplified the music's power.

The themes were based on the Angels' symbolic identities, the first four movements titled "Light," "Sea," "Sky," and "Land." My music sparkled and glowed, and then waves of sound receded to the back of the auditorium, even as gentle zephyrs swept down like waterfalls from the corners. A pounding whirlwind built to a peak of tension, then I triggered a release—a long sustain into a slower tempo, a softer dynamic, in subtle variations of minor chords.

I created monumental landforms out of sound so that the listener sensed immense chasms, towering mesas, and vast formations of red rock. I built fantastic landscapes from tales of the great deserts overseas and the legendary lands of the far north, Ultima Thule—a mirage of tremendous glaciers under dark skies that danced with shifting veils of colored light, then a tower of sculpted rock, solitary and eternal, with stars wheeling around its upraised finger.

Gradually, I raised the percussor's pitch and the tempo, and the music raced faster, louder. I created darkness, a chill, then slashes of white heat. This began the fifth and most important movement of my symphony: "Quintessence," and its musical language and images might only be understood by the Watchmaker. Chords swirled around the room like desert dust devils, while frantic bursts of notes flashed like lightning. Volleys of drums thundered, while others beat down like heavy rain, or dripped from imaginary eaves. A chorus of ethereal voices seemed to cry out against the tempest.

Forgetting myself and my audience, forgetting everything but the music, I had programmed the crescendo to the very edge of restraint and control, then the percussor concluded with a massive chord that faded away into a flicker of purple fireflies before diminishing into a dark blue forest and the gentle fall of diamond snowflakes.

As the last vibrations fell silent, I stood dizzy, with shaking joints. I knew it had been good. I turned to look at the faculty and, more importantly, at the Watchmaker. Surely he had experienced and understood! Some of the other professors were smiling, but most remained stony-faced. The Watchmaker himself sat erect with a slightly puzzled frown. No one spoke. Everyone waited to hear the Watchmaker's assessment.

Finally, he said, "It is an admirable example of clockwork motion and the intricate synergy of components, but I fail to grasp the purpose. What does it do? How would you add this to my Angels? And why?"

"It is … *music*, sir. Rhythms to touch an audience, to move them. Imagine it in Chronos Square, with the Angels watching from above."

The Watchmaker sat still. "I've never been fond of music, though over the years I have come to tolerate it. I realize that some of the lower classes take comfort in it, however, and to deny them that small pleasure would be counter-productive to the Stability. But I would expect the students in my Alchemy College, and my professors, to be more concerned with important matters. I fail to see how this would improve the Clockwork Angels at all."

The Watchmaker stood up along with his black-uniformed Regulators, preparing to leave. "Your grasp of clockwork engineering is indeed impressive, Professor Russell, but we will not be using this device to accompany my Angels. I would suggest you devote your efforts toward something more tangibly useful to my Stability."

He departed, leaving the other professors to mutter amongst themselves, reaffirming what the Watchmaker had said, now that he had said it. They all departed, leaving me alone in the echoing lecture hall with my magnificent but supposedly useless clockwork percussor.

Despite my disappointment, I took heart from the smiles I had seen on some of the faces. While many were deaf to the rhythms, others did hear and enjoy them. But my music would never be a part of the Clockwork Angels.

The Watchmaker's lukewarm response was a crushing blow, but he had not *forbidden* any further performances of the percussor. In fact, he had complimented me on my design and engineering skill. Maybe the students would learn something from the mechanics of my demonstration device, even if they couldn't hear the drumbeats for what they were.

I decided to move my grand mechanism and let others see for themselves.

But my body had not stopped shaking, and I felt weak. I couldn't complete my mission unless I controlled myself, and again my best recourse in this difficult situation would be to rely on artificial means. I wanted to move quickly, before word spread throughout the College.

I returned to the alchemy storage vault, presented my standard authorization to the Red Guard. "I require another sample of quintessence for a very important experiment." He didn't question me; the Red Guard had never questioned me. My legs were wobbling as I climbed the ladder to the high shelf. Even the Alchemy College had only a limited supply of quintessence— but I had my needs, which I considered sufficient.

The marvelous, shining substance felt warm and effervescent as I removed a droplet the size of a pearl, and applied it to my trembling hands, my arms. I felt immediate relief. I was steady again, seemingly younger, and ready.

But even quintessence couldn't last. I would accept what I had now, and I would make it count. I hoped that more of the students would feel and recognize the rhythms.

I reassembled my clockwork percussor in the courtyard between the student dormitory and the looming laboratory building. The process took hours, during which time curious observers watched me, muttering about "odd Professor Russell." I ignored them as I tinkered and adjusted, calibrated the articulated arms and ran my trembling fingertips across the percussor's smooth copper head, the rounded cylinder of the torso that contained a tiny fragment of quintessence. I felt a greater stamina now, and I kept going without rest.

"What is it, Professor?" asked one of my students from the second term mathematics of music class. "An industrial machine? A device designed for the manufacturing lines?"

"Not at all—something much better."

I hadn't summoned a crowd, but they came anyway, hundreds of students ranging from the freshest novices to the elite graduates. They all watched me as I prepared the percussor, tested the pressure gauges, and finally turned to survey my audience. I gave no introduction this time. I would let the drumbeats speak for themselves.

Pounding out a long sequence of irresistible rhythms, my percussor performed so magnificently that I was swept away in the beat, feeling my pulse increase. Even my returning tremors matched the tempo—the music made me feel as alive as the stolen quintessence did. Some students joined the rhythm, patting their sides with their hands, tapping their feet, but most looked disoriented.

When the percussor finished its intricate programming, the last of the steam vented out, its armatures reset themselves and folded the drumsticks close to the central torso. Silence rang loudly in the air.

There was some applause, but it died quickly. I looked around to see a gathering circle of frowning alchemy priests. Behind them came a group of uniformed Regulators, and my heart sank.

I was stripped of my professorship, my classes assigned to other instructors; my recalcitrance was bad enough, but when it was discovered that I had fraudulently procured some of the vital quintessence, I was told to pack up and leave the Alchemy College.

Even with my disgrace, however, I didn't let myself fall into the depths of despair, knowing the great—even impossible— thing I had achieved. In one small measure of mercy, the Watchmaker did allow me to keep the core of my clockwork percussor. His cryptic message said, "My alchemists and my Regulators have no interest in your device, but the average may have some use for it. I only regret that your obvious talents could not have been directed toward something worthwhile."

Worthwhile … If only the music could have joined the Angels high above the city square.

Years have passed, and only this remains. A much smaller device than my original elaborate construction, not much more than a sideshow act, really, but it is the best I can do now. And my percussor is still very good. When the people come to see each performance, some of them can hear what I hear.

The Regulators do not bother me as my device performs to crowds in the streets. Despite the degeneration of my own nerves and muscles, the percussor rolls out the rhythm perfectly, every single time, never missing the tiniest beat, exactly the perfection I had intended to create. It has become more and more difficult to obtain the spark of quintessence my percussor needs—that *we* need—but we manage.

I can still program my percussor, change his performance, add new complexities to the drumming. Perfection in the mathematics of music requires two things, both passion and precision. Because the heart of his mechanism still has that fragment of quintessence inside, that tiny bit of soul, I can experiment. Because that is the only way a person—or a clockwork drummer—can grow.

Now he can *improvise.*

This is perhaps my favorite story set in Tucker's Grove—with time travel, dinosaurs, and a lonely old farmer. It's a very vivid tale for me, and I can picture every scene perfectly, and the character is drawn from an ancient, bachelor farmer who lived next door from us, Mr. Reindahl (I also mentioned him in a previous story.) As a boy, I would run across the hayfields and keep him company, climb the big box elder tree in his front yard, and listen to his stories. I spent a summer helping him bale hay (which was really hard work!). All that time, I didn't know I was collecting ingredients for stories.

"Drilling Deep" is so vivid it has always haunted me.

DRILLING DEEP

I can only stay a week, Dad." David sounded apologetic. "The other paleontologists are already out digging in Montana, and they can't survive very long without me."

"That's okay." Arne Christensen gave a nothing-bothers-me shrug. "I'm glad you came at all. It's been so long."

David opened the cupboard above the sink where Arne had kept the jelly jar glasses for the past twenty years. He removed a glass and turned on the faucet, but only a thin, murky trickle crept out.

Arne leaned forward in his worn overalls, making the kitchen chair creak. "The well's gone bad, Davey—and what does come out tastes like salty muck. I'm getting Harry Warner's rig out here to start drilling a new one."

David tasted a drop with a simultaneous smile and grimace. "It's called *connate water*, Dad—fairly unusual. It's the salt water from ancient seas, trapped underground when the rocks were formed a couple hundred million years ago."

"No wonder it tastes like dinosaur piss."

"You're off by a few years, Dad. But no matter." David always liked to explain things, and Arne listened with full attention, since he'd never had a chance to go to college—too much work to do on the farm. Nevertheless, he found the world endlessly interesting, with or without scientific explanations.

Arne smiled, and his single gold-rimmed tooth flashed in the early morning light. He had always (jokingly) watched the gold prices in the paper, threatening to sell his tooth if things got too bad on the farm. Fortunately, things looked good this year; he had rented out most of the usable farmland, keeping only about ten acres for himself, now that he was alone.

David set the glass back on the cracked Contact paper in the cupboard, as if he hadn't actually wanted a drink but simply needed something to do. Arne ran a dirty fingernail along the edge of the gold-flecked Formica of the kitchen table. "What is it your team is doing out in Montana, again? More dinosaur bones?"

David knew the subject would fascinate his father. "We're looking into the K-T extinction event. Sixty-five million years ago the dinosaurs and a whole list of other animals just *died*, all at once, probably because of an asteroid impact. To find out more details, we have to dig down sixty-five million years and look at the rocks."

Arne frowned. "How do you dig down millions of years?"

David relaxed while talking about his work. "In geology, new rock layers are laid down on top of the old ones. Like a stack of bills—new ones on top, oldest ones on the bottom. The deeper down you dig, the further back in time you go."

Arne's old fatherly interest had never dimmed despite David's occasional intellectual coolness. He was proud that his son knew so many things that he himself had never figured out, although David couldn't help but feel superior to a "hick farmer" who had no real geology training.

"But because of upheavals and weathering," David continued, "the past is closer to the surface in some places—and it just so happens that sixty-five million years ago is close to the surface in Montana."

Though the red-winged blackbird's song sounded like an unoiled hinge, Arne enjoyed the flavor it added to the early morning peace. Regretfully, he started the generator on the well-drilling rig, drowning out nature's noises with more civilized racket.

David had been away from the rise-at-dawn farm life for many years now, and he was still asleep inside the old house. The well-drilling rig made one hell of an alarm clock, though, hammering the bore pipe like a piledriver with percussive violence.

Thunnngg

The pipe bit into the dirt.

Thunnngg

The rig pounded it below the surface, like a disoriented mole tunneling toward the center of the Earth.

Arne mused to himself, "I'm drilling back in time." Though he didn't entirely understand it all, he was fascinated by David's geological analogy. "Digging down a million years." He would chew on the concept as if it were an old piece of tough jerky.

If you went back in time by digging down into the ground, then were all the people in those underground earth-homes literally "living in the past?" He grinned at his own joke; he would have to tell it to David as soon as he woke up.

Thunnngg

There, now the rig had sunk the pipe all the way into yesterday.

Thunnngg

And the day before.

Thunnngg

Picking up speed. Now David was still in college, and his mother had just died.

Thunnngg

David a little boy.

Thunnngg

David just born.

Thunnngg

Arne and Elizabeth first married.

Thunnngg
And that was World War II.
Thunnngg
World War I.
Thunnngg
The Civil War.
Thunnngg
The Revolutionary War.
Thunnngg
In 1492, Columbus sailed the ocean blue.
Thunnngg
King Arthur and the Knights of the Round Table.
Thunnngg
Jesus Christ.
Moses.
Thunnngg
The dinosaurs.
Adam and Eve.
Thunnngg
Even though morning coolness still clutched at the air, Arne discovered he was sweating.

Day after day, the rig hammered each section of pipe up to its neck in the dirt. Arne screwed together another section and set the rig in motion again, letting his thin probe bore through the ancient strata.

The work wasn't too hard, it wasn't too monotonous. The hose dumped water down the shaft, and the rig hammered it into muck, pounding the pipe sluggishly downward. Arne pumped up the gray sludge, spilling it across the sloping farmyard like a dead lake of wet cement.

Two hundred feet down.

Arne's eyes bounced up and down, watching the center pipe in the rig as it rhythmically rose and fell, like the pendulum on the biggest grandfather clock of all. He could easily run the rig himself, but David did his best to seem helpful (which mostly entailed standing around and talking a lot, keeping his father company). The summer stillness was broken only by his conversation and the cyclic *thunnngg* of the rig.

The insert pipe came up, spilling battered sludge, but now a glistening black stain swirled in the gray clayish ooze, like a shadow from the past. As the mud continued to spew from the shaft, the black became darker. David bent down in the mud and ran his fingers through the black ooze. "You just struck coal!"

Arne was both surprised and proud to see his son so willing to get his fingers dirty. "Coal? Like real coal?"

David sounded like a lecturing teacher again. "It's not too uncommon to hit coal when you dig a well, Dad. This is probably low-grade stuff, but I can take a sample to a friend of mine, so he can analyze it."

Arne was genuinely amazed. "So, how far back did I drill?" Seeing David's puzzled look, he added, "I mean how many years down did I go? To hit the coal?"

"Oh." David's face looked like a jumble of jigsaw puzzle pieces falling into place. "Of course. Let's see, coal would be about three hundred million years ago, during the Carboniferous period. Not too bad for six days work."

Arne beamed. David saw the expression, smiled, and described the picture for his father. "Lots of swamps covered the land. Towering fern-trees, giant insects, big lizards. Volcanoes. The air hot and steamy." He raised his eyebrows. "Do you know what the coal is, Dad? Why it burns?"

"No." He knew David wanted to explain it to him.

"Rocks don't burn. Anything that burns had to be living at one time. Wood burns because trees spend their lives soaking up sunlight, storing 'solar power' in their trunks. When you burn wood, you release that sun-energy again.

"Coal is from those big, steamy swamps of three-hundred million years ago, all the vegetation crushed under layers and layers of rock over time, squeezed and concentrated. When you burn a lump of coal you're releasing 300-million-year-old sunlight."

Arne let out a sigh. "Ah, Davey, you should have been a teacher."

Less than an hour later they struck water.

The sun nudged toward the southwestern horizon, and Arne stood in his mud-splattered overalls, hoe in hand, at the edge of the vast garden. He realized he looked like an old cover from *Reader's Digest*, the kind that were "Rural with a Vengeance" according to David.

Each spring Arne planted a garden six times larger than he needed for himself, but he enjoyed the work, and he enjoyed giving the vegetables away. And if he didn't feel like harvesting everything that ripened, he threw it all in the compost pit; the vegetables didn't care if they were harvested or not.

Inside the farmhouse, David had cooked a fancy farewell dinner for himself and his father. Arne usually cooked for one, and—thanks to the fouled well—he had become accustomed to not cooking at all in the past week. David had filled a few old milk jugs with water at the neighbor's to tide them over until the new well could be hooked up to the house's existing plumbing.

By himself outside, Arne waited in the expectant silence, looking out across everything he had known. It had changed very little since his own childhood. The unplanted half of the garden stood in black, hard chunks, just as the plow had piled them a month before. The garden seemed transformed in the reddening sunlight of the dying afternoon.

Arne stared at the lifeless earth, amazed at the lack of weeds. Although there had been no rain for two weeks, several viscid puddles lay in the dirt, covered with slimy green. He hadn't noticed them before. As he watched, the pools seemed ... alive, crawling, oozing, glittering with ancient secrets: algae groping for a foothold on the blasted, sterile landscape of a newborn Earth.

When Arne pulled in a hitching breath, the air seemed oppressively damp and steamy.

Suddenly, something felt wrong. The sun hung motionless on the horizon, but as he watched, it picked up speed in the opposite direction and heaved itself above the edge of the world, like a fiery red behemoth whirling from west to east. The huge clock-hand of the sun moved backward, counterclockwise.

A thousand conflicting thoughts battered on his mind, terror yet awed fascination at the same time.

What if, in his thoughtless drilling, he had punctured a bubble of the past, a cyst buried three-hundred million years below the surface? Like the primordial water that had invaded his old well, causing it to dry up? What if that ancient past was even now seeping toward the surface?

Arne blinked, and the illusion of the sun's motion vanished, leaving it half-sunken on the horizon. When David called him to come in for supper, he almost ran to the house.

That night, Arne had no nightmares because he never slept at all.

He lay tossing on his creaky bed, smelling the taint of brimstone in the air. He and David had sat up and talked next to the fireplace, where Arne insisted on burning a few old lumps of coal he had found in the basement. His eyes sparkled with childlike fascination as the 300-million-year-old light spilled into the present.

David had to leave the next morning to catch a flight to Great Falls, Montana, and already Arne felt more lonely than he had been in years.

In the numbness of night, Arne could hear the echoing drip of the faucet in the kitchen. How could a faucet drip with no water pressure behind it? The dripping pounded deep into his consciousness, into his imagination.

Drip drip drip drip drik drik trik tik tik tick tick tick tick

Nature's own clock. Time was passing ... but he couldn't tell which direction it moved.

From outside, through the window screen, came night sounds he had never heard before, awful and primeval. Eerie calls and haunting burbling noises as of something moving slowly through a swamp. The air in the bedroom felt hot and humid, intensifying all sounds.

A thrill of fascination traced Arne's spine, a thrill of fear. He had immersed himself in something strange, a true mystery of nature. He didn't know whether to be eager for morning, or to be terrified of it.

Arne stood on the porch in the still-wakening dawn and stared out into the new universe of what had been his backyard. His jaw hung open in an unabashed expression of awe.

He took a step off the porch, compelled to walk toward the misty, primeval swamp that had appeared during the night, seeming to stretch beyond his distant fields. Ruddy sunlight shimmered and reflected in the steamy air, as if slowed down by plowing into the past.

The ground felt spongy and damp beneath his work boots. He could smell the bizarre vegetation and the sultry ooze lurking in the swamp. He paused, torn between his fascination and the urge to run and hide under the bed.

He thought about calling for David, but the sense of wonder clouded all his fear. Arne was experiencing something no one else had ever imagined. David would never believe this; in fact, Arne feared that his son might not be able to see it at all. This simply couldn't be real.

The air was hushed and brooding, as if noise-making creatures had not yet evolved. Far off, beyond where neighboring Tucker's farm would someday be, Arne could see the smoke-belching crown of an ancient volcano, but the rumble had been reduced to a low drone in the steamy air.

Giant rushes and wide-spreading ferns rose around him, dripping star-points of dew. Huge fern-trees towered overhead, some rising almost a hundred feet high. Primitive evergreens and trees with no flowers clustered in the wet undergrowth. When a sound like a chainsaw whizzed past, he gawked at an armored dragonfly with a wingspan of two feet. The dragonfly circled Arne's head and then sped deeper into the swamp, as if beckoning him to follow.

He walked along, hypnotized by the primeval beauty.

Billowing seed-ferns and giant, cactus-like club mosses shed green reflections into the heavy forest. A large beetle scuttled sluggishly down the fallen trunk of a fern-tree, picking its way across a wet mass of algae.

Arne pondered beside a quiet, glassy pool crowded with bored-looking fish. All around him was a pervasive, relaxing hum, like a cicada's song played backwards. A spider the size of an apple watched him from a scale-tree but did not seem interested in prey so large.

Arne felt a delicious lull in himself and enjoyed a moment of peace. He had always known there were mysteries in the world far greater than himself. This made the most profound religious experience seem like no more than a sneeze. He wished David were here with him. He decided to return to the house—at least to within shouting distance, so he could rouse his son. No one should miss this!

Arne didn't think he had stayed in the swamp for long, and the sun still hung low in the morning sky. He hadn't gone far, but when he turned back toward the farm house, the prehistoric swamp had swallowed everything, and stretched for miles and miles in all directions.

The past sprawled forever and ever before him, and he had to go three hundred million years to get home again.

PREVIOUS PUBLICATION INFORMATION

"The Blood Prize," copyright © 2016 by The Aradio Brothers, first published by WordFire Press, 2016.

"Canals in the Sand," copyright © 1996 by WordFire, Inc., first published in *War of the Worlds: Global Dispatches*, edited by Kevin J. Anderson, Bantam Spectra, 1996.

"Change of Face," copyright © 1995 by Kristine Kathryn Rusch and Kevin J. Anderson, originally published in *Amazing Stories* vol. LXVI, No. 1, 1992.

"Cold Ice, Red Blood," copyright © 2022, WordFire, Inc., first published in *Weird Tales 366*, 2022.

"Drilling Deep," copyright © 1986, WordFire, Inc., first published in *The Horror Show* Winter 1986.

"Final Performance," copyright © 1985 by WordFire, Inc., first published in *The Magazine of Fantasy and Science Fiction*, January 1985.

"Frog Kiss," copyright © 1991 by WordFire, Inc. First published in *Marion Zimmer Bradley's Fantasy Magazine*, Fall 1991.

"Make a Wish," copyright 2024, WordFire, Inc., first publication.

"Mirror, Mirror on the Wall," copyright © 2011 by WordFire, Inc., first published in *Tucker's Grove*, Arc Manor, 2011. An earlier version of the story was published in *Beyond* no. 7 (year unknown).

"Mythical Creatures," copyright © 2011 by WordFire, Inc., first published in eBook form from WordFire Press (2011).

"Quest Prize," copyright © 2022, WordFire, Inc., first published in *Animal Magica, Volume 2*, ed. Tanya Hales, Mythic Mongoose Press, 2022.

"The Reign to Come," copyright © 2018 by WordFire, Inc., first published in *Pulphouse Magazine* issue 1, 2018.

"The Rhythm Method: The Percussor's Tale," copyright © 2015, WordFire, Inc. and Pratt Music, first published in *Clockwork Lives*, by Kevin J. Anderson and Neil Peart, ECW Press, 2015.

PREVIOUS PUBLICATION INFORMATION

"The Sacrifice," first published online in *Daily Science Fiction*, 2018.

"Sea Wind" copyright © 1985 by WordFire, Inc. First published in *Theshold of Fantasy*, Winter 1985.

"Skeleton in the Closet," copyright © 1985, WordFire, Inc. and Ron Fortier, first published in *Bringing Down the Moon*, ed. Jani Anderson, Space & Time, 1985.

"The Stranger on the Ice," copyright © 2023, WordFire, Inc., first published in *Double Trouble*, ed. Jonathan Maberry & Keith R.A. DeCandido, International Association of Media Tie-In Writers, 2023.

"Tarzan and the Martian Invaders," copyright © 2013, ERB, Inc., first published in *Worlds of Edgar Rice Burroughs*, ed. Mike Resnick and Robert T. Garcia, Baen Books, 2013.

ACKNOWLEDGMENTS

To me, this set of my collected short fiction is the epitome of how publishing has changed in recent years. If you've looked at all the books, you know what a tremendous effort it was: seven complete volumes, more than 130 stories, each one with a personal introduction. It took me a lot of time and effort to put it all together.

But if I had taken this proposal to any of my major traditional publishers—where I've had numerous bestsellers and sold millions of copies—they would have laughed me out of the building. Seven volumes, in hardcover, of reprint short fiction? Not even a specialty publisher would be interested in such a large undertaking.

But I knew in my gut that my fans would feel different. I really wanted to do the Kevin J. Anderson Short Fiction Library, and I wanted to do it my way.

In the old world, I would write up a proposal, send it to my agent, who would shop it around among my editors. If an editor was interested, they would try to convince their marketing departments. If that worked, the publisher would produce the book, then send out their sales reps to the bookstores, who would order some copies, and then finally offer the book to readers in the store.

Instead, thanks to Kickstarter, I could just present this project directly to my fans—no middlemen, just me and the readers.

During the three-week campaign, over 900 people stepped up to the plate and put their money down, expressing their faith in me and my writing. With their direct support, I was able to make this project happen, and very quickly.

Because I had done so much of the work ahead of time, I was able to deliver the entire ebook set, all seven volumes, within weeks of when the Kickstarter ended. On the very day the surveys closed, I had the final numbers, and I could put together the print order for the hardcovers and trade paperbacks.

No traditional publisher could have done that. No traditional publisher would have even considered it.

I'll say it again: I could not have produced the Kevin J. Anderson Short Fiction Library without the overwhelming support of my readers and backers. To show my gratitude, I am listing every one of their names here, 912 Kickstarter backers, in order, who made these books possible.

I think this is a real landmark in my career. You're a part of this project, and now you're a part of this book. Thank you from the bottom of my heart.

Kevin J. Anderson

Martin Greening

Christian Meyer

Ben Wallace

Daniel Cruson

Casey J Bowen

John Crouch

Three Ravens Publishing

Saud Abdulaziz

Kevin A Davis

Erik Fischer

Kevin Halstead

mdtommyd

Mike Bavister

Sean Smith

Luke Herstedt

Belinda Asbell

Tod Casasent

Ian Harris

Rob Carlsen

Eva Holmquist

Jeanne QTF Baker

Mark Leslie

Ryan Danger Congdon

Wes Kullhem

Anonymous

Jason Kristopher

Jamie Davis

Rowan Stone

Eric Stallsworth

Robert Prinzing

Erik K. Booth

Joseph e Evard jr

Kerensa Ward

pjk

Dr Douglas Vaughan

Angelica

Mark Carter

Michael Rosenberg

Charlotte Glaze

Kevin Miraglia

David H. Hendrickson

Ronald Heere

Albene Dictine

Dave Holets

Joe Dube

Sherrilyn McQueen

Nate H

Deborah Hinkley

Robert Bishop

David Pierce

Russell Fisk

Ryan Scott James

R. Dylan Stewart

Thor Nolen

Timothy Cobb

Siona St. Mark

Kris Alexander

James R McGinnis Jr

joe dicker

Joe Gillis

Scott Casey

Heiko Koenig

Steven V

Remiam7

Michèle Laframboise

Star Eagle

Jim Gotaas

Monster Ivy Publishing

E.M. Middel

Bryan Spaulding

Joe Davidson

Chris coker

Rebecca M. Senese

PM

Timothy Walket

Peter

Peter Michael Gray

Jimmy Guikema

James Palmer

Zack Fissel

EnricoB

Chad

Kraig Krueger

Jason 'XenoPhage' Frisvold

Stephen Ballentine

Ryan Honsl

Lois Bartholomew

Pierino Gattei

Rick R.

Charlene Solonynka

Jared Nelson

Kate Worthington

Holmes Harrison

Eric Sands

Dirk-Pieter Smits

Doug Campbell

Zarko Hauschberger

Luis Roco

Donna

Joana

Mike Vance

Sherri Mines

Terri Connor

Nathan B. Dodge

JG Morales Villanueva

Jean VERNEY-CARRON

Clinton Sands

Anonymous Reader

Dan Andrews

Kevin G. Farnam

Raja Thiagarajan

Mary Jo Rabe

Cherrie Newman

Richard Rose

Daniel Ljungberg

Emilie Thiessen

Lee Alexander

Chris Maxwell

Jemma

Scott & Somone Bull

James Cleverley

Fred

Kal Powell

Patrick Hay

Jakob Suhr Nielsen

Teri N. Sears

Dirk Leyers

Steven Crane

Tim Jordan

Leslie Lauderdale

james m landis

Martha Carr

Connor Whiteley

Rick Parker

Ken Hoover

Bill Kohn

Janice Galeckas

Carolyn Rowland

Angela Saunders

Joe Monson

Eric Goebelbecker

Rod Haller

Christa Pipo

Simon Dick

Theresa C. Davis

Eduardo Rios

Alex James

Matt McCormick

David and Debby Horst

Sam Knight

Leroy S. Gutierrez

Ben A

Daniel Rouk	Conor Stephens	Lucas Battershell	Michial K. Warrington
Steven Bastien	Alvin Dousip	Martin van Blerk	Kevin Reid
Jennifer Brinn	Claire Rosser	Kaitykat	R. L. King
Stace Johnson	Talesdrin	The Freeman Family	Carol Hendrickson
Jessica Meade	embyrd	Steve Barnett	Alex Baughn
tim torres	Shellie surles	Shana	Mark
dgabrielson	Dina Barron	Kerry Frey	Andrew Monk
Hannah Sheldon	Максим Стоялов	Lumla	Brendan Moylan
Darren Fry	Thomas Baird	Sarah Ehinger	Deslea R. Judd
Franziska	Elmdea Adams	Tomasz Pik	Eric W Wei
Heather Jones	Brad Kane	Eve Borkenhagen	GhostCat
Jennifer Carson	Patric Ryan	M. Scott Phillips	Jim Phillips
GA01	Jessica Springer Guernsey	Eiseg Feuer	Emilia Pulliainen
Sean Hennigan	Judy McClain	Laura Eaton	Darren Wall
Akos Nagy	Gaurav Karanjkar	Stuart MacDonald	Jeff Eppenbach
Jennifer V Gray	Chip Thomas	Tony McCowan	Scott J. Dahlgren
Susan O'Fearna	Mischa Borgnaes	Jason Bittner	Greg Masztal
Eric & Nikita B.	Annmarie SanSevero	Denis Boisvert	Nicole Toscano
Beyls Alexandre	Old Man Peck	Michael Cohen	Audrey Hackett
Randy McCallum	Andrew Saxby	Josechu Sanmartin	Rex Moss
Kristof Mols	Per Møller Jensen	Capn Vrag	Dimitrios Lakoumentas
MW	Christine Tucker	John Broxson	Tim Williams
Zach Heflin	Fr. Andrew Kinstetter	Dean Wesley Smith	Timothy Stark
Paul Rose Jr.	Raymond Croteau	Stacey Anderson	Robert Lynem
Trevor Boyd	Monika Kielbus	Peter Engebos	Dwayne Plain
Eva Eldridge	Alexander H.	Charles M. Kersey	Eric Jordan
Marek Fukas	Mary Barzee	Stephen Taylor	Neil Musser
Christopher Pallone	Natalia Botto Pérez	Mike Rayburn	Dave
Thái Thiện	Scott Kohtz	Julia Deutsch	Paige Brage
Philippe Le Cerf	Thomas Bull	Andrew ten Broek	Ronald Clemons
Amanda Goodell and Joshua Murphy	Chris, Sam and Emmie Foster-White	The Graduate Program in Creative Writing at Western Colorado University	Mark 'Aahzmandius' Montgomery
Tobias Treter	Jens Bejer Pedersen	Peter Gary Bauer	Silver
Robert Long	John Barone	Mel Ladner	Max
Anja K.	Lucas Battershell	Erhard Larry Schmidt	Robert M. Kerns

N. Karen Fonville

Andy fytczyk

Scott Zirkel

Laura Eaton

Chad Bo

Ronald L. Weston

Stephen Jack

Kelly Adams

David Hamelin

Jess

Kevin Ikenberry

Nicholas Stegelman

Daniel J. Lyons III

John Wolver and family

Andrew Bulthaupt

Margaret A. Menzies

Darin

Bailey Finn

Steve711

Hermes Astacio

Edward E Tucker

Phil Beneker

ObiBobMcHobo

Mark Wibaux

Bruce Seiler

Dan Marsh

WildCard

Clifton Field

Sharon

Zay Inked

Karen Bulgarelli

Jonathan Kurtz

The Beltram Clan

krinsky

Shadowfall

John Idlor

Xanthis

Terry A Aue

Céline Malgen

Brooks Moses

Kate

Michael Pleier

Danielle Monique

CthulhuChris

Phillip H

Steve Camp

Niklas Nord

Kyle "Fiddy" Pinches

Scott S Sikora

Roy Wassink

Randy Iber

Luis Manuel Sánchez García

dennis chambers

Richie Halsey-Watson

David Emmons

Palli

Ryan Gilgallon

Louis

Mark Phillippi

Richard Hebson

Garrett Sever

Garrick Dietze

Michael Fenton

Trinity Turner

sepak

Thel3rain

Chet King

Erin M. Brown

Michael Chrisman

Rob Bakker

Michelle and Perry Swenson

Dione Marie Basseri

Swedish Meeples

Robert J. McCarter

Max Beckman-Harned

John Wenskovitch

Bradley J. Birzer

C. Scott Kippen

eerian sadow

Jeff Martin

Rick Shaw

Pepita Hogg-Sonnenberg

Brad Kabosky

E Stafford

Erwin H. Bush

Eric Brown

TranDinhDuy

Hans de Wolf

Tom Boucher

Afzal Mawji

Herlander Simões

Michelle Yost

Joseph McGuire

Jon Haël Brenas

Joerg Mosthaf

Brian Hagman

Daniel Morris

Kenneth Givens

Leona Jackson

David Charlap

Kathleen Werry

David Arbuckle

Sandra

August Elliott

Leigh yelle

Andy Anderson

Tara & Paul Smith

Jessica Enfante

Alexandr Machula

Tracey Patterson

Jamison Ousley

Janet Berkman

Pierre Sullivan

John Fritz

Chris Massam

KenderKim Green

Mr Andrea Casamassima, MD

bernard teuben

Joost van Ginkel

Brandon L'Amoureux

Lyndon Perry

Duncan Wilcox

Folker Schmidt

Darren Lipman

Shay Dinur

Colleen Feeney

Fearlessleader

Rajasekaran Senthil Kumaran

Christopher Paul Carey

Dave Rendell

Grayson Sheldon

Bryan and Luisa Shirley

Richard O'Shea

Patrick Douglas

Andy Konecny

Barry Hunter

Barry Midwinter

Holly McMiller

NightmareNewt

Adam Rajski

Faz Nishib

Jeffrey Harlan

scantrontb

MICHAEL

Wei-Hon Plasma Chen

Anders Skov

Wolfgang Knebel

Krzysztof Piszcz

Dean Carroll

Kurt Adam

Billie Kellar

Chip Frederick

Frank Kiss

Haraldur Johannsson

Deak Long

Joshua Gerdes

ben bugby

Jeff Wolfhope

Beth and Maggie Stillman

J

Tomasz Pluskiewicz

Jessie

mrreynolds@bellsouth.net

D Michael Martinez - TheF8photo

Rob Johnson

Patricia Ingram

Eric

Allan Halme

Kyle Bergeron

Rachel2

Mikel J. Wisler

Alex Helm

Peter Marsh

John E Fallon

Siretchisketch

Michael Barbour

Brynhild Corona

Lisa Kruse

Jen BenJamin

Andy Ransom

Robbie Reilly

Ward Edwards

Ryan M. Williams

Lori Lane Gildersleeve

Bruce Paulik

Ben Morgan

GMarkC

Richard Boehme

Jason Doyle

Joshua Easter

David Kiesewetter

DaveHotspur171

Craig

Carmen Bovard

Dan Balkwill

Peter Boyles

Elias Hunt

Laura Landry Sypien

John Davis

Damion and Cathy Gilzean

Henry Kaufman

Valhalar

Tommy Chu

David Rabbani

David Peterson

John Ladley

Raeli DaPra

Eric Rohnen

Sirrah Medeiros

Hisham Barazi

Elivin Mendez

J.R. Johnson

carm

Joel Mattson

Daniel, Trista, and Eleanor Robichaud

Richard Freeborn

Richard Freeborn

Chris Ruybal

Alastair Fairman

Susan E. Wilson

Justin paul

António Matos

Kodi Cutler

John Thompson

Aimee Hudson

leigh

Sean

Jay Mullen

Adrian Bellis

Ruth Ann Orlansky

Kenny M.

Simon Waugh

Harry Fischer

Bert

Chriss Glaisyer

Kevin La Rue

Mitchell Cutler

James T. Lambert

Quek Han Yang

Elizabeth Blair

Thomas Melfi

Robert Brown

aniket

B. Wad

luciano

Salvatore Puma

Nicolas Petterson

Ferran BD

Edward knowlton

B. Daniel Blatt

L. Douglas George

Liz Madden

chrisl0r
James Zahler
Seamus Sands
Yvan Le Verge
Greg Gagnon
Stuart Walters
Justin Speck
Hayley Rae Johnsin
David Kisloski
Beau Craner
"filkertom" Tom Smith
William Graves
Henrique Falcão
Suneé le Roux
Nancy
Eric van der Sluis
Bridget Cowne
Joanne Lanham
Amric S Manku
Jaron van Boheemen
Mustela
Sarah Chesterman
Theodore Paxinos
Brazz Official
Lacey Luvian
Jennifer Flora Black
Chris Larlee
Juha Mäenalusta
Benjamin Guy
Mike Andrews
Christoph Dimpker
Rainer Ziller
Phillip Jones
Daniel Müller
Sharan Volin
C. East

Jonathan Kurts
John
Dritzz
Alenary Luckovsky Sorkin
Seth
Will
Philip Cloud
Marshall McGowan
Kirsty Steele
Ryan Yeats
Alex Jucan
Jacob_Hamblen
Joeseph Simon
Kenesha Williams
Philip H.
David Kimmel
Jake W.
LN Emmert
Ivan Mogos
Tim Peele
Simon Prior
andy99000
Paul Osentowski
Florian Bambl
Tony Henthorne
Matthew Smith
The Good Doctor
Elenna
Matthew Rancourt
GuyAnthonyDeMarco
Guejazi Navarrete
Stephen Taylor
Linda Edwards
David Schwarzkopf
Sara Rebennack
CHERYL ANDERSON

Danielle W.
Michael BenJamin
Barry Finn
Gretchen L Anthony
JHMcKeen
Amanda Daggett
Derek Sweetman
Bailey Johnson
David J Ham
Renee M. Boucher
Elizabeth Stanway
Shane Gardner
Scott Santaella
Tyler Damon
Donald Evans
Marie Findlay
Martin Glöckner
Bouke de Boer
Colton M Davis
Gwyneth Gibby
Mike Shaffer
Phillip A. Leavenworth
James Aylett
Earl Brawley
Judith Bramlage
Kevin Parma
Rachel Hadaway
Michael Pickett
Sakar Weng
Michael D Boatright
Evan Smith
Marcel Kuipers
Jessica Phillips
The Belina Family
John Lamar
A.K.Meek

Arend van 't Oever
Keira Blondin
Justin Couchot
Storm Humbert
J.R. Murdock
Bradley Wilken
Jason Hanley
Debbie Hayward
scott
Gary Weaber
Paul Leaney
John Williams
Jalane Locke
Tania
BefuddledPanda
Justin T
Corinne Brucks
Laura Ware
Scott Smith
Nickie Kaylee Irvine
Bob Fritchen
Chad V Holtkamp
Pleiades
Doc Ezra
Tyler Barbee
Cody Browne
Yosen L
Travis Dubaich
Thomas @ Altminus
JJ Johnson
Kari Kilgore
John Rickert
Markus Morrice
Sarah Cuypers
Scott Hipp
Michael Roedelbronn

Amy Schriever

Konrad Karczewski

Rich Van Cleave

ChuckB

Michael Howie

Christopher Larson

Peter Ehm

Lindsey Watson

M.Beaujean

Katy Board

Brittany Tilley

Brook & Julia West

Jacob shlagel

John Maloney

Joe Lawry

Mark Miles

Caroline Denicourt

Matej Kianicka

Tim Tucker

Scott Hajek

Paul Go

Tom B.

Laura Williams

Henry Poland

Draddog Family

Hiram G Wells

Peter Wolf

Cameron Anderson

Ronald Miller

Annie Reed

David Hutchins

Jan Kotouč

Tanja Neubacher

David Blockley

ErikH

Seb Fabre

Kevin & Ashley Childs

Joel Jansson

Dan Schu

Michelle Yvon

Moist Jimmy

Steve Sanchez

Blake Elliott

christopherhchoi@gmail.com

R.H. Campbell

Clay Stewart

Diane McRae-Hardin

Caleb Kofahl

Rick Ohnemus

jmarkusbradley

Vincent Van Dyck

Steve Ryder

Weogrim

Jacob Ihle

Daniel

Ryan Cunningham

Maddy Marie-Rose

Joel Aguilar

medaloffairness

Figworth

John Harlacher

ElderMillennial

Chali Wertz

Daniel Carter

Felix Augustsson

Jason Tucker

Andy Reisdorf

Daniel Lowenstein

Todd Sloane

Ben Bagamery

Richard Sanchez Jr

Rob Rooney

Aidan Doherty

Thomas Krech

Shawn West

Steven Sabatke

Peter C Miller

cheapweed

Joel Rand

Michael Henderson

Raphael Bressel

Adrian Thomas-Prestemon

Christopher P. Menkhaus

Benjamin Kohler

Braiden Olds

Lucas Ecker

Stephanie Good

Matthew Ceplina

Hugh Oh

Richelle Holland

C. Myers

Angry Prophet Games

Matt Knepper

Adam Schreiner

Nick Conklin

Foxtales

Kegan Cunningham

Serecac

J.B. Fearns

Kelly McMahon

Michael Shane soencer

Steve Kertes

MrBen

Jonathan Martens

Mike Oney

PowrSteve

Maxime de Hennin

Spike K

Nik Batistich

Angelica Molly

Funyaripka

Weevilst

Lauren O'Byrne

Ray

Ian Pedoe

Bjarne D Mathiesen

Josh Kergan

Logan O. Uber

Kai

J.A. Johnson

Joe Rosa

Adam Shiflett

J Mills

Jamie Miner

Amaryllis Jeanne Quilliou

Craig S. Weinstein

Nicola Thompson

Amanda Barton

Andrew Keller

Wiktor Matslova

Andrea Clerici

Anonymous

Don Hoban

Ed Schulte

Hugo

Sirhawk

Jose Olivenca

Darrell Z. Grizzle

Judith Dohmann

Jasmijn van Zuidam

Matthew Apsokardu

David Scoggins

Tom Karpel

Jose Maisog

Bill Garcia JR

PippiMD

Ferdinando Martino

Cynthia Jones

S. James Abbott

Arno Hautala

Michael

ldjessee

Steve L

Chris Harris

Rona Horn

Kenyon Wensing

Steve Esmaili

aurinko

Alex B

Bradley

Lee Clark

Morgan Mayhew

N/A

Patrick McNerney

Wayland Chang

Haden Lively Cookson

Khadija Hussain

Wendall Nicholson

Ayla Heisinger

Dennis Andrews

Bejay Cleary

Simon Horvat

Sean Patrick Phelan

The Smallwood Twins

Kevin Taylor

Eugene M john

Ruben M.

Jackie Payson

David Walle

Steven Rietveld

Manuel Dornbusch

Darren L

Jon Boese

CJG

DarkSphinx

Todd L. Caron

zabbas

Steven Epperson

Anonymous

Nathan Huster

Terry Moore

Gareth Hill

Adrian Gamble

Thiago Miliante

Georgios Fotopoulos

Jordan Isler

Jeff Blackshear

Kristin Selzer

John Bredesen

Brendon Hudnell

Alan Winterrowd

Eric

David Brafman

Christopher Heß

C. Edward Sellner

Stuart Frowen

Preston Watts

Chris Cheek

Tamás Bodnár

John K. Patterson

Robby Gaspard

Shane Berg

Matt Blackwell

Timothy Helbing

Alexander Shrewsbury

Per Stalby

Hans Stuer

tonel

N/A

Trevor Parkinson

Anonymous

Michael Johnson

J. Kyle McLaughlin

Felix Meier-Stephenson

Caleb Frambach

Kate Dane

Monica Kershaw aka Game Raider Official

ABOUT THE AUTHOR

Kevin J. Anderson has published more than 180 books, 58 of which have been national or international bestsellers. He has 24 million copies in print in 34 languages.

He has written numerous novels in the Star Wars, X-Files, and Dune universes, as well as the unique Clockwork Angels steampunk trilogy with legendary Rush drummer Neil Peart. His original works include the Saga of Seven Suns series, the Wake the Dragon and Terra Incognita fantasy trilogies, the humorous Dan Shamble, Zombie P.I. series and the Dragon Business series.

He has edited numerous anthologies, written comics and games, and the lyrics to two rock CDs as companions to his Terra Incognita trilogy.

Anderson is the director of the graduate program in Publishing at Western Colorado University, and he and his wife Rebecca Moesta are the publishers of WordFire Press.

IF YOU LIKED ...

If you liked *Fantasy Stories: Volume 2*, you might also enjoy other WordFire Press titles by Kevin J. Anderson.

Our list of other WordFire Press authors and titles is always growing. To find out more and shop our selection of titles, visit us at:
wordfirepress.com